D0273353

...y Davis

The Course of Honour
Rebels and Traitors
Master and God

Falco: The Official Companion

THE GRAVEYARD OF THE HESPERIDES

Lindsey Davis

HODDER

First published in Great Britain in 2016 by Hodder & Stoughton
A Hachette UK company

First published in paperback in 2016

I

A CIP catalogue record for this title is available from the British Library

Paperback ISBN 978 1 473 61339 3

Printed and bound by CPI Group (UK) Ltd, Croydon, CR0 4YY

Hodder & Stoughton policy is to use papers that are natural, renewable and
recyclable products and made from wood grown in sustainable forests. The logging
and manufacturing processes are expected to conform to the environmental
regulations of the country of origin.

Hodder & Stoughton Ltd
Carmelite House
50 Victoria Embankment
London EC4Y 0DZ

www.hodder.co.uk

THE GRAVEYARD OF THE HESPERIDES

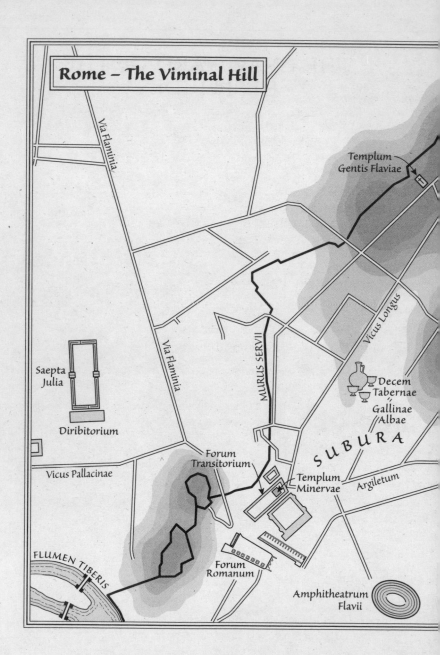

Rome – The Viminal Hill

Via Flaminia

Templum
Gentis Flaviae

Vicus Longus

MURUS SERVII

Saepta
Julia

Via Flaminia

Decem
Tabernae

Gallinae
Albae

Diribitorium

S U B U R A

Vicus Pallacinae

Forum
Transitorium

Templum
Minervae

Argiletum

FLUMEN TIBERIS

Forum
Romanum

Amphitheatrum
Flavii

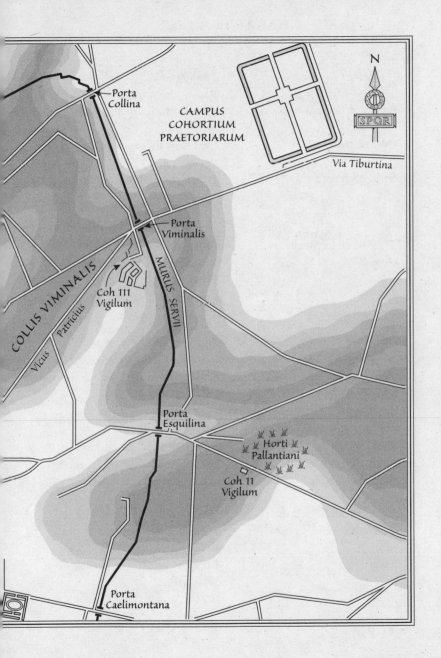

N

SPQR

Porta
Collina

CAMPUS
COHORTIUM
PRAETORIARUM

Via Tiburtina

Porta
Viminalis

COLLIS VIMINALIS

MURUS SERVII

Coh 111
Vigilum

Vicus Patricius

Porta
Esquilina

Horti
Pallantiani

Coh 11
Vigilum

Porta
Caelimontana

CHARACTER LIST

Home . . .

Flavia Albia	a happy bride
Tiberius Manlius Faustus	very straight, her lucky man
Julia and Favonia	her sisters, his wedding planners
On the bride's side:	Far too many other relatives to mention
On the groom's side:	tricky Uncle Tullius, scratchy Aunt Valeria, unhappy Fania Faustina, objectionable Antistius, three whiny boys
The Fabulous Stertinius	a rhapsodising citharist
Genius	the celebrated chef (who doesn't cook)
Larcius	a dependable works foreman
Sparsus and Serenus	two daft labourers
Trypho	a have-a-go watchman
Lares and Penates	bent

. . . and Away

Julius Liberalis	a have-it-all bar owner
Old Thales	a popular landlord (deceased, thank goodness)
Rufia	a do-it-all barmaid (disappeared mysteriously)
Nipius and Natalis	two louche waiters (all too present)
Artemisia and Orchivia	two Dardanian virgins (honest)
Menendra	a woman of commerce (looks dishonest)
Nona	the wise woman (in business, don't ask)

Costus	your best bet for religious sacrifice
Passus, Erastus and Victor	who will do the deed with:
Snowy	a sheep (tomorrow's mutton broth)
Staberius	an obliging augur (ask whatever you want)
Silvinus	an undertaker whose trade is quiet
Prisca	everybody's grandma
Gavius	one of hers, a marble-supplier
His parents	very proud of him
Aglaia, Euphrosyne, Thalia	the Three Graces, big girls
Appius	an honest second-in-command
Lepida and Lepidina	snackery proprietors
The Macedonians	providers of other services
Chia	a very young Macedonian
Rhodina	a wants-it-all mother
Morellus	of the Fourth Cohort, a rough-and-ready officer
Macer	of the Third, just as rough but even less ready
~~Juventus~~	*[sensitive information redacted]*
Pudgy	grandmother to the Three Graces
A chicken supper	probably
The Egyptians	sought-after provender-sellers
Rabirius	a failing gangster (not been seen for a while)
Roscius	his rising heir (lying low, but not for long now)
Gallo	doesn't want to know where the bodies are buried

ROME,

25 August AD 89

Eight days before the Kalends of September
(a.d. VIII Kal. Sept.)

I

Everyone knew a dead barmaid was buried in the court-yard.

The Garden of the Hesperides was a large but otherwise typical eating house on a busy street corner, with two marble counters, five pot-holes for containers of food, three shelves of cracked beakers, an unreadable price list on a flaking wall and a faded picture of nude women. The daub seemed to have been painted by a shy artist who had never seen anyone naked. In a nervous line of three, his nudes huddled beneath gnarled boughs from which dangled dingy fruit. Hercules set about his scrumping task, watched by a bored snake instead of by Ladon, who ought to be a fearsome, hundred-headed, never-sleeping dragon. A snake was easier to draw, no doubt. The legendary Golden Apples were so pockmarked I personally would not have sent Hercules to climb the tree for them. Hard to tell with all the dirt whether it was just poor art or the paint was now peeling off the wall.

No doubt when the bar was open for business it had waiters who were very slow to serve anyone and pretty girls who did all the work. A room upstairs was used for assignations; you could bring your own or hire the staff.

Its landlord, a famous local character – that horrible type – was believed to have murdered the missing woman years before, then hidden her body in the courtyard, where customers could sit outside under a pergola. Regulars referred to the tragedy matter-of-factly, only adding lurid details when they wanted to get into conversation with newcomers who might buy them drinks. Anybody sensible thought it was a myth – yet it was odd how the myth did specify that the barmaid's name was Rufia.

About six months before I first went to this bar, the old landlord died. The new one decided to make improvements. He had been waiting for years for his predecessor to pass on, so he was full of ideas. Most were terrible. Instead, a firm of renovation contractors convinced him he needed to pretty up the courtyard; his bar was, after all, named for the most famous garden in the world. What he should do, they assured him earnestly, was to improve the dank, uninviting area by creating a delightful water feature that would tempt drinkers to linger. They said it could easily be done. If he really wanted to be authentic he could plant an apple tree . . .

He fell for it. People do.

They promised to give him a good price for a timely job. In the way of their trade, that meant they would overcharge, delay for ever and mess up the works until, after weeks of not being open to customers, the despairing owner would be left with a leaking canal in a garden that now had no room for tables. The tree, if one was ever supplied, would die the first summer.

All normal so far.

Not long after the old landlord had his last drink on earth, the owner of the building company died too. I am a private informer and she had been a client of mine. About

4

five months later, the man I had just set up house with decided that at close to forty years of age it was time he found his first job. Perhaps he feared that keeping me in Lucanian sausage might not come cheap. He may even have noticed that I, who did have work as an informer, was just as wary of him possibly sponging off me. Whichever it was, since he knew my ex-client's heir, he bought her empty house, together with her decrepit builders' yard and failing construction firm. It appeared to be a mad idea, though in fact he had his reasons because he was that kind of man. Also, as my family pointed out, if he took up with me, he must be brave.

When Manlius Faustus first acquired the business, he found the Hesperides job still on the books. At that point, it was the only order his workforce had. They would toddle along to the bar every couple of weeks with a handcart of inferior materials, stay for half a day, then disappear again. The client was disgusted, as people who try to renovate property so often are. He had not realised the company had almost been wound up due to a death and the heir was a cheesemaker who took no interest in it; he was extremely lucky my loved one was the new proprietor. Faustus may never have held a job before, but he was currently a magistrate. He could organise. For starters, he let the workmen know they were about to be supervised, by him in person.

Faustus then walked down to see the bar owner, who was amazed to be visited by a quiet man in a clean tunic who handed him revised drawings, plus up-to-date costings and a new timetable. What's more, completion was to be the end of August, which was this month.

He may have been less thrilled to receive an invoice for

work done so far. I had helped work that out; it was not perfect, because nobody had been keeping records. But it showed how things would be from now on. The barkeeper agreed he had been warned. He wouldn't argue over payment. He just wanted to be able to reopen and sell drinks.

Faustus was proving himself. Privately, I was reassured too. I would never knowingly have lived with a sponger – but it's an easy mistake. I had had several clients who needed me to extricate them from layabouts' clutches. Layabouts can make themselves look attractive and they know how to cling.

But as I had hoped, my new man was applying himself. A month after we started living together, Faustus was extremely busy. As a magistrate, a plebeian aedile, he worked hard; that would continue until his year in office ended in December. He distinguished himself, turning up at the aediles' building by the Temple of Ceres almost every day. It was unheard of. When I first met him he was having a fine time adopting scruffy disguises and going out onto the streets to catch wrongdoers in person. At the moment he was also preparing for the Roman Games, a great festival in September that the aediles organised. Patrolling markets, baths, bars and brothels himself might be optional (they had a permanent staff to do this) but running the Games was not.

Faustus had also chosen to renovate the house that came with his building firm, where we intended to live. So he had three jobs. Some days I hardly saw him.

We were in love. I wanted to see him all the time. So, one particular morning when he was over at the Garden of the Hesperides, I packed up a little basket of dainties and took him lunch. Yes, he was working at a bar, but it was closed due to the works. Besides, I had convinced myself that only I could make my man a proper picnic, assembled the way he liked it; Faustus went along with that, all soft eyes and tender murmurs. We had not been together long. We would settle down. Probably by next week we'd be ignoring one another.

While the drooling still occurred, however, he and I were sitting side by side at one of the bar tables, with hard-boiled eggs and olives set out on a napkin. In between drinking from the same beaker, I was wiping olive oil off his firm chin and he was accepting my solicitousness. He liked it. He didn't care who knew that, even if his workmen snorted.

We were devoting almost all our attention to each other, yet we were observant people. We both did work that relied on sharp eyes. It was stupid of two builders to hope they could sidle out of the courtyard without us noticing that among the dug-up rubble they were carrying away in a basket slung on a pole, interesting items stuck out. They had found some bones.

2

'Stop right there!' instructed Faustus in a quiet voice, but meaning to be obeyed. He had the knack. He had tried it on me a few times, though had now given up. Nobody gave me orders.

His workmen shambled to a halt. They stayed there, still holding the pole on their shoulders. One was a young man called Sparsus, to whom the others always assigned the worst work. He put up with it, accepting this as his role in life. The other was Serenus, a bandy-legged lag with a squint. Though short, he had managed to adjust the pole so all the weight fell on Sparsus.

Faustus finished the hard-boiled egg he was eating. I licked salad dressing off my lips. In our own time, we both stood up and walked over. Faustus signalled for them to put down the rubble basket and pull out the carrying pole. He took the container's double handles with a strong grip, then emptied everything out onto the courtyard, shaking hard so the rubble scattered as it fell. He began picking through the stones, old tiles and brick ends that had been left behind, buried under the courtyard surface when previous builders had finished some job. Patiently, he sorted out the bones, setting them on one side. I had seen him do an evidence search before. He was thorough.

The foreman wandered up, looking innocent. He had

probably been watching Sparsus and Serenus trying to take the spoil away surreptitiously. They all knew full well what was there. They knew they ought to have mentioned it and not tried to secrete the bones in a skip. They liked a pretext to stand around gabbing, but if the job was now suspended they might not be paid.

Faustus straightened up. He gave me a sardonic glance. 'These look human. Seems we have found the famous Rufia.'

'Well you're far too busy to investigate. I'd better take this on,' I answered, with both resignation and curiosity. That's a dangerous mix, well known to people in my trade.

My treasure grinned. 'Don't expect me to pay fees!'

'Oh, is your wife keeping you short of pocket money?'

'She's a tyrant. Gives me nothing.'

'Get a new one,' I advised him.

We were both smiling now. The matter of us being married was taking up yet more of this busy man's time and effort. He wanted us to have a formal wedding. I had told him to forget that. I was rude, though it achieved nothing; famously stubborn myself, I knew how he could be when he was determined. He was organising a wedding anyway. No wonder the idiot was so often exhausted.

Now he had this to deal with.

3

Tiberius Manlius Faustus, my gutsy new lover, was thirty-seven, broad-shouldered though not too heavy, grey-eyed, astute and quiet. He strigilled up well, when he wasn't in a tunic covered with building dust. A plebeian, but from forebears who had made their pile – he never had to sell fish or hammer copper. Until recently he had lived at leisure with an uncle in the warehouse trade, from whose complex affairs Faustus was now trying to extract his own money. We needed cash to set up our new business. I had yet to find out why he wanted to be a building contractor – a decision he seemed to have taken entirely alone – or what had convinced him he could do it. But he was an interesting man. I suspected he could learn anything and be a success at whatever he chose.

I was a tricky, more complicated mix. I grew up in Britannia, an orphan of unknown parentage. Under Roman law, as I have been assured by lawyers, foundlings always rank as citizens. Rome won't risk even one little free person being denied their rights, just because their parents lost or dumped them. Mine probably died in the Boudiccan Rebellion. Nobody knew who they were.

Freedom belonged to me, which was crucial in the Roman Empire. As I scavenged for food and dodged cruel blows as a child, it ought to have been comforting. Sadly, at the time I didn't know. In my experience, a foundling feels like a slave.

Originally fostered by rough cabbage-sellers in downtown Londinium (a town where 'rough' means grim and 'down' is rock bottom, though the cabbages are robust), I sensed problems coming so I ran away. Of course I was picked up by a brothel owner. In the nick of time, I was spotted and pulled off the streets by Marcus Didius Falco and Helena Justina, he a crusty middle-rank informer and she a lovely woman of senatorial birth. They brought me to Rome, city of wonders.

So I had seen some of the best and all the very worst of life. I now occupied an awkward position where my acceptance by other people could not be relied upon. Yes, I was freeborn, adopted into the middle rank and brought up by a senator's daughter – but I had a scavenger's eyes and temper, and was even whispered to be a druid. The fact that, like Father, I worked as a private informer made me even more frightening to snobs. Rome was packed with snobs. For the past twelve years, since making my own way in the world, I had tried to keep my head down and avoid their notice. As an informer, I was probably on a vigiles watch list, which never helps.

Faustus had enjoyed a different life as a big-city rich boy. He had been married briefly years ago. His ex-wife, Laia Gratiana, despised me. I loathed her. Our opposing views on what Faustus deserved would never be reconciled. She could not understand my kind feelings for him; she was jealous of his open attraction to me. In whimsical moments I suggested to him that since she remained on the edge of his social circle, he ought to invite the aloof Laia to our wedding, if we had one. This almost convinced him to drop the idea.

I too had married when much younger, but was widowed when my husband died in an accident. I had never expected to find anybody else. Then Faustus swanned into my life.

Another fine concept in Roman law is that it simply defines marriage as an agreement by two people to live together. So, once Faustus brought his luggage to my apartment and stayed with me, I was a wife again. His wife. It felt right, he seemed calm, but I was still a little nervous.

My mother, Helena, had never felt the need for a wedding ceremony. I had expected to follow her example. Who needs a show? According to Mother it saved money that would be better spent on good food and books. In their early days, just like Faustus and me, Helena and Falco could barely afford either.

Also, Mother told me, you want to avoid ghastly wedding presents. She had had a doomed first marriage where the awfulness of the gifts was prophetic. According to her, she sent out the notice of divorce with the same messenger who was still taking round her thank-yous for the hideous vases.

A woman with a conscience, Helena Justina always writes polite thank-you notes, even when she hates a gift, or if she already owns three manicure sets. Of course she does have three, because she has three daughters; from time to time she must have owned at least six sets because Julia, Favonia and I often forgot what we had given her at a previous birthday or Saturnalia. She would just say, 'Oh it doesn't matter; this is a much nicer one!' – as if she meant it. As a mother she was a fine example, as our father often pointed out. That was his idea of imposing discipline. 'Be like your mother, you rascals, or you can leave home.'

I counted myself lucky to have been adopted by Falco

and Helena. They gave me security, education, comfort and independence. Humour. Rebellion. Loyalty, too. Falco had taught me the craft by which I earned my living. Both my parents encouraged my rampant curiosity.

Being a well-trained informer would enable me to find out what had happened to Rufia, the missing barmaid. It may not be what you want for your daughter, yet ask yourself: why not? As I set up with Faustus, I would think about this. Does the ability to tackle a mystery about a bunch of bones from under a courtyard mean an informer cannot be a trusty friend? An elegant companion? A useful contributor to the domestic purse? A sweet daughter? A loyal wife? Even a good mother? Although that was certainly not on my horizon, if the apothecaries' products did their duty.

Above all, an informer's task is good; we enable justice. If anyone had ever cared about Rufia, I now hoped to find them, to provide explanations and perhaps consolation. If anyone had done her fatal harm, I would make them pay.

When we first saw what we presumed were the barmaid's remains, Faustus and I closed our lunch basket and discussed how to proceed. We were now alone. He had told the workmen to stop what they were doing; he sent them back to the Aventine to their normal evening job, refurbishing the house at Lesser Laurel Street. I hadn't been much involved with that, so I still found it hard to accept it as 'our' house. Faustus had said I could decide whether to live there once I saw it renovated. But I knew I would agree. Meanwhile we lived in my apartment – and, like most people in Rome, spent as much time as possible outside the home.

Here, we were sitting on one of the bar's crude wooden benches, which we had pulled out of a stored pile so we could snuggle up to share our lunch. Our seat was an old, worn, splintery contraption. Perhaps the landlord would purchase a handsome new set of garden furniture when his project was finished, though I doubted it. The Hesperides had never been that sort of place.

It was a workaday bar. Most customers stood in the street, probably at the main counter, which was longer than the return around the corner. They had the usual food vats, never washed out. For a sit-down drink, you came in through a purpose-built gap in the crazy-paved marble worktop, squeezed by the inner tables and service area, maybe glanced at the unreadable drinks list painted on a wall by the beaker shelf, exchanged a word with whoever was serving, walked down a very short corridor with a dark staircase, then emerged into this not very airy, so-called garden.

It was larger than you might expect. Rustic trellis used to divide up semi-private table positions. I saw no trace of climbing greenery, though two empty birdcages hung on the rough-hewn trellis posts. A canopy shaded one part. There was a half-dead bay tree in a large pot with a rim piece missing. I had yet to work out what kind of customers would ever have used this interior. In Rome, we tend to socialise on the streets.

The bar owner had never mentioned the mystery, but our foreman, Larcius, had told us the public rumours with a grin: 'The site is supposed to be haunted. They say some murdered waitress was buried out here years ago.'

Faustus had given him a cool look. He and the workforce would have to feel their way together, though it seemed to be working out. They had realised he was no soft touch. He would turn up on-site, where the conversation soon showed them he fully understood what they were doing and anyone who failed to get on with him might lose his job.

'Not afraid of ghosts, are you, Larcius?' I asked dryly. Larcius did not bother to answer.

'I find it hard to believe,' said Faustus, playing the serious-minded aedile who discouraged gossip, 'that drinkers have downed their tots here for decades, knowing a corpse was right beneath their sandals.'

'No one remembers much about her.' Larcius seemed to think that justified it. 'She's just always been "that missing barmaid".'

Not any longer. Now we had found her.

It would be to her advantage that she had been found by *us*.

So, after his men left, Faustus and I considered what we could do. We discussed whether to tell the landlord yet, but decided to keep quiet for the time being. I would begin discreet enquiries about Rufia: who she was, why people believed she had come to a sad end, when it happened, what suspects fell under suspicion originally, what new ones we could identify. I might have wondered why nobody made a real fuss at the time, but I knew. People hate to interfere. Nobody invites trouble. Regulars are always loath to start a hue and cry that might end with their favourite bar being shut down. Many things can be excused as 'loyalty'. It's pathetic, but it's how people think.

Before we left that afternoon, we took a last look at the bones. The jumbled haul would not make a complete skeleton. Possibly there were more bones to be found, if they had not decayed completely. These were definitely old, though impossible to say how old. But for hearing past mention of Rufia, they could have been dismissed as really ancient, some prehistoric ancestor who lived here even before Rome was founded. If we were pious, they might have been collected up and reburied in a pot in a proper cemetery, though to be honest, most people would deposit them on the nearest midden heap and walk away fast.

Faustus pulled down the awning to wrap them. It was stiff with what could well be mould, but Rufia would not complain. We left her bones there, though we carefully locked up. The back gate onto a narrow alley was always left very secure, to stop anyone coming in to steal tools or materials. Faustus blocked the passage to the courtyard with a heavy old door (all building sites contain old doors that don't belong anywhere, don't ask me why), piling sacks and timbers against it. Fortunately he employed a night watchman, who had probably heard what happened today because we found him in the main bar; he had come early.

This was just as well. We had no chance of keeping the discovery private. A small crowd of sightseers had already gathered in the street.

Faustus used his authority as an aedile to order these ghouls to disperse. They were not impressed, freely ignoring him, and there was a danger that others would join them. He made the best of it with an announcement: 'I presume you have heard that human remains have been found. I am aware of the rumoured disappearance of a waitress some years ago. There may be no connection. But anyone who knows anything pertinent should come to see one of us.' He indicated that I was included, though I was his wife now, so he didn't bother with introductions. I smouldered like an appendage who would cause trouble at home later. 'Now please, go about your business quietly.'

Had the Hesperides been open for business, he would have stood no chance of moving people on. As it was, some shuffled off but many simply shifted themselves to the Medusa or the Romulus along the street, then stared across from there.

Because of the public interest, we went back and, helped by our watchman, reopened the passageway indoors so we could fetch the bones safely away with us.

After that, since too many people already knew, we set off to inform the landlord after all.

4

Pedantic people will probably wonder where these events took place. Extremely pedantic bods with fixed narrative ideas will ask why I have not mentioned it before. Look here, you write things your way, Legate. I shall draft my case notes just how I want.

So! The Garden of the Hesperides stood in the city's Sixth District, the Alta Semita, or High Footpath. The bar occupied a corner on the Vicus Longus, which is an extension of the famous Argiletum, the main road north from our fine new imperial fora. The latest, Domitian's Forum Transitorium, would add some lustre when it was finished, but the Argiletum's reputation had always been unsavoury, especially the area called the Subura. It was allegedly famous for booksellers and cobblers, but in the Subura trade of all kinds flourished, and I do mean *all*.

The Hesperides, Medusa and Romulus stood in a dirty enclave called the Ten Traders. There certainly were shops, as *Decem Tabernae* implied, but bars and eateries abounded, some keeping so quiet about the brothel upstairs it looked as if they only sold wine and stuffed cabbage leaves. No one was fooled. This area had no temples to virgin goddesses.

The Garden of the Hesperides seemed popular, though not quite as lively as its immediate neighbours, the deafening

Four Limpets, the raucous Soldier's Rest and the utterly appalling Brown Toad, where bisexual prostitutes openly solicited from front benches. The Ten Traders sits on the southern end of the Viminal Hill, the smallest of the ancient Seven Hills of Rome. It is a dull ridge that is mostly passed by, with roads either side taking people to more interesting places.

The landlord lived in Crab-apple Alley, in a rented apartment above a potter's, just around the corner from his bar. He could go home for lunch. From what I guessed about the Hesperides and its daily menu, he would probably want to. His proximity meant we could not expect to keep anything quiet; in fact, highly excited neighbours must already have rushed around to burble what had happened. Luckily for us he had been out – we met him as he fiddled with his latch-lifter on his way back in. Nobody had spoken to him yet, giving us the theoretical advantage of surprise.

I felt that if he knew anything at all about Rufia, his surprise would be slight. Surely he must have suspected the workmen would find something? Since the skeleton seemed incomplete, a curious informer was bound to wonder whether he had actually made an attempt to find and remove evidence before any work started. I asked Faustus; he knew of no prior digging, but he had not been in charge of the project at its start. I told him to question his foreman. He meekly promised to do so.

The landlord was one Publius Julius Liberalis, as we knew from the building contract. Three names, all Latinate – a free citizen. Rome's finest, and somewhat typical: a short man with a large head. On it was robust silver hair, which he parted in the middle. That suits nobody. Two silver horns of hair sat over his temples with matching sideburn points.

He enhanced the four horns by twiddling them when he was nervous. I tried not to dismiss him as a wrong 'un just because he had a bad hairstyle. But it set the tone for me.

He looked between thirty and forty. That mattered, because according to my impression of the timescale, he would have been young when Rufia vanished. Possibly even too young to go into bars, though boys start young in the Subura. Drinking is not the only thing they start early, either.

I had met him casually on-site, though he showed no recollection of it. This time, Faustus gave me a proper introduction, as if he might have caught my frosty glance just now at the bar. 'Flavia Albia is an informer who works with me when something needs special investigation. We are about to be married, I am delighted to say, so I'll have even better access to her expertise. There is a problem at your bar. We need to talk to you.'

Liberalis had at first assumed Faustus needed a decision from him on something to do with the renovation. Faced with the unexpected threat of special enquiries, he grew flustered, gabbling that he never had visitors so had left his apartment in a terrible mess. I just reached in and helped him with his latch-lifter while Faustus pushed the door. When somebody is reluctant to admit an informer, it only makes us more determined to get in. Did he have an ulterior motive?

Actually, no. When we pushed past the quavering Liberalis and stormed his citadel, it was indeed stupendously untidy. Tangles of clothes and old wine flagons covered every surface, no rubbish had been emptied for weeks, sandals lived on the windowsill, lopsided pictures dangled off bent nails, and if you wanted to sit down you had to forage for a stool then offload armfuls of detritus. Whatever you moved had to be added to teetering piles of other stuff. He probably claimed he knew where everything was, as idiots do, but that would be impossible.

'Well done!' I exclaimed, since there was no point pretending not to notice. 'I've known adolescent boys who would envy what you have achieved here.'

'An old biddy comes and does, since my mother passed away, but she's been off colour . . .' I saw her point. This was clearly not a man whose mother had taught him he must tidy up before the cleaner came.

There was no wife. So long as this remained his bolt-hole, there would never be. To me he had a distinct mother's-boy air, old-fashioned, innocent, probably selfish, ill-at-ease in company. Like many people who hanker to run a bar, he was poorly equipped for it. Perhaps the Hesperides had been there so long it would run itself despite him. He wanted success and was not tight with his money, as we knew from the work he was having done. I presumed he could afford it because he had no social life and no other calls on his cash.

Since refreshments would never be forthcoming, Faustus and I sat ourselves down, waited a moment in a friendly fashion for Liberalis' nerves to settle, then waded in.

'The workmen have found a human skeleton, or parts of it. I had to stop them working so we can investigate. Fortunately Flavia Albia has a talent for this so if I don't have time, she will conduct some checks. People have mentioned a disappearing barmaid, someone called Rufia?'

Faustus had begun, while I watched the way Liberalis received the news. He took it like any householder with a project: 'Will this hold up the job?'

Faustus ignored that, as if waiting for our news to sink in and Liberalis to speak more decently. 'Is the barmaid story familiar?' he asked sternly.

Liberalis became more guarded. 'I may have heard rumours.'

'Do you know when she is supposed to have vanished?'

'Oh, I'm not sure. Many years ago.'

'You knew her?'

'Yes.' So going by his age, her disappearance could not have been quite as long ago as the rumours suggested.

'And people believe somebody killed her?'

'Hazard of her job.'

'It didn't put you off taking on the bar?'

'Not at all.'

'You thought it was merely a rumour?'

'I am not afraid of ghosts.'

I leaned forwards as I suggested gently, 'I think you ought to tell us more about your connection with the Hesperides, Liberalis. Were you waiting for your predecessor to pass on so you could take over? I have the impression you had been planning how to renovate, once you obtained the premises. Is that correct?'

'We were distant cousins. He was older. He had no one else to leave it to, we always knew it would come to me one day. Yes, he'd had the place a long time so he probably lost interest in change, while I sometimes thought about better ways to run the place. I used to have dinner there. I would look around and imagine what I could do with it, that's natural.'

'No animosity?'

'I wouldn't have wanted to upset him. It was harmless daydreaming that I don't suppose he even noticed. I think

22

he was glad to know his place would stay in the family. But we rarely spoke about it.'

'What was his name?' Faustus interjected.

'Thales. Everyone always called him "Old Thales".'

Thales was a Greek name. So the barkeeper may have been Greek. Or more likely not. The Greeks are famous for travelling abroad to resettle for economic reasons, yet I could not imagine they would come to a notorious part of Rome and buy a dingy bar. Immigrant Greeks were either slaves who became very high-class secretaries or financiers in high-end trade or banking.

'Thales was a well-known local character?' I asked, concealing how much I despise such types.

'Oh yes.' Liberalis looked a little jealous. 'Everyone knew Old Thales. He had a great reputation.'

'What as?' asked Faustus, keeping it light.

'Oh, you know.'

We sat quietly, with raised eyebrows, implying that we did not know. The truth would emerge if I started asking around, but it would have been useful to know first how Liberalis assessed his predecessor. They must have been opposite types.

'A rather colourful landlord?' I hinted eventually, determined to extract more.

'Larger than life,' agreed Liberalis with another tinge of envy. I tried not to groan.

'So what exactly is this story about his missing barmaid?'

Liberalis shrugged. Faustus and I again waited for him to elaborate. Finally he caved in, though he was sparing with real facts: 'Rufia was a waitress at the Hesperides. Everyone who went there knew her. One day she suddenly disappeared, without any warning. Nothing more was ever

23

heard of her. Old Thales was the owner at the time. That is all I know.'

'So people thought the landlord did her in?' I demanded bluntly.

Liberalis shrugged again.

'Unfounded rumours or grain of truth?' Faustus tried, but it still took him nowhere. 'How long ago was it? Did you know Rufia yourself?'

'I told you, everyone who patronised the Hesperides knew Rufia.'

'Including you? You weren't too young?'

'Including me.'

'But you wouldn't describe your relationship with her as close?'

'That's right. She was a barmaid. She put my dinner on the table; she didn't bother to chat. She knew me as one of the family but she treated me as a customer, a young one, too, in those days.'

'What kind of barmaid?' I put in.

'The normal kind,' answered Liberalis calmly.

'She gave the full range of services?'

'She was a barmaid,' he insisted, not even blinking.

We all knew what he meant.

5

Consulting each other with a glance, Faustus and I stopped the interview. We would find out more from other people before, if necessary, pressing Liberalis harder. So far, he had only confirmed the vague rumour that had hung around the Hesperides for years. It could be all he knew. It could be all anybody knew nowadays. But instinctively I felt he was holding back.

The person to question next, were it possible, would be the previous landlord, but Old Thales, colourful character and chief suspect, was inconveniently dead. I decided not to question his successor about him any more at this stage, since Liberalis might feel too much gratitude to be honest, after the bequest of his coveted bar. I would ask around locally, starting soon, before there was daft gossip and people were lured into 'knowing' that mere supposition was fact. That crowd who had headed off to the Romulus would now be standing there deciding Rufia's history. Loudmouths with their elbows on the counter would be telling how it was, on the flimsiest evidence. I had seen it too often. The wilder their stories, the more the rest swore they had personally seen it all happen – and they would soon genuinely believe they had. Then I would never shake them.

Before we left, Faustus reminded Liberalis he was a

magistrate. As well as general responsibility for neighbour-hood order, aediles had a particular remit for the good behaviour of bars. The Sixth District was not in his formal jurisdiction, though of course Faustus worked closely with the relevant colleague. There would be consultation. The colleague would take an interest, though he might leave the problem to Faustus. (Bound to, I thought.) The local vigiles would also be informed. Faustus himself felt obliged to tell them, though they would obviously hear about the bones anyway; he hoped they would be reassured by his presence on the spot and would leave him to deal with the problem.

Liberalis took this well. He was assuming a helpful manner now. He started to express shock at the grisly finds today. He wanted things to be sorted out as painlessly as possible and would be all too ready to cooperate if anyone told him how. He even thanked Faustus for taking charge.

More fool Liberalis.

In reality he must have thought most builders would quietly parcel up the skeleton and scatter the bits in another district. It was his bad luck to be employing a firm that had been taken over midway by a magistrate – and that rarity, one who had scruples.

After we left the untidy apartment, I tackled Tiberius about my proposed enquiries. Nothing would have stopped me taking an interest. But if this was to be done properly, he would have to acknowledge a logistical problem. Tiberius himself had already found it hard to visit the site, even on an infrequent basis. It would be worse for me because I would need to be present every day. Our Aventine home was a long stretch from here; you had to come down from our hill, negotiate the huge valley of the Circus Maximus, pass around into the Forum, batter through the crowds, and come onto the Argiletum before beating up the Vicus Longus. Going home was worse because you had to slog up the Aventine at the end, when already exhausted.

'Darling, I shall need to come over all the time. There-and-back travel will be much too tiring.'

Tiberius conceded the point. We would rent somewhere to stay; he would come as well, which made it much more attractive. I knew there was accommodation at the Hesperides, which I had not seen, but those rooms could only be tiny, and currently they seemed to be home to the bar's un-employed waiting staff. Besides, who wants to sleep in a fug of concrete dust?

Our nightwatchman had found himself a half-decent billet to sleep in during the day. It was upstairs from a feltmaker's, so a grade better than living above a bar, though right on a busy crossroads. We took the bones there for safe keeping overnight. Tiberius instructed Trypho to move out and sleep in the Hesperides. Now that the site was a crime scene, having it guarded was doubly wise.

If my beloved was to scrape a living, I might need to monitor his costs. I said nothing yet, since I had no wish to be a married woman who nagged about the family busi-ness — except when there was a clear need, in which case I would certainly not hold back. Gaining my trusted advice was why Tiberius had taken me on, surely?

I did not want to be formally married at all, which was another reason for moving here, away from the wedding furore. However, the dogged Manlius Faustus had other ideas: 'I will have to go over to visit the aediles' office sometimes, for my duties,' he said. 'Don't worry, I can see how the wedding plans are progressing then.'

What a darling.

I sweetly assured him I was not intending to worry, since I myself did not want any progress on his terrible idea. He remained relaxed. I was beginning to see how he handled me, never becoming excited if I dug my heels in. It would probably work.

He had found helpers for his project. Two dark little handmaids had inveigled themselves into his confidence, wedding planners who could have organised Pluto's union to Proserpina in the Underworld, all wailing and downturned torches: my sisters, aged sixteen and fourteen. Tiberius had promised them a free hand, so long as they created a huge splash that would tell everyone on the Aventine he and I were married. Julia and Favonia were thrilled. They knew everything that ought to happen, much of it mythical in origin. They had no idea of common sense or cost.

'This mystery must not cause a delay,' Tiberius told me fondly. 'We shall just have to solve what happened to Rufia before our wedding day.'

'A race against time, eh? My favourite kind of case!' I have had pressures on investigations often, but never the deadline of being a bride. There was a date set. I had been ignoring it. Our ceremony was to be the last day of August. That was only six days away.

I wanted to begin investigating quickly anyway, because that is the best plan when a body turns up. I sent off my bridegroom to pick up things we would need from our apartment, while I started at once.

'Bring clothes, bath things, writing equipment – and absolutely our own bed sheets. Don't worry about food. I'll obtain something during my enquiries. The bakery is always a good place to start asking for gossip.'

'You're wonderful!'

As I said, we had not been together long. He would drop that adoring pose soon enough. I was human. I couldn't stand the strain of living up to it.

6

The nightwatchman told me where to find acceptable public facilities. One of my father's rules for informers was: always go out on reconnaissance with an empty bladder. You cannot be hopping at a crucial moment, and it's worse for a woman. He at least could pop down an alley and pee on someone's house wall like every other man in town.

'Acceptable' was Trypho's definition, not mine. Still, the crude latrine was fine if you stepped carefully, and it was usefully sited for my mission, with a well-established bread shop just over the road.

This bakery was not promising. Like most retail premises and workshops, it had a one-room-wide interior. You didn't go inside. Every morning the owners pulled the shutters and arranged their produce around its opening; they came to the front to serve buyers, who stood outside on the pavement. These particular bakers had a high counter, with servers leaning down over it, so you had to inspect the bread on tiptoe.

A good baker has his own millstone, often more than one. If you cannot hear big grinders being trundled by a lopsided donkey in a back room, the goods will be hopeless. Dough needs to be made on the premises. If flour is bought in, quite often ready-made loaves and rolls are too. Once products are obtained from a middleman, you can bet whatever you buy will be stale.

Here either the donkey was taking her nap or they had no grindstone. It was late afternoon on a hot day in August, so we were at the rump end of today's bread batches anyway. As I waited, I realised the assistants would be no use, for they were two young girls, perhaps sisters. They could not have been working here in Rufia's day. Sometimes an informer should be prepared to change tack and go elsewhere for information but I was drowsy in the heat, so I stayed put.

The servers looked rough, a feature of this area, though they turned out to be surprisingly sweet-natured. In front of me was an old woman, so poor she begged them to cut a dinner roll in half so she could afford it; one girl winked as she passed down a whole white roll, apparently making no charge at all. I suspect this happened every day. I thought grumpily that, unlike my menace sisters, this nice young pigtailed pair would never go cosying up to a man, organising his wedding for him despite all protests from his helpless girlfriend. . .

Now it was my turn. I bought a loaf, hoping its thick, segmented crust would have staved off the sun as it lay at the bottom of the basket. But we would need strong teeth. Giving out the last on sale cheered the girls, who willingly chatted. I was right; they had never heard of Rufia until today, but this afternoon customers had told them her bones had turned up at the Hesperides. I saw no point hiding what I was doing, so I asked, 'If you were me, trying to find out what happened, who would you go to around here; who's best for knowing things?'

They thought. They had an involved conversation together, in which more than one name came up. There was nobody waiting to be served, so I just let them reach a conclusion in their own time.

31

'Nona. You should see Nona, the wise woman.'

'Well thank you!'

They gave me directions. 'Good luck!'

'Thanks for that too.'

'Wise woman' is a standard euphemism. I would have no problem achieving an interview, which would be in private. A woman my age can always manage to gain a quiet word behind closed doors with the local abortionist.

Yes, she received me alone in her one-pot kitchen. I shrank from looking closely at what was simmering in that pot on the brazier. Thick, viscous gravy glooped blackly, as if made with blood. I didn't want to know where it came from.

Nona was of indeterminate years and hunched bearing. Thin, with a pointed nose, she had the straightforward manner of a woman in a solitary profession, accustomed to doing business on her own account, used to imposing her terms. Money up front and no time-wasters. Well, I was like that myself.

Her glance was swift, assessing me with hard eyes. I felt glad I had no need of her gynaecological expertise. I would have felt unsafe – though no doubt most women set about terminating pregnancies with a sense of dread. Even if you are guilt-free and have no doubts, the process is upsetting and you know it will be dangerous. Fortunately I had never needed to do this, though of course I knew women who had. I was also aware of others who were suspected of going through with it in secret. Sometimes that's slander, but often not.

'I am Flavia Albia. I won't mislead you about why I have come,' I admitted immediately. 'If I lived in the High Footpath district, you and I would be on the same vigiles watch list – I practise as an informer.'

Nona was delighted by this rare chance to look down on someone else.

I felt curious about how she had become what she was, yet she offered neither her past history nor information on the social service she gave. I wondered what she charged. She had no price list on display, since her services must be concealed. I guessed she assessed each client according to her accent, clothes and jewellery – or lack of it – then asked for as much as she thought she could screw out of them. Some might weep, a few might flee, but most would pay.

I explained the situation at the bar and what I was trying to do. 'The contractor is an aedile so he cannot ignore it. I am helping him find out what happened. Whatever was hidden in the past, it all has to be brought into the open now. Do you know the Hesperides?'

'Oh yes!'

Despite a tacit understanding that her work was known to me, we had not spoken of it. So at that point I made no suggestion that Nona had ever gone to the bar for professional reasons. It was quite likely. For waitresses, pregnancy is a routine hazard. Usually there is no known father. Invariably the girl cannot afford a child, while a barkeeper is nagging her to get rid of the problem as quickly as possible in order to be back at work, available to sleep with other men.

If randy regulars spot a barmaid with a bump, they shy away, thinking they may cop the blame. Even those who are new in town are scared. Well, let's face it, travellers are most at risk; strangers fresh off the boat can so easily be set upon with a false accusation, however ludicrous, and held in the local lock-up until they pay to be set loose.

'So, Nona, do you remember Rufia?'

'Everyone knew Rufia. Is there a reward for information?'

'Not so far. At the moment I am acting out of public duty.'

'Stupidity!'

'Well, the man who owns the building firm, Manlius Faustus, is a friend. It's a favour for him.'

'You sleeping with him?'

She had a professional interest in my private life. I produced a slight smile, trying to be discreet. When you have only had a lover for a few weeks, memories can be embarrassingly vivid. 'He wants to marry me.'

'So he says!' scoffed the wise woman. Her first principle was that all males past puberty are bastards. You cannot go wrong with that. 'You surely don't believe the old marriage lie? They all use that to gain their dirty desires and it brings me most of my custom.'

'I know. Plenty of my clients, like plenty of yours, do fall for false promises and live to be full of regret. But Faustus is solid. I told you, he's an aedile, and a respectable one at that.'

'You know your own business!' cackled Nona. She meant, *No, you don't, you're a fool, young woman.* I made no attempt to argue. She would never believe Julia and Favonia were at this moment planning their bridesmaid outfits.

They did not have to plan my costume. I would be in a traditional saffron wedding veil, which belonged to my aunt Maia. She wove it herself in her youth when she worked for a tailor and was marrying her first husband. The veil had already been lifted reverently from the chest where it resided – only to reveal that after all these years and quite a few borrowings, it was full of moth holes. There were more holes than woven sections. Julia and Favonia had wanted to try weaving a new one but there was no time for them to learn, even if they had not been butterfly-brained. Just my luck. I had been informed we were using the mothy monstrosity anyway.

'Well, *you* may have managed to find some man to look after you,' said Nona, as if I had latched on to Faustus merely for cash, not joined forces for companionship. 'Rufia had to work. For a caupona waitress, there will never be pretty nuptials with a priest taking the auguries from a sheep's liver.'

'Oh don't! I am dreading the damned sheep will wander off.'

'Well, you're in the right place here. Get yourself a decent sacrifice. Costus runs a *victimarium*, professional sheep-despatchers, right along the street. He's been there for years, covers most of Rome; everyone who knows the score has their religious business done by his lads. They are fine fellows and well known for their kindly rapport with animals. Book yourself in when you leave here, then your worries on the big day are over.' From the way she advertised, Nona sounded like Costus' loyal auntie. 'But Rufia only knew those lads as customers she served with drink,' she warned me guardedly.

'And other things?' I asked, not falling for that.

Nona gave me her hardest stare, a fine adamantine product.

I still resisted the pretence. 'I dare say Rufia did what was expected of a bar girl. I don't blame her for it. As you said earlier, she had to earn her money in the best way she could.' The only way. That's life.

We were sitting on stools, almost knee to knee. This would

35

be how women negotiated with Nona as they pleaded for her help with an unwanted baby. I lowered my voice. Probably the women did the same, when they reached the point of saying how far gone they were and why it was so important that they did not have to bear the child.

'The question is, Nona, was there ever conflict with the landlord over what Rufia had to do? I can think of various scenarios. She worked in a bar, so of course it was assumed she also went upstairs with men. Maybe she didn't like it, or after a time it became too much to bear. She could have acquired her own boyfriend, so wanted to stick with him. Maybe Old Thales used to impose on her. Maybe men who fornicated paid Thales, then he gave Rufia nothing – or not enough, in her opinion. Maybe it went the other way: she took the money directly from clients, but Thales suspected she cheated him of his right percentage. Maybe there was a fight over her. Maybe someone had a fight *with* her, over something else.'

'You ask a lot of questions, Flavia Albia.'

'Questions are unavoidable. This is how I do my job.'

'Leave it alone. The past is dead and buried. Don't disturb it.'

'Too late. A bunch of workmen dug up the past today. If it's Rufia, she has come back to claim justice.'

'If she's dead, she doesn't care any longer.' Clearly Nona had no belief in an afterlife – an advisable stance for an abortionist. She wouldn't want to be wafting through the Underworld one day and meet up with the tiny ghosts of foetuses, all furious with her for being snuffed out prematurely.

How did she achieve the fatal snuffing out? She was too unfriendly to ask.

36

'You seem eager to protect the barmaid's memory,' I commented. 'Is that because Rufia was an old customer, I wonder?' She blanked it. 'Come on, Nona, I know what you offer. Had you ever helped Rufia escape an unwanted pregnancy?'

'I would never have done that,' the wise woman assured me, stony-faced. 'Killing a child in the womb is against the law, as you well know, my girl.'

Abortion is indeed illegal, even though prevention is awkwardly tolerated. Aborting a live child denies its father his rights. We must protect men's rights. Meanwhile the poor mother cannot refuse to carry and bear a baby, even if its father is unknown or married to somebody else, if he thumps her, drinks all their income, unfortunately dies on her, or the horrible pest has simply bunked off.

Once I might have persuaded Nona to be more open, but I saw that being associated with a magistrate worked against me. Juno, I had become part of the establishment. People would stop sharing confidences.

I must learn from this. In future I would only mention Manlius Faustus being an aedile if it positively helped.

'So you cannot tell me anything?'

'I don't gossip.'

That must be a useful attribute in her profession. Sadly it was no help to mine.

After I left Nona, I happened to stroll past Costus' victimarium, which she had mentioned, so I went in to speak to the proprietor. The place reminded me of an undertaker's; it had very little on display to upset people by open reference to its trade. Costus worked in an anodyne office that could have housed a bookkeeper, not a slaughterer.

Unlike Nona, he had a readily available price list, as I discovered when I admitted I might be hiring.

In our family, we have to avoid allowing my aunt Junia's husband, the doleful Gaius Baebius, ever to fulfil his lifetime dream of acting as a priest. He once took lessons in sacrificing, but still doesn't know how to do it. Julia and Favonia were foolishly lining up this pompous uncle, assuming his legendary backache allowed him to function, but I now decided to overrule them.

Costus, a practised salesman in a long tunic, ran through his patter. 'The best deal is the full threesome: your *victimarius* to gently lead in the selected beast, your *popa* to stun it with his trusty mallet, your *cultrarius* to slit the throat neatly and slash open the stomach for inspecting the organs.' Triple fees, I thought, without rancour. 'We can put you in the way of a decent seer to read your entrails. Staberius is who we recommend. Very reliable. Just write out your required omens for him and he always fulfils his brief. You can buy your sheep, porker or bull from us too; beautiful animals, they come from our own farm. Just give advance notice if you want any unusual bird or creature. I warn you now, we can't get flamingos for love nor money at the moment.'

'What am I supposed to have?'

'A pig is most popular for weddings.'

'Who wants to follow a trend? Can I change to a sheep?'

'You're the bride! We have a glut of mutton. Black or white?'

'It's a wedding.'

'Snowy then.'

'I hope "Snowy" is a tint off your fleeces colour chart, not some pet's name.'

'Oh you're a one! Who's the lucky couple?'

'My man and me.'

Costus leapt back, surveying me with what could be new respect – or possibly derision. '*Congratulations!*'

'Thank you.' I was amazed how calmly I said that. 'The do will be at my pa's house on the Marble Embankment, below the Aventine.'

'Absolutely not a problem. Now come and see the boys.'

'Oh lovely. Is it pick-your-own?'

I think he suspected his new customer of too much levity.

Olympus, his boys were lush! It had been a hot day but in any case, the sacrifice experts liked to show off. They would work barefoot and bare-chested, with wide sashes holding up long wrap-around skirts – and this was how they sat around in the backyard, waiting for potential hirers. To butcher a bull you need a very strong physique and steady nerves. They looked seriously up to it. They must achieve their stunning ripples by gymnasium exercise, after which their toned torsos, arms and calves were oiled to display the results. They all had well-tended curly hairstyles and had been manicured. I bet the eager girls gave them free nail buffs. The men now preened like peacocks and gleamed like polished rosewood. You couldn't have statues of them in your home, it would be too exciting.

'We train them to behave well with the public,' Costus assured me. 'Your guests will find them respectful.'

That might not be how the bare-chested ones would find my irreverent guests, but by then it would be too late.

Playing it cool, I took my pick. Things were looking up. My entire flock of female relations, plus those belonging to Faustus whom I had yet to meet, would appreciate the

39

care I had expended on obtaining a decent sacrifice, carried out by trusted experts – with beautiful muscle tone.

'I look forward to seeing you at my father's house. Together with Snowy,' I cooed, smiling my gratitude at Passus, Erastus and Victor, my chosen trio of hunks. 'Now don't be offended, but you look like lads of the world . . .' Though no longer lads, they were far from offended. 'So tell me something, if you can. Did any of you ever know a barmaid who worked at the Garden of the Hesperides – name of Rufia?'

They all did, including Costus.

7

They seemed willing to talk. At least that was my first impression. I admit I was reluctant to harbour doubts about such handsome samples of manhood. A bride is entitled to hanker for the freedom she is losing. Isn't she?

Victor said they all drank at the Garden of the Hesperides, had done for years and still did in theory; as soon as it reopened for business they would return. 'It's a good bar.'

'Would you say you had some special relationship, or were you just ordinary customers?'

'Just normal.' Their profession gave them a thirst. The Hesperides was good for lunch and evening meals too, plus you could have a flutter on horses and chariots if you wanted.

'And other things?' I asked, trying to look matter-of-fact. Nobody volunteered an answer, so I added, 'Or are you all good, clean-living boys?'

Erastus said Passus had never been good or clean-living; they all guffawed. He obviously had a reputation for playing around, which perhaps the others envied.

'Oh come on, you can tell me. I'm a woman of the world and in my profession I've seen everything. If you go upstairs with waitresses – or with waiters, for that matter – it's your business.' I saw no sign that any of them preferred the male sex, though I kept an open mind. 'My only interest is what you can tell me about Rufia, who disappeared.' Still no admissions, so I changed my angle of questioning. 'At least if you all knew her, can you describe her for me? So far she is only a name. Was she pretty? A good waitress? Was she well liked?'

Erastus did the honours. 'She was never much of a looker, but she was good at her job. She got on with everyone. She knew how to be friendly.'

'Could she be *too* friendly? Get herself into situations?'

'Rufia could take care of herself,' Costus weighed in. 'She was the one who chucked out troublemakers if ever a strong arm was needed.'

'A woman had to break up fights? They do have male staff, don't they?'

'Natalis and Nipius. But nobody argued with Rufia.'

'What she says goes,' Passus reinforced his master. So stern had been this legendary waitress, he still used the present tense. 'Besides, if Rufia was trying to eject someone and they declined her invitation to leave, everyone else in the bar would come and help her.'

'Ho, ho! Her word was law?' That was slightly unexpected. 'It doesn't sound as though it would be easy for someone to overpower Rufia and do her in – which must be what happened, if those are her bones in the courtyard.'

'Overpowering is always doable if it's tackled the right way,' Passus disagreed. I reminded myself that these experts spent their time persuading enormous specimens of cattle to go willingly to their deaths. It was essential that a sacrifice did not protest, or you had to start again.

It would have been impolite to suggest the victimarii had murdered Rufia. They seemed too good-hearted. (I know! That old cliché. I would never accept it from a witness, but of course my own judgement was trustworthy . . .) I momentarily envisaged them hanging a garland around the barmaid's neck, walking her to an altar with gentle encouragement, then, *Kneel down for us, Rufia, don't worry – whack . . . stun . . . whizzo . . . slit – gather up all her spurting blood in special bronze bowls . . .*

Presumably not. Whatever happened to Rufia was most likely sudden, messy violence carried out by an enraged acquaintance, or perhaps done by a stranger. A stranger would probably be untraceable now. An acquaintance might be an easier prospect.

'Did Rufia have a boyfriend?' They sniggered. Apparently not. So much for my most obvious suspect. 'Do you find the suggestion amusing?' I pressed.

'She was not exactly the type,' claimed Erastus.

Passus added, 'No one would have dared.'

'Being the bouncer? I am gathering that Rufia was a force of nature. Was she quarrelsome?'

'Not if you did things her way.'

'You're implying people generally did? Anyone hold a grudge against her?'

Without obvious consultation, the victimarii all shook their heads. They were positive. Too positive? Sometimes you just catch a hint of conspiracy. Had I noticed flickers?

'All sure about that? Well, if you remember anything, please let me know.'

They each nodded again, good honest fellows. All not looking at one another.

Were they simply convinced there had been no grudges? That Rufia was a genuinely lovely girl with a sweet personality, whom everyone liked? A lovely but very strong-armed girl who could (and would) expel louts and generally make people follow orders? I had seen barmaids like that. They enjoy their power. Bars being what they are, I do not blame them.

'Do you remember that time, when she disappeared?' There were nods, freshly helpful. 'Was it known immediately? The same night or next morning? Or did people only gradually become aware she had gone missing?'

This question seemed to puzzle them. 'I suppose it was gradual,' decided Costus.

'The bar had other staff, so Rufia dropping her shifts might initially pass without disrupting the place?'

'There was some cursing from the waiters!' Victor grinned.

'Bars tend to have a shifting complement,' I mused. 'Staff do come and go . . . How quickly did the dark rumours start? The suspicion that she had been murdered?'

They could not tell me. Stories of her being killed and buried in the courtyard seemed to have grown up slowly until all the world just knew about it.

'What did the landlord, Thales, have to say?'

'He harrumphed and made no comment. That was how he was.'

'Was he suspected from the beginning?' Again, the landlord's supposed involvement developed subtly. There was no public outcry and no one investigated. Although people guessed Rufia had been killed and he was guilty, no one said so too loudly. 'Were people scared of Thales?'

'He was not a man to cross unless you wanted to be barred.'

'Oh wonderful! Nobody thought about Rufia, only whether their own drinks were at risk!' It had a horrible ring of truth. 'In general was he violent?'

'Not particularly,' said Passus, the one who was supposed to have the filthy lifestyle.

'For a bar owner,' chuckled Erastus, a much quieter

character. He had a birthmark down one side of his face that might put off some of the girls. When he was conducting a sacrifice, he would have to mask it with face paint so he looked perfect.

'Hmm . . . Do I deduce Rufia did not live on the premises? I know there are rooms above the bar.'

'When the place is up and running, those rooms are always in use,' said Costus.

'For travellers to rest their heads – or the purposes I mentioned earlier?'

'For all kinds of things,' he swore, pretending all these things were of an innocent variety. A sewing club met there? A group of pastoral poets?

The main point was that Rufia lodged somewhere else, which made it less likely anyone would go and check on her if she failed to turn up for duty. 'I imagine she had a room not too far away?'

'Mucky Mule Mews, I believe.'

'Desirable area?' I was wry. They shared the joke.

'Very exclusive!' scoffed Costus. Erastus said his cousin lived there, but he always had, so he didn't know any better.

As they told me about Mucky Mule Mews, I could see they were sharing some amusement at the thought of me going there. Was it also dangerous? I wondered. Would there be a risk to me if I went?

'This could explain what happened to her,' I said. 'There are plenty of instances of weary bar staff leaving in the dark, after their workplace finally shuts in the small hours, then being waylaid as they make their way home. Especially women. Robbery may feature if the money's easy to grab, but perverts are really after sex, sex with a vulnerable lone victim.'

'They would have spotted her in the bar?' suggested Passus, clearly not liking the thought.

'Either just that night, Passus, or perhaps they have been watching for weeks,' I told him. 'Sometimes they have even made an approach and been rebuffed; more usually they have never spoken to the victim, who has never noticed them.'

'Scary!'

'It is. From what you say about Rufia, I would expect her to be streetwise, but she could have been suddenly jumped in a spot where she had no chance of escape, with nobody to hear a cry for help. Anyway, she would be tired after a long evening, off her guard.'

There was a flaw in this argument, which I did not mention. Why would a killer who attacked Rufia in the street bring back her body to the Hesperides afterwards? She could have been buried anywhere, or just left. Why tie the murder so closely to her place of work?

I felt convinced that whatever misfortune had befallen Rufia, it must have happened at the bar. Either she never left that night, or she herself came back. But unless a lot of people witnessed her death and had since kept strictly silent, the event could only have occurred in the dead of night, after the Hesperides emptied and the other staff had gone home.

That would fit a fight with the landlord, as the rumours supposed.

8

I could take my questions no further at this stage. I needed more of a lead. When I left, Costus and his staff escorted me to the door with elaborate gentility. I glanced back and waved. I knew the men stayed there in a group to watch me down the street. While I would like to think that was because they found my questions apt and my person attractive, I suspected they had another motive. My visit had felt vaguely unsatisfactory. They knew something. I for my part did not yet understand enough to probe for it.

It was likely to be some time longer before Faustus returned. Not only was the Aventine a good step from here, he had given himself too much to do: aediles' business, wedding plans, fetching luggage and visiting Lesser Laurel Street to see what his workmen were up to. I hoped they would not dig up any more human remains, or I too was liable to be overstretched.

Of course finding bones was possible in any city, especially in Rome, which had such a long history. The rule against burying a corpse within the city boundary was good public hygiene, but it must always have led to the surreptitious concealment of bodies. It was not necessarily the result of misdemeanour. Many of the poor could not afford a niche in the cheapest columbarium, let alone a tomb in a necropolis. Even to bury ashes in a broken old pot, they would first have to pay for cremation. So, when digging anywhere in Rome, there was a good chance of finding bones that should not be there. Skeletons of babies abounded, though if a child died in its first four days it was permissible to bury the body at home. It was better to tuck your stillborn under your own threshold than cast its sad corpse onto a rubbish heap with the risk of dogs, rats, carrion crows and witches, let alone youths looking for something horrible to kick around the streets.

I decided that Faustus and I had better try to identify whether the bones we had were truly those of a woman, one who had vanished in living memory. There was no point me chasing down what happened to Rufia if this was not her at all. By the look of it, the Garden of the Hesperides had been a bar since the Republic, so given what tended to happen in bars, it could have a long series of sad little waitresses who had met untimely ends.

Now I was despondent. Why had I so easily got involved? Why did I never learn?

I tried a small bathhouse, only reminding myself how disgusting they can be. At your local, you stop seeing the scum. Here floating dirt and oil lapped in the basins and pools all too obviously, while the floors were slippery with other people's scraped-off filth. The customers looked like people who peed in the plunge pools.

All right; you can't tell from appearance. But they all looked like people who were just asking to be insulted.

Emerging glumly, I explored more stalls and shops around the Ten Traders area, buying provisions that I carried back to our hired room. The bag of bones silently greeted me; I tucked it away under the bed. While I waited for Faustus I took more note of the location.

The room was directly above a teeming crossroads. Behind a battered shutter, I found a balcony onto which you could take one step, if you really wanted to stand on a ledge like a pigeon. Teetering there I could see people thronging the Vicus Longus, with all the usual extras: smells I tried not to identify, mules braying while their drivers yelled themselves hoarse, strident women arguing with hoarse neighbours, artisans singing as they worked, copper-beaters hammering, carpenters rasping wood with adzes that set my teeth on edge. Someone was scraping out a huge cooking pot into the gutter and a sad child was bawling for attention it would never receive. Nine feral dogs in a pack came rampaging down the road, scarily barking their heads off, then bystanders yelled after the dogs.

By now I had identified some of the smells, and wished I hadn't. I braced myself to keep looking because I wanted to get a feel for the neighbourhood.

People came from all levels and the whole fabric of society. Groups of the idle hung about waiting for life to improve, making more noise than seemed wise, given that while I watched a bunch of the Urban Cohorts marched in, looking for people to harass. A few mature women who looked quite respectable were going home with shopping baskets. These women would want places for religious observance, though temples were nowhere in evidence. The closest thing to incense was the pungent after-waft of some public slaves who had been given garlic soup. Perhaps it was so they wouldn't notice the odour of the dung they were brushing from the road.

At least it was swept. These folk should try living in Fountain Court, which never was.

As the afternoon ended and evening began, people of the night started to emerge. Workers in the entertainment

49

trade, bar staff, musicians, odd types who sold themselves in very curious ways, were all heading for their places of work – places that would be loud and lively far into the night, and I bet in this district their customers really lingered. An evening out at a bar was how they socialised and even did business; it staved off the misery of going home, when home was dire. This was not a quiet nook to live in, nowhere to live at all if you had any choice. Many people had none, so these miserable souls, with their children, aged parents and animals, would be venting their frustrations at all hours.

Looking down the smaller street that crossed the Vicus, I could see a couple in a clinch against a grimy wall down one alley while in another a cluster of men had their heads together as if inspecting stolen goods. Going into the ginnels was only to avoid being trampled. They did not care who was watching. Their activities were carried out in full view and even the heavy boots of the Urban Cohort soldiers failed to make them pause. I had better not let my lover take the air on our skinny balcony, or he would be faced with a crisis of conscience. He had enough to do, without wanting to clean up another aedile's patch.

Fortunately, when he finally arrived it was dark, though as I let him in I saw him look back over one shoulder rather thoughtfully. He had his slave, Dromo, grumbling under the weight of luggage they had brought for us. I fed them both, then took Dromo to the Hesperides where he would have to sleep in any space he could find. When I returned to the room, Faustus was lying on the bed, spark out.

I stretched beside him quietly. He woke enough to murmur. A light kiss on my forehead from him served for our goodnight. We were so close now, we had already passed beyond needing to fuss. I spent a few moments thinking how hard the mattress was and then, lying close against his side, I too tried to sleep.

No use. I spent many more moments listening to the hubbub from outside. Added to the unfettered hum of voices, the Romulus had live music; on hot August nights like this the castanets and tambourines were brought out into the street, where the clientele joined in with stamps and clapping. The Four Limpets competed with a solo lyre, well played if you like loud weeping string instruments in the hands of a mad dramatic singer. Meanwhile a persistent pest with pan pipes travelled around all the bars, tootling at drinkers until they paid him to move on.

At least I was getting the measure of this district at night, the low-grade noisy hot spot where poor Rufia was said to have been murdered.

Eventually Tiberius sensed through his slumber that I was struggling to find rest. He roused himself enough to gather me closer with one arm, then dropped off again immediately. I lay with my head on his shoulder, thinking about this. He had passion, when not poleaxed by weariness. Even tonight, he wanted to grip me tightly, as if I might escape him while he was lost in dreams. So here we were, utterly at ease together. Together for life now, I knew it. I would not need the wedding augur to foretell this by peering at a dead sheep's liver.

Not that it would hurt to have him prophesy happiness to our families. They didn't believe us. Tiberius was right: maybe the relatives would have more faith if a stranger in a dirty head veil told them.

Smiling to myself at the incongruity of having a husband I agreed with, finally I fell asleep.

9

The Ten Traders street life gave me nightmares.

As a rule, I tried not to dwell on the unfairness of my childhood, an orphan of the Boudiccan Rebellion, living among unaffectionate people and then fending for myself as a scavenger. Sounds assailing me here threw me back to the cold unpaved streets of Londinium, where I once haunted dingy eating houses for any crust to stave off hunger, amongst the dross of degenerate tribes, transient merchants, unhappy soldiers and criminal incomers.

I started awake, with a dry mouth and fast heartbeats. If I tried sleeping again straight away the bad dream would return. Slipping from the bed, I went and stood by the balcony.

The streets below lay in darkness. The noise had dropped, the musicians were silent, yet a low burr of steady voices told me people were still here. No one even tried providing street lights in such an area, and where there was an occasional oil lamp for bar customers, it gave only a tiny blur of light that barely covered the table or counter it was set on. As my eyes grew accustomed, I could see waiters still moving to and fro with trays on their shoulders. I thought I heard the sharp click-clack of gaming counters, with cries of reaction as dice were thrown. I scanned the darker shadows, imagining I glimpsed some waif cringing in an alley, as I had once done.

'What's wrong?' Tiberius thought something outside had disturbed me.

'A bad dream.'

I heard the soft approach of bare feet, felt warm arms come around me from behind – comforting, not controlling. 'Be easy,' he murmured. I leaned back against him, accepting his affection.

'What goes on down there on those streets was my world once.'

He said nothing. That was Tiberius Manlius. Perhaps he sighed a little.

'Did you know?' I persisted.

'Always been obvious.' He took one of my forefingers to a scar on his palm where once, before I knew him well, I had stabbed him with a fish skewer. 'Nicely brought-up young ladies from regular homes do not do that.'

'So you want danger and thrills from me?'

'I just want you. I don't think you are dangerous, not to people you love.' After a moment he added, 'Your mother told me I ought to know you had a very bleak childhood.'

For a moment I was angry with Helena, before I saw that she was protecting me. She did not want Faustus to find out later about my experiences. No hope and no safety. The physical blows, emotional famine, rape by a brothel-keeper . . . All Tiberius knew from me was that afterwards I had had a happy marriage, though tragically short.

'She gave no details,' he said. Nor did I now. I was not ready to risk it. Maybe I never would be. Even so, I muttered, 'Helena Justina warned you for good reasons. What did you say to her?'

'I told her I grieve for your suffering, which I had always suspected, but I love you as the woman you are. You can

53

tell me,' he offered in a low voice, still standing behind me. One of the soft things we had said when we first acknowledged our feelings was that we could tell one another anything. Mostly we did so, though people fool themselves. It's always dangerous. Even the best of men might find my experiences impossible to live with.

'Not now.' Tiberius thought he could bear anything but I was loath to test his tolerance. 'I try to forget.' Of course I never would entirely. You are made by your past.

Can you be remade by the present? I turned around to embrace him, enjoying the shape and feel of this body I was learning to know, moulding myself to his ribcage and stomach. We were both naked. Until recently I had slept in an old under-tunic; probably he had done the same. Now, except for a few days a month, that seemed unnecessary.

We kissed gently, then I went back to bed with him. My bad memories were hovering nearby, but the nightmare would not reimpose itself tonight.

Tiberius held me close. 'While I live, Flavia Albia, you will be safe. If I have any influence, you will be happy.'

'I know.' I was always happy with him, and being happy makes you feel safe.

26 August

Seven days before the Kalends of September
(a.d. VII Kal. Sept.)

Five days before the wedding of
Tiberius Manlius Faustus and Flavia Albia

10

Breakfast was our special time. This had started when we would meet as if by chance and sit together in my aunt's caupona. At the Stargazer, you had to converse to stop losing your grip on life. Talking together was easy, we had found, even though we were both by nature reticent. So, we became friends over the Stargazer's granite bread and fatty meats. I would watch Faustus mentally assessing how the waiter, whoever it was that day, had given us the least possible number of olives he could serve without having the pottery saucer thrown at his head. Those bite bowls are small but carry weight, as any scavenger knows. I had had them flung at me, back in Londinium.

After a few Stargazer breakfasts, I noticed Faustus was not in fact auditing the nibbles but taking an interest in me.

Now we were living together, he would probably go back to real olive-counting. He was an aedile. Monitoring behaviour was his favourite task. I let him get on with it. Supervising waiters was better than imagining he could supervise me.

In daylight today, we were able to spot remnants of the ancient market that must have originally given the Ten Traders its name. There were single-room shops each with a vaulted roof and a room above, like the one where we were staying. Early in the morning the bars were closed – well around here you could still get a drink and I don't mean water – while shops we had not seen yesterday afternoon now opened and revealed their presence. Dry goods and fresh greens mostly. One of the scroll-sellers for which the Argiletum was supposedly famous. A cutler, so people in the bars could buy bone-handled dinner knives to stick into other people they argued with.

A sign said an apothecary lived in one of the upstairs rooms, ready to run out with salves for any non-fatal knife wounds. He claimed he also sold love potions. He risked having an aedile raid him, to root out magic. Like plenty of others the seller clung on, purveying herbs that worked and incantations that didn't, pills that put you on a bucket all night and powders that claimed to make you irresistible to others, but might kill you.

On the Vicus Longus we found a streetside snackery that was being swept clean by a worn woman, while her thin-faced daughter served a few rolls and cheese wedges to passing workers. Rather than have us clutter up their counter, they put out a bench for us to sit on.

We each reported on yesterday's efforts. When I expressed anxiety that Tiberius was wearing himself out, he reassured me. He said nothing about progress on the house, although I gathered he had been there. He had told the aediles' office he was 'going to his villa at the seaside'; apparently no magistrate was ever expected to work in the August heat, although Manlius Faustus must be the only one in history who was too poor to own a holiday home. He was arguing with his uncle over his right to draw cash from their family finances. He would never prise money out of Uncle Tullius for luxuries. Business deals were hard enough to fund.

Meanwhile he had left Julia and Favonia with a wedding-guest list. When they applied themselves to something they wanted to do, my younger sisters could be meticulous. They had Katutis, Father's secretary, writing out invitations; between them there was no chance any awful relative would be left out. Any day now, this event would be scribbled on everyone's calendar. I was stuck.

I mentioned that I had myself hired victimarii and an augur. My bridegroom looked annoyed. He pointed out, mildly, that since I had refused to take any interest, he and his helpers had fixed all the details; we must avoid duplication, he pompously decreed – practising for the day he could thunder around as head of the household. Practising how to ignore that, I said Julia and Favonia would be delighted when they saw the hunks.

'You're marrying me, remember. Not some bastard bunch of bare-chested bull-despatchers,' growled Tiberius. I smiled dreamily. 'What?' he demanded.

'Remembering you in bed!' I murmured, so he pretended not to blush, while sweetly proud of himself. Men are so easy to manage.

Faustus nudged me in the ribs with an elbow, fully aware of my tactics. 'And what kind of horrible heart-throb is your augur?'

'Haven't seen him. Supposedly he is top quality – all we have to do is send a note beforehand and he will foresee everything we ask for.'

'Can't he "foresee" what we want without being fed instructions? I'd like a long life with a darling wife who is never cheeky.'

'Sorry, sir, I can't do lack of cheek. That omen has been discontinued. Even the gods have limitations.'

While Tiberius chewed the rim of his beaker, I recapped what I had learned yesterday from my various interrogations, especially from Costus and his crew. 'I discount the possibility that Rufia fell victim to some stalker who grabbed her on her way home to Mucky Mule Mews. I think she must have been killed at the bar. So we have *either* she was an abused girlie bashed by a degenerate landlord claiming employer's rights, probably drunk at the time, *or* she was a stroppy piece who quarrelled and, if you believe in the concept, "brought it on herself". I'm not there yet – I need to ask around more.'

Tiberius agreed we should persuade someone with anatomical knowledge to examine the bones. We had brought them out with us, like some pet that needed exercising. He was going to the local vigiles, the Third Cohort, to report our find, so he would ask if their doctor or someone else with expertise could pronounce for us.

We settled our breakfast bill, which meant I paid it, because of Uncle Tullius.

Gazing at the older woman as she counted in the coins, I was sure she had been listening to our conversation. She said nothing but I knew what this wily bird had been up to while she innocently wiped down her counter.

'I presume you're not a customer of the Garden of the Hesperides?' I asked, gently letting her know I had spotted her eavesdropping. Now it was the daughter's turn to listen in. She too said nothing.

The Hesperides was just out of sight, though very close by. The mother shook her head, pinching her mouth. She was a hard-working scrap who looked affronted at the suggestion that she might lower herself to take a tipple in a wine bar. 'A body has been found there. I expect you heard about it?' Again, she pretended to look shocked. *I do not listen to common gossip, Flavia Albia!* Classic. She could have been my Aventine granny biffing me with a dishcloth for impudence.

I spotted her having a good squint at our bag of bones.

Faustus and I went to the Hesperides.

Immediately we were assailed by Dromo, complaining. He couldn't be expected to live in a place full of dead bodies, he hadn't had a wink of sleep, the watchman had been cruel to him, and nobody had given him any breakfast.

'Come with me,' said Faustus calmly. 'I'll buy you a flatbread on the way.'

'You tell your kindly master all about it, Dromo!' I had listened carefully to the slave's moans in case he had seen anything useful. After all, he had spent the night at a newly discovered crime scene. Anything could have happened. I did not spell it out to him, but perpetrators sometimes do return.

'I don't find my master kind, Flavia Albia.'

'Yes, he is. Be good and maybe Manlius Faustus will let you carry the bag of bones.'

'I'm not going to touch a dead person!'

'Lucky for you, then, these are in a rubble basket,' his master barked as he handed over the remains; they set off, still bickering in their normal way. I went into the courtyard, which the watchman, Trypho, opened up for me before he curled up to sleep on a pallet in the bar. Alone, I gazed around, considering the place with new eyes.

The project, which I considered ridiculous, was that the small outdoor area would be given one of those canals people create in fancy outdoor dining rooms, down which lamps and little food dishes are floated, generally to sink with their contents. Opposite the bar end, a daft grotto had been created, with shell decorations and a small mosaic of Oceanus wreathed in sparkly glass seaweed. A so-called specialist had provided that; I knew, because Faustus had had a row with him because he was preoccupied with some designer villa and had sent his apprentice. The apprentice had never been properly taught, though he was a bright lad who learned on the job. His right-hand seaweed ringlets were much better than his left. Customers in the know would be asking for the table by the fig tree, on Oceanus' good side.

The fig tree was new. They were fan-training it on one courtyard wall, in theory. The builders must have planted it; nobody had told them to contain the roots. In a few years the monster would be forty feet high so when hard, unripe fruit fell from the topmost branches, gravity would make it bounce on the drinkers' heads with knock-out force. Or worse, the figs would splash into their beakers, spilling their drinks.

That would be if the tree lived. The sapling looked sick. There was no water on-site at the moment. The workmen had filled in a well with concrete. They were supposed to be arranging a connection from an aqueduct to supply the water feature, and include the kitchen, but the new landlord had just been told its horrifying cost. He had baulked. Faustus, who had inherited all this barmy design, had promised to quote for other options, although now the well was out of action there were none. Like any experienced contractor, Faustus was simply waiting for the client to give in and pay, knowing Liberalis was desperate to have his bar back.

Rufia's bones had been below the opposite wall to the fig tree. As far as I could tell, the men had only been digging there so that they could bury their lunch wrappings and a smelly sack, the traditional way builders avoid removing rubbish from a site.

Returning to the corridor that led back indoors, I spotted a narrow staircase. It must lead to the upstairs rooms where customers obtained 'extras'. It was steep and dark, with dirty treads and dusty walls. Pulling my skirts in, I climbed up to explore. Three curtained doorways clustered around a top landing that was fit only for mountain goats. With no natural light, it was barely negotiable. I banged my head on a suspended phallic lamp. That would help at night, and gave a clue as to what went on here, although no one but an idiot would blunder up accidentally. Still, idiots do go to bars.

Poking back the first spidery curtain, I found a bare cubicle with an unmade single bed. No surprise. There was no other furniture. No hospitality tray (I jest), not even a chamber pot. As a bower of delight it was crude, though much as I expected.

'Five star!' I exclaimed out loud, sarcastically allocating the kind of mansio grade you see on high-class travelling maps. I did not suppose many high-class travellers ever found their way to the Hesperides, but strangers in a city can make mistakes. Well, who hasn't accidentally wandered into a den of sin when merely looking for a quiet chickpea supper?

As I turned to investigate the other two rooms, I received a shock that nearly made me tumble downstairs. Somebody was there.

'Hades!' I was scared, I admit.

A man in a one-armed unbelted tunic had stuck his head out of a room, looking to see who I was. The occupant of the other room zipped back his door curtain too; *he* was naked. He had an extremely hairy chest; I tried not to look any lower down. I fancied I heard females in the background, though with these narrow doorways people inside the rooms were hidden. Judging by how the two men looked, anyone they had lured in here could not be picky.

Though startled, I managed to accost them: 'Nipius and Natalis, I presume? You work here when the bar is open? Well, I am Flavia Albia, looking into the unpleasant finds the workmen dug up yesterday. I suggest you both put your clothes on straight away, and come downstairs to help with my enquiries!'

I I

By the time they sloped down to the courtyard, I was sitting down, looking cool. Being enthroned while others stand is a sign of superiority in Rome, though waiters never subscribe to such etiquette. A waiter can be lying on the dirty ground pushing a wedge under a wobbly table leg, but he will still behave as if you are an upstart slave, unreasonably complaining, whereas he is of royal birth. You can stand up, sit down or cavort like a dolphin with hiccups, but you won't obtain respect. All waiters in any establishment occupy the position of power. Julius Caesar must have had his nose put out of joint every time he fancied a half flagon of house red while he was out shopping.

All right. I concede that old pomposity Caesar may never have nipped out for an onion – not even to gain a few minutes' peace from Calpurnia's nagging him about her dreams.

Nipius and Natalis gave me their *What do you mean, you expect faster service?* faces. They had been waiting at tables so long, it was their first line of defence.

'So!' I positioned my note tablet on one knee, stylus in hand, fully composed. 'Which of you is which?'

Grudgingly, they told me. In daylight, I was looking at two semi-mature cheeses. Not exactly cave-ripened until their fine flavour knocked your head off, but they were theoretically old enough to have been here when Rufia was on the payroll. Both were easily twenty-five and probably more, so by my very rough timeline they would have been lads in their first employment. Nipius was taller, with joined-up eyebrows and pustules. Natalis was heavier with only half as many spots, the hero with the chest fur; its wiry black hairs were peeking now over the neck of his crumpled workwear. It would be the only tunic he had, clearly bought when he was slimmer. He was no advert for bar snacks.

They were in similar green tunics, like a uniform; Natalis had put ragged brown braid on the hem of his. At least, he'd persuaded some girlfriend to do it. Nipius expressed whatever personality he possessed via a piece of string around his neck, from which dangled a big pebble with a hole in it. He must have expensive tastes. Natalis had prob-ably learned that a necklace would snag in his chest hair so he wore copper bracelets instead. He had had them so long he didn't notice the verdigris.

I decided I wouldn't trust either of these scallywags to serve up the drink I had asked for or to remember my complimentary pistachios. Nor would they would go back for the nuts, even on the third time of reminding. But I bet they would still demand a tip. They gave the impression they might be aggressive about it.

I could see that, in the way of waiters, they were wondering if there was any point trying to flirt. I gave them the frosty treatment. 'I am doing this for Manlius Faustus, the contractor. He is a magistrate, a busy man, and he is my fiancé. I shall take down your story, then see what he wants to do about you.' There could be no harm suggesting they might find themselves in trouble. 'You both work at the Hesperides when it is open? How long have you been here?'

They confirmed that they had started as lads. 'So you knew the barmaid called Rufia?' They gave me the common verdict: everyone knew Rufia.

'What was she like?' They looked vague. I tried specific questions, which worked better. Rufia was the normal height and build for a waitress, with no special characteristics. 'Black eyes? Brown eyes? Skinny or curvaceous? Did she nick olives out of the customers' titbit bowls? Would she commandeer all the tips?' This got me nowhere further. Anyone would think that when ordering the dish of the day, I had asked if the chef could leave out the oregano. 'Nipius and Natalis, either you are utterly unobservant, or you're playing up. If she was a customer, I would expect you to say "We see so many, we can't remember" – but Olympus, you worked with this woman!'

Possibly they looked shamefaced.

'Right, you hopeless pair. Tell me what happened when she disappeared. Her duties must have fallen on you, so please don't pretend you knew nothing about it.'

They stared. I glared. They decided they had better say something or I might become cantankerous. Wise boys. They were the kind who would make sure they never looked your way when you signalled for your bill; still, when someone finally grew angry, they deigned to notice. (You don't believe bar staff *accidentally* fail to meet your eye?) 'We just came in one morning and she was no longer here.'

'What did the landlord say?'

'Only "the bitch isn't here" and that we had to cover for her.'

'Was that how he always described her?'

'Nothing unusual.'

'Old Thales sounds unpleasant!'

67

'He was a normal landlord.' Every time Natalis spoke to me, he looked shiftier.

'Really?'

'Yes, he *really* thought himself special – though he wasn't,' Nipius told me with some venom, fiddling with his pebble necklace.

'Expand, Nipius.'

'Thales was a bully and a bore. He traded on his reputation.'

'Which was?'

'Being a wonderful character.'

'I've met some of those!'

'He just hung around cadging drinks off the customers.'

'He had a horrible laugh!' This detail from Natalis, the one with the bracelets, came unexpectedly. 'And what he laughed at was usually not funny.'

'How was he with his staff?' The waiters hung back from answering. 'Grabby?' I guessed.

'There was a whole lot more than grabbing,' grumbled Nipius. I felt unsurprised.

'Only the women?'

'He preferred the women. He was never choosy.' Both folded their arms, a defensive position, as if they had been groped by Thales when young. Maybe even after they grew up. Maybe worse than groped.

'Did that include Rufia?'

They both guffawed. 'Sounds like you know nothing about Rufia!'

'I would, if somebody told me!' I snapped back. I was growing tired of this. 'Thales is supposed to have murdered her and buried her, right in that spot over there.' I gestured to where the ground had been disturbed; the pickaxe Sparsus

68

had been using yesterday still leaned against the wall. The waiters looked away, as if they feared Rufia was still decaying in the garden. 'You two have been treading on the poor woman on a daily basis. The least you can do now is help me find out what really happened to her, so we can give her ghost some rest.'

At that, they said that no ghost of Rufia's would ever lie easy in Hades. She would be organising the other spirits within an inch of their lives, or what had once been their lives. Nipius joked caustically he was surprised there had been no reports of Underworld protests.

'Now I am starting to imagine her! She bossed you around, I take it?' Actually I was on her side. This pair of loafers were bad enough now; as aimless youngsters in their first job they must have been dire. 'Were you working here on her last night?' Nods. 'Remember anything out of the ordinary?' Head shakes. 'Was the bar full?'

'Lively.'

'All regulars?'

'Yes,' said Natalis.

And 'No,' Nipius contradicted, before he noticed that Natalis was signalling him to hush. I waited. 'We had a party of salesmen in.'

'Part of the time.' Natalis downplayed it. He picked at his acne, which could be his way of taking his mind off something difficult. I doubted he knew he was doing it.

'Out for a good time?' I asked dryly, knowing what dealers and distributors are like. The waiters groaned in confirmation. 'Did they cause any trouble?' No. 'Did Rufia serve them?'

'Yes, Rufia looked after them.'

'What does that mean?' I was sharp. 'Come on, I know

69

what happens. Did the party of salesmen stop at drinks, or did any of them have extras?'

The salesmen all had sex. Of course they did. They were salesmen.

When I demanded more details, Natalis and Nipius admitted this had happened in the rooms upstairs. They said they were unable to supply positions, time taken, or whether there were interesting twosomes or threesomes. I ignored their sarcasm.

'Twosomes and threesomes are never as interesting as people hope. Too mechanical, they have to be. Positioning the bodies requires a commissariat.' Nipius and Natalis raised their eyebrows at my inside knowledge. 'I read widely!' And I listen to other people's conversations. 'Lads, I take it this was a regular happening? How much did it cost?'

They feigned ignorance of sordid details.

'Come off it! Upstairs is where I found you two this morning. You know exactly what goes on there. Is it where you have always slept?'

No. Since the upper rooms were out of use for commercial purposes at the moment, the waiters had taken them over. After their late-night shifts, they slept in for most of the morning, except when people like me came along to disturb them.

What shifts? I asked how they earned their living while the Hesperides was being renovated. They had obtained temporary work at the Four Limpets. According to them, Liberalis knew all this, was perfectly happy, let them scrounge beds meanwhile, and would give them their old jobs back when he reopened.

'He seems a very kind landlord!'

It could be true. Well, he was new.

Bar staff do come and go; they are even sometimes lent out to rival establishments on special occasions. The only reason you get served by your usual waiter at Saturnalia is that he wants his holiday bonus from you so he makes sure he's there, not two doors down. Count yourself lucky if he reciprocates with a complimentary wine flagon. Even if he does, don't drink it, just use the stuff as skillet cleaner or, if you must, to colour gravy.

'So who was it I heard upstairs with you today?' Nobody, they claimed. I gave them a level stare, though kept my response light. 'You must think I'm deaf or daft, boys!'

We did not pursue the issue.

As with the victimarii yesterday afternoon, I felt these chancers were being cagey. These witnesses were male. I won't say I see men as unreliable, but maybe I could extract more from a woman, especially one who had been on good terms with Rufia. Whoever was being concealed upstairs might provide what I wanted. Once the men were off the premises, I would rootle their floozies out.

In the meantime, Manlius Faustus came into the courtyard. He must have left Dromo somewhere, probably squatting on the kerb outside, which was where slaves usually waited for their masters. Faustus was carrying the basket of bones himself. He set it down, and stood waiting as I closed my interview.

'Does the Four Limpets employ you at lunchtimes? Better hop along there now and start laying up tables.'

The notion of setting out nice napery and cutlery sets was as alien here as in most of Rome. Nipius and Natalis had no idea what I was telling them to do, but since they were keen to escape my questioning, they stared curiously at Faustus, then went off to work.

He remained where he was for a moment. We both wanted to be sure the waiters were out of earshot. 'Pointless waste of time . . .' I tipped my head to one side, considering him. 'Aedile, you have something to tell me, I hope. Cheer me up,' I said. 'None of my witnesses has parted with any information.'

'Nor mine,' he answered gloomily.

12

Tiberius came and joined me, with the basket of bones, which he shoved under the bench. I turned and kissed his cheek, merely a greeting. He leaned sideways a little, rubbing his head against mine briefly.

'So, how was the forensic examination?'

'Up to scratch for the vigiles.' He sounded depressed. 'The Third Cohort claim to be poor overworked slaves who don't have the time or capacity for ancient murders where the chief suspect has died anyway. One of their half-baked investigators took a peek, but only when I acted up.'

I would have liked to have seen that: Tiberius Manlius Faustus, magistrate and man with a conscience, explaining to a cohort who had never met him before why the demands of public order meant they should do what he wanted. 'And?' I asked sympathetically.

'They are human bones, it seems.'

'We knew that.'

'Quite.' He sounded annoyed.

I told him about the waiters. Faustus immediately wanted to know what kind of salesmen had been in the bar. I realised I had not thought to ask, so I turned tetchy on him. Who likes to be shown up?

I had initially supposed they were passing trade, visitors on a spree who would now be impossible to track down.

Strangers. Irrelevant. Merely indicative of how the Garden of the Hesperides operated when the bar was humming. But they were here that particular night and Rufia 'looked after them'. Curses. They mattered.

'Albia my love, it's hardly a disaster.' I had chosen such a reasonable husband. Damn. Why could he not be a self-satisfied swine I could kick? 'Ask the waiters later.'

Not so easy if that pair of conspiratorial swine had put their heads together on the way to the Four Limpets, and agreed to keep quiet. 'Of course I will, darling.'

Listen to me! I was a wife already.

I suggested that the next time one of us was going over to the Aventine we could take the basket then toddle along to the Fourth Cohort, our local, and consult Morellus. He was a truculent bastard too, but we worked with him. Faustus had given money to his wife while Morellus was on prolonged sick leave after being attacked on duty. Morellus owed him. Even so, Faustus was now too glum to cheer up.

I took his hand. He squeezed mine back automatically. But we relaxed. Late-morning sun beamed down on us, unfiltered by foliage or awnings; in due course we would have to move into a shadier position but until then we let lethargy seep into us.

We sat on our bench in silence, thinking. No, I do not mean canoodling. We were practical enquirers, simply reflecting on what we had learned, or not learned, and considering where, therefore, we could look next.

The courtyard hardly seemed like a murder scene; it was peaceful. Out here, you could barely hear the teeming Vicus Longus. Most people who used to have lunch or a drink here probably failed to notice how muffled the street hubbub was; they would have their own concerns, the society of their friends, their irritation at the serving faults of Nipius and Natalis . . .

We were so still and silent you might suppose no one was here.

Scuffling noises on the staircase made us glance at one another. Someone was coming down. 'All quiet down there now; the interfering bitch must have scarpered.'

Tiberius lifted an eyebrow, amused. I flashed back a smile. We stopped holding hands but otherwise stayed motionless.

Into the garden came a couple of no-hope, high-trussed bust-band, barefoot sluts, sneakily creeping downstairs.

'Hello, girls!' I greeted them cheerily. They wondered whether to run for it. 'Come on down, my dearies, don't be shy.'

They came down. From the start, these Hesperides honey-pots were not in the least shy.

13

'I was wondering when you would deign to show your faces. Do come and join us. Now you are ready to socialise, I have a few questions.'

'Oh shitty shit!' observed the first one, immediately identifiable as a whore who cost less on a tavern bill than donkey fodder.

'You said the nosy cow had gone!' groused her dishevelled friend. She was refined (she thought); she had a snake bracelet with red glass eyes. She wore it on her ankle.

'Don't be like that,' answered Faustus in a mildly reproachful tone. 'Flavia Albia only wants to know what *you* know about Rufia. Where is the harm – unless you were the killers?'

This produced indignant denials. Faustus made a soothing gesture, palms spread. I just gazed at the couple thoughtfully. The first one noticed my coolness. She believed she could bamboozle men, but grasped that I would be more difficult.

We established their names, Artemisia and Orchivia, and that they were not from Italy. They said their homeland was Dardania.

'What shitty place is that?' I asked, deciding on a Dardanian adjective in the hope we could communicate. She looked blank.

'Part of Moesia,' Faustus told me. Moesia is one of the

eastern provinces, bordering on barbarian Dacia, where our Emperor was currently at war with a ferocious king who cut off the heads of Roman officials and merrily slaughtered our armies. This king, Decebalus, had made several attempts to expand his territory into Moesia. A troubled mix of Thracians, Dacians and Illyrians, which made a curious slurry at the best of times, Moesia clung on as a Roman province by bloodied fingertips. We sent tough legions and not very renowned governors, men who could be spared if they should happen to be decapitated.

Apparently Moesia's chief export was bar girls. Artemisia was short, wide-faced, grubby and stroppy. She wore a slouched tunic that showed off her big bust and sturdy legs, and she was topped by a high-piled tangled mop of black hair. No bathhouse coiffeuse had ever attempted to tame it. Orchivia was squinty, with even stragglier, browner hair. She had at some point asked a stylist to tackle it, but the results were hopeless.

The girls told me in their high-minded way that Rome was shitty, Roman men were shitty shits and Roman women shittier. I decided to wait before asking what they thought of Rufia.

They were not slaves. They had been lured here by professional traffickers of sex-trade workers, who promised them a better life than anything available to young women of poor background (that is, all of them) in Moesia. So, compared with slaves, they came of their own free will. Using a rough and ready business plan, before that they had learned their craft by servicing the legionaries who defended their home province from its annexation by whooping head-loppers. These noble men with money to lavish in the shanty towns that clustered outside their forts had spoken of Rome – a city, I knew, many soldiers in the legions had never actually seen in their lives. Nevertheless, they eulogised its monuments, palaces, theatres – and its golden opportunities. Artemisia and Orchivia had listened to the squaddies then joined a mule train to Italy.

Now they worked here, taking customers upstairs. They did not mind telling us. They said someone had to do it, though the job was disgusting, the old landlord wanted horrible favours and the new one was a shitty nobody, while both then and now their earnings stank. No need to ask of what.

Faustus questioned them about their hopes for the future. They responded to him better than I expected, saying they would go home, but they still owed fare money to the man who brought them here, a toothless drover in a hairy cloak who had told them he knew their parents. Everything he said was shit. However, they were scared of him and what he could do to their families. Besides, in their hearts they still hankered to find those golden opportunities the legionaries had promised, which they still believed existed somewhere.

While they were answering Faustus, I tried to gauge how old they were. They pretended to be nymphs but had the faces of hags. This was a common result of poverty, let alone the work they did. Bad diet and degradation had left both with poor skin, dull eyes, bruises, pocks and a washed-out, grey appearance under whatever poisonous potions they painted on. I could see a lot of that; they would die before their time. But they were too young to have known Rufia.

They were too young to die, too, though I concede that was irrelevant to my enquiry.

They confirmed they never met the missing woman. However, they knew people who had. Well, for one thing, they screwed Nipius and Natalis. From the waiters, if from no one else, they had heard the rumours about their luckless predecessor's fate.

'Was she Dardanian, or any other kind of foreigner?'

'Who knows?' said Artemisia.

'I do!' boasted Orchivia. 'She was a shitty Illyrian.'

'Who the buggery told you that?' demanded her colleague scornfully.

'Menendra.'

'What does she know?'

'She knew Rufia.'

'Shit!'

'Is there,' I interposed quickly, 'any way I can speak to this Menendra?'

A shadow came over Artemisia and Orchivia, as if they regretted mentioning her.

'She's around,' Orchivia muttered. 'Off and on.'

'Well, if you see her, will you please push her my way?'

Orchivia said she might do, though Artemisia looked as if she did not like the idea that this other woman might find out they had been talking about Rufia with me.

'Is Menendra another scary one, like Rufia?' I asked, on the off chance. They laughed. They were pretending to dismiss that suggestion – while obviously agreeing with it.

'Does she also serve drinks at the Hesperides?'

'No.'

'Where then?'

'Nowhere special.'

'So how does she earn a living – assuming she doesn't own a fancy man?' Few waitresses had pimps; in general their custom was straightforwardly controlled by the bar owners, who saw no reason to let others muscle in.

'She supplies the bars,' said Artemisia.

'Supplies what?' asked Faustus, butting in. He so much adored finicky detail.

I like detail myself; I prefer to work up to it my own way. 'Supplies what?' I echoed, putting my own stamp on the question.

'Anything they need,' Orchivia replied dismissively.

'That's nice and vague.'

Both women gave high-shouldered shrugs, as if my insistence was unreasonable. What passed for expressive in Dardania meant nothing in Rome. Faustus and I stared.

'Fruit,' explained Artemisia glibly. 'Menendra is a fruit-seller.'

That, I felt certain, was a bare-faced Dardanian lie.

Getting nowhere, and hoping I could track down Menendra myself, I went back to Rufia. Did the women have any idea of when she disappeared? Surprisingly, they put a date on it. Someone had told them it happened in the first year of the Emperor Titus. Titus only reigned for two years, which was sad for him, but helpful here.

I joked with Faustus, 'I remember his inauguration, plus all the festivities when he opened the Flavian Amphitheatre, made it necessary for bars to obtain a great deal of fruit!'

'Happy hour,' he returned light-heartedly. 'Raining pomegranates. Cornucopia with every wine cup. Can you two remember anything else about when Rufia disappeared?'

Artemisia and Orchivia reminded him they had not been in Rome then; it was even before they left their mountainous birthplace and went north to sell their valuable young virginities to the Fifth Macedonica and other fine legions in the Danube forts.

'Despite the pleas of your weeping relatives?' Faustus suggested, being wicked as he went back to probing their lives.

'Oh, they couldn't see us off fast enough.'

'They were heartbroken but they knew none of us had anything else to sell; for everyone's benefit we had to sacrifice our little cherries. We were young. We looked as if we could be real virgins.'

'And how many times did you manage to peddle those precious commodities before the randy soldiers twigged?'

'About six or seven.'

Orchivia claimed she could still sell hers if she put her mind to it, on a good night in winter when the lamps weren't lit.

Artemisia laughed hysterically at that. Then she mused, 'One trumpeter bought mine twice.'

'Why was that?' enquired Faustus. 'Because he enjoyed it so much the first time?' For a serious man, he could come out with comments that were very funny. But only I saw the joke.

These were hard, untrustworthy, filthy, foreign working girls, yet Tiberius and I were in danger of feeling sorry for them. They, on the other hand, would lie, dodge, and diddle us at every opportunity. I saw no likelihood of squeezing anything more useful out of Artemisia and Orchivia today, so I said they could be off to wait at tables in the Four Limpets or wherever they had employment.

'The Brown Toad.'

'Juno! You don't care what dump you work in . . . I expect you know the old phrase, don't leave town.'

They looked puzzled.

★   ★   ★

81

As they were leaving, their paths crossed with those of two very different damsels. Strangely, both pairs nodded as they passed, each without being at all affronted by the other.

Artemisia and Orchivia sashayed off, while we were joined by a dainty couple of young girls who shrieked, 'Ooh what a *horrible* place!' They were thrilled.

The Dardanians called back over their saucily bare shoulders that the Hesperides was indeed shitty. I would get the blame at home for this: my little sisters had learned a new catchphrase. 'Just *so* shitty!'

Orchivia popped back. 'If you two think you're going to work here, don't even try it. We own the franchise!'

I could feel Tiberius shaking with laughter.

14

Julia Junilla Laeitana had been given a third name because she was born in Spain where our father had had to deliver the baby himself and save our mother from near death – as he boringly reminded us on occasions. After these horrors, he badly needed to swig the local Laeitana wine and named his firstborn after it.

Sosia Favonia was birthed at home by our two sober grandmothers, so only had two names, but that suited her because she was traditional; a private, austere girl, she regarded her sister as frivolous, not least for her excess of names. She was called Sosia for a long-dead cousin. There was some tragedy involved, so nobody used it. Don't ask me to explain: some long-ago family business.

Julia was sixteen, tall and slim, desperately bright. Favonia was fourteen, sturdy and gruff, with deep-grained, practical intelligence. I was old enough for us never to have squabbled; I had lived elsewhere for much of their childhood. When I visited home, they often did my hair, or altered my clothes and jewellery, as if I was a big doll in their toy collection. I loved them to bits.

These were my daft, spoiled, innocent, lovely young sisters, who were ecstatic to be roped in by Faustus for our wedding. No one had entrusted anything important to them before.

They were arranging things better than I ever would, though with no regard for my wishes, my father's willingness to pay or my mother's good taste in social matters. It was the best fun they had ever had – and now they had capped that by coming to a shitty bar where they were hoping to see dead people.

'How did you get here?' I nagged. 'Don't tell me you walked, not down the Argiletum?'

They had seen we had a bench, so were busy sorting out another for themselves. Soon the building site looked like a picnic spot. Julia took charge. 'We did walk. Good heavens, that's an interesting street. Wigs and false teeth!'

Along the Argiletum, they would have tripped past barbers and slave-sellers, butchers, linen merchants, makers of iron goods and suppliers of all kinds of food. The teeth and wigs were certainly exotic, but oh dear gods, not as colourful as the whores, bumboys and people who called themselves actors and were openly bisexual. I hoped the girls would not go home to our concerned parents all full of it. But I knew they would.

'Who were those fascinating women who left just now?' demanded Favonia. 'What is the job they warned us off?'

'Prostitutes. You couldn't do it. You don't have the application and you're both too squeamish.'

'But it is steady work,' suggested Faustus. I was really discovering his provocative side today. 'They were telling us just now how their speciality is selling their virginity.'

'Oh, that's so neat! How much could we make with ours?' asked Julia, apparently a serious question.

I growled. 'Not enough to buy you dress pins.'

The girls sat down side by side on their bench (having

84

thoroughly dusted it) and smiled at us. Neither had yet
realised how beautiful they were, not even Favonia, who
was the more observant; thank goodness for the murki-
ness of mirrors. They had dark hair, dark eyes, strappy
sandals, fluttery stoles, complicated girdles they had
created themselves from streamers of ribbon, and so much
jewellery I knew they must have sneaked out of the house
without Mother spotting them. The whiffs of peculiar
perfume were ripe. Flies were dropping dead all over the
courtyard.

'Who brought you? Please don't tell me you came un-
escorted.'

'No, no, don't fuss, Albia. We have Katutis.'

'*Where is he?*' Favonia mouthed, anticipating my next
demand. 'Outside, talking to Dromo.' Father's Egyptian
secretary and Faustus' awkward slave had struck up an
unlikely alliance while Dromo was guarding some scrolls
Faustus had 'borrowed' from his uncle and Katutis was
transcribing the transaction history of Faustus' inheritance.

'Tiberius is such a nice man,' said Julia, apparently to
me, though she was aiming the compliment at him. 'But
have you noticed him slyly getting people to do things for
him? He is very clever, Albia!'

'Rich boy,' I answered. Faustus smiled easily, unfazed by
my sister's outspokenness. Or even by mine. 'So, gorgeous
girlies, update me on my horrible wedding plans.'

'Leave it to us. Just turn up and let it happen,' commanded
Favonia sternly. I told you she was practical.

'You will enjoy it, you will, you will!' Julia pleaded,
desperate for me to do so.

I snorted that I *was* taking an interest and that I had
myself arranged the augury. Like Faustus, they shrieked

about duplication. I described the victimarii, laying it on thick. Wide-eyed, they backed down. They even wanted to be taken along to Costus' office to inspect the heavenly hunks *right now*. I vetoed that.

Instead, Favonia ran out to Katutis, returning with a set of note tablets from which she and Julia read aloud selected items. I tried suggesting that because I had to investigate the courtyard bones, we should delay the ceremony. My sisters cheerfully slapped me down. They had already chosen the date for me. They were the wedding planners; I was merely the bride.

They reminded me of their limited options. The Kalends, Nones and Ides of every month, plus the day following each, were unlucky. Various extra religious events interfered. August had a great festival of Diana on the Aventine; it also had a celebration of Consus, a fertility god, in which all the beasts of burden were given a day off, prettily garlanded, then led about the very streets we would be needing for our own procession; among other things in the calendar, there was one of the days when the entrance to the Underworld was believed to be open, so we had to avoid any danger of ghosts popping out. Even more importantly, in September Faustus would be one of the officials organising the Roman Games, which would take all his time and concentration. Julia and Favonia pointed this out to me, much as if I was failing in my wifely duties by not trying to relieve him of stress.

'Obviously I shall take care of Tiberius when he comes home exhausted from the races and plays.'

'No, you must be right at his side through all the events! Flavia Albia, it will be to his public credit if he is a proper married man.' Being paraded at festivals as his domestic

86

dear was a role I might dodge. As he listened to the chatter, Tiberius twinkled at the thought. He did know what he was in for with me. I, however, had not previously considered the full horror of being an aedile's wife.

I had one more possible weapon. 'I believe a widow who is remarrying, by tradition ought to choose a public holiday or major festival in order to conceal her shame that, instead of being a one-man woman, she is committing the social blunder of a second marriage.'

'Ha! Don't try it!' scoffed Julia.

Favonia leaned forward. She explained to me as if to a dimwit: 'The purpose of your wedding, Albia darling, is to demonstrate publicly that the brave Tiberius Manlius Faustus is committing himself to you, our eccentric sister, and that from now on he wants you to be invited to supper parties with him. Even though we have told him you will be rude to his friends.'

'So he thinks I'm starving; it's to get me more prawn nibbles?' I chortled.

Favonia rolled her eyes at my beloved. 'We warned you. She is incorrigible. If you want to back out, do so now before it's too late and the wedding guests are travelling.'

'Ah, but she is the woman for me!' He took my hand tenderly but firmly.

My sisters then looked at each other, miming *This is just so-o-o romantic!* It lasted a few moments before they lost interest. They had known me since they were babies. In some ways they found it inconceivable that I might have a love life – let alone with a man they had come to perceive as very old (by their standards) yet nevertheless nice (even by their standards).

He took them seriously. They liked that. In fact they had

slightly grown up while fixing this wedding for him. I knew our parents were impressed.

The madcaps had been talking about one subject for as long as they could manage. Now they turned to what had really lured them here from the Aventine.

'Can we see the bones?'

I frowned. It made no difference. 'Show some respect, Julia.'

'We do. We know it was a person once. We want her poor spirit to rest easy. But can we see the bones, can we? Is that them there, in that basket Tiberius has under his seat?'

Before we could stop them, they flew across the court-yard, pulled out the rubble basket and like competent navvies carried it over to their own bench. In fairness, they opened it carefully. They could have tipped it out all over the yard, but of their own accord they spent time lifting out each bone, or piece of bone, individually. They handled each with cautious reverence.

Julia and Favonia set out the collection on the ground, to some extent composing a skeleton. Father's work as an informer meant they had acquired strange gobbets of know-ledge, anatomy being just one subject they would one day have to conceal from respectable husbands. Pa had taught them to play dice too. Favonia even had her own – she had filched a set of counterfeit ones that turned up once at the auction house.

Now they were absorbed, heads together, as they pored over the remnants of the skeleton.

'Where is her skull?'

Good point. These flighty bits could notice significant things. A skull certainly ought to survive in the ground, if other bones do. The workmen had not found it.

'Her head is not here. This will not do! There needs to be more digging,' declared Favonia. Julia always seemed to be the leader but Favonia was a born organiser. Then it was she, my thoughtful youngest sister, who noticed something else, something crucial: 'Look, this is not right. These leg bones are different sizes. Either the barmaid was deformed, or the bones come from two different people.'

15

I let Tiberius tell my disappointed sisters that they could not come with us to see Morellus. We were seeking a favour, so it would be bad practice to arrive in a noisy crowd. We would need to flatter Morellus. 'Albia will need to restrain herself. This won't be the moment for her to tell him his faults.'

I bridled. 'Husband-to-be, are you chastising me?'

'Never, my darling!'

'How wise of you, Aedile.'

I watched Julia and Favonia accept what Tiberius said as they would never have done with most people. Instead, while we walked along in a posse, I was treated to a list of wedding guests. I had the odd experience, even though Tiberius was here, of my own sisters enlightening me on his family relationships: 'First, Uncle Tullius. He is a famous molester so if we talk to him we always have to make sure there are two of us there.' I saw Tiberius wince, though he did not dispute the description.

'That's if he comes. He may not, because of Tiberius demanding his property rights.'

'No, it will be all right. Father went to smooth things over.'

'I'd like to have been at that meeting!' I commented, stepping around a recumbent beggar.

'Oh no. It needed diplomacy.'

'Well, thanks, Julia!'

'Father told Mother all about it, so we know what happened.' This was not because Helena Justina had confided in them but, in the family tradition, the girls had shamelessly listened outside the door.

'Father said he fully understands why Uncle Tullius feels unhappy; he wanted Tullius to know the marriage is nothing to do with him. Falco has his own misgivings, which he hoped Tullius would not mind him setting out briefly. Flavia Albia is his eldest daughter and Falco had always hoped any new partnership would reflect our family's status, with him being a confidant of the great emperors Vespasian and Titus; also, we have two uncles in the Senate, which is evidently important.'

I choked quietly.

'Uncle Tullius then blamed Falco for putting Tiberius up to trying to get his own money back. But Falco said Tiberius had the idea himself—' Lies, devious Father! Falco had suggested it. 'If it comes to court, Falco's advice would be to back away fast. But of course, Tullius doesn't need advice from him or from anyone, he's a famously sharp businessman.'

'So what,' asked Tiberius wryly, 'did my sharp Uncle Tullius respond?'

'Oh we don't know, we only heard the sounds of Mother throwing a cushion because Father is a reprobate. Then Father threw it back, but he missed and broke a vase. I think it was a kantharos. Things were said. About the kantharos, I mean.'

'As in "This is a fine Etruscan drinking cup with two vertical handles"?'

'No, Albia. As in, "Didius Falco, you are a trial to live with".'

'Next, Mother invited Uncle Tullius to dinner and, to the surprise of all, he came. She didn't use our cook – she borrowed a good one.'

'Father got ours, Tiberius. Hopeless as usual. He just can't buy slaves.'

'Helena Justina tucked his napkin around Uncle Tullius with her own hands, complimenting him on the fine job he has made of bringing up his lovely nephew. She murmured to him that it would be best for both families to grit their teeth and show support. Tiberius and Albia both being so headstrong, she thought that was the only way – otherwise there was a danger you would run off to be beach bums on a Greek island.'

'We never even thought of that,' I marvelled.

'Still could!' suggested Tiberius in a low voice.

'Falco said our mother was a wise and wonderful woman. So, he was prepared to withdraw his own objections and pay for the ceremony, as a gesture even if it choked him, provided Uncle Tullius found it in his heart to unbend as well.'

'Which Tullius had to?' I asked.

'Of course!' Julia scoffed. 'Our ridiculous parents have some uses.'

We had reached the Forum. I gathered the girls closer. Favonia excitedly continued her chatter, oblivious to her noble surroundings and the squalid crowds bustling therein, very keen to feel her up or steal the purse from her girdle. 'So Uncle Tullius *will* come to the wedding. He can look magnanimous announcing that it's the right moment to give Tiberius more say in their family business. That will make everyone happy. Tiberius will get at the money, so he can go out and buy lots of things, especially for your house.'

'We can help with choosing things to buy,' Julia told him hopefully. Gently moving a persistent sausage-seller out of our path, Tiberius managed to seem distracted; he had mastered the art of looking non-committal. As a wife, I might see a lot of that. I was ready for it.

'Now listen, Albia,' Favonia ordered me. 'The other new relatives we are expecting are these.' She ticked them off on her small fingers. 'An auntie from Caere who is elderly and infirm, but if she can come we have to be nice to her even though she is a bit grumpy these days. Tiberius has a sister, her name is Fania Faustina. When their parents died, they were split up. Tiberius was taken by Uncle Tullius in Rome while his sister was brought up by Aunt Valeria in Caere. Tiberius was once very close to his sister but she married a husband that Tiberius can't stand; they have three little boys whom he hasn't seen for a long time because of the gruesome husband.'

Julia had a say: 'We shall have to decide who they stay with. Aunt Valeria will refuse to be at Uncle Tullius' house because he is so deplorable. He's not her brother, so she can't order him about. Mother says they may all have to stop with us.' I imagined Helena had mixed feelings about that.

'Your mother has been very kind,' Tiberius told me.

'And Falco?'

'He's just being Falco,' Julia sniffed. 'Don't worry, we have him under control.'

After further discussion about my own relations, mainly who we wanted to omit from the guest list (though they would come anyway), we rounded the Circus Maximus and arrived at the foot of the Aventine. Katutis and Dromo were deputed to escort my sisters home safely, while Tiberius and I climbed up the hill to the vigiles station house.

First we stopped for a rest and a drink of water at the Stargazer, my aunt's caupona. There I tried miming to my deaf cousin Junillus, the waiter on duty, that I was having a wedding to which he was invited, but he would have to inform his father, the doleful Gaius Baebius, that I had appointed someone else to conduct the sacrifice and augury.

Junillus, a bright, good-looking seventeen-year-old, let me struggle for a long while before he suddenly and silently reacted. 'Jupiter Tonans! The poor old sod will be mortified! You can bloody well tell him yourself, Albia.'

The cheeky lad understood more than he usually let on and was a brilliant actor.

We went on to the Fourth Cohort's secondary billet. Tiberius shouldered open a crack in the heavy gates, despite the vigiles' attempts to deter the public from bothering them.

Various ex-slave troops were lolling in the courtyard among pieces of firefighting equipment. They whistled at me on principle, regardless of my being under a magistrate's protection. This was no surprise. The first time I came here I was with my father, yet only narrowly avoided being gang-raped on a heap of esparto mats. We were collecting a lost dog. Even she looked slightly ruffled, as if she had fought off unwanted attention.

A dark closet halfway down a dusty veranda housed Morellus. After a night's long shift he could have gone home to his family, but as usual he was asleep, carefully wedged on a stool with his back against a wall and his feet up on a table. His booted heels were dropping road dust on the scroll that listed last night's arrests. For once the miscreants were not shouting protests in the cells. Drunk or sober, they seemed to be landlords who wouldn't comply with fire regulations and were now resignedly waiting for slaves to come from their bankers with the necessary bribes. Morellus must have stayed late in order to extract his cut.

I banged a metal spoon on his dented food bowl. Like all ex-soldiers he had the knack of waking instantly, on the alert. Seeing us, he did not bother to lower his boots.

'Flavia Albia! Word is, you're now screwing that aedile who was sniffing around you.'

'I am here,' the aedile pointed out.

'I see you!' Morellus did not call him 'sir'.

'Good to have you back,' returned Faustus, mildly.

'I thank you, Aedile. It's bloody good to be here and not dying in my bed with four upset nippers all bawling their sad little heads off and throwing porridge about.'

Once overweight, a vicious poisoning attack had left Morellus a shadow of himself. He had the shaved head all the vigiles favoured, and wore the standard red tunic, stylishly crumpled, with muted accents of gravy stain. His belt was wide, his boots tough, his feet showing through the battered straps were dramatically blistered, his manner was truculent, his career had stalled for the past ten years. In all of this he was typical. Of Rome's various military or paramilitary forces, the vigiles were the lowest grade.

'Come over here and have a big squeeze,' the horrible lout enticed me, still ignoring Faustus.

'No chance, Morellus. Haven't you heard? I'm getting married.' I would never have gone anywhere near him anyway. 'Show some respect to my fiancé, will you?'

Jumping his feet down floorwards, Morellus sat up suddenly, letting out the customary cry of amazement. 'Fiancé! You don't say! When is the wedding?' He laughed raucously. Tiberius did not. 'I'll have to get a new smart tunic for that!'

'Who said you were invited?'

'Don't worry, I'll invite us myself. Pullia will be delighted.' His wife, Pullia, was a surprisingly nice woman, though she must have been sozzled the day she agreed to share her life with Morellus. I wondered whether they would bring the four little porridge-flingers. Probably have to. They were children no aunts would willingly look after. Anyway, Pullia liked them to all go out as a family. It would increase morale, she hoped, poor optimistic woman.

Tiberius placed the rubble basket on the table, a heavy planked affair onto which officers traditionally slammed the heads of witnesses they were interrogating. Having a smashed face was supposed to encourage people to tell the truth.

'Presents? What's this, Legate?'

'We are hoping you can tell us. We think it may be some of the bones of a dead waitress, but as Albia's bright sister remarked, if that's right, she had interestingly mismatched legs.'

'Just my type. I love a woman with a physical quirk. Let's see your luscious legs, sweetie!' Morellus hauled himself upright so he could peer salaciously into the basket. Pullia was in fact a good-looking woman; there was nothing wrong with her. Well, except for her judgement in men.

Morellus upended the basket, scattering the bones all over the table where, I knew, he regularly ate and drank. 'Ooh, these will look attractive in your cabinet of curiosities,

Manlius Faustus. I take it you'll display them for visitors, when you and the luscious Albia socialise?'

Faustus went along with it genially. 'So how shall we label them?'

Morellus shifted bones left and right on the tabletop, sorting them. His movements were swift and decisive. 'Woman's thigh, woman's ribs, male thigh bone, indeterminate spine knuckle, probably toe – could be anybody's – female pelvis, child-bearing age, looks as if she has carried some to term, poor unhappy cow . . .' He continued like this through most of our cargo before speeding through the last few items. 'Can't tell, can't decide, can't tell, could be a dog, bound to be poultry.'

'You're good!' commented Faustus.

'Practice. Tell you one thing.'

'What?' I asked since he had clearly paused for emphasis.

'This one, this male thigh bone, has been sawn.'

'Deliberate dismemberment?' asked Faustus. Nodding, Morellus showed him the cut. 'So we can assume at least one of the bodies, perhaps not the dog or the chicken, died from foul play?'

'Well,' Morellus drawled, being clever. 'Whether you call it foul play will depend if your victim was a bad waitress. If she often fiddled bar bills, I'd call it justice.'

16

It was now the hottest part of a sultry summer day. We were up on the Aventine, a long way from the crime scene but temptingly near my apartment. We went there. Supposedly we wanted to consider options.

As we walked the short distance from the station house, I wondered why the street life in your own area always seems safer even if it's no more salubrious than other places. There must be as many sordid bars here as in the Ten Traders enclave. The food stalls were as dowdy, their fare as unappetising. But where you live, in general the whores don't shout invitations at you. You know, so you mainly dodge, the pickpockets. Feral dogs ignore your passing. Somehow you just feel more confident, less anxious, more at home, less oppressed.

The Eagle Building, Fountain Court, was nearing the end of its long life. Constructed in the Republic as a six-storey block of basic tenements, its decayed structure now creaked at every puff of breeze, so that mould and dust flittered from the increasing crannies. Fortunately in August breezes rarely blew. As the hot sun baked the minimal apartments, remnants of their meagre paint were flaking more every day. The building stayed upright only because it had settled like a plant on its rootstock over many years. But one slight shock and it was done for. If a god laughed in Olympus, it would crash.

Tenants had thinned out recently as my father, who owned Fountain Court, tried to find them other places to live. He had a conscience. Nobody was grateful, but he carried on, seeking to edge them out elsewhere before he finalised a sale to a senator who would pull down the apartments to build his own private house. He was Spanish. Pa had told him this was a desirable area. According to Falco, the Thirteenth District was crammed with amenities.

It is true that on the Aventine there are many temples. Sometimes you can't move in the local bars for disreputable priests engaged in illegal gambling with their awful acolytes. A spotty altar boy loses, goes mad about it, and cuts off a priest's ear with a fruit knife. If the gossips are lucky, it is subsequently discovered that the priest was using loaded dice . . . Lots to talk about.

I concede that a senator could be very private on the noisy, smelly, rumbustious Mons Aventinus. Nobody would ever come to bother him at his house. Maybe Ulpius Trajanus was not so daft.

While the Eagle Building still remained, I kept my rent-free niche in one of the better apartments (where the comparative 'better' is a reckless term to use). I had lived there during my first marriage and ever since; I also used an office on the top floor, which had once been Father's. There would be nostalgic pangs for both of us when we left Fountain Court for good, but it was time. Nobody wants to be crushed under collapsing rubble.

Father declared he would reject any compensation suits from hurt tenants because he had given formal notice that the place might fall down any day. Staying on was now at their own risk. My two barrister uncles, the Camilli, chortled as they said they looked forward to fighting that one on behalf of the tenants. In the family we viewed Aulus and Quintus as wild boys, though there was evidence that they knew how to choose winnable cases.

When Tiberius and I arrived that day, Rodan the porter was nowhere to be seen. That saved me having to ask whether he had found another job yet, but it meant anyone could walk in. With luck, burglars did not operate in the heat of midday. Indeed, some of them lived upstairs so they did their thieving elsewhere to avoid annoying their own neighbours. Otherwise, when property is half-empty it tends to exude a message that there will not be much worth stealing. The Eagle Building teetered on the cusp, visibly dying but not yet sufficiently deserted to attract squatters or moonlit salvage teams.

Tiberius and I went into my apartment.

In the bedroom, I quickly sorted earrings to take away to the Viminal. Tiberius followed me quietly. I straightened up from the side table.

'Hmm. Options!' he remarked, sliding my dress brooch to one side so he could caress my bare shoulder.

We had not been at ease in our hired room, which we could guess had been the scene of many purely commercial couplings. We had not liked the narrow bed with its sagging, much used, wool-stuffed mattress. Here we were now, standing together beside our own fine antique bed, on an afternoon when it was still too warm to walk about outside for any distance. We also had that secret thrill of nobody knowing where we were . . .

I said in a businesslike voice, 'It's obvious what we have to do next. Tiberius Manlius, you must summon your work-force from wherever they are snoozing over midday, make them bring all the spades and picks they have in the yard, then we must dig up every foot of the outside space at the Hesperides, to see who else is buried there.'

'I could do that.' Tiberius nuzzled my neck.

Enjoying his attention, I softened. 'Or collect them later?'

'Absolutely. Flavia Albia, I would never make the men go outside in stonking heat. I care about their welfare. I don't want them fainting.'

'So the poor Hesperides corpses will have to lie a little longer underground?'

'Delay is reprehensible but we can make up time later . . .'

He did not care about the excavation being delayed. As my dress pins scattered on the floor mat, the most excellent Tiberius Manlius had only one thing on his mind. It did not involve finding buried bodies.

17

By early evening we were back at the bar, with a packed courtyard. The cooler hours before sunset were genuinely best for heavy digging. Tiberius and I had returned, relaxed, bathed, refreshed by one another then by cakes and mulsum, ready for whatever grim discovery awaited.

Nosy, self-nominated experts came to witness our opening of the ground. As a row of workmen set about digging up the entire courtyard from its outer wall to the bar interior, first Morellus turned up. This was not his jurisdiction; the inquisitive swine claimed he was here to help Tiberius and me decipher any evidence. Such goodness of heart!

Officers from the Third Cohort, those tiresome men who had previously dismissed the request for advice, soon joined us too. It was their patch; crime was suspected; they could not be turned away. Fortunately they took to Morellus. The group settled down as sideline observers, heads together, bringing a sombre, militaristic presence. None of them offered to help dig. Tiberius Manlius put them to shame when he stripped to his under-tunic and weighed in alongside his men.

I had learned why he looked so much at home doing this. That afternoon we had grown closer. For a start, I was seeing how our future life would be, with its pleasurable mix of working and living as a couple.

At home earlier, I had contrasted the intimacy and fulfil-ment we shared in bed against the paid, time-limited, one-sided sex that customers bought in bars and brothels like this. I had balanced our ideal pleasure against the trade other people indulged in: mechanical action with faked climax, the risk of assault, joylessness, guilt. And now the sorriest consequence of this particular bar's commerce was to be revealed.

As Tiberius put his back into digging, I now knew he was born to the building trade. On our way back here, I had asked how he could settle so readily into it. He explained that his grandfather, on his father's side, had been a contractor. When the Emperor Augustus boasted that he found Rome made of brick and left it marble, the elder Manlius Faustus was one who installed that marble. He worked on public monuments, then later he built homes in the country for other plebeian families who had made good and were retiring from city life. His own son moved out to the country, becoming an estate farmer and never working in the family business.

The grandfather carried on until his death. I had heard Tiberius speak passionately of marble, and I now under-stood that; as a lad he had loved to visit building sites with his grandpa, who had been delighted that his only grandson took so much interest. Tiberius observed and absorbed every kind of knowledge.

His parents' marriage had been a love match; their fam-ilies became acquainted because one of his grandfathers supplied warehouse storage for the other's costly marble. So, when Tiberius was orphaned, it seemed natural for his mater-nal uncle, Tullius, by then in charge of the warehouse empire, to take him in. One day Tiberius would inherit everything. That had never encouraged the suspicious Tullius to involve him closely. So now there was friction and argument, occasioned by Tiberius branching out, back into the business on his father's side. I wondered whether Uncle Tullius regarded warehouse management as a clean-hands occupation, while perhaps he looked down on building.

He would loathe seeing his nephew at this moment, covered with dust, organising trenches, unearthing gruesome finds, wielding a hefty pick as if he had always done so. Uncle Tullius and I had clashed already, so I knew he would resent seeing me here too, itemising finds, plotting them on a map I had drawn of the courtyard, in a team with his rebellious nephew. For Tiberius, this new life fulfilled the wish of someone he had specially loved, and I could see that mattered to him deeply. He also cared that I played such a willing part in it.

That was why the Garden of the Hesperides would be an important experience for us. It was an ordinary bar. Even the fate of its missing waitress was mundane, common enough for a woman in that world. However, with this project Manlius Faustus had begun rebuilding lost family connections. It made him happy. I was happy for his sake and even began to accept the wedding ceremony he wanted; it would publicly mark this turning point in his life.

Of course I might still niggle him about the wedding. But, whether in Roman peristyle or British round hut, niggling was what a wife did. A good husband shrugged off, or maybe even enjoyed, the tussle.

It made me think more keenly about Rufia. Had she cut up rough in some domestic argument that nobody shrugged off? Whereas I had independent free speech with a tolerant man, had she been cruelly battered to death for her outspokenness?

* * *

We had brought back the basket of original finds from the Aventine. Waiting members of the vigiles took out Rufia's bones, which they passed around with their usual terrible, out-of-place jokes, although those were superseded by sucked teeth and heavy silence as the workmen made grisly new finds. The troops always used graveyard humour to make tragedy endurable, yet they had a basic respect for the untimely dead. They were slapdash, untrained, unsystematic hard men, but it was not entirely their fault; they were, too, undermanned, poorly supervised, despised by the public and shoved into all kinds of danger on a daily basis, generally without thanks. Someone had to investigate. Under the shabby bravado, they did want a proper resolution. Their methods might be crude but, according to their practice, they would see it through.

Our men soon produced plenty to cause deploring head shakes.

Right at the centre of the courtyard we found a single burial that seemed very old, just a cluster of fragmented bones, together with a crude pot and several unmatched coloured stone beads. Faustus decreed this burial was unconnected to the rest, rather some ancient interment whose history we could never learn. Morellus and Macer, the chief investigator of the Third, exchanged mutters in a huddle, then agreed. But the next finds were different.

Around the edge of the yard were a set of surprisingly neat burials. They appeared to be all of one date. The bodies were laid out straight. Nothing was found with them. 'Stripped,' said Morellus laconically. 'Every stitch removed. No wrappings. No grave goods to help them down in Hades.'

'Not even a coin to pay the ferryman over the Styx,' added Macer. He was a wiry tyke with bandy legs and a dismal attitude. 'That will upset the thieving guild of river boatmen!'

Morellus decreed, 'I think we can assume these poor sods were not planted in the earth by loving sons, pious wives or freed slaves honouring their kind old masters.'

'They all are nicely set, no bent legs, hands in their laps, no heads off,' Macer commented. 'Me, I do like to see a bit of care in an unlawful burial.'

'So we're looking for a surveyor?' joked Morellus, bending low to peer at the nearest skeleton while eyeing it up as if using a straight edge.

'Oh just a landlord who wanted to remember where he must not let his gardener plant lavender.'

'You have a sweet imagination, brother!'

'Herbs in a bar garden, always welcome! Brings the bees. A bee might sting your girlfriend, so you get to go down her tunic and soothe the pain for her.' They glanced at Tiberius and me.

Ignoring their lewd asides, I decided to impose professionalism. 'I count five now, plus the one we think is Rufia. Her grave was badly disturbed before anyone realised what it was, so her bones are a bit jumbled. But the odd leg we dug up yesterday seems to have come off number four. Can't tell whose was the dog Morellus identified, nor who took a chicken supper to Hades with him.'

'Bright bint, your scribe,' Macer said to Tiberius.

'Future wife. We're promised.' Leaning on his pick, Tiberius rested. 'I'd have given her an iron betrothal ring, but she asked for a laundry slave instead.' This was not true. 'Had the party and everything.' Well, we went to dinner at my parents' house. 'Got drunk with her father, faithfully promised her mother I'll look after her – or were those the other way around? . . .Yes, she's bright. She'll help me solve this for you, if you don't have the capacity.'

'Old crime. Landlord did it. He's dead. No point,' Macer replied. That was frank. It was also as I expected.

'It would be good to work out who they are,' I suggested. 'The barmaid will have no advocate, but the rest may be persons of status, who should be identified if possible.'

'Nice little row of other barmaids,' Macer disagreed. 'Pitiful. Old Thales must have bumped one off every week. His weekly treat on market day: bash another one.'

Morellus stirred unhappily. 'No, number four is a man. Others could be.' I wondered whether he would have raised this objection had he not given his verdict on the male to Tiberius and me that morning. Would he have kept quiet and let Macer close the case? Put it all down to a perverted landlord, now deceased? No effort required?

'Perhaps the bastard also fancied waiters!' Macer sounded bluff, but was obviously less confident now. I didn't mention that Nipius and Natalis had confirmed Thales had assaulted them; I thought they would have told me about any history of serving boys actually disappearing.

Instead, Macer dwelt on what might have happened here. 'This was all done at the same time, if you ask me. Horrible to think about. Must have been some night. Bloody massacre of six people, then endless torchlit digging while they concealed the remains.'

'Old Thales can't have done it alone. He must have had helpers,' I said. 'Multiple conspirators and aggressors. One man could never have killed so many, let alone buried them all – and so tidily, as you pointed out. This was no hurried, chaotic dump. It must have taken a lot of time, all done before the bar opened as usual next morning.'

'Did it? Did it reopen as usual?'

'So the waiters say.'

Macer quizzed me sharply about that. I told him what I learned from Nipius and Natalis about Rufia's disappearance. I decided not to mention the two Dardanian prostitutes, let alone that third woman I had yet to find. Artemisia and Orchivia were not in Rome when the crime happened, and whatever Menendra's role was, I wanted to investigate myself.

The troops were making acquaintance with the Dardanians anyway. Artemisia and Orchivia had joined a group of sightseers congregating outside in the street. The women were soon offering their services to the vigiles, who, according to their custom, did not rebuff them.

Purists may think investigating officers and their witnesses ought to remain segregated. The Third and Fourth Cohorts were neither of them pure.

18

Morellus and Macer pretended they were above such behaviour even if, in the spirit of good community relations, free tricks were offered. Macer instructed his lads to scarper, which the lads took to mean go and get their oats somewhere else, not here under a plebeian aedile's nose. Macer must have decided telling them not to fraternisc at all would be a waste of time.

Surprisingly to a cynic like me, it was made plain that the Dardanian dreamgirls would not be allowed to bring clients into the Hesperides, which was a crime scene. They grumbled loudly, then simply took the men down to the Romulus, 'for a quick drink'. Perhaps they even did have a drink prior to whatever else happened. There were so many troops they must have formed a queue. Flagons would undoubtedly be ordered meanwhile. Any landlord would ensure that. One bar's tragedy was another's boost in trade.

Left behind, four of us stood in the newly peaceful courtyard, looking down at the burials. Morellus and Macer favoured Tiberius with their professional views; I was allowed to listen. I baulked privately, but tolerated their attitude. For one thing we might need their cooperation later. For another, Macer could always claim this was *his* crime scene, sealing it and making life impossible for Faustus as the contractor. Faustus made no secret of his aims: to obtain any new evidence in one go, have the skeletons removed tonight, then retake possession of the site so he could finish the refit and be paid. I was marrying a true plebeian.

The bodies had been buried around the edge of the yard. A good two feet of spoil was packed on top of them; these graves were not shallow. The victims' heads abutted boundary walls; their feet came forwards into open ground. Three were positioned on one side, Rufia and one more were at the far end, the last was on his own opposite the three others. He might have been fitted in alongside Rufia, but there was a gate to the outside alley. It must always have existed so its rutted pathway posed a discovery risk.

'Can you tell what kind of fight happened here?' I asked.

'Not a clue.' Macer, a natural misery, enjoyed saying no.

Morellus was slightly more helpful. 'Number five has a little dent in his skull, though not enough to have killed him. Number two had his neck broken.' He showed us.

There were no defensive cut marks and, except for the one possible neck injury, no bones had been broken peri-mortem. We found no tips of knives or spears among the bones or left behind, stuck in them. Rufia might have been strangled (clearly that was the method the two vigiles would use on a woman they wanted to silence for ever) but without her head no one could tell. Poisoning, drowning, suffocation would none of them show up.

We still had not found a skull for Rufia, though we had looked carefully. All the rest, who we agreed looked like male skeletons, had their heads still attached to their spines. Only number five, with his dent, had any sign of a head wound. The only disarticulated bone was the lower leg with the cut marks.

'If it was his arm you would think,' Morellus pontificated, 'he had a knife, so somebody hacked off his limb to stop him using it.'

'Wouldn't it be easier just to grab him and take the knife away?' I asked. 'Haven't we agreed there must have been several people involved in the killing?'

Morellus spat, but that was just because I was a woman arguing. He liked to spit. It was his way of expressing a repulsive personality. 'You've never seen a really vicious fight, girl.' I had, but forbore to argue.

'What happened to Rufia's head – and why?' demanded Faustus. 'My men were thorough when digging. If there was a skull, we'd have found it.'

'No, the men never missed it,' agreed Macer. 'The barmaid's bonce absolutely isn't here.'

'So why is she different?' I asked. 'If by your verdict all these people died at the same time?'

'Same incident. Has to be.' Morellus was definite, defending his theory. 'Look how they are all put in the ground – Rufia and the man beside her spaced exactly like the trio over there. All the same depth. All placed exactly the same. All the bones have weathered equally, come to that.'

'Why then would someone have taken her head away?'

'In case the bodies were dug up too soon and she was recognised?' suggested Morellus.

'More likely nabbed as a trophy,' Macer argued.

Even Morellus assumed a pained expression, thinking his colleague an amateur. 'Well, son. Some perpetrators do take trophies. Your normal killer wants a piece of jewellery or a lock of hair to remind him of his exciting experience. Those things can be hidden in his armpurse, but a whole head can cause him a problem. You don't look too good, walking away down the street with someone's head under your arm. Well,' he finished disparagingly, 'that's how our lot do it on the Aventine. Your villains may have a different system in the Viminal.'

People who lived on the other Seven Hills regarded the Aventine as foreign; for Morellus, born and bred there, ours was a sophisticated haven; other hills were alien places. Their occupants all had unspeakable characteristics, with no rule of law applying to their unregulated streets.

'Morellus, you ever-comical swine,' I chastised him, bantering as we generally did, 'you speak as if mass killers are a professional group, with traditions, apprenticeships, annual guild dinners. And no doubt a funeral club. How handy for when they have fatal fights in dodgy bars!'

'Whatever went down here,' Macer of the Third carried on conversing with his colleague in what he perceived as a fair-minded way, which meant ignoring me, 'after the fracas ended, with one lot all lying quietly dead, someone rapidly got organised. Someone hoofed off for spades. Maybe there was building work nearby so they could nick tools, but they probably put them back afterwards or a big theft would have been reported later. Questions would be asked.' I noticed Faustus huff quietly, as if in his experience the vigiles never took much interest in thefts of building tools. 'While the corpses cooled, a group of people methodically made graves. They dropped in the bodies. They cleaned up. They flattened down the earth. They rearranged the tables and seats to look like normal.'

'They wiped down the tables and patted the dog,' I added satirically.

'I bet they unsealed an amphora and had a bloody big drink!' scoffed Morellus.

'Of course the killings may have been planned,' Faustus brooded. 'Some old quarrel. Weapons and burial tools may have been collected earlier.'

'Yet nobody talks about a feud like that existing,' I reminded him. 'The only rumour says the landlord murdered Rufia. It sounds like a domestic. All too usual. Five men must also have disappeared the same night, but when this rumour comes up, who mentions them?'

'Out-of-towners,' Morellus answered at once. 'Nobody cares.'

Macer agreed. 'Grockles.' It was a term my father used for visitors to Rome who came for business or pleasure, gaping at sights and having their travel bags stolen.

'Easy pickings,' I conceded. 'You shout "Look at that!" then pick up their luggage while their heads are meekly turning. Alternatively, you lure them into a bent dice game or fleece them at Find the Nymph under the Cup. Fair enough – but Morellus, Macer, nobody needs to murder them.'

'And the barmaid serving them,' Faustus backed me up.

'So did Rufia get in the way?' I pondered. 'Had these five men given her a big tip, so she liked them, then she objected to them being set upon and got bludgeoned herself for her pains?'

'Had her head cut off for interfering?' Faustus mused.

'A woman barging into men's business,' I agreed sourly. I had seen that a few times. 'She received double punishment.'

'We don't know that, love . . . So, officers,' Faustus asked slowly, 'when you look at these bones, nothing tells you how the victims were killed?'

Of course I had asked that at the start, but those bastards

Macer and Morellus took him more seriously. They let him see they thought he was being obsessive, however. 'Very careful garrotting could leave no signs,' said Macer, now playing the silly ass.

'Or extremely neat throat-cutting,' added Morellus. This disreputable pair had by now mastered working as a tight team. Either alone would have been a trial to a curious aedile; together they were a boot-faced, two-man pack. Their verdict was deemed to be expert, its unhelpfulness was final. According to them nobody could get any further with this.

From experience, I felt that if we mulled over it until another day dawned, new ideas might come.

All of us were tired, depressed and aware that there was very little to steer us towards what really happened here, let alone who might be pursued for it. The two vigiles officers lost interest. They looked at one another. Each gave the other a slight nod, some well-established private code. Morellus, since he knew us, made it official. He announced that Faustus and I were the best people to investigate.

'Let us know.'

'Keep in touch.'

The two useless brutes went off, almost arm in arm, heading to join their men for refreshments down at the Romulus.

We made no move to follow them.

19

At last we could mull this over together in private.
Tiberius and I were silent for a time. He and I never
needed to be constantly in conversation. One of the first
things I ever heard about him was that he was a listener,
a man who made up his mind before pronouncing. This is
rare. Most give a rash opinion before they hear the full
facts. Usually they get it wrong.

We paced around the yard together, gazing down at each
skeleton as we reassessed these secret burials. The layout,
depth, consistency of them. The oddities. The disarticulated
leg. The missing head.

'The men are all of a type,' Faustus said at last. 'Not tall,
stocky build.'

When I got down low to look closely at number four, with
his severed lower leg, I spotted that his other, the one still
attached, had a markedly deformed bone. 'Look here, Tiberius.
This man suffered an accident in his lifetime. His remaining
leg had been badly crushed. He had a horrible fracture, as if
something disastrously heavy fell on him – a millstone, a huge
piece of masonry – bones were broken, a compound fracture
that probably stuck through the flesh. He must have been
lucky to survive. But it had all mended long before he died.'

Tiberius took it further: 'He would have had a very
conspicuous, awkward gait. This man stood out. Everybody

would have known him. I wonder . . . Albia, if we think Rufia's head was taken away to prevent possible identification, did somebody also decide to remove the damaged leg for the same reason?'

'They cut off the wrong one!' I exclaimed.

Tiberius let himself grin, then grew more serious. 'Could be understandable. We say they were well organised, yet killing six people has unimaginable horrors. There must have been huge tension by the point of the burials. A mistake was made. Let's face it, even surgeons have been known to carry out wrong amputations. Someone realised the error, but they couldn't face hacking off a second leg, so they cursed, gave up, and tossed the wrong one back into the trench after the body, hoping for the best . . .'

'Gruesome.' While I still crouched beside the limping man, I swung around to make comparisons with his next neighbour. 'Same wear on their teeth. Same diet.'

Tiberius followed my reasoning at once. 'Same origin?'

'Likely, though it's nothing exceptional. Same habits, certainly. Gritty bread. Fruit. Acid wine followed by acidic belching.'

'You make them sound lovable fellows!'

'Who all drank in bars,' I reminded him, with a smile.

'But you are not going so far as to identify their home village?' He was teasing me.

'Could even be Rome. My point is, they all hung around together, leading the same lifestyle. In the same trade, I bet. And somehow they must have made a common enemy.'

'But was it Old Thales?' Tiberius now frowned. 'Did Thales himself, helped by his staff, attack these five men? If so, why?'

'Had the five men somehow killed Rufia, so Thales ordered punishment killings?'

'Surely we have no reason to believe Rufia meant that much to him?' I made a note to start asking people just what she did mean to the landlord, while Tiberius continued suggesting alternatives: 'Or did a completely separate group have a set-to with these fellows, while Thales either kept out of the way or stood on the sidelines pleading with all parties to stop fighting in his bar?'

I snorted mildly. 'I don't think he was that kind of land-lord. But his bar was well ordered. We know he had the no-nonsense Rufia to stop trouble – she sounds as if she would have kicked him into action if mayhem started.'

'Ah, *that* kind of woman!' murmured Tiberius gently, as if to no one in particular.

I shot him a cool glance. 'If he didn't himself arrange the attack, who could the antagonists be – people that Thales was scared to interfere with, and too frightened of even to report their crime afterwards?'

'Soldiers?' suggested Tiberius.

'Serving soldiers would have been missed. Absconding from the army is one crime that does get taken seriously. Especially if it happened in Rome, which is awash with units who could look for deserters.'

'So the victims shared some trade, physical though not extremely hard by the look of their bones? Thales either was so scared of the killers, or so closely in league with them, he allowed them to fill his yard with corpses. He must have agreed to these burials. The killers must have relied on him keeping the graves secret, especially making sure afterwards that nobody dug up anything accidentally.'

'Now he's dead, the killers have lost their security. Do you think they know he's gone?'

Tiberius lifted his shoulders, saying, 'If they are anywhere local, they must find out now. They will hear that we have the bodies, so the authorities will be looking for perpetrators.'

I chortled. 'If they hear the vigiles came down here to reconnoitre, and danced off for a drink, they may not be too worried!'

Tiberius returned a rueful look. 'So will they realise that you and I are investigating instead?'

I reckoned it was safer for us if they didn't find out our track record. 'Darling, I'd like to think I have a reputation as a dogged enquirer and you as a meticulous magistrate – but luckily on the Viminal we are neither of us known. Here you are merely the building contractor and I am—'

'The contractor's sparky wife!'

He enjoyed being able to say that. Fortunately, I never felt diminished; he saw us as an equal partnership. In fact, he viewed me as essential. We two would, in every respect, jointly run our family business. The reason I loved Tiberius was that he had never envisaged anything else.

Our foreman, Larcius, came into the courtyard, quietly waiting until we were ready for him. He had been off and found a local undertaker to collect the bones. There were too many, and it was all too public, for us to simply shunt them into a big hole somewhere. Besides, no aedile – well not this aedile – could be so impious.

Tiberius gave instructions that the skeletons were to be kept for a time, in case our enquiries necessitated further inspection. Besides, we liked to be hopeful. We wanted to believe we could identify the dead, giving us a chance to allow their relatives to hold funerals.

The undertaker's cart came. One by one, the collection was lifted and taken away. It was now so late we saw off the bones by lamplight. Then, finally, the courtyard at the Garden of the Hesperides lay in darkness, deserted and empty.

20

Tiberius and I went for a light supper. On our way down the street we passed the vigiles, still gathered at the Romulus. We did not join them.

I noticed they were quiet enough. Those who were having drinks either leaned an arm on the bar counter in twos and threes, pecking at snacks and casually talking, or sat in loose groups at tables. Two had called for the draughtboard.

The other customers, there and at similar places we passed, were behaving in the same relaxed way. None seemed drunk. None were loud. Certainly no one was fighting.

People were here because most had no cooking facilities at home. At least it cut down the number of house fires. But people need to eat. They come out to streetside eateries and either tuck in with company or take food home and get blamed by the family for forgetting to bring fish pickle. This is daily life in Rome.

For some reason I found myself thinking about home – oops, Londinium. As I remembered, social behaviour was much the same, except that British bars were just so cold, dark and grim that more people bought takeaway food – ooh look, it's exotic Roman turnips. They then rushed home to eat these treasures, thinking it was civilised. Also, more people than here cooked at home as their ancestors had done, brewing up nettle broths on tiny hearths; even with experience they were still capable of burning down their horrid huts. Londinium always had the smell of damp smoke. It could be a bath furnace. It could be manufacturing. It could be a bakery ablaze. Or it could just be Ungulandivericundius warming up some pigs' trotters.

Here, the bars with marble counters were where the majority routinely ate. It was easily warm enough to stand outside, indeed, too warm not to. Either I was mistaken about the ominous mood last night when I looked out from our room, or this was a quiet evening, or simply too early for trouble. Sometimes street violence flares in waves then for no obvious reason dies down. Maybe this was a lull.

Now I began thinking about the night Rufia disappeared and those men were murdered. It could have coincided with a big holiday. There were many in the calendar, as my sisters had found when choosing my wedding day. A religious parade, the gladiatorial games, theatre. Oh all right, everyone ignores drama. So say it was religion or the arena, the staples of Roman entertainment. Harder drinking, wilder festivity. But nobody so far had mentioned a festival in connection with Rufia. If the barmaid had vanished on such a particular night, it would have lingered in the memory, surely? Artemisia and Orchivia had said it was the year the Amphitheatre was consecrated, but the games held for that went on for over a hundred days, which did not really help me.

I talked about this with Tiberius while we were still strolling, before we identified a caupona we liked the look of. In a strange area it's always tricky. We never went into anywhere that had no visible customers, nor anywhere that was throbbing. This one had a few people but some empty places at tables inside. It turned out to be run by a woman. I have no reason to think that was significant – though I found it pleasing.

She was neat and capable. Her helper was a boy of about twelve, presumably her son. She served a decent house red, with a jug of cold water and honey too, then offered us a stew of hot lentils with celery. So she even obeyed the food laws that stipulated no meat. Tiberius Manlius complimented her on that, though did not say he was a magistrate.

He muttered to me that it was so well run, he could not imagine this caupona could ever be a haven for political conspiracy (the daft idea was that by only serving pulses, plotters against the government would be discouraged from gathering to eat out). I smiled, privately thinking that the neat domina and her apparently law-abiding place would provide the perfect cover for fomenting threats against the Emperor. No one would suspect her.

I said nothing. I had yet to ascertain whether the man I was marrying would approve if Domitian were assassinated.

I stopped thinking about that. Even to dream of removing our tyrant was dangerous. I looked around at the other customers nervously. Domitian had spies who could sniff out your private thoughts, even in a haze of lentil steam.

We ate a quiet meal. As we paid, I asked the hostess whether she knew anything about the Hesperides. She claimed not to. Maybe it was too far along the street. Certainly, she was reluctant to gossip.

This was a different kind of establishment. No fornication rooms upstairs. The woman and her son probably lived there, but they kept their own space private. Her clientele were local couples, families she had known for years, passing workers who bucked the trend by wanting breakfast and dinner somewhere congenial and clean.

We walked back to our hired room. When we passed the Romulus, the vigiles had left. Now it was dark, they would need to sign on for their shift, patrolling the streets to look for fires and wrongdoers – or at least householders they could fine for not keeping their fire buckets brimful.

Artemisia and Orchivia had gone from the Romulus too; we saw them talking to other men down at the Four Limpets. They were sitting with their potential clients, pretending to listen admiringly to the conversation. A lanky man in his fifties was actually serving food and drink, with Nipius and Natalis vaguely hovering indoors. In any case, I remembered that the women's current nominal employment was supposed to be at the Brown Toad.

Their places of work seemed curiously fluid. It hardly fitted their official designation as 'waitresses'. People always spoke of Rufia as routinely attached to the Hesperides. Was she an especially loyal kind of barmaid, or did Old Thales keep a tight grip on his staff? Otherwise, were Artemisia and Orchivia specifically whores and exempt from carrying trays?

While the Dardanians were with customers, I would not interrupt them to ask. I wanted my bed, with my lover Tiberius, who had already indulged in a very different kind of wooing today.

27 August

Six days before the Kalends of September
(a.d. VI Kal. Sept.)

Four days before the wedding of
Tiberius Manlius Faustus and Flavia Albia

21

Next morning Tiberius first started his men back at their renovation at the Hesperides; later he intended going to Lesser Laurel Street. I joked that builders always keep two jobs on the go, so whenever you want them, they can say they are over at the other one.

'Oh yes, I'll be getting drunk in a bar all day!' replied Tiberius affably. I had never seen him really drunk, though the night he went out with my father to gain approval for our future together was supposed to have had epic qualities.

'You won't want lunch with me then.' I must have sounded disappointed. It was obvious he would have no time to come back; he had to see a painter about colour shades for doors, apparently. For him, too, our not having lunch together was a matter for regret. 'This had better be for the front doors, nothing less!' I grumbled.

'Our public face,' he conceded. 'Vital.'

'Choose cream and dark red.'

'Yes, that's a classic look and it's what I've gone for. The base must be not too light, but warm with the sun on it, the fields and features picked out for contrast. But I have to match the cream correctly, and it must be the right red.'

Olympus. Ought I to have known him longer before tying myself to this pedant? Would his niggling drive me mad?

He could see what I thought. Wickedly, he said no more.

The whole conversation might be a tease. He would always keep me on the hop; I would never be bored. Oh I loved this man.

I myself was planning to visit the landlord, Liberalis. I wanted to challenge him about the new death count. However, before I could set off to his untidy home, he turned up of his own accord. 'I heard the news. How appalling, how terrible!' The man was flapping to a degree that roused my interest. Was he merely perturbed to have other corpses found in his bar, or was there more to it?

He peered anxiously around the courtyard as if he expected it still to be an ossuary. Perhaps he wanted to frighten himself with something gruesome. He may not have known that it can be traumatic if you have to look at murder victims in a location that's very familiar to you. It would be better not to.

Faustus, who was still here at that point, explained that the bones had been taken away last night, then he suggested, po-faced, that as owner of the premises Julius Liberalis must be responsible for paying for their funerals. From an aedile this sounded credible; Liberalis looked horrified. I knew public funds would probably be found; Tiberius would rather Liberalis kept his cash to pay the renovation account.

While the workmen started to reinstate the ground, I took Liberalis over to the Romulus for a private talk about our discoveries. The bar opposite was empty. The morning shift seemed startled to find customers, but the atmosphere was perfectly pleasant. They even brought us an olive saucer. I personally view four olives between two as miserly, but they saw it as a wildly hospitable gesture.

At this hour the Romulus was seemingly a quiet haven

of refreshments. A mother could have stopped there for a drink of water with two toddlers and never realised she had chosen a place that served as a brothel at night.

'Publius Julius Liberalis!' I gave him a long thoughtful gaze. He started to speak but I carried on in a sombre tone, implying that he was in trouble. 'Six corpses, five males and a female, have been found buried on your premises. What do you have to say about that?'

'I know nothing about it! This has nothing to do with me!'

'Well I warn you, you may have to prove your innocence to a very senior magistrate. I'm sure you heard, the vigiles came down to view the crime scene. They went away to consult their superiors, but you know how they operate. They will look for somebody to blame, and as the owner now, you fit their suspect profile.'

Liberalis exhibited a mix of bafflement and self-defence. It can characterise the genuinely innocent – or else it's how the guilty try to bluff. 'Surely I cannot be held responsible for things that happened before I owned the bar?' That may have seemed common sense to him, but the vigiles were not renowned for logical thinking.

I smiled, acting more sympathetic. I had been to Egypt. I could shed crocodile tears. 'Yes, I am so sorry they are crude. It makes life awful for the innocent. You know what they do, of course . . .' He had no idea. I would enjoy telling him. 'They pinpoint someone they can say looks likely to have done it, then they beat him up until he confesses.'

'What if he hasn't done it?' gasped Liberalis. 'He's not going to confess then, is he?'

'Oh he is! They use a torturer, you know.'

He had not known. He was so naïve, definitely a mother's

boy. I wondered what his mother had been like. Sometimes those who mollycoddle are as dim as their offspring; other times they are needle-sharp. That can especially apply when an inheritance is looming. Mothers of unworldly only sons so often know how to get their hands on the legacy. 'You are not serious!' he quavered.

'Afraid so. If someone says he is not guilty, the vigiles only take more time to make him own up. His pain lasts longer. They like that.' I smiled again, in fact I giggled. 'Listen to me! I sound as if I've spent my life in a station house . . . Well, an old uncle of mine was an enquiry chief for many years. I grew up with this kind of thing. I don't want to shock you, but it taught me a lot, Liberalis. Lucius Petronius is a lovely man in a family situation, but dear gods, I would never have wanted to meet him at work! In fact, one of the officers who came to look at your bar is his replacement, Titus Morellus. Definitely woven on the same loom. He's Fourth Cohort, but very thick with the Third over this. It's a multi-cohort initiative now, in view of the number of corpses and the gravity of the case.'

Oh come, Flavia Albia. That's a fine way to describe the multi-cohort drinking bout for which the Third and Fourth found occasion yesterday. I doubted that those two would ever be back. It would not even be 'case closed' because I knew neither of them even intended for a file to be opened.

Liberalis appeared to be shitting roof tiles. He fell back on pompously asserting, 'I am not talking to you. I will only speak to a magistrate!'

I had learned never to argue with a man who tried to go over my head. I led him quietly back over the road to see the aedile.

★   ★   ★

130

Manlius Faustus had not yet left. He leaned against a door frame, listening to me explain how our witness was feeling demoralised. 'Darling, he doesn't believe I, as a mere woman, can know all the ins and outs; he will only trust your judgement.'

'Fair enough!' said Faustus to the anxious landlord, briefly calming him but causing me momentary trepidation. As Liberalis relaxed, Faustus then turned back to me. 'So what do you want to ask him?'

'Oh, you are just acting in concert!' Liberalis complained.

Smiling, Faustus reached over; he took my right hand in his own for a moment, the traditional pose of married couples. 'We speak as one, my friend. Well, Flavia Albia? The floor is yours.'

'I want a neutral questioner!'

'Of course you do, Liberalis.' Faustus remained unmoved. Annoyingly, he agreed with the landlord's protest while not allowing it. Classic Roman justice. 'That is the bonus of you having two of us. Checks and balances. I am happy to be present, if you request it. You gain the benefit of a witness – while afterwards, when I discuss you with my wise young wife, we shall have a double perspective as we evaluate your answers.'

Once more, he signalled for me to begin. Liberalis resigned himself.

I didn't gloat; it never helps. I remained grave.

'When we interviewed you previously, Julius Liberalis, we were considerate. You happened to be the unlucky owner of premises where a woman had met an untimely end. She died long before you took over. You gave the impression you were too young at the time to know anything about it, while perhaps not even being in the bar that night.'

I saw Liberalis lick dry lips. He followed up with that nervous twining he did with his silvered hair. I was not making eye contact with Faustus. This was my interrogation. He stood very still and let me proceed alone.

'Now we know there were many corpses. If Rufia is one of them, her death appears to be associated with the murder and concealment of the others. So, the conclusion has to be, that night a terrible event happened. A big fight went down, Liberalis. This was no private altercation between the landlord and a staff member. Not a domestic incident at all. It was planned. It would have been loud, crude and highly organised, and it could only have been carried off with helpers. At the time you were practically family – you told us you and Old Thales were related.' He had said 'distantly', but also that he was the obvious heir from a long time back. 'I want to know now, with no more prevarication, what you have to say about this.'

'I can't change my answer. I won't. I know nothing.'

I grew much tougher. 'I think you were there.'

'Not me.'

'I believe you were in on it.' He was only intending to repeat his denial so I cut straight across him: 'Who were the "salesmen" I have been told were in the bar that night?'

'I have no idea.'

'Were they trying to sell specific goods to Thales, or was their presence coincidental? They just happened to seek their evening entertainment here?'

'I don't know. I don't know who they were or what they wanted. I was not party to management at that time. Sometimes I came in for a drink because I lived nearby, but Old Thales did everything his own way and kept it all to himself. How the bar ran was never my business.'

'Well, if that's true, you can help me find people who *were* taking notice! I want names. Who were the other customers that night?'

'I don't even remember which night!'

'Don't lie. This was a major event for the Hesperides. Even if the bar was a den of criminal violence in those days, this deed would have stood out as extraordinary. Anyone close to Thales – as you admit you were – would know all about this drama. Six people died. Six people were then stripped and buried, very efficiently. Six graves were raked smooth by somebody with nerves of iron, then tables were set out upon them so it all looked innocent. To anybody who was there, the night must be unforgettable.'

Liberalis shook his head. He was highly distressed.

'You know who those bodies are.'

Another head shake. He could not even bring himself to speak the lie out loud.

'You know who killed them.'

This shake was smaller and tighter, barely visible.

'You know why.'

Almost nothing this time. He was holding on and holding in, but I could see him shaking. I saw panic. I saw fear. He could not bear to remember. Whatever had happened here was a horror from which he had hidden for years. He still dreaded to think about it.

Now I was certain: I was not the only sleeper in the Ten Traders district who had suffered nightmares after we found Rufia.

22

Sometimes you have to back away and leave them with their anxiety for a time. Of course you then risk finding them hanging from a beam in a barn. That way they will never answer your questions.

Since we were in the barn-free city, I hardened my heart. I sent Julius Liberalis off, advising him to think about his responsibilities. Faustus said dourly that he would ask Macer if the Third Cohort had an empty cell. I played the kindly one, for once. Pretending to intercede with my brusque fiancé, I told the landlord to go home, quickly. 'You're not under arrest yet. Come and see us when you are ready to talk.'

This established that *he* knew that *we* knew he did have something to say.

He left.

Still maintaining his austere persona, Tiberius Manlius now set off for the Aventine. With the manner of a particularly pompous consul, all he gave me was a nod, no kiss. I blew him one, exaggerating the gesture. Unless he softened up, his paint-supplier was in for a sharp meeting with snap decisions. I ran after them and called out to Dromo to make sure his master had a midday snack to relax him, because I didn't want us ending up with myrtle when oyster shell would be a better foil for the oxblood features. The slave looked at me as if I was even crazier than normal; Tiberius kept walking but raised an arm in salute. Even though he had his back to me, I knew he was grinning.

I stood behind the counter of the Hesperides, watching them go, feeling intense. Once before, I had sent off a husband for an ordinary morning walk, then had him returned to me, dead before lunchtime. I would never entirely recover.

'Take care,' I whispered, though Tiberius could not hear me. It was a charm for myself. What's the point of supposedly being a druid if you cannot chant magic to protect those who are dear to you? *Take care, my love. Dromo, take care of him. Come back to me . . .*

I stayed where I was for a time, thinking. Life is uncertain. Tragedy can strike unexpectedly. Five wives, if the victims were all married men, once lost their husbands for ever in this bar. Five women somewhere must by now have accepted they were widows.

I turned around, looking back towards the courtyard while I imagined it previously. The workmen were out there now, reinstating the garden area; I was able to erase them mentally, taking myself back to that night ten years ago.

The garden was most likely where the trap was sprung. Outside in the street beside the marble-topped counter would have been too visible and too risky − the intended victims might break away and escape. Inside would muffle any noise, though shouts and screams were probably routine around here. Subduing five men would be a difficult prospect, even if the attackers could rely on surprise. The aim must have been to take them out fast, before they could react. Whoever planned the attack would have wanted to prevent a real fight ever starting. That would cause too much damage, damage that would be obvious to customers the next day – wounds on the attackers, breakages that would need to be replaced before the bar could operate.

The Garden of the Hesperides had opened as usual the following morning, that was clear from statements. Everything had looked fine. No one, no ordinary member of the public, had realised anything had happened there.

Five men disappeared, but it would seem that nobody ever came looking for them.

Strangers? Up from the country or, more likely, foreigners. Men who had never been here before? Or men who had been before, yet nobody at home, wherever that was, knew of their links to the Ten Traders district in Rome, let alone their connection to this specific bar.

Had it been too far to come looking, too expensive to make the journey, had any chance of finding out what had happened been too uncertain?

Alternatively, perhaps these men's deaths had served as a warning. No one came searching because people were too scared of the same fate befalling them.

That seemed unlikely. Old Thales sounded a social menace, but not particularly scary. If I thought someone like him had murdered five people I knew, I would not hesitate to wreak revenge.

Not everyone was like me. Just as well, you may say.

All right, if you were a peace-loving, timid type yourself, you could at least report the crime to the authorities. This was Rome, city of ancient justice. Well, it was Rome, city of interminable legal wrangling. You could hire a barrister to sue all Hades out of Thales. If you had the money, you could demand justice.

If not, you would have to make a complaint to the vigiles. That was not entirely pointless. The Third Cohort were shirkers, but for sudden disappearances and presumed killings, they might at least prepare a scroll so as not to be caught out if anything else happened later. Cover your backs, my uncle Lucius would say. Write up some notes, so you have notes to consult, notes to present if and when your case is raised again by busybodies.

Macer had apparently known nothing about a past crime until he came and saw the bodies. Possibly he had now gone back to his station house to hunt up old reports, though I wasn't confident.

If the five men could afford to travel here, their associates at home probably had access to funds too, so ought to have been able to follow them. I reckoned the associates could not have known where to come.

And what of the woman? If it was Rufia, she had lived here. When trouble started, did she get in the way? Did one of the aggressors kill her accidentally? Or was she deliberately punished by someone for being too friendly with the victims? More likely, with one victim in particular? This was harsh, but it would by no means be the first time a jealous man had lashed out and murdered a woman on those grounds. Come to that, it wouldn't be the first time a man had planned it in advance.

Why was her head removed, and what happened to it afterwards?

I turned around so I was facing the street again. No one outside had spotted me. Everyone knew the bar was closed, and I was standing still beside a post that held up the roof. No one had any cause to look over this way. I was not noticed.

From there I could see across to the Romulus, now empty, and beyond it the Four Limpets. At the Limpets, I recognised Nipius and Natalis, leaning on the bar counter, not serving but apparently having a late breakfast themselves. At a table in the street were Artemisia and Orchivia, though they seemed to have finished eating. Artemisia was leaning forward on her elbows, yawning, Orchivia sprawled backwards. Another woman stood on the edge of the pavement, talking to them. She looked less blowsy, definitely older.

I had the impression they knew her, though the relationship was muted. They appeared to listen as required, but were taking little notice. She spoke to them; they let her talk. I could not make out any response. Well, I knew they were a stroppy pair.

While I watched, the older woman glanced across the street. I was uncertain whether she noticed me. Three mules, all laden with heavy grain sacks, came to a halt between us while their drovers called at the Romulus; whether for delivery or for refreshments was unclear. The woman broke off her conversation and swiftly took herself off in the uphill direction, patting a mule on the rump as she passed. The Four Limpets was far enough away that if I had started after her, she would easily have lost me. Besides, the beasts were in my way. I let her go.

For some reason I felt that I had just seen Menendra, the woman the Dardanians had mentioned before, who once knew Rufia. If so, this Menendra had no desire to talk to me.

23

A public slave came down the Argiletum, sweeping. When I say he came down the road, it was a slow progress, with many stops to stand still and gaze around pointlessly.

I had somewhere in mind to investigate. Not wanting to alert any bar staff to my intention, I asked the slave if he knew Mucky Mule Mews. Normally no one spoke to him. I politely ascertained that he did understand Latin, since it is not always certain that they can talk our language. Some public slaves look after temples or imperial baths, so they tend to be of acceptable quality, but the rest are cheap labour given menial, dirty tasks that even the poor don't want; many public slaves are as bad as that implies. This one was sent out every day by himself, so someone must trust him. Still, where would he run to? Who would pay him anything for his snaggled old broom if he stole it?

He grew jumpy in case I was suggesting he ought to have used his broom in the mews. I reassured him. Once his panic receded, he gave me directions. I thanked him, donated a copper for his pension fund and set off. His directions were wrong. I have no reason to think he did that on purpose, though my father, who is deeply suspicious of everyone, would have been certain.

Once I realised, I asked again of passing locals. I had reasoned Rufia lived fairly close to her work, so the alley I wanted must be nearby. It was. Nothing had been lost, except a few moments' anxiety on my part because I dislike ending up somewhere I don't know, without planning to be there. In the end I found the place.

It was no worse than Fountain Court, but I was so used to my own horrors I barely noticed them. Not so here. Even if the road sweeper had been ordered to this deplorable cul-de-sac, one man with a besom could never have achieved much. There must be a stable hereabouts. I had never seen such high piles of mule dung. They looked old; they smelt fresh. Any mules who created these deposits were probably half wild and spiteful-tempered. Their drovers could well be the same.

I looked around, making sure I knew where the exit was and how deep the potholes on the way to it were. I did not want to find myself stuck down this lonely alley with a feral animal-driver, let alone a bunch of them. I knew what they would be like. No teeth, big whips, depraved ideas. If Rufia had had to make her way down here every night in the dark, I knew why she had become aggressive. I felt weary and angry just imagining what she went through.

Perhaps late at night when she came home, the drovers would all be snoring in the stable. And perhaps they were in truth sweet-natured, honest heroes who would come running to the aid of any female in distress . . . I would not want to test their response to screams. The swine would come running all right – every man of them pulling up his tunic, whooping with glee, ready to join in the gang rape.

It was very quiet at the moment. I felt glad of that.

At first I thought no one could live here. Blank black walls loomed above me on both sides. Gradually I began to spot dark doorways in the filthy walls that shadowed the dank, unpaved lane. There were arched windows too, their brickwork caked with centuries of dirt and pigeon guano. Shops may have lined the street once, but were long gone; nor could I hear any sounds of manufacturing. I pulled my skirts in tight, trying to avoid puddles of ominous liquid. I wished I was not wearing jewellery. I took off my necklace and put it away in the satchel where I kept my note tablet.

It struck me that nobody knew I had come here. Tiberius would say I should always tell him where I was going; he would be right. I must learn to do it. Well, one day perhaps, but I had survived on my own for twelve years so I saw no urgency for change. I had no intention of living in my husband's pocket like his little pet mouse. He would have to get used to that.

If nobody else knew I was coming here, at least no one with bad intentions would have trailed me, no one would have come ahead to lie in wait. Only the people who lived here posed any danger.

They did not seem to exist. It was excessively quiet. To reach this place I had only walked down a short side street, yet the racket on the Vicus Longus was completely muffled by the intervening buildings. Though the mews was grimy and oppressive, as a professional myself I could see that a woman who worked late and who wanted somewhere to sleep undisturbed by day might find the isolation helpful. Rufia could have overlooked its sordid aspects, much as I did at Fountain Court. It would take a brave acquaintance to come bothering her at home. Any stalkers who followed her unbidden might give up at the end of such a horrible alley. In view of the time since Rufia had disappeared, I nearly gave up myself. What was the point of hoping some-body here would remember her?

I jumped: a shadow came out from a doorway. Quite suddenly I was passed by a little arthritic old woman with a basket on one arm. Such an ordinary apparition, her sheer normality was startling. I pulled myself together to run after her, calling out: 'Granny, stop, will you!'

She looked round, squinted at me with near-blind eyes, then told me to get lost. If she could have scuttled away, she would have done. Instead, she kept going, at her slow but steady pace. Here was a ninety-year-old biddy in flat shoes and a ragged stole going out for a melon and a pinch of powder to take away her pains. She had no intention of talking to a strange young woman, let alone of being helpful.

'You must have known Rufia!'

The only reply was a *humph*. She would have said that if I had asked the way to the Forum, told her she had come into money, or pretended her landlord wanted to put up her rent. Her own long-lost love child would have received the same angry rebuff. She managed to creak up into the side street ahead of me and was gone on her way.

Human contact revived my confidence. I started knocking on the dismal doors, even though my first attempts brought no answer. Eventually I summoned a housewife who claimed no knowledge of the barmaid and I believed her, but she did suggest another woman, who pointed out where Rufia had once lived.

'Did you know her?'

'Not to speak to.'

Further questions were clearly unwelcome.

I crossed the alley, nearly turning my ankle in a rut. Thumping the door eventually brought a fragile, stooped man, who said I should speak to his wife. He closed the door on me. Just when I was about to give up and leave, it reopened; she emerged, looking fearful.

'It's all right, I'm not a door-to-door fishwife, so you don't have to pretend you have no call for razor clams.' She looked baffled. I reined in my wit. 'Forget it. I am so sorry to bother you. I am an investigator. I have been told that Rufia used to live here.'

I could have pretended Rufia was a friend, but I was too young for the claim to look convincing and I knew too little about her. Everyone thinks informers are constantly adopting disguises, but you can tangle yourself up for no purpose that way, while you inhibit witnesses. So I use an honest approach.

Unexpectedly, the woman unbent. I wondered if she had been waiting all these years for somebody, anybody, to show an interest. But perhaps not, because she asked, 'Menendra sent you?'

I was startled. 'No. I've never met her.'

'I don't like that one.'

'Any reason?' I demanded, recovering.

'No. Better come in then.' She let me through the door. I saw a room to one side that must be where she lived with her husband; I could hear him wheezing inside. Narrow stairs led upwards. 'You can take a look, if you have to. But I'll come in with you. It isn't right. There's all her things.'

'Have you kept her possessions all this time?' I was amazed. 'Was she your lodger?' I asked. As we went up the woman confirmed it, though she was too breathless to elaborate. 'And you have never re-let the room? Really?' They were clearly as poor as most people in Rome. If the old fellow had ever worked, he was past it now. She looked younger, though none too sprightly.

'I didn't like to. I'm not in a hurry to have other people. We get by. And who knows?'

Who knows what? I was struck by the oddity of this, but we had reached the top landing so I wanted to give all my concentration to where Rufia had lived. There were no more stairs beyond us even though I had seen from outside that the building had further storeys. Anyone who lived higher up must have another entrance. I guessed that when Mucky Mule Mews had had more life, this part had once been a self-contained shop or a workshop, with living quarters above it.

The peeling door was not locked. The landlady pushed it open, then sent me in first. She followed only as far as the threshold, watching closely, but she let me enter to look around unhindered.

Sometimes such a room can feel as if its occupant, the dead person, has only just left that morning. Not here. There was no sense of her.

'Have you touched anything since Rufia disappeared?'

'No, it's all just the same.'

Despite the landlady's claim that I would find 'all her things', there was not much.

'Did anyone else ever come and take away possessions?'

She shook her head. I gazed at her, not so much doubting her as puzzled. She was, as I now took in properly, a worn, faded soul who looked as if she had worked hard all her life, probably for other people. She had thin colourless hair, scraped untidily together, brown liver spots, bony hands, a scrawny neck poking out of the loose opening to a dingy tunic. While she stood watching me, she plucked at her long sleeves and reorganised her tunic neck, pulling it tighter as if she felt cold.

I turned back to my survey of the room. It was small, of course. As a single working woman, I might have lived somewhere like this, had I not been fortunate to have a father with a tenement he wanted to fill. Otherwise I too would have spent my days in a dire cubicle that was part of someone else's home, with no cooking facilities, a bucket for washing and sanitary purposes, a small high window I could not see out of though it had a pigeon looking in, one bed, one cupboard, a stool, a hook behind the door and a moth-eaten rag floor mat. Most of those, I guessed, came with the room.

So what was Rufia's? An inventory of personal possessions could be written in three lines. Of course a barmaid would earn little and own little. But if I assumed Rufia had gone to work in her clothes the day she died, she had left behind hardly any other personal items. No spare tunic (well, that might be correct on a barmaid's wages), no accessories, no cloak for winter.

At least she owned her food bowl, beaker, cheap bent cutlery. There was a pair of beaten-up backless slippers, kicked under the bed, one with a sole long gone. She had had small feet. With no other clothes to guide me, I could not picture the rest of her. On the rag rug, I noticed a hairpin. That was surprisingly nice. Probably some ordinary bone, though it masqueraded as as ivory. I picked it up. Sniffed it, finding no relic of perfume, not that there could have been after all this time.

'Tell me about her.' I was holding the hairpin on the palm of my hand. 'Was Rufia a girl who used cosmetics?'

'Don't they all?'

'Where are her paints and powders then?' For heavens' sake, everyone owns at least a pot of cream. Rufia almost certainly had to wash the Hesperides' bowls and beakers, because I could not imagine Nipius and Natalis doing that; so she would have had dry, cracked hands.

'I told you, I've taken nothing!'

'I was not accusing you.'

'She kept her stuff at the bar where she worked, I suppose. That was where she would have wanted to look nice. Nice for the customers.'

Hmm! 'Did she ever have a boyfriend?'

'I never knew of one.'

'And she never wore jewellery?' People who do, however basic it is, generally have more than one piece so they can swap around.

'Don't look at me! She had a bangle that she always wore. I never took it.'

Fine.

'I was just thinking,' I said sadly after a while, 'this is so little to show for a life.'

The woman from downstairs settled; she liked me showing sympathy. 'I took her pillow. That was all I ever came and took out. For the old one down below, when he has trouble sleeping. I could have returned it if she ever came back.'

'She is never coming back.' I wondered whether to say we thought we had found Rufia's body, but stalled at the woman's next remark.

'No. That's what the other one said.'

24

She had turned around and was making her way down-stairs again. Although our discussion about Rufia ought to have been sad, she seemed to take it matter-of-factly. I cast a rapid glance back at the room before I started down but there was nothing there to detain me longer.

'Who was it?' I demanded, once we reached the ground again. 'This other one?'

'That Menendra. I told you, I didn't take to her.'

'She came here, and recently?'

'She came yesterday.'

'*Yesterday?* What did she want?'

'To see the room, like you. Only I just showed *her* from the doorway and wouldn't let her go inside. I never liked her attitude.'

'You knew her already? I have been told she was some-thing to do with Rufia, I don't know what that was – friends, or they worked together?'

'They worked. That was all. I met her once with Rufia. That was enough for me, thank Juno.'

The landlady had a tight mouth, disapproving of the other woman. Somehow I knew she regarded me more favourably. With luck, she would talk to me.

'I have not met Menendra yet, though I shall have to.' I

spoke openly, on equal terms. 'I am not sure what to expect. Can you tell me what she's like?'

'Pushy. You won't like her. I can tell you're not that kind.' That would be news to my friends and family, who all thought me an obstreperous fiend.

'Is she foreign like some of the others?'

'Something. Speaks with a funny accent. Don't they all?'

'Barmaids, you mean?'

She let out a hard laugh, loaded with meaning. 'And the rest!'

'She is a prostitute?'

Now my informant retracted. 'Not for me to say!' Her voice told me, however, just how she regarded Menendra; whether she thought the same of Rufia was unclear, though I thought not.

'So why did this Menendra come now? Why was she interested in Rufia's room?'

The worn landlady drew herself up, becoming a pillar of rectitude. 'That I don't know. I wouldn't want to know her reasons. But what I can say is this, young lady. That Menendra came here in the morning. I gave her the run-around and saw her on her way, quick as I could. The same night, and yes I mean last night, someone else came and they tried to break in on us!'

I was shocked. This was a harmless couple with nothing to steal. 'That's terrible. What did you do?'

'Our son was here,' she replied, relishing this. 'Bad luck for them! He calls in to see us most days. He had his three big dogs with him – they are sloppy things but they bark loud. So whoever it was, they stopped trying to get in the door and they scrammed.'

'Did any of you see them properly?'

'No, they hopped it too quick. Our lad ran down the alley after them, but it was no good. He'll be back this evening,' she assured me, seeing I felt great concern for the besieged couple, especially the frail old man. 'He's going to bring materials to make the door safer. One of the dogs will stay here with us; the other two cry if they're not in their own bed.'

Rome was full of mosaics saying beware of the dog, with portraits of fierce curs in big spiked collars. Few houses actually had a guard dog, or if they owned one, he was gentler than his portrait. Of course we had the usual men who wanted to look tough, leading about horrible curs they could not properly handle – and also families with much-loved pets who wanted to greet strangers with ferocious licking.

'That's good. All good. I'm very glad you have someone to look out for you.' I let the woman see me thinking hard. 'What's your name?'

'Annina.'

'Look, Annina, if the people who tried to break in had something to do with Menendra's visit, they must want to find something.'

'That was what we thought.' These people were savvy. She and her husband and son had debated this. Their conclusions were the same as mine. The burglars and Menendra were connected, and they all wanted something. Something they thought Rufia had had, something they wanted to get to before me.

'Did any of you go up and search?'

'We know there's nothing.'

'May I take another look?'

She nodded at once, almost as if she had been hoping I

would ask. She let me go back by myself. This time I searched hard, scoured the room like a professional. I went through everywhere, hunting for hidey-holes. Not simply under the mattress and behind the cupboard, but seeking out loose boards, removable bricks, hollows in plaster above architraves. I found the secret places that Rufia may have used when she lived there. But they were all empty.

25

As I left Mucky Mule Mews I remembered to stay alert. When preoccupied by odd discoveries, it is all too easy to become so abstracted you fall prey to villains. Wise informers wait to start their brooding.

Even so, I was wondering what people might think Rufia could have left behind.

I walked carefully back to the Vicus Longus. The main thoroughfare, which had once seemed so insalubrious, suddenly felt familiar, populated and safe. I took a long breath and relaxed, as if I had narrowly escaped a scare. It was ridiculous. Nothing had happened, not to me. But I had enough experience to know what was possible in obscure places.

I went along to where Tiberius and I had enjoyed breakfast. I sat down with refreshments, fruit juice and a complimentary almond biscuit. Of the two who ran the stall the mother was alone today, so she joined me in the sunlight. We exchanged names. She was Lepida, a good Latin designation, so I asked whether she had lived around here long.

'Born and bred.'

'That seems fairly unusual. A lot of people I've spoken to are incomers.'

'Too many slaves and foreigners,' Lepida grumbled. It

was a classic complaint: unwanted low-class persons flooding in from overseas, taking all the work.

I decided not to mention Britain. With brown hair and despite blue-grey eyes, I had no really alien features. No stuck-out Pictish ears, no eastern steppes high cheekbones, no unusual skin tone. No one could tell my origins, unless I told them. Any bright occupant of the Empire can soon pick up Roman gestures and habits, learn to speak conventionally, then blend in. If anything, what marked me out was having too well-bred an accent nowadays.

I kicked out to scatter pigeons as they pecked too near. One of the automatic traits you soon learn eating out in the Mediterranean.

Cradling my beaker, I sat deep in thought, letting my jadedness show. 'How is it going?' asked Lepida sympathetically. I pulled a face. 'You're trying to find out what happened at that bar, aren't you?' I agreed, deliberately leaving her to take the initiative. I remembered how yesterday, with her daughter present, she had held back.

'Working as an informer,' I said, when she stalled, 'isn't always easy.'

'What are you stuck over?'

'Oh pretty well everything!' I sipped my drink, gazing vacantly across the street. 'Who died? Who killed them? Why? Five men and a woman vanished from their daily lives, yet nobody seems to have missed them. I know a few people who admit being in the Hesperides that night, but they are all keeping mum. I'm sensing fear – which is understandable. And now an innocent couple, who merely happened to be Rufia's landlords, have been attacked in their own home.'

'That's terrible!' breathed Lepida, wide-eyed.

'It's connected. Has to be. Digging up those sad old bones from the bar is starting to have repercussions.'

We sat in silence for a while. I knew when not to apply pressure.

The street lay bathed in August sunshine. At noon, this was an ordinary-looking thoroughfare. Sounds and scents of people having lunch at home in apartments all around us. Mothers nagging children to eat their bread nicely. Men whose work involved late shifts rousing from sleep, starting to make their presence felt in a world that had managed without them for the past few hours; wives resisting as they tried throwing their weight about. Dogs standing up and stretching their long backs. Dogs lying down again in diminishing patches of shade. Shops closing up for a lengthy siesta.

'I never knew that Rufia.' Lepida was opening up. 'I never spoke to her.'

'You knew who she was, though?'

'I had seen her. If you pointed her out, I could have told you her name. I was young then. But I never mingled with women of that sort.'

'Barmaids?'

She pursed her lips and didn't answer. We drank our juice.

After a while she suddenly came out with, 'Things are not the same around here.' She paused, reflectively. 'It's all got very rough.'

Although I was surprised, I merely said some people would think the whole Subura had always been a rough area.

'Oh it wasn't too bad,' answered Lepida, who had presumably never lived anywhere else. She seemed unaware her local district was historically notorious. 'All the usual things went on, but it was . . . oh, I don't know. In a bar like the Garden of the Hesperides, yes, if a man wanted to go upstairs, the landlord probably had a daughter or a cousin who would oblige for a copper. But it was casual, you know what I mean. More of a favour than a business. Now it's all much more . . . professional.'

I absorbed this. 'Was Rufia like somebody's daughter or cousin?'

'Yes, I think she was one of those types to start with.'

'She changed?'

'Oh I would think so!' Lepida exclaimed, though I could not see why she was so exercised. 'Don't you, Flavia Albia?'

'You mean she worked here a long time and acquired some respect?' I remembered I had been told Rufia was not native-born. 'Somebody told me she came from overseas; Illyria was mentioned.'

'I don't know about that.'

'So why do you think she changed?'

'Maybe she got used to running things.'

'The bar?'

'Anything that needed sorting.'

I started to doubt that Lepida knew anything useful. This conversation was meant to steer my investigation in a friendly way, yet her attempt to help was pretty vague.

'So is it your impression, Lepida, that what happened at the bar was connected to the rougher elements who have come in?'

'I don't know. I'm just saying what I think.'

No, she was *not* saying much, and perhaps not even thinking. But that's witnesses.

26

Sometimes when you are looking for someone, they come looking for you. This is generally bad news.

I had finished my juice and said friendly farewells to Lepida. Tiberius and I would be back for more breakfast another day. With no clear plan for taking things forward, I had wandered back towards the Garden of the Hesperides. I reached the bar, but hesitated, because there was no reason for me to go in. I could hear our workmen inside, talking in low voices, chipping with spades. From where I stood I could not actually see them, nor they me.

'Here, you!'

A hoarse female voice accosted me. I knew it was me she wanted. There was nobody else around. It was Menendra. As Lepida had said, like so many in Rome she had a heavy foreign accent. Earlier she had avoided me. Now, from her stance, feet apart and arms folded, she had sought me out deliberately. Her attitude was not friendly.

Behind her stood two large men. They never directly threatened me. Their presence was enough. Everyone understands a pair of heavies like that.

Instinctively I glanced back to the bar, but we all knew that by the time I could attract attention, it would be too late. I had better cooperate.

27

I felt as distrustful as when I had seen her earlier with the Dardanians. Close to, she was around fifty, with the air of an angry matriarch even if in fact she was not a mother. She was at least as old as Lepida, and much unhappier in her spirit.

She carried a powerful aura, full of confidence. She looked like someone who would matter-of-factly drown unwanted kittens. She might also drown me, if I happened to offend her and there was a handy barrel.

From time to time people passed in the street, though nobody gave us a second glance. That could mean that once they identified Menendra, they were careful to look away.

'You!' Her voice was throaty. Either she made a habit of yelling at people or she had spent too much time amid the smoky oil of late-night lamps.

'Me?' I queried demurely, stalling.

'Yes, you! The magistrate's bint.' Faustus would smile at that. I gave her my *I am my own woman* stare. My attempt was as much use as trying to wash a dog that's rolled in dung without getting dirty yourself.

She came nearer. I would have stepped back but I was already against the bar counter. Menendra was a hard-faced ratchet who could not be called attractive, though she looked as if she had never been held back by that. She wore a dark green gown with a fierce belt, but she had let her body run to seed so her belly flopped over it. The necklace hanging heavily from her dry, creased neck must have cost plenty, though if she had money she did not waste it on skin lotions. She also wore large metal earrings of an exotic ethnic type. Taking those together with her accent, wherever she originated was a long way from Rome.

I never despised anyone for that.

'You want to speak to me?'

'Yes I do, if you can find me a moment, dearie.' I could see this woman forcing herself to sound milder. She wanted something, or she wanted to make me do something; it would be bad policy for her to start out too rough. I was equally uncomfortable. Everything about her, including the lurking heavies, made me feel too dainty. The urge to simper and tuck in locks of hair felt strong, though I have never been a hair-twiddler, thank you, Juno.

'Well, I am Flavia Albia, as you seem to know. And you are . . . ?'

'Menendra.' I gave no sign of having heard the name, but asked what she did. She ignored that, so I asked what she wanted. 'Just a word to the wise, dearie.' This is the usual euphemism when somebody is warning you to back off. I played innocent. She kept pressing. 'You don't want to get yourself in any trouble, do you?'

I refused to understand her. At moments like this, I like to be my mother's daughter: educated, well off, well mannered, sweet-natured . . . Well, maybe not sweet-natured. I pursed my lips slightly, but I folded my hands gently at my waist and raised my eyebrows, looking merely amused at her tone of voice. Then I simply waited. I wanted to see how far she would commit herself.

It was an interesting situation. Menendra clearly struggled, as if she was addressing me in a foreign language. The codes she normally used with people she bullied – and I reckoned bullying was her medium – were not working. She was desperate to make me comply; she did not know how to go about it. She had a reputation, but I seemed to have no fear of it. She saw that an open offensive would be counterproductive. Since I was a magistrate's woman, anything stronger than wheedling would be risky, because Faustus could come down very heavily on her.

I refused to help. Let her flounder. Let her wonder whether I was too dense to see what she meant – or actually laughing up my sleeve at her.

'Now listen, dearie. You just tell that man of yours, whatever happened was a long time ago and it's better for everyone not to stir it all up again.'

'Why don't you tell him?' Even to myself I sounded haughty. 'Of course he will ask what is it to you? Were you involved? What do you know about the people we have found dead?' I paused for a single beat. 'Did you kill them?'

Still controlling her manner, Menendra gave me a reproachful look. 'Now, you don't want to go around accusing people of killings.'

I stopped being a nice senator's granddaughter. 'It's what I do.'

She blinked.

I smiled with false sweetness. 'We seem to have got off on the wrong foot. Shall we try again? I am formally investigating the events that led up to six bodies being buried in the courtyard of this bar. Manlius Faustus, the plebeian aedile, wants to know who they are and who put them there. Apparently, you don't think we should interfere, but you're too late. As soon as the first bones turned up, that was the end of keeping things quiet. So, before we discuss the corpses, Menendra, why don't you tell me about yourself and your connection with the Hesperides? I have heard you act as a supplier to the local bars. Fruit was mentioned.'

'*Fruit?*' Menendra now definitely thought I was making mock.

If what she really supplied was flesh for the upstairs-room trade, 'fruit' could be a witty word for it. But Menendra lacked my sense of humour. I noticed that after her first outburst of disgust, she failed to correct me. To me, that confirmed what she traded was sexual. 'I am in commerce, yes that's right. I work with all the neighbourhood bars. They all know me very well.' But for what? She had no intention of explaining.

'And they don't mess with you!' Flattery was worth a try. But again she completely ignored it. This was a hard, shrewd woman who expected to be in control.

'Were you at the Garden of the Hesperides on the night the six people died?'

'I was not.' Menendra spoke with a nasty smirk, daring me to try to prove otherwise. I felt sure she would lie to me. If I was ever to put her at the scene that evening, someone else would have to tell me. First I would have to find them, then convince them it was safe to risk Menendra's wrath.

'Did you know Rufia?'

'Who told you that?'

'I can't remember,' I bluffed. A wise informer protected her sources. Otherwise, if Menendra got to them with her hints about keeping quiet, backed up with her heavies' meaningful looks, those sources would dry up rapidly. 'Several people.'

'Yes, I knew Rufia, knew her very well. What of it?'

'Do you believe one of those bodies they dug up is her?'

'Well she vanished, didn't she?'

'She did so quite unexpectedly?'

'I heard that.'

'Somebody tried to burgle her old room last night. I wonder what they were looking for?'

'Oh what can it have been?' sneered Menendra, not even troubling to deny her involvement.

'Rufia isn't the only puzzle. There are five more bodies. That night she disappeared a group of salesmen were in the bar. You're in commerce. Do you know anything about them, or who they were?'

'I never heard about any salesmen.' Really? Nothing she said was reliable; she actually flaunted that.

'Rufia looked after them.'

'You seem to know all about it, Flavia Albia!'

I knew damn all, and this witness was not helping. I recognised what was going on. Her aim was to find out how much I did know, but not to enlighten me further.

I toughened up again. 'Oh I think you are the one who knows, Menendra. So if I can hand out quiet advice myself, it is let me find out by my own civilised methods. Don't compel me to call in the men with hot irons and weights.'

'You don't scare me!' She leaned towards me, full of menace. 'I said, leave it all alone!' She intended to petrify me. She turned to her two heavies, her intention plain.

'Call them off, Menendra.' Measuring distances by eye, I let her know I could get to her before her men could get to me. Then I spoke like a street urchin who had taken part in every kind of street fight: 'Scram them! Or I'll pull out your eyes with my bare hands before your brutes can move a step.'

28

Everything shifted.

I took a step forwards, pointing my right forefinger. 'Move them back!' My tone made her believe I would carry out my threat to her eyes. It almost made me believe it too. That's all you need.

Now she saw that I too had an unforgiving past. No one crossed her; nobody crossed me.

After a beat of disbelief, she made a slight, angry movement to her men; the heavies slowly walked across to the Medusa, leaving us.

A chill sweat trickled down my neck and under my tunic, but I made sure no anxiety showed. I was not so foolish as to think I had outfaced this woman. 'That's good. Now answer my questions, Menendra. Better to speak to me than officials. It's your choice, but you are not stupid.'

Her chin came up though she did not object.

'Tell me how things were in those days, back when Rufia vanished. Thales owned the Hesperides, Rufia worked there. What about you? Were you providing your "supplies" in those days?'

'Not me.'

'Too young? You hadn't started?'

'I built up my little business afterwards,' she acknowledged.

I looked her up and down. From the way she dressed,

her business could not be so little; she was comfortably decked out. 'Everything was more casual back then?' That was what the woman at the snacks stall had told me.

'I suppose so.'

'Where do you come from, Menendra? Where were you born?'

'Lycia.' In the north-eastern Mediterranean. Pirate country. Not much else there.

'Slave or free?'

'I am no slave!'

'Never have been?'

'Wash your mouth out.' I saw her scanning me, wondering. Plenty of people assumed I myself must have slave origins. It was a possibility. I would have to live the rest of my life not knowing. In moments of depression, I felt that any slave had better luck than me; at least they understood their place in the world. Still, I was a happy bride now. Happy and fortunate. Happy, fortunate and free.

'All right. So you came to Rome of your own accord, for the pickings – was that when you met Rufia?' She begrudged me a curt nod. 'You were friends?'

'She was decent to me. Took me under her wing. Taught me how to survive here.'

'Oh, all girls together then? I'm trying to imagine how it was.'

'You're wrong.' Menendra cackled as she anticipated my discomfiture when she explained. 'Way wrong. Rufia was hardly a girl. She must have been easily fifty. Could have been older. She had worked at the Hesperides for decades. She was older than Old Thales himself, and she looked every day of it. She was like a grandmother to me.

So you haven't been seeing the picture at all, have you, dearie?'

I pulled a face, openly admitting that I had misjudged everything. Believe me, I was cursing.

29

Our conversation ended. I was too nonplussed to sustain it.

Menendra turned on her heel and made off down the main road. A jerk of her head drew the two heavies after her. If I managed to interview her again, she would gloat and I would flail. The only option next time was an official interrogation. She would resist and only if we had direct evidence could she be leaned on. I had lost this game.

I was left to feel I had so far been foolish. Nobody ever told me Rufia was young; that was my own stupid misapprehension. Now I knew, I had to work through everything all over again. I had quite wrongly perceived the kind of event that must have happened here; I understood nothing about it.

Nowhere in the Twelve Tables is it legally enshrined that in the city of Rome a barmaid must be some cute young girl. Of course they generally are, unless the landlord can acquire others so much more cheaply that he puts up with a lack of youth or beauty. Some landlords have to employ their own relatives, who may be any age from eight to eighty and look as ugly as their employers.

I wouldn't care how old Rufia was, except that all my previous theories about her fate suddenly became unlikely. The kind of predator I had imagined attacking a barmaid would want young flesh; that kind of sexual killer hardly ever stalks an older woman. Even if he is brave enough to take her on, her tough maturity insults his manhood. Perverts want them luscious. They need to snatch youth, which is for them unobtainable because of their own oddness; they yearn to punish the lively women they have seen with other men.

The idea that Old Thales had bumped off Rufia also took a new twist. If she and her employer had had any relationship, it could not have been as I once thought. If they had quarrelled, it must have been a different kind of quarrel. Why Rufia was then killed along with five men became an even more intractable puzzle.

At least the stories of her quelling any trouble in the bar now seemed more natural. Experienced women tend to know how to quash obstreperous men. I could easily envisage this Rufia throwing out troublemakers. I could see them meekly leaving as soon as she said go. Regulars, who knew her, would probably not even start being loud while she was serving. She had been here for years. This bar ran the way she decreed.

Nipius and Natalis groaning at her bossiness now made more sense too. And I could see why they had sounded so astonished when I suggested they had gone upstairs with her. Menendra could not have been the only one who saw Rufia as an old woman.

While I was coming to terms with all this, Sparsus and Serenus, two of the workmen, appeared from behind me with one of their baskets of rubble, which they dumped in the gutter. Perhaps a cart had been arranged to pick up the mess later. Perhaps not. I was too preoccupied even to give them a reproving glance.

They asked if I was all right. From habit, I immediately said yes. I had looked after myself for twelve years as an informer. It would be hard to accept that I was becoming part of a family group, with staff who might take an interest, people who might want to protect me. Even so, I followed them back into the bar and through it to the courtyard, where I sat down, feeling more secure in their company.

The men got on with their work, consolidating the ground where the bodies had been dug up and starting a trench for the water feature. They must have been able to tell I was only giving them half my attention. I really wanted quiet time to readjust my thoughts.

This was hardly the first time a suspect had startled me, but I admit I felt like Prometheus having his liver pecked out. Perhaps being a bride was unsettling my guts. Hades, Albia. We hadn't even got to traipsing out at dawn to cut the flowers for the bride-and-groom headdresses yet. Stinging nettles, if I had my way . . . I was in a foul mood.

I gazed around the courtyard, once again mentally peopling it with drinkers at tables, then trying to envisage how the customers had been attacked. Well, I presumed the victims had come as customers.

Now, instead of picturing a young, agreeable barmaid joking with them and perhaps upsetting her jealous landlord by seeming overfriendly, I superimposed a much older woman. She would be competent, yet not flirtatious. That would make customers cringe and Thales scoff. But I doubted that Rufia ever chatted up men as she served them. So, when the attack started that night, I wondered if the victims had grabbed her as a shield or a hostage. Maybe that was how she came to be killed in the scrum.

Musing, I wondered if Rufia had been the kind of barmaid who effortlessly remembered the exact round of drinks that had been ordered, or whether she was a vague one. If she was as stern as people implied, I bet no one argued when she banged down a wrong flagon. Once she came out to the garden with what she deemed people wanted, only a brave customer would send her back indoors for something else . . .

The workmen stopped for lunch. Huge chunks of bread, raw onions, fruit. Fruit . . . It was a while since their breakfast so they believed they were due a break. They tended to take many. I had heard Tiberius chivvying them, though mildly. Mostly, unless he was with me, he joined in. There was another wifely task; I would have to watch his weight.

Larcius, the foreman, came and plumped himself by me. Like the others, he asked if everything was all right. I must have looked properly shaken.

'I had an unpleasant set-to with a woman I needed to interview. I'm used to it. Don't say anything to Faustus. I'll tell him myself in due course, but it's nothing he needs to worry about.'

'Who was that?' asked Larcius, nosily.

'Her name is Menendra. She sells some commodity to the bars around here. Ripe young whores, I expect.'

He nodded. 'Seen her.'

'Oh! Do you know what her game is?'

Regrettably, he shook his head. 'Only that she comes and goes a lot. As you say, in all the bars.' Did that mean the workmen had tried them all?

'Has she been here?'

'Once a week, on the dot. Keeps wanting to know when the Hesperides will reopen. I tell her we don't know and shoo her out again.'

'Does she get aggressive?'

He grinned his toothless grin. People who enquired about the works were nothing new; he was an old hand at seeing them off. Neighbours often tried to extract information from builders, who (I was learning from Tiberius) either stalled completely or, if they were feeling mischievous, invented a mad story to cause consternation.

I sat and pondered.

Sparsus and Serenus, to whom ludicrous stories came easily, were in deep discussion as to what they were likely to encounter if and when they made a connection with an aqueduct for the water feature. They started talking about sewers. The fact that the builders made little distinction between the supply of fresh water and the removal of effluent could explain why so many households have plumbing work go badly wrong. Certainly the underground world was a source of thrills to our men. I heard mention of gigantic rats, discarded pet crocodiles, ghosts coming up from the Underworld, and – their favourite fright – large pulsating blobs.

'Worms!' called Larcius, hoping this detail would insert realism into the conversation. 'Big tangles of worms.' No use. Sparsus and Serenus were not looking for facts, they wanted to scare themselves silly. Discussion of the legendary horrible blobs continued. They decided that if they should find one of these, Larcius could be the brave person who poked it with a stick to see what happened. He patiently agreed he would – if it was ever necessary. He had worked with them for years. He let them ramble.

'Flavia Albia's been telling me she had a run-in with that Menendra.'

'Who's that?'

'The miserable hag who comes around.'

'Oh her!' scoffed Sparsus.

'She's a one,' agreed Serenus. 'She can see we are nowhere near finishing, but she's always on the niggle.'

The workmen had a kind of easy acceptance that the world was full of idiots, whom they had to fend off patiently. They possessed technical expertise while all members of the public were irritating amateurs. People love to stare at holes in the ground. They think they know all about hole-in-the-ground engineering and management. Works in a bar made it worse because gormless passers-by could so easily prop themselves against the marble counters, leaning in to ask time-wasting questions.

'So why is the finish date so vital to Menendra?' I queried, not expecting answers. 'Do you know what she does?'

'Sells them their olives?' guessed Serenus. At least it was a variation on fruit.

'Ever seen her bring a storage amphora to any of the bars?'

Serenus looked offended at my pernicketiness. Proving a theory with evidence was new to him. If he continued to work for Faustus, he would have to sharpen up.

'I can ask her,' volunteered Larcius. 'The next time she invades the site, nagging about when we're handing it back to Liberalis, I shall say, "What do you need to know for?" Then she'll tell me.'

He was an innocent.

I just told him if he could find out, I would be grateful. He seemed proud to take charge of this task.

The day was growing very hot. The men said that once they finished lunch they were to close up and gently trek over to Lesser Laurel Street. I did wonder what exactly

Tiberius was having them do there, but he would show me in his own time.

I left the bar, went to our hired room and had a quiet lie-down.

30

I skipped lunch myself. Failure dulls my appetite.

In the room, I peeled off my tunic, kicked off my sandals, then lay down on the pallet that passed for a bed, perspiring. The midday heat oppressed me. Today there was so much humidity in Rome, it was difficult to breathe. I knew I would fall asleep from sheer exhaustion, but first I would relax. I would empty my mind, to let my opinion of the case restructure itself naturally. Mulling is an informer's best weapon.

It was clear that people knew more about what happened at the Garden of the Hesperides than had originally seemed likely. Both the new landlord and Menendra were concealing information. Liberalis, at least, may have been present when the dead met their fates. Menendra knew far more about Rufia than she wanted me to discover.

Since Rufia was such an enigma, I revisited what I knew about her one-time protégée. Artemisia and Orchivia knew Menendra, though this morning at the Four Limpets their attitude to her had looked truculent. If she knew they had already met me, I wondered if she had been trying to persuade them to put the frighteners on for her, with them refusing? With those two, being uncooperative was their normal reaction to anything.

Menendra was a wily, self-assured piece. The two girls

were stroppy, but younger. Had she tried to control them? Had they rejected her? Was it possible that what Menendra sold to the bars was organised sexual talent – but sometimes the talent rejected her services? The Dardanians, with their youthful experience in the Danube forts, would not easily submit to a brothel mother. Not when they reckoned they could find punters for themselves.

Others might go along with it. A system could exist. Was running the bar girls – and boys – a trade that Rufia once dabbled in? Since her disappearance, had Menendra taken over? It would explain why Menendra was so interested in when the Hesperides would reopen, bringing back a lucrative bar into her market. Lepida at the snacks stall had said providing extras to customers had become very professional. There must be a lot of money to be made.

I did not suppose Menendra's business was invoiced, or that she paid taxes on her profits. So long as she could say she herself was not working as a prostitute, she would never need to be registered with the authorities. That could mean she operated below their line of sight; Rufia must have done so too. Macer of the Third Cohort knew what happened in bars in his area, but he seemed unaware how it was controlled. From what I knew of the vigiles, their idea of 'local knowledge' was being able to find their own station house.

Rufia, who had supported Menendra when she came to Rome from Lycia, may have taught her the business. Had Rufia used her as an apprentice, let Menendra become a trusted assistant – only to be removed because she was in Menendra's way? Was Menendra behind Rufia's disappearance?

Menendra would still have been junior, but it was not

impossible. The younger woman might even have attached herself to Old Thales and used sexual favours to persuade him to dispose of her less attractive rival. Menendra was leathery now, but ten years ago Thales may have welcomed an offer from her to oust the stroppy Rufia.

When Menendra went to search Rufia's room, it may have been in case Rufia had left something incriminating behind. A diary or letters, saying Rufia had been nervous that Menendra was trying to supersede her? Seemed unlikely.

Usually people who conduct a search like that are seeking valuables. Surely if Menendra thought Rufia had left treasure behind she would have looked before – as soon as Rufia had gone missing. Why now? Because of Tiberius and me poking our noses in. But Menendra's search attempts had been very obvious, and ultimately bungled. Just because she ran a network of sex slaves did not mean she was intelligent. Going around with ugly bodyguards did not make her clever. Her burglary only drew attention. A truly shrewd woman would have kept out of sight.

All this was one theory. I had already wasted time on others, and there could be more yet. But I began to feel more content. Finding new questions always peps me up. Satisfied that I had my new line of enquiry, I dozed off.

In the suffocating summer heat, I slept much longer than I meant to. By the time I woke, the temperature had cooled and become more pleasant. Sounds from the street outside had changed from lunchtime lethargy to late-afternoon reopening time. Bathhouse bells rang to proclaim that water was hot and doors open.

After my previous poor experience, I decided against the bathhouse, but stripped off and washed down with a cloth and bucket of water. I dressed, changed my shoes then went out. Briefly forgetting that the workmen had gone over to the Aventine, I made my way automatically to the Hesperides. On the threshold I remembered that nobody was here this afternoon, but by then I had spotted that the passage from the bar to the courtyard had been opened up and someone had aimed something heavy at a corner of the counter, denting and cracking the marble pieces. The old door with which the men secured the passage had been pushed aside.

Everything sounded quiet enough, though investigating on my own would be stupid. That didn't stop me. It was too early to expect our nightwatchman. I made a tentative entry. When I stepped out into the garden area, I found a scene of devastation.

Horrified, I swore out loud. All today's work had been destroyed. It must have been done with brute force, for most of the workmen's tools had gone with them to Lesser Laurel Street. That had not deterred the intruders. The careful trench that was meant to form the water feature had had its neat sides trampled down, then spoil and rubbish kicked in. Formwork to hold a poured concrete wall had been pulled away, so the as yet uncured mixture was setting in an irretrievable mass. I went across to look, in case I could push back the wooden shuttering, but there was nothing I could do. The gate to the back alley stood open; I did close that.

I felt distressed for Tiberius. He had lost time on his job here while his men, too, would be upset to see this carnage. I would have sat down and sobbed but, to complete the mess, all the old bar furniture lay scattered and smashed.

The message was clear. This was not casual mucking about by local menaces. It was crude, deliberate and shocking. Yet ultimately it seemed pointless. Whoever had done this intended to warn us to stop our investigation. All they had really achieved was to advertise that questions were worth asking. And I now believed the perpetrators of the old crime were still in this locality.

Some criminals have no idea that all they have to do is nothing. Lie low, and if there was never evidence in the first place, no more will appear.

Start sending messages, and we will know interested parties are definitely out there.

I was angry and anxious. Then, just when I was making attempts to tidy the broken benches, someone else arrived, coincidentally adding to our problems.

It was a couple who looked very out of place in this area. They turned up in a hired litter, which they kept waiting, ready for a fast exit. They were not hopelessly imagining they could buy drinks; they had come here on a mission. She, she told me, was looking for her brother, Tiberius Manlius. Oh dear. Our wedding guests had begun to arrive.

For her big visit to the city, Fania Faustina was wearing white, with modest jewels. When she was younger, people must have told her she had a sweet nature, on which she still traded, though she was losing it more every day. That was due to her husband, by name Antistius. He was in a brown tunic, accessorised with bumptiousness. Nobody could ever have called him sweet.

'This is a monumental mess!' He surveyed the scene superciliously. 'I didn't expect Faustus to have much idea, but it's a lot worse than I imagined!'

Manlius Faustus was right. His brother-in-law was detestable.

I brushed down my skirts. Dusty and flustered, there was no chance that I looked a convincing bride for an aedile, but I had to introduce myself. I watched my bridegroom's sister wondering whether she ought to kiss me, then she decided it was not yet called for. That caused relief on both sides.

Since there was nowhere to sit, we stood around awkwardly. My new in-laws explained they had arrived that day with others in their party whom they had left with Uncle Tullius, though they were hoping Tiberius was intending to house them all somewhere else, in view of Aunt Valeria's rigid antipathy to his uncle. Thanks to my sisters, I knew about that. I was able to express sympathy, though I pretended I was unsure what the alternative plans were . . .

I did know my mother had been hoping this influx of strangers would not happen so soon. She had tried to convince herself only the austere aunt who loathed Tullius would request somewhere else to stay. Aunts were absorbed into our household whatever they were like, but I could picture my father's expression when exposed to Antistius.

These country folk had wasted no time. As soon as they hit Rome, in between eagerly searching for Tiberius, they had managed to acquire at enormous expense (they told me) many tickets for a cithara recital by a famous musician, the fabulous Stertinius, to which everyone was now invited as their contribution to the wedding celebrations. They thought it was a fine way to meet my family. My mother would agree politely, though again, I feared what Falco would say.

I had heard of the popular lyre player, but no one I knew would have gone to hear him. I had no idea how Tiberius would view being made to sit through a public concert by a musician of the moment, without any warning, at the end of an extremely long and physically exacting day. With the bar's destruction, his day had become much worse than he yet knew.

'We tried to find my brother at his new house, where we had been assured he was, but nobody answered when we called,' said his sister, sounding peevish.

'Well, that's builders for you.' I shrugged.

'We were definitely informed he would be there,' her husband complained, in high irritation. 'I don't know how long we stood in the street banging at the doors.'

Not only Tiberius, but all his workforce ought to be at the house now. I had a sudden inkling that he had looked discreetly through a grille, could not bear to face the brother-in-law, so told the workmen to stay quiet while he hid inside . . . 'Are our doors beautifully painted now?' I asked serenely. 'Tiberius has gone to endless trouble choosing the colour scheme . . .'

'That's hardly the point,' Antistius growled.

Until now I had not felt domestic, but I found myself hoping these visitors had not touched our doors while they were wet and permanently smudged them with fingermarks. It would be sickening to remember Antistius every time I got out my door key.

Nevertheless, I knew what I must do. I smiled as if I meant it, gushing how thrilled we would be to go to the sought-after concert by the extremely famous cithara player. I can be charming. My mother taught me. If you can act it is easy, at least with people who have never met you before.

Luckily we were all distracted then. I had misjudged

Trypho, our nightwatchman, when I assumed he had not been on guard. Now he hove into view, limping down the street, with blood all over him. Ignoring my future relatives with a fine sense of who mattered, he told me that he had found an intruder wrecking the works, so he had beaten up the man then chased him off.

'What did he look like? Will you know him again, Trypho?'

'He'll have a smashed nose. You bet I will.'

'Good. Come and be mopped up. Fania Faustina, do please excuse me while I attend to this emergency in your brother's absence . . .'

It would have been good to think my new in-laws were impressed by the competence and composure of the bride who was joining their family. But they just made it an excuse to scamper into their litter, then order its bearers to hare off.

31

It is generally accepted that the cithara is an extremely demanding instrument. To most people that means it is difficult to play. Even those who adore its softly stroked strings in the hands of a skilled performer may find themselves in a situation where enduring the music is hard. I mean, when dragged to a concert by people you don't know.

At least a promised couple can sit together and discreetly hold hands. If Tiberius began dozing, I could squeeze his paw to keep him more or less awake. If my head lolled upon his shoulder, he could shake me upright.

It started not too badly, as we were preoccupied by disrupting everyone else while we took our seats. Originally we were even joined by Uncle Tullius; his niece and family did not omit inviting their host. However, Tullius took one horrified look at the stairs we were to climb, then beetled off to buy himself another ticket; he ensconced himself among the business community in their excellent seats lower down and we never saw him again all night. Everyone else was slightly relieved.

Fania Faustina thought my sisters were lovely. Her husband, too, was giving them the eye. Julia and Favonia pretended not to have noticed, though there would be a lot of giggling back at home in private. For now, their whispered discussion was all about ghastly young men in the audience.

My mother clearly felt Tiberius' Aunt Valeria was sensible and not half as tricky as she had been painted. Shawled up and reeking of liniment, Valeria knew when to fetter her bile; she could play the sweet old lady, she just didn't believe in doing it. She had managed to win my parents' good opinion so tomorrow she could shuttle to their house. She did foolishly say she could only stomach a little light gruel for breakfast, to which Mother responded gaily that mornings were casual at our house. Auntie Valeria was welcome to visit the kitchen and brew up her own gruel just the way she liked it.

My father loudly said they had no room for anyone else. They did, but the three small boys were whiny and Falco prides himself on intolerance. It had been claimed the little boy in-laws were keen to meet my brother Postumus. That was before someone told their parents he had just been sent home in disgrace after a foray into the Circus of Gaius and Nero while in the custody of his birth mother, a snake dancer. His visit had ended abruptly when he involved himself in the escape of a lion, a fire, an accidental death, financial strife and several divorces. He was a lonesome child, who liked adventures.

Our side made jokey comparisons between the ancient Theatre of Marcellus, the concert venue, and the circus that Postumus had supposedly burned down. Postumus maintained it had only been a little fire and was all the lion's fault. Fania Faustina and Antistius expressed alarm, while we all smiled mysteriously.

My weird little brother was to be in charge of their precious boys in my bridal procession. They would carry flaming torches, a tradition that could so easily go wrong. Postumus assessed his proposed team with cold unfathomable eyes. That was how he looked at everyone, though the Antistii seemed worried that their innocent heirs were being consigned to a maniacal tyrant. They missed the point. My brother, who was twelve but had grand ideas, believed the wedding was for his personal glory. He intended to run the torchlit walk smoothly, to reflect well on him. If the three whiners failed to meet his standards, they were out.

Plectrum-wielding intervened, thank you divine Apollo of the golden hair and lovely sandals.

The cithara music was amazingly beautiful and transporting, or so said the commentator who introduced the repertoire. Many of the audience did assume attitudes of being carried away by rapture. Not our lot. Most were still muttering in undertones, unaware that the concert had started.

I smiled at Tiberius. He smiled at me.

Gazing up at the theatre's fine architecture as announcers told us we would be treated to the poignant Phrygian and mournful Hypodorian modes, I drifted into my own reverie. My relatives settled down, after other members of the audience clucked reproaches.

We were in one of the largest theatres in the world, at least it had been until the Emperor Vespasian created the Flavian Amphitheatre to outshine them all. Coolly clad in travertine, it had ancient grandeur, with elegant arches on each of three classic pillared tiers and its upper level decorated with huge marble theatre masks. The building was fitted with the usual ramps and tunnels that enabled spectators to leave the theatre rapidly, though of course one was expected to remain in one's seat during the performance or be deemed a barbarian. The stone seats were surprisingly comfortable, especially if you had the forethought to bring a cushion.

Vespasian had restored the stage, which had been damaged in the civil war that brought him to power. The stage fronted the river; our seats were a long way from it. We were right at the top, which was why we could be seated men and women together, because the Antistii had inadvertently bought tickets for the women's and slaves' tier. For an intimate musical evening to hear a delicate instrument this was not good. We could never see the player's skilful hands, and despite generally excellent acoustics, we could not hear even the manly and stirring Dorian mode that is supposed to inspire soldiers going into battle.

I don't think so. How can an army be fired up by the gentle twiddles of a one-man harp? Have no musicologists ever seen, let alone heard, the racket of a legion marching?

The cithara maestro's hands slithered on his seven strings – or more than seven when he deftly changed instruments to demonstrate what a sterling virtuoso he was. I thought I liked music, but I had never been trained to understand it. Although my father inherited a pan pipes player from Grandpa, we rarely had other instruments or singing in our house. We dealt in ideas, expressed with words. That could be colourful enough. Grandpa's pan pipes player ran away, feeling unappreciated.

Struggling to hear the faint and far-off beauteous improvisations gave me plenty of time to reflect. Ignoring my relatives, both old and new, I realised I was seeing another aspect of Rome from the street life around the Ten Traders. Here we had monumental imperial architecture, refined entertainment, a boisterous family group on the eve of a wedding. We were well-fed, well-off people enjoying a leisure experience, or at least enjoying it in theory. Our young were full of hope and privilege. Our old were cared for and brought among us, even those who made it plain they would rather be somewhere else, sipping gruel.

Stertinius received loud applause, which woke up anyone who had dozed off. At the interval Aunt Valeria admitted she was tone-deaf; also, the three little boys were bored, so they all went home. Tiberius was obliged to go down and help find them transport. Luckily litter-bearers do form a queue outside at the midway point of concerts because they know there will always be people who have had enough. Even the fabulous Stertinius could not please everyone.

Those of our party who lacked an excuse to leave were able to spread ourselves on the narrow upper-tier seats. Antistius tried to get to sit with my sisters, but Father deftly outmanoeuvred him, claiming this was a rare opportunity for a fond old papa to enjoy the company of his girls. Julia and Favonia rolled their eyes, but knew exactly what their watchful parent was doing.

My mother closed her eyes and seemed to pay close attention to the gorgeous cithara. She had wrapped an affectionate arm around Postumus, which stopped him getting up and wandering off, as he liked to do. I watched how Helena Justina handled this whole stressful situation. With a vague smile, Mother let chaos carry on, provided there was no bloodshed or hysteria – or not too much. She was a good wife and mother but would not be overwhelmed by others' clamorous demands; she subtly detached herself mentally. Helena led her chosen life. I made a note to do the same.

My father saw me observing her so thoughtfully. As was

our habit, I winked at him before he could get in first and wink at me. Tiberius noticed that.

The fabulous Stertinius treated us to a lengthy set in sensual Hypolydian. Good little bride that I was, for the benefit of my in-laws, I managed to appear entranced.

28 August

Five days before the Kalends of September
(a.d. V Kal. Sept.)

Three days before the wedding of
Tiberius Manlius Faustus and Flavia Albia

32

Tiberius and I scuttled off from the concert, claiming we had to rush back to the Garden of the Hesperides. I had gone to the Aventine before the concert to tell him of the damage and to pick up a formal outfit from my apartment. I would have seen for myself the famous newly painted front doors, but a protective cover hid the porch. I never saw inside the house either; I could not concentrate on frescos. Later, I warned myself that many a new wife has a bad shock on discovering her man's taste in art.

At the end of the evening, before our relatives could suggest following the concert with a getting-to-know-you nightcap, we floated our 'Hesperides emergency' excuse then, unknown to anyone else, we fled up the Aventine and stayed at Fountain Court that night.

'I know my brother-in-law quite well enough already!' grouched Tiberius. He realised I too had had enough of Antistius. Our agreeing over such idiots reminded me of my parents. They would put on a polite face in public, then later see who could devise the most killing insults. I would have started to teach Tiberius to play that game, but so far I was pretending to be a sweet wife, the peacemaker in our home.

Tiberius was perhaps not fooled.

★   ★   ★

Next day we woke at first light. We had breakfast at the Stargazer, our usual haunt, then made our way over to the Argiletum while decent shopkeepers were still emptying out water buckets to wash the pavement and sweeping off their frontages. Scents of new bread and fresh flowers filled the air.

Yesterday, after I told him about the damage, Tiberius had been thoroughly depressed, though as was his way he held back from exploding until he had seen it. He had sent a message from the aediles' office to ask the Third Cohort to exercise that slippery commodity 'extra vigilance'. This was to apply both at the bar and also at Mucky Mule Mews where burglars had been chased off. The security measures Tiberius requested meant that, certainly at the Hesperides, a few members of the vigiles sat outside all night. In their eyes, they were making their presence felt to keep an aedile happy. If anyone had been so foolish as to try a new invasion of the premises, they would probably just have said hello.

When we arrived in the morning they had gone. However, there was a draughtboard drawn on the pavement, lots of crumbs and an empty amphora to prove we had had protection last night. An extremely sordid pigeon was gobbling the crumbs. We shooed him away despondently.

Tiberius found Trypho in the courtyard with Serenus, hammering the benches back together. Having proper seats to sit on and moan was their priority. Reinstating the works could wait until the others arrived. In fact, I knew it would wait until they had arrived, taken a gloomy look around, discussed what had happened in endless, ponderous detail and then gone out to buy breakfast to take their minds off the calamity.

I watched how Tiberius tackled this. The spoliation clearly made him furious but he wasted no time complaining. Looking pale (which could be the after-effect of an evening spent with relatives), he surveyed the scene. He jumped on spoil heaps, clambered into what remained of the trench, prodded, kicked the ruined concrete, tossed timber aside. Then he fetched out a note tablet and quietly began making a list of what could be salvaged, what had to be rebuilt and the order in which his men should tackle everything. He was set-faced, yet a practical man who simply began repairs. Larcius arrived. Tiberius handed him the list. The foreman read it, then nodded his approval.

Trypho's bruises were colouring up well. We said he looked like a painted Greek temple. Tiberius quizzed him about the man he had taken on. According to Trypho it was a giant with leather wrist guards, an urban Hercules. 'That's appropriate,' I said, indicating the bar's signboard. Trypho stared blankly.

At that point, I had no doubt that the perpetrators of the Hesperides damage were Menendra's surly bodyguards. It seemed logical. I would have liked to link them to the attempted break-in at Mucky Mule Mews but nobody had seen those burglars close up. Still, both attacks were so obvious it was stupid, so perhaps that in itself showed a connection.

Logic can let you down. As we set about tidying up the site, with me helping, Macer turned up with a group of his men, dragging along Menendra's heavies for Trypho to identify. To my surprise, he said neither of them looked like the man he had found damaging the works. Besides, neither had the nose damage he had inflicted.

Macer decided that since the pair had been arrested, he

would keep them in custody anyway. 'My torturer has nothing else to do today, so he can put in a spot of practice with his weights and chains, maybe do some red-hot-poker work. There must be something these lags will confess to. We'll see.'

Now I looked closely, the prisoners were both burly and cauliflower-eared. That could be because they had a history of fights, or else they had brawling wives who owned particularly weighty frying pans.

As they slumped in the arms of their captors, it looked as if they had already been softened up with a few vigiles rib-thumps. I marched up and asked what they did for Menendra. I had a fair idea, but would have liked to know what job description they gave publicly. One made a feeble attempt of muttering 'Who?' When I pointed out I had seen them all together yesterday, the other just spat on the ground. He made sure to avoid me. Even so, one of the vigiles gave him a great shake. 'Naughty!'

'It's all right,' I returned in my mildest tone. 'Some people cannot help being barbarians. I expect these came to Rome to get civilised. The etiquette lessons are simply not working.'

'Where do you think they hail from?' Tiberius asked Macer.

'Some cesspit in the east. I could send them back to swim in their home dung, but to save the expense I'd rather wheel them out for the lions.'

In the arena, criminals who felt too nervous of the big cats were indeed placed on little wheeled trolleys and pushed forwards. An uncle of mine had that happen. It made a good story at Saturnalia, provided his children weren't listening.

'My quota for the amphitheatre is a bit low this month,'

Macer continued. 'I could use a higher tally to impress my tribune. I get a free ticket if I send enough lowlifes to the beasts.'

Perhaps he was joking to worry the prisoners but he sounded as if he meant it. I still thought these men had been involved in the attempted break-in, yet they were clearly exonerated from smashing up the bar. I told Macer to have the old couple and their son from Mucky Mule Mews take a look at them.

'You don't want to waste helpful witnesses, Macer.' Of course neither they nor their son had really seen the burglars but we were all bluffing. To the enforcers, I said, 'If you tell me what you went to look for in that burglary, I will intercede for your release.' No use. 'I see you're too frightened of Menendra and not scared enough of me!'

'They will learn!' scoffed Tiberius cheerily.

He went back to attend to his site, so I followed. Not knowing what else I could do next on my enquiry, I decided at least my presence would boost his morale. To my surprise he suddenly took me in his arms. 'Don't worry,' he urged, as if he thought I was afraid life with him might always involve pillage and property-wrecking.

I helped where I could. I can carry a bucket. While we were sorting out the mess, his brother-in-law appeared on-site again. Until Antistius came, we had been making good progress. Larcius had hired in a couple of extra bodies, wide-chested jolly labourers who set to with picks as if demolishing ruined concrete was their idea of a picnic on the beach. Our usual men cleared the rest of the site. Tiberius had been off with Sparsus for more materials; when I joked that 'going to buy materials' was a good old builders' excuse, he cheered up enough to smile and aim a spank at me. (He missed. I saw it coming.) Then to spoil our day, we had our visitation.

Antistius hinted again that what happened here was caused by Tiberius somehow failing to exercise control. Viewing Tiberius as an amateur, the swine was sneering today as much as yesterday.

We were lumbered with him. He had escorted Aunt Valeria to my parents' house this morning, which had let him shed his wife and children. Fania had taken the boys to the imperial menagerie. I disapproved. In our family my mother would choose expeditions, but normally my father tagged along. We would all be disappointed if he could not come with us; only significant business ever stopped him.

Antistius had no excuse. Here he was, bringing his young-sters to the city for the first time, yet he preferred to slither off to annoy other people. He started to give us pompous theories about what the workmen should or should not be doing; they shot looks at Tiberius, who washed his hands in a bucket of water then hauled Antistius out of the bar to let them get on.

I suggested we take morning refreshments at one of the open bars. Antistius selected the Brown Toad. We advised against it. He ignored us. This unpleasant place was the last Tiberius and I would have chosen, but Antistius over-ruled us, despite our experience as locals. Exchanging a glance, we gave in and let him choose.

'You two never have much to say for yourselves!' he commented. That became even truer when he started to interrogate Tiberius about his financial tussles with Uncle Tullius.

I kept well out of that. I knew how much the current strain over money upset Tiberius. It had almost led to complete estrangement, after twenty years of harmonious living. Having met Tullius Icilius, I guessed what he must think of Antistius. He would loathe an idiot stranger taking interest in his close-guarded financial affairs. The alacrity with which he had left us at the concert last night was an indication. He went his own way and didn't care whom he offended.

The Brown Toad had dusty counters and a smell. Two tables were in the street, which was strictly illegal. We took one. At the other sat a group of women whose occupation anyone could guess. Most had barely three stitches holding together their tunics' side-seams. I could see snake bracelets. None had beakers in front of them. They were not girl-friends out for a gossip; they were waiting for custom.

While the men talked family business, I concentrated on ordering what passed for snacks from a tired waitress who had not wanted to start serving this early. In a short tunic and bare feet, she had a button nose and a fine line in lethargy. I could not suppose she owned the bar, though if there was a landlord he never showed his face.

'I would like to know,' boomed Antistius, 'whether Tullius has any money in his hands that rightly belongs to my wife?'

Tiberius had already told me that he had been very fond of his sister when they were growing up. He missed her after they were taken in by different relatives. He was sorry she married a man he could not stand, preventing Tiberius from visiting her. 'Nothing of Fania's is managed by Uncle Tullius.'

'You certain?'

'Fania is well provided for, as you must know.'

'Main attraction when I married her!' bragged Antistius.

Not the best way to impress her brother. Tiberius would rather she was valued as a good woman and loyal home-maker. She certainly was a dedicated mother; few of us could have loved those unhappy sons.

It was obvious Tiberius distrusted Antistius. The couple must have had the usual dowry. If Fania had inherited any other family property, Tiberius could have ensured her husband never heard about it. When their grandfather and parents died, legacies might have slyly remained not even with Tullius as Antistius suspected, but quietly looked after for Fania Faustina by her fond elder brother. If so, I wondered if she knew? Would it suit her that something of her own was squirrelled away?

Up to a point I liked what I had seen of her, even though her husband infected her with his self-importance. If ever they reached a crisis, she would feel she had to stick with her marriage because of the three boys. I would never have done it; I would send Antistius a notice of divorce, encouraging him to exercise his paternal right to custody of the tiresome trio. Fania was trying to give her boys her ameliorating influence. It was pointless. They would grow up like Antistius.

The waitress brought what I had ordered, dumping a tray on our table. I placed beakers in front of everyone, then began pouring the drink I had asked for – posca, honeyed wine vinegar infused with herbs. Not enough herbs, I could immediately tell.

'Good gods, this is peasant fare! Army rations. I'd rather have wine!' Antistius declared. 'We men should have ordered. Your girl has no idea, Faustus.'

'You can order what you want,' Tiberius replied calmly. 'I have to work this afternoon. Albia knows that.'

Antistius jumped up and went to the counter, intent on finding something that suited him better; he clearly had not drunk much wine in Roman bars. With luck, he might actually pay for his own hooch. While he was away from us, I shuffled along the bench, nearer to Tiberius. He brushed my cheek briefly with a forefinger. I patted his thigh.

I noticed that Antistius took advantage of speaking alone with the waitress. He pretended he was asking for directions to the facilities; he probably believed he was discreet, but I was sure he asked how much it would cost to go upstairs with her. Her reply was loud enough for us to hear. 'Sorry, I don't have time.'

I was intrigued that she did have a choice. It is all too easy to assume bar girls are forced to accommodate their customers whether they like it or not.

As Antistius rejoined us, I decided he really believed himself a perfect husband. He would never have done this in their home district, where Fania might hear about it. But in Rome it meant nothing. This was one of the city thrills a man could sample, just as his children were visiting the emperor's exotic animals and Fania had had her cithara concert.

Tiberius looked furious and disgusted. I made a moue to say there was no point him saying anything.

The waitress went and spoke to the women at the other table. When she brought Antistius his wine flagon, she leaned over and told him, 'I can fix you up with one of the Macedonian girls, if you want, sir.'

Antistius barely bothered to look sheepish. But as Tiberius scowled on his sister's behalf, he did decline.

He was offhand. The waitress looked annoyed. She had

chosen to involve the whores, for nothing. She probably claimed a finder's fee if she introduced customers. But she had lost that, then we heard them raucously abuse her when she went and reported that the client had chickened out.

33

Tiberius drained his posca cup and stood up so fast he nearly pushed the bench over backwards with me still on it. I rose too, seeming to have more composure. Although this time I chose to play the gracious bride, it was temporary. If the brother-in-law ever came to Rome again, he was for it.

Tiberius threw coins on the table, clearly only enough for what he and I had had. 'Since you found your own way here, I'll assume you can get back.' He strode off.

I gave the brother-in-law a nod, not bothering to make it look sincere. 'We shall see you at the wedding.' I meant he had no chance of other socialising. Then I too walked over to the Hesperides.

Out of curiosity, I glanced back to see whether Antistius had changed his mind about the Macedonians. They were still there. He had gone. For Fania Faustina's sake, I was glad. I would not have wanted her to find she had a mysterious weeping disease. I would not want to see her bemusement when a doctor told her what it was.

She wrote to her brother regularly, with mild complaints about her life. I preferred not to have my new husband rampaging around our house after he had heard what ailment his horrified sister had acquired, and knew how she had caught it.

At the same time, I had been dreading what Tiberius would make of my more bothersome relations when he met them, so I felt comforted to know his were as bad.

Of course many a daft wife has thought 'that makes us even then' – only to learn it does nothing of the kind. Still, he was a fair man. I often told people so.

Back at the bar, I sat out of the way of the workmen. After a while, I went out to see if any Macedonians were still at the Brown Toad, then I went over to them.

I thought one was now missing. I could guess why. Now I looked closely, what struck me about the rest was how young they all were, a couple barely past childhood. The career span of a working girl is short. They tend to start early and perish prematurely. At least I knew these floozies could not have been here when the Hesperides killings happened.

They were tall but scrawny and looked half starved. Hailing from the homeland of Alexander the Great had not improved their luck in life. Most were blondish with good bone structure, though no one would call them beauties because their manners were so uncouth. They knew no better.

They stared at me as if I was something novel. I said I wanted to apologise for our brother-in-law messing them about. He was up from the country and a numbskull anyway. They pulled faces, agreeing the last part. Uninvited, I sat down with them, which they allowed. I expect they were bored. Any distraction was fine, until the next mark wandered along and responded to their catcalls.

I made it straightforward. I said I would buy them all an early lunch, if they would talk to me. I saw raised eyebrows (they pared their brows to tiny charcoal lines) but none disagreed when I called over the waitress. I asked for wine and water, telling her to bring as much good food as the Brown Toad could come up with. I had few hopes, but it turned out there was a large pot of meaty stew bubbling on a brazier inside, which someone's grandma came in and made every day for the staff. The waitress openly expressed her unease about Faustus finding out, with him being a magistrate. Whispers had circulated all the bars that while he was constantly around they should be careful.

I said if he didn't know, he couldn't fine anybody. Besides, his own fiancée was paying today, and I gave her the 'fair man' story. We had a little extra conversation, because the grandma normally never gave the whores anything; they were visitors, like street pigeons. I put money on the table. In her own time the dreamy waitress served up steaming food bowls and a basket of bread. The Macedonians fell upon this fare as if they hadn't eaten properly since they sailed out of Thessalonica.

I sighed gently to myself. Thinking like my mother, I reckoned that if only they all sat down to a decent meal together every day, while they were socialising they might decide to cooperate and better their lives.

I had wine as well, to show I was not snooty. After a sip I left most of it. There are limits.

While the others ate, I talked to them and discussed their way of life. Their initial wariness faded. I guessed I was the first person who expressed any human interest in them since they came to Rome. This was so because, at the end, one of them complimented me on not being stand-offish.

By the time we finished, I knew their existence was terrible. What I learned was intriguing.

Unlike the Dardanians, their trip to Rome had been far from self-motivated. They were all slaves. Most had been sold to dealers by their own relatives, or people to whom relatives owed money. Dragged off to Delos, the filthy Greek island where thousands of slaves came onto the market every day even nowadays, they had been purchased by a Roman dealer who transported them here, then sold them on to a pimp to be run as prostitutes. It had always been their end destination. No one had ever intended them to do needlework or hairdressing. No one bothered to lure them with that pretence.

They lived in, and operated out of, a local district just south of the Ten Traders. It lay close by, at the start of the Viminal Hill. From what I could tell, theirs was a smaller version of the big brothel area in the Second Region, the Caelian, around the Amphitheatre and Nero's Great Market. That was one of the most densely occupied parts of Rome; it was crammed with bars, stalls, barbers, cheap souvenir shops and barracks for soldiers on temporary assignment here. The Second Region was thus an ideal spot for brothel owners to colonise, so it was grim. I had worked on the Caelian recently, but tried to stay on the opposite side of the hill.

These girls had a base up here, from which they were sent out to cruise nearby streets. Their sordid home district was called the White Chickens.

What the Macedonians also told me was that, as I had already realised, there were two levels of tavern prostitution. Individual waitresses who had genuine jobs serving drinks could be hired for a casual bunk-up. It worked happily or unhappily for them, depending on their work premises. But there were also professional whores.

The professionals lived in brothels of various sizes, some of them rooms in otherwise normal properties. Perfectly respectable people would hire out a space on an hourly basis and think nothing of it. Prostitutes had pimps or they had mothers – who were not maternal according to high Roman ideals and, in fact, were rarely related to them at all. The girls' work was organised by these people, who treated them ruthlessly. They either suffered long, soulless hours in cubicles, or they could be sent out to cruise the streets.

They were slaves. They were constantly watched, frequently beaten, brutalised by their pimps, poorly clad, poorly fed, given no relief from misery. Most of the money they earned was immediately taken away from them by their pimps or brothel mothers. They would work until their dingy charms no longer attracted clients, or until they died. If they managed to stay alive but were no use, they would be cast out like so many enfeebled slaves and would die anyway, on the street or under a bridge or beaten up by louts. Even the hospital of Aesculapius on Tiber Island, which generally gave a refuge to old, dying slaves, tended to reject prostitutes.

'You will never earn enough to buy your freedom and give up this life?'

They stared at me as if I was mad for even suggesting it.

34

Now they were talking freely, at my urging they revealed more about how brothels like those in the White Chickens operated. Some were directly owned by a pimp or procuress, who installed girls to work there, and occasionally boys too. Others were owned by property agents who hired out rooms to independent workers as direct subtenants. As we discussed more details, there was giggling about the kinds of men who paid for sex, which led to variants, for instance fine Roman ladies visiting incognito for a thrash with a gigolo. Further laughter followed, as the Macedonians harped on about such women coming back for more.

We all chortled at the thought of Roman fathers not knowing that their children had been sired in the stews, then the talk swung to the risk that women thrill-seekers might afterwards find themselves in trouble; a pregnancy meant their adventures would become public knowledge. They would have to get rid of it. At least the well-to-do could afford a quick solution, we agreed.

One of the girls, Chia, went rather quiet at this point.

I made a face at a girl with a mole sitting near me, who replied behind her hand that I was right; Chia could be expecting. She looked to be the youngest. I could see she was extremely anxious. She frowned a lot, moved jerkily, picked at her cuticles.

It would be her first time. That was bad enough for most women. But the worst problem for Chia was that soon it would prevent her from working. The pimp would beat her and give her no pocket money, so she was liable to starve. Even if she came through and managed to produce a child, there was nowhere to keep it, no one to look after it. The poor mite would be a slave anyway, probably taken away by the pimp as soon as it was saleable. Masters of that type don't hesitate to separate mothers and babies – and they do not sell slave babies to be nicely taught to read and write as docket clerks or secretaries. Girl or boy, it faced abuse.

None of us spoke to Chia about her predicament. That did not make us unsympathetic. I picked up a silent understanding that first she had to be sure she was pregnant, then she must face up to it and decide what she wanted to do. After that, if she wanted help, she could ask.

Finally, I tackled my reason for approaching them. 'You know that some bodies have been found at the Garden of the Hesperides. One is a woman.'

They all nodded. 'Rufia.'

Rufia's story had reached even women who were too young to have known her.

'It must have been before your time, but have you heard anything about her? Why I am asking is because everyone calls Rufia a barmaid, but I am starting to wonder. I certainly have the impression most people were in awe of her, and she kept the Hesperides running her own way. I know there are women who organise and control other working girls. They tend to be powerful characters. I am trying to find out if she ran things.'

The Macedonians listened. They considered. They said they had never heard of Rufia being *that* kind of barmaid, although of course it was possible.

Then I asked, 'There is another woman now, once connected with her. Do any of you know Menendra?'

Brighter than I expected, the one with the oddly placed mole on her cheek asked, 'Do you think she does that?'

'Organises girls?'

'So you think she runs a racket.'

'Am I wrong then?'

Several of them shrugged. If Menendra did control a vice ring, it did not include these young women. They had a pimp. They admitted as much, pointing him out. He was a lean dandy with a slick hairdo, sitting outside the Romulus with one knee elegantly crossed over the other, holding a small cup between three fingers, enjoying a tisane. Watching whatever they did.

I loathed him on sight, but he was theirs. In a grim way they accepted him. I dare say they knew worse men.

I had a cold feeling that later that vermin over there would batter every one of them because they had been talking to me. They were risking it. Maybe he would have battered them all anyway. I wanted to hope our conversation was an act of defiance on their part, but I did not wish it to cause them harm.

'So how do you girls know Menendra?'

A glance passed among them, which I could not interpret. 'She lives in the White Chickens.'

'In a brothel?'

They sniggered. In their world any house might be used for sexual commerce, any room was a potential location for trade. If it had a bed, that clinched it.

Menendra rented a place of her own over a cookshop. They had never seen her take men there – or women, giggled the one with the uncombed goat-girl curls. But that meant little. There were plenty of nooks for assignations. What they seemed sure of was that Menendra did not have other prostitutes using her own premises.

I believed that. Any woman of business needs her private place for after work. So Menendra kept a room that was her personal retreat, just as I had my apartment.

I asked where exactly hers was. They told me an address. I asked where they themselves lived. They were cagier. I did not press them.

With a decent meal inside them, the girls were reluctant to resume working. As we sat there at the Brown Toad, out of habit one or two made desultory attempts to lure men off the street, but they were half-hearted. Their pimp had left the Romulus. Speculating among themselves, they reckoned he had gone off to a dice game. They were obliged to work that evening, but decided to take time off this afternoon, behind his back.

We drew our conversation to a close. I thanked them, and that was when I told them I came from Britain. We laughed; it made them feel they were the high and mighty ones. Well, I was used to that.

On the verge of parting, the one with the wild curls gave me a narrow look. 'What we've been talking about didn't seem to surprise you.'

Another backed her up. 'Is it from personal experience?'

I gave them a wan smile. 'Close.' I took a deep breath. 'I escaped. But I do know what it feels like to be fourteen, hungry and worthless in your own eyes, then some filthy brute picks you up, calls himself your friend, promises kindness – but curses and kicks are all you get as he grooms you. You soon become too scared to refuse to work for him.'

'And all the time he's telling you, this is what you deserve,' said the one with the mole.

I nodded.

'So what happened to you, Albia?' asked the curly one, in a hard voice.

'Luck. Some rich people saw me and thought I would make a cheap nurse for their babies.' Better to put it that way. 'I just want to tell you – if I could get out, you can too.'

The Macedonian sex slaves knew it wasn't true for them. That was the worst aspect of the life that had been imposed on them. They had absolutely no hope.

As I left I ventured to ask whether they were afraid of ending up like Rufia. I was surprised that they showed no fear of sharing her fate. Any one of them was vulnerable to being beaten up, all of them risked death on a daily basis. Presumably they had to blank that.

I left them and went back to the Hesperides. The workmen were still hard at it, with Tiberius in charge. He broke off when he saw me returning.

I sat down and told him some of what I had learned. I said that increasingly I thought this bar might once have been the centre of a prostitution racket, with Rufia strongly implicated.

'All bars are brothels, officially,' he answered.

'Well this one has only three rooms upstairs. I am wondering if Rufia carved out a wider empire.' That would fit with what witnesses had told me, how everyone in the neighbourhood knew her.

'So who would the five dead men have been? Clients? Someone who decided not to pay?'

'I don't know.'

If a whore's customer refused to hand over her fee, he had to expect a violent reaction – though killing five would seem extreme, and the neat, organised burial at the Hesperides surely argued for advance planning. As a general rule in business, if somebody fails to honour a bill, you don't kill them – you want them alive to pay up. Mind you, there had probably been plenty of Roman executors who were asked to settle debts for sexual favours procured by the deceased. I expect favourite prostitutes were sometimes even passed on as bequests.

'If Thales was a brothel-keeper, wouldn't it be recorded somewhere?' I asked Tiberius.

'Brothel-keeping is not illegal. Prostitution neither. If Old Thales profited from vice, so long as he declared his income at the census, and duly paid his taxes, that was his only responsibility. The state's interest is not moral, merely fiscal.'

I laughed gently. 'The government never minds the source, so long as cash clinks into the Treasury! But I thought prostitutes counted as outlawed non-citizens, along with actors, gladiators and the like?'

'Whores only. Their masters not. Perfectly "respectable" people fund their lives by the sex trade. You would be surprised how many society people have fortunes that come from brothels.' I could see Tiberius thought as I did, that this was hypocrisy. He added, 'The Emperor Caligula levied a direct tax too; each prostitute has to pay a one-off to the

Treasury, whatever she charges per man. It was an unheard-of measure when he introduced it – but quickly became accepted, given how lucrative it is.'

I kept niggling. 'I know you have records. Aediles keep them. So who does have to be registered?'

'Any woman acting as a prostitute.'

Again, Tiberius saw my disapproval: I thought it typical that only the women were monitored so closely. That was in addition to their being tied to pimps and brothel-keepers. Everyone had power but them. Meanwhile, those who organised the game escaped censure. 'I want to understand the rules. Tell me?'

Tiberius shifted uncomfortably. 'This has not been my favourite aspect of the job . . .'

'All right, I'm not accusing you.'

'Every prostitute has to register with the aediles. She must present herself, give her correct name, her age, her place of birth, and the pseudonym under which she intends to practise. If a girl turns up who looks young and respectable, we try to persuade her to change her mind.'

I shot him a look. He managed not to squirm. 'Look, we do our best! Well, I have tried always to . . . If she is adamant,' he continued, still looking abashed, 'we are bound to issue her a licence. She tells us what price she intends to charge. We enter her name in the roll.'

'Can she be removed if she gives up the trade?'

'No. Never. It's permanent.'

'So no prostitute, even if she is forced into it at a very young age, by other people, can ever repent, reinstate her good name or be forgiven by society?'

Tiberius agreed dourly.

★   ★   ★

I knew better than to blame him for this. He acted as an instrument of government policy. If he refused the task, someone else would do it. I would rather he was checking the legality of market weights, but if an aedile had to be involved, better it was Manlius Faustus. He was straight. He had a charitable attitude.

I bet there had always been different magistrates, men who exacted a trick when they registered a woman. Their free sample. 'Checking that her price is value for money.' These men had a duty to protect the public from rip-offs, after all. They would claim they must test out the goods. Compared to the majority, mine was oddly innocent.

I gave him a hug, to show I did not regard him as tainted. Then, without telling him my plans, I left him at the Hesperides while I went by myself to have a look around the district the Macedonians had mentioned, where both they and Menendra lived. From what they said, I too would soon feel soiled, merely from going there.

35

Some people know *Ad Gallinas Albas* as the whimsical name of the elegant imperial Villa of Livia at Prima Porta. Supposedly an eagle soaring overhead once dropped a white hen in the empress's lap, bearing a sprout of olive in its beak. Waste not, want not, so the great lady kept both, planting an olive grove and keeping a poultry farm, with the bonus that on occasions they presaged the deaths of emperors. So useful. If I ever have my own olive tree, I want it to wilt when the daggers are about to be plunged into Domitian.

The poultry area by the Ten Traders may boast the same name, but it is as different as anything could be from the fine rural retreat on the Via Flaminia that was once the possession of Livia Augusta. Forget the desirable residential areas that did exist on the Viminal further on. Was *Gallinae Albae* ever a farm? If there had once been hens, they must have been hoarse, pox-ridden laying-fowl that produced soft-shelled eggs. Their eyes would weep, their lungs would clog with the foul seepage of diseases of the dirt. The human birds who lived in this sour valley bottom now, scrawny creatures pecking for clients, were little different.

Not all the prostitutes were brought in from abroad. Not all were slaves. A few were freeborn women, lured here by want, vulnerable souls in distress who were so desperate they had to turn to vice. They disappeared from their former lives, in total thrall to their procurers.

More often than you may want to believe, the people who controlled their daily acts were women. Many of those women had once been working girls too. They were callous; they felt no pity for the new generation. I suppose they were simply glad they themselves had grappled their way into a slightly better position. By then, abuse was all they knew. When perversion was not being imposed on them, they imposed it on someone else.

I was coming to see this as Rufia's way of life, and Menendra's too. This pair, I decided, were power players in the sordid game.

I wished I had not gone to the White Chickens alone. It gave me a terrible sense of dread. The reason I knew all about what went on here was that thankfully brief period when I myself had been kidnapped by a brothel owner. It had only lasted a day, though it was the worst of my life. At the time I was a forlorn child, who believed his lie that he would take me to a safe place. But when he violently turned on me it was no surprise. Living on the streets had taught me what goes on.

I would have given in and done whatever that man made me do, because I had no other recourse. No friends, no family, no home. At that time, to be wanted for his filthy purposes was better than not to be wanted at all. I could have pretended to myself that his lies were real. I could have spent the rest of my existence on earth in that dire condition.

But Fortune offered one kind nod. Didius Falco and Helena Justina gave me a better life. At the end of this month they would see me married to a good man, and I knew they would both shed tears for my happiness, knowing their own part in it. They had come across a child in misery and instinctively plucked her from it. They never dwelt on their benevolence. But on my wedding day, they would be prouder than most parents.

I felt troubled here, being reminded what they had saved me from. A deep-seated fear always lurked that my rescue was an illusion; security could be snatched away. Coming to this area, on top of my admissions to the Macedonians, unnerved me. As for them, I wished now that I had not taken them into my confidence. I hoped they never told anyone what I had said.

As soon as I started looking, I knew nobody in the White Chickens brothels stood a chance of escaping to respectability. Ordinary people could walk down the Vicus Longus or the Vicus Patricius, the long highways that ran on either side of the Viminal Hill, and never notice what was here. Once you stopped, once you began to see it, the area was dire.

There were entire tenements given over to brothels, each with the procuress either lolling outside on a wooden stool or just visible as she lurked indoors. Working women hung around on the streets, openly eyeing up potential customers, calling out invitations. Men lingered, hardly distinguishable, whether they were prospective clients or the sorry pimps and enforcers who were attached to the brothels.

Suddenly I saw Chia. She was alone now and at once I hailed her. She greeted me with a wan smile on her child-like face. I went up to her and said in a low voice, 'I wouldn't wish this on anyone, but in case you absolutely want an abortionist, the one in the Ten Traders is called Nona.' I could hardly forgive myself for telling her, but I pitied her position. 'Ask at the bakery stall opposite the public facilities, Chia; the girls serving bread will direct you. They call her the wise woman.'

'Have you——?'

'No. Not me. I had to speak to her about my investigation.'

Chia was perfectly open: 'Thank you. I have to find someone. There is a person the brothel uses, but I don't like her.'

She asked what I was doing in the White Chickens. I said I was looking for my sister. I had to give a reason; a search for a runaway made sense. Chia was too immature to work out that I had another motive. She seemed to be heading to her room. As sweetly as my real sisters taking a girlfriend home for almond cakes, she offered to show me where she lived.

It was a full-scale brothel, reeking so much of dirt and lamp soot that after I left its smell would be ingrained in my hair, clothes and the very pores of my skin. Extending up for several storeys, all completely occupied by working girls, the building was divided into many similar small, windowless rooms, so oil lamps were everywhere, some smoking langorously even by day.

The place was better run than I expected. The accounts manager, on a high stool with a record tablet, could have been chief clerk in any respectable business. They had a hairdresser (who looked as though she probably served her turn on a pallet when required) and a boy with a water basin so clients could wash afterwards. Maybe the girls could use that basin of his, though somehow I thought not. His towel looked as if it was used by everyone for days on end without being laundered. Even the boy himself had a used look. Men could certainly bugger him, probably without paying extra.

Chia led me upstairs to her cubicle. On the way we passed other rooms, some with closed doors as they were in use, some open so visitors could see the wares on offer. Half-naked women were visible inside, most looking far from erotic, more like schoolgirls lolling in their bedrooms. I almost expected to see dolls and miniature farms on show, but I was a realist; these young people had probably never owned playthings as children. All they knew now were sex toys.

House-proud whores had draped curtains across their doorways, some looped up with string tie-backs while they were waiting for a customer. Each had a painted sign above the door showing a couple (well it was usually a couple) engaged in whatever sexual position that woman performed. The variety made me blink. Each room had a sign dangling from a hook, giving the occupant's name and price, then 'engaged' when she turned the tablet over. It was lunchtime now, so quite a few rooms had closed doors. I heard few cries of pleasure from within. Trade here must be a mechanical, laconic business.

Chia's little cubicle was dark, mean and as smelly as the rest. I suppose after a time the women got used to that notorious brothel odour. Inside, she had a basic single bed, covered with a threadbare blanket and graced with a lifeless pillow in a striped case. When she was in, the room was lit by one pottery oil lamp. Chia took it in order to light it from another in the dark corridor.

I could then see that unlike my room or my sisters', this was not littered with clothes, shoes, scarves, cosmetics, jewellery boxes, pink glass perfume bottles shaped like birds, miniature statuette collections, musical instruments on which somebody had once had three lessons, scroll sets or vases. Chia's cubicle had no clutter at all. At least that saved her being nagged to tidy it. I saw no evidence that this building was ever subjected to housework. The crud on the floors and door frames looked prehistoric.

'So this is your little nest, Chia!'

Again, she gave me that sad, wan smile. She had dark hair and soft eyes; the customers probably thought her a pretty one, though she was simply young. The skinny mite had tiny hands and baby fingers; she looked no more than fifteen, unformed and a little backward with it. I think she could see she broke my heart.

'It's all right,' she urged, as if reassuring me. 'I'm used to it. They give me food and clothes. I have a job. The other girls are like a big family.'

She spoke as if she thought herself lucky; she just had to stick with it.

I sat beside her on her bed, trying not to imagine who else had been there or to notice what traces they had left behind. How could any man with self-respect come to a place like this – let alone carry out what ought to be an intimate act among such public squalor? 'Do you do well, Chia?'

'Oh yes,' she agreed seriously. 'I look young. A lot of the men ask for that.'

At this rate she would soon look older. Then how would she fare? 'So do they treat you nicely?'

'Some.'

'And the rest?'

She pulled a face, though seemed acquiescent. 'They

215

want to call me a naughty girl and punish me.' She saw my look. 'Oh it's just a game, Flavia Albia. Close your eyes and forget it. Soon be over.' That must be what the pimp had told her.

'So,' I said gently, 'I am wondering about you. I am thinking, can you manage to escape being downtrodden? Will you one day grow into a force to be reckoned with, like Rufia at the Hesperides?' It was a ridiculous thought. She was so pallid, I knew the answer.

'Or Menendra?' Giving me a sly look, Chia knew what my interest really was.

'The elusive Lycian? Apart from issuing threats to all and sundry, I am still not clear what Menendra does. According to her she supplies bars, but it's very vague what she supplies them with.'

Chia seemed to be considering. We were friends now, special cronies for the moment. I did not trust it to last, but I might as well exploit it. 'They didn't want to tell you,' she said.

Ah. One of those moments. An informer lives for this.

'Your Macedonian friends? Didn't want to tell me what, Chia darling?'

'Menendra does go round and sells stuff to the cookshops. But I told you.' I raised my brows, puzzled. 'She's that one I said about.' Chia seemed surprised I had failed to grasp this. 'She's horrid. She scares me. That's why I don't want to go to her for help. It's her this place uses for the girls—' She spelled it out for me, almost exasperated I was being dense about it. 'Albia – she gets rid of babies.'

36

Chia was wanted. A large tanner came to her door. He seemed diffident, asking politely if she was busy at the moment or could she could 'do' him? He was ordinary, almost likeable, though he did stink of his work.

I left.

Before I thanked her for our chat and freed her to ply her trade with the tanner, the girl had told me how to find the cookshop where Menendra lodged. I came upon it easily enough, but when I went up the stairs at the side of the building, her door was firmly locked. She had a name sign on a hook, like those I had seen in the brothel, but when I turned it, the back was blank, no 'engaged' notice. So people came to find her here, but not to fornicate.

Retreating, I bought a pie from the busy cookshop. It was surprisingly good, given the area. That's Rome for you.

I walked slowly back to the Garden of the Hesperides, eating as I went. I could not help thinking what a wondrous treat it would once have been for me to eat a warm pie in the street. Once, when I was homeless in dreary Londinium.

Today the weather was mixed, with small clouds scudding in between gladdening bursts of sunlight. The temperature was cooler than earlier in the week, so walking about was more comfortable. Still, this was the Golden City, with its climate so different from the one I grew up with: Rome, where you could go bare-armed even while the sun was hidden. Rome, where my family all laughed at me because if the sun peeked out in December, I would throw off my cloak, raise my face to the warmth and start smiling . . .

Tiberius, still at the bar, caught me brushing pastry crumbs from my lips. Since he looked envious, I walked over to the Brown Toad to ask if they could supply a bowl of their stew for him. Nobody was about. People could walk past and not be accosted by the transvestites. Any lunchtime clientele had gone. I went inside, looking for the lethargic waitress. She wasn't there, but I found an aged woman washing out food bowls; she must be the granny who cooked up the daily cauldron.

'Where is the girl?'

'Having a lie-down.' I interpreted that the lewd way. Maybe I had spent too much time investigating bars.

'Any of your meaty hotpot left? I have a hungry man to feed over the road.' I did not mention that he was an aedile who ought to enforce the pulses-only rule. Not knowing who I wanted it for, she obligingly scraped the last of it out of her cauldron.

I grinned. 'If you're like my old gran on the Aventine, you're pleased to see the clean bottom of the pot.'

She was like my old gran all right. Beaming, she let me run a finger around the inside of the cauldron, cleaning up the last of the gravy. I thought I had better try some, since I had not tasted this famous broth when the Macedonians had lunch on me. Anyway, I had a long history of licking out cooking pots. All my family liked to do it; when a bunch of us gathered in a kitchen, there could be squabbles.

I congratulated her on the flavour. I was polite; besides,

it really was good. I liked remembering that eating places were supposed to be for eating in.

She had a small bowlful set aside under a cover, put away for herself, but she was eager to see her labour being enjoyed by someone else; she pushed me onto a stool, insisting I have it. Despite my pie, I downed the stew as well. Brides need nourishment. Both my own grandmothers would have said that. At the moment, I was feeling nostalgic for them.

'What do people call you?'

'Gran.'

'Can I have your recipe, Gran? My aunt runs a caupona up on the Aventine; they could really do with serving up meals as delectable as this. You've made the meat really tender!'

Naturally she pretended she just threw in whatever was to hand that day. That might be true, but she knew how much to throw and what else would taste well with it. 'It's top beef. I get it from the victimarii.'

'No, really? You mean Costus and company?'

'You know them?'

'They are doing the augury for my wedding.'

'Oh that will be lovely for you. Just tell old Staberius what you want him to prophesy.' I managed to assume the correct dreamy look, as if I was really looking forward to the ceremony. Grandmothers have standards. They know marriage is a lottery, but they expect a bride to be full of joy on the day. There will be plenty of time later for her to admit she has made a horrible mistake.

'So how come the handsome sacrifice boys have a butcher's shop?'

The granny tapped her nose, but told me. 'Oh they have

a lot of little sidelines. One of my grandsons is in that crew; I have to stop him telling me the horrible things that go on . . . It's not a shop. You have to come round to the back gate on the right day . . .' So if a sacrifice went wrong, if a large bull was slaughtered and there were leftovers, if a beast came up from their country farm then was not wanted by a fickle client, Costus let favoured neighbours buy choice cuts on the quiet.

'If the gods don't get a sniff of altar smoke, they won't know what they've lost?' I smiled.

'Gods only have wafts of offal anyway. The main meat is handed out – after the bastard priests have had a good dinner first!'

'My grandma on the Aventine reckoned offal was the best meat.'

'She was brought up poor if she thought that!'

'Yes, she was,' I agreed soberly.

'All the better for it, girl.'

'She had a hard life.'

'But she lived to see her grandchildren thrive.'

'Yes.' Including the interloper from Britain. Junilla Tacita had viewed me at first with intense suspicion, in case I did down her 'real' family – but she mellowed.

She, too, would have come and wept at this wedding I was to have. She enjoyed a good cry on a happy occasion. I suppose it made up for all the tears she had bravely bitten back during tragic times. She had known plenty of those.

I gazed at the Brown Toad's cooking granny. 'So tell me, old one: did you know the famous Rufia?'

She cackled with loud laughter. 'Who didn't?'

I took a chance. I decided she was honest and would

speak her mind. 'This is an unpleasant thing to ask but I have to: did Rufia run a vice ring from that bar?'

That was when the granny snatched back the bowl of stew intended for Faustus. For a moment I thought she was offended and he had lost his lunch – but she only wanted to stand his bowl on the brazier to keep it warm. It suggested we were in for a long chat. Excellent! (Faustus could wait.) She pulled up another stool for herself and squatted, groaning as her joints protested.

'So! You're wanting to find out what happened over at that place.' This old dame kept up with gossip and was brazen about doing so. Luckily, I had never seen much point in keeping our investigation a secret. The crime was old and it helps to have the neighbourhood aware that you are open to offers of information.

My companion was now behaving as if I was a grand-daughter whose schoolwork needed to be supervised – by someone less indulgent than her goofy parents. 'I dare say other people have been giving you the runaround. You should have come to me first, Albia.'

I felt a surge of hope. 'Six dead. It must have been a ghastly night. Do you know what it was all about?'

'I do not! I keep my nose out of things like that.'

After this outburst of sanctity, she paused. I had to encourage her into talking anew: 'Gran, like what? I can't tell what kind of bar the Hesperides is because it's closed for works. The new landlord may intend it to be respectable – or he thinks he does. But did it have a very different history?'

'No worse than other places,' she assured me compla-cently. I managed not to look around the Brown Toad, which had lousy staff and low customers, especially at night.

It gave bench room to the Macedonian whores, while the waitress who had gone from sight could herself now be having her 'lie-down' upstairs with a paying customer. Judging by those I had seen catcalling outside, the lethargic waitress could even really be a boy.

Unlikely; she was not pretty enough.

My confidante settled in to share her knowledge. Close to, she was no piece of art. Most of her teeth had fallen out, her hair was going the same way and nowadays she was warty. She wore an old tunic that might have belonged to a couple of other people before she picked it out as a bargain on a recycled clothes stall.

According to her, in Old Thales' time the Hesperides pretended to be quite reputable – 'If you didn't look too close.'

'There are rooms upstairs.'

'And they used them.'

'For regular prostitution? Was it organised?'

'Oh no.' She was dismissive. 'If men wanted it, they could get it – but not from full-time prostitutes. Apart from the fact there wasn't a lot of very dirty activity in those days, Old Thales hadn't the gumption to organise a piss in a public latrine.'

'You didn't like him?'

'I never really knew him. My husband did, and called him lazy, all talk, and not trustworthy. He puffed himself up as the happy landlord, but Rufia was the busy one at that place.'

'What was the relationship between her and Thales?'

'She worked there. He made out he was the big wheel, while he let her get on with it. The place would have gone to the wall without Rufia.'

'No affair?'

'Oh no. Not between them. I don't think Rufia trusted men. She never had a regular fellow, and never any children.'

'Did she go upstairs with customers?'

'If she had to. I don't count that.'

I did wonder if Gran had ever done the same herself. I could not ask. She would have denied it indignantly. Nowadays she was grandmother to many and had a decent reputation to sustain. The past was formally quashed.

'Routine services? Did she do anything else, anything involving the other bars?'

My witness leaned forward confidingly. She had sweet breath as if she sucked apothecaries' pastilles for some ailment. 'Other business? Not like you mean. What she did was act as a mother to all the women.'

'"Mother" as in brothel madam?'

'No, more "mother" as in mother! You know . . .'

I did not.

'She looked after them. Plenty of the girls who have to do that work are very young and ignorant. She taught them how to take care of themselves. Keep their spirits up. Keep as clean as possible. Watch out for each other, especially if they knew there were any nasty types of men around. How to deal with violence. And, if they was unlucky and fell for a you-know-what, Rufia quietly took them somewhere private and did the necessary.' I gazed at her. 'So that the baby went away. You know!'

'Yes, I know.' So it was Rufia who taught Menendra, who now carried this out for the White Chickens girls. 'What about Nona?'

'So you know Nona? She's all right, though I hear she

charges enough . . . Nona came in afterwards. Same thing, of course. Well, she makes the babies go away; I don't think she bothers with the other stuff. She *really* doesn't care for men. She doesn't much like the girls either, she does what she does to make money out of them and their misery. That was what made Rufia special around here. Her proper mother-ly approach.'

'She had no family, you said. Was that because she got rid of her own too?'

'Oh no, I don't think so. Well, you get a feel for these things – I always thought she was one of those women who just couldn't conceive. She had plenty of chances. Being a barmaid – you can imagine!'

'Did she want children?'

'I suspect so. She always spoke really nicely to my little ones if she met us in the street.'

'So, Gran, she looked after the good-time girls instead?'

'That's right. That brought out her caring nature. She was a hard woman in many ways. I expect if she'd had her own, she might have been quite different.' The granny laughed, reminiscing. 'Well, you have to stay calm then, don't you? I say she was hard, but that was just her attitude. She talked hard. She stood no nonsense. But you knew where you were with her, and she was never unfair. People liked her for it.'

I put aside my food bowl. 'Somebody failed to appreciate her. She was killed at the Hesperides.'

'Was she?' The granny assumed a vague, watery-eyed look. It was the kind of disassociation my own would have used. *I am just a poor old body who can't answer anything difficult* . . . 'Well, I don't know about that, dear.'

'So you know nothing about the five men either, whose

bodies we have dug up?' She shook her head with determination. I tried pressing her, though I knew it was hopeless. 'They could have been salesmen – it's been suggested. I don't know what they were trying to sell.'

To my surprise, the old one suddenly perked up. 'Oh that would have been the cladding-sellers,' she cried. 'Gavius and his crew. They were always coming round in them days. They used to love a night out drinking at the Hesperides.'

'Oh! But that was in the past?'

'Fell out with Thales. He was like that. Took against people for no reason, never mind if they was good customers. Stupid kind of man.'

'Or they stopped coming because they are all dead, Gran.' She looked at me quizzically. 'If they fell out, would Thales have gone so far as to have them murdered?'

She now stared as if I were barmy. 'No,' she explained, with a pitying manner. 'Old Thales was a coward. But none of those men are dead. Whatever gave you that idea, Albia? They are as alive as you or me, same as always. Alive and decent enough boys, for salesmen. They live in Mucky Mule Mews. As I recall, Rufia used to lodge in a cheap room above Gavius and his parents, when he lived with them.'

I drew in a deep breath. Then, since she seemed to have no more to tell me, I took the warm hotpot off the brazier and carried it across the road to give my man his lunch.

37

'Albia! You took your time.' Ravenous, my bridegroom sounded as sharp as if we were married already. Could our bliss be over – so soon?

It seemed worth reviving; I kissed him. 'I apologise, darling. But I bring holy broth made from bootleg beef, if you don't mind stealing from the gods—'

'Sorry, divine ones . . .' Tiberius grasped the bowl of hotpot, already pulling his folding utensil set one-handed from a pouch. He kissed me back – so there was hope for us – then leaned himself against a pile of full sacks, falling to. Although he was a pious man, he seemed unfazed by benefiting from a bull that had escaped sacrifice. Nor did he take any notice of Dromo, who had been drawn into the courtyard by the stew's enticing scent, looking hopeful.

Dromo was pushed aside by Julius Liberalis, the Hesperides landlord, arriving in a bate. I took over, so Tiberius could eat without harassment.

'Liberalis! Your contractor is busy. Come and talk to me instead.' Tiberius was listening in, so I pitched my voice so he could hear and catch up on my latest discoveries. 'I have been learning some dirty things about your precious bar – not least that it once was a centre for local abortions.'

'Rubbish!' Liberalis blustered, unconvincingly. 'These premises are wholly above board.'

'Possibly now. It will be up to you how you choose to run your hostelry, won't it, genial proprietor?' Playing fair, I allowed he might alter the bar's character for the better. 'You need to buck up though. Since Old Thales passed on, the Garden of the Hesperides has already come under vigiles scrutiny – and you haven't even started yet.'

'Is it my fault you dug up a load of old bodies?'

I felt my chin lift. 'Bodies that are assuming a more mysterious role than ever. I now know about the salesmen who were in the bar on the night of the tragic events. They were locals, a group of men who are still well known in the Ten Traders. They simply stopped coming because Thales quarrelled with and then barred them. My sources reckon the falling-out was most likely unprovoked.'

Liberalis had the grace to nod. 'Yes, he was rather like that.'

'Don't model yourself on him then! Ever heard of Gavius?'

'I know him. He sells marble as a fascia for bar counters. Acting as a middleman for all the big quarries. He re-clad both of our worktops recently.'

In that case, it was indefensible that Liberalis had previously claimed to know nothing about the salesmen and their evening drinks. I wanted to know why he had lied, then more about the salesmen, possible witnesses, and their connection with the bar. 'Was this work done after you took over, or was Thales still living?'

'No, he'd gone. It was my first improvement, straight after the bar came to me. What of it?'

'Well to start with, you were present the night Rufia vanished. So when I asked who was here then, you strung me along deliberately.'

'All right, I thought it might have been them.'

'No, you knew! Now if the Gavius crew are not our five buried skeletons, I ask you yet again. What other group came to the bar that night? Who are those dead men?'

The new landlord applied an innocent expression, still pretending he was quite different from his more raffish predecessor. 'Sorry, I can't help.'

'Maybe Gavius will tell us,' Tiberius mumbled through a mouthful of stew, trying to scare Liberalis for me.

'Good thinking, love.' I played along. 'I'll call on him next. The marble crew won't remember drinking or shagging a barmaid ten years ago; they probably do that every night. But having a big row with Thales should have stuck; they can tell us who was here then. They may even say what Julius Liberalis was doing that evening, since his own memory is so vague.' Liberalis shuffled anxiously.

Had Thales quarrelled with the marble-suppliers deliberately, to make them go home before the real trouble started? Was he clearing the bar, to leave no potential witnesses to what he already had planned?

'So tell me,' I broached Liberalis, changing my tone, 'what brings you here today, looking so anxious?'

I hoped he had had a serious rethink. No chance of that, unfortunately. 'I came to see the damage to my bar,' he grouched instead.

I refused to sympathise. 'Well, you came too late, man. You're using a good contractor; it is already cleaned up and reinstated.'

'Yes, I can see. But Manlius Faustus sent a message about what it was like this morning.'

Manlius Faustus stayed on his sacks, methodically spooning up stew.

'I saw it myself, a total mess. Liberalis, all you cared

about from the start is whether this will hold up the work.' Exasperated, I went fully onto the attack. 'Of course the real problem is that we have uncovered a serious crime, the culprits are clearly still out there, yet nobody – especially you – has the sense to tell us who they are. There would have been no damage to your place if we had had these people in custody. It's time for you to cooperate, I'd say!'

Liberalis looked shifty but made no reply.

'Oh come on! You already admitted it was Gavius in the bar. So who else did you see that night?'

He shook his head as if the answer was nobody. I had never believed that. So he was still stubbornly lying.

I snapped at him to get a grip. I was thoroughly riled. I mentioned how we once presumed Menendra's heavies were involved, although our eyewitness discounted them. That was when Liberalis finally burst out with a completely new complication: 'Eyewitness? If somebody saw who did it, you tell him to be careful! I don't want anyone else getting hurt. These people mean business.'

'What people? What business are they in?'

He sighed. He was pulling at his hair again as he admitted unhappily, 'The bar business. If I'm right, Flavia Albia, this was aimed at me.'

For once he had startled me. Even Tiberius stopped eating. While he, like a sharp contractor, probably began thinking that if the site intrusion was a customer's own fault, the customer would have to pay for the damage, I asked severely, 'What have you done, Liberalis, to deserve such punishment?'

He squirmed, his usual reaction to pressure. Then he finally owned up: 'I told them I saw no reason to pay any protection money while the bar was closed for work.'

'*Protection money?*'

Out of a corner of my eye I saw Tiberius pass his bowl to his slave. Dromo complained it was empty, then started to lick out the gravy. His master came over to us, mopping his mouth with a napkin and, full of official interest, demanding that Liberalis explain.

It turned out all the local bars paid a gang for 'protection', which of course meant bribes not to harass their premises. This came as no surprise; it is a centuries-old crime that the authorities will never stamp out because bar owners are always too scared to complain.

Tiberius was growling under his breath at the landlord's accepting attitude. When pushed, Liberalis told him that in the High Footpath neighbourhoods, including the Ten Traders, the leading villains were the Rabirius gang. Tiberius glanced at me; we had come across them during a previous case.

'I'll just have to pay up now.'

'You could try reporting it!' Tiberius answered sternly.

Liberalis shrugged, very matter-of-fact. 'It's only an overhead.'

'No, it's extortion.'

'I don't want to watch my bar burn down.'

'Is that how they intimidate you? Who does it? The elder or younger Rabirius? Roscius is the young blood's name.'

'Not sure. They send agents. Thales knew Rabirius quite well,' said Liberalis. 'Old cronies, or pretended to be. I've never had a personal visitation, just a couple of henchmen come round like door-to-door sponge-sellers. Only they are not vending anything, and they are very menacing. They stand up close, then don't smile.'

'Shark tactics!' This situation annoyed Tiberius. 'Rabirius

is supposed to be getting on in years. The next generation want to wrest control from him – we anticipate a crime war. Are threats the only way they lean on you?'

'That's all. Leave it, Legate.'

'Have they tried the trick of forcing a man of theirs on to your staff?'

'A plant?' Clearly Liberalis was worldlier than he appeared.

'That's what I mean. Observing you, taking charge of the cash box, creaming off profits, letting you know *they* know everything that goes on in your place?'

'No, it's simple protection. If I pay them, we all rub along fine. This is how things are done in the trade.'

Ideas were jumping at me. 'So did Thales always pay up?' I wondered whether the five dead men could have been enforcers; had Thales fought back? He would have been a brave man, which did not fit with what I had heard. But his heir assured me Old Thales paid up sweetly. There had never been bad feeling. 'Do the Rabirius men habitually drink here?'

'Oh no. They have their own places where they spend time, they never mix business and leisure. All they ever take from us is a quick hospitality beaker of wine.'

'Formally sealing the deal? So civilised!' I scoffed.

Liberalis missed the point. 'Well, we've always given them our top quality, the flagon we hide in the cupboard, to make sure they leave happy . . . You need to explain to her,' he told Faustus crossly, 'how the business world works!'

'I think she knows,' was the quiet answer.

Liberalis was feeling the pressure; he flounced off. Over his shoulder he threw one last barb: 'You ought to be ashamed of yourself, Flavia Albia, buying a meat dish from a bar. You should know that contravenes the Emperor's food regulations!'

I knew that too. But sometimes the law is plain ridiculous. For me, if a decree seems outrageous, I stand up to it.

Of course if it's a decree from Domitian, I do it discreetly. I'm not stupid.

38

When I went looking for Gavius, I took along Tiberius. Marble was his speciality. He wanted to come and meet the supplier.

Tiberius took the bowl back to Gran at the Brown Toad. He thanked her for the hotpot (angling for more another day) and followed his usual routine of asking a nit-picky question; this time he wanted to know *whose* granny the old granny was. Flattered and giggly, she said 'pretty well everyone in the High Footpath district'. He asked if she knew where the fascia salesman might live nowadays and she then said in Mucky Mule Mews, which she had told me already.

I led him to the dungheaped alley, where we could ask the man's parents for the actual house Gavius lived in nowadays. They let us pat the dog Gavius had left with them, a slobbering, happy creature who greeted us like old friends even though we were strangers. But she was a large girl, and when we first arrived she let out a sonorous bark. It might deter intruders, if they were cowardly. The parents gave directions to the other end of the mews, only for us to find Gavius was out. If he was working, he could be anywhere; he might even be visiting a quarry miles from Rome.

We became a little despondent, then we heard his other

two dogs barking loudly indoors. So he was coming back eventually and could not have gone far. We walked to the street end to escape the high smell of sun-warmed dung, but decided to wait. This was a hazard of being an informer; it was not all mint tea and walnut cake. However, Dromo spotted a stall selling fruit tarts so he dragged us over there. While we were watching his meticulous choosing process, Gavius arrived home to give his dogs their afternoon exercise. We knew him because the stallholder called out a greeting. So he was popular.

We followed Gavius back to his house, though not for long.

'They're barking so much because they heard you and thought you were me coming to take them out! You will have to trot along with us. The girls will go mad if I don't take them straightaway now they've seen me.'

Apparently these dogs took precedence over everything else, but he let us accompany their walk. I was still digesting my lunchtime pie, plus stew, but was now forced on a hike the whole length of the Viminal. Most of our journey was uphill. Nothing else, we were assured, would do for the Three Graces (including Euphrosyne, whom Gavius had collected from his parents as we passed).

'I can't leave her behind; she'll soon let me know what she thinks of that.'

At first we humoured their owner and let him warble about his pets. They originated in the Pyrenees, so were quite unsuitable in Rome. They were huge flock-guarding dogs, with long, white, merrily shedding fur that was thickest over the folds of flesh on their great shoulders; on all three, the white fur had large dark blotches over their heads and upper bodies. Gavius actually said he bought them as pups

234

'from a man in a bar'. I had not thought people really did that. But of course crowded bar counters are packed with dodgy dealers selling all kinds of things.

According to their owner, the Three Graces possessed the gentlest, calmest natures; they loved children, adored having visitors to count, but would ferociously protect their home and family against intruders. (Despite our experience of being happily slobbered at his parents' house?) They adored going on walks so they could look around, check out the neighbourhood and make as many friends as possible. We saw them even try to lick a potter's raven through the bars of its cage. The bird told them to get lost. Well, it was ruder than that, but they wagged their long tails anyway.

Gavius himself was sized in proportion to the dogs he doted on. In his case it derived from many hours of leaning on bar counters, sampling snack bowls as he discussed marble requirements. He was unmarried and, apart from visiting his parents every day, even his social life consisted of drinking with his colleagues, as he freely told us. I would never have guessed this heavily paunched, fat-faced, easy-going fellow was the son of the worn, fleshless, anxious-seeming couple I had met. When they were all together he must look like an outsized cuckoo in a meadow pipits' nest.

After we had worked through enough canine lore, Tiberius opened a discussion of marble. Every caupona, popina, thermopolium and mansio throughout the Empire has one or more counters faced with stone crazy-paving pieces. These make food shops instantly recognisable, besides being attractive and easy to clean down.

Gavius was knowledgeable. He liked to chat. Tiberius had begun by mentioning that the counters at the Garden of the Hesperides had just suffered damage. 'Some idiot looks to have landed a couple of blows with a lump hammer.' Gavius exclaimed in horror at that; he had provided the marble so recently. They discussed repairs.

Gavius quickly saw that Tiberius had the kind of professional knowledge he respected. 'Well, you know how it is around here, sir, they want everything for nothing, with goat bells on. We provide whatever they will pay for, and sometimes I do squeeze a commission with exotics – Cipollino, Brescia. But the bars around here tend to have a mix of Luna and Pentelic, same old white and grey you see everywhere, not much of a challenge for me and the boys.'

'Do you mainly supply reclaimed pieces?'

'It's legit!' Gavius protested, as if Tiberius was suggesting his supplies were stolen.

'I know, I know. The reclaimers even have a guild in Rome. I am not criticising you, Gavius. It's understood – when a property is to be rebuilt, the contractor has a right to any materials he takes out, which he is allowed to sell on. Do you have contacts in the building trade or the quarries?'

'I know everyone. That's good business.'

'How long have you been doing this?'

'Fifteen years, easily.' Gavius thought Tiberius had merely asked a polite question but it was useful to me; the marble-supplier had definitely been trading as long ago as the Hesperides killings. 'We do obtain offcuts from quarries, though I mainly pick up suitable pieces after renovations. I often buy on spec, keep the bits at the yard. One source for me recently was Domitian's Temple of the Flavians. Nice and close. Absolutely slathered in gorgeous new marble – have you seen it? He was so choosy, they had a lot of rejects. The builder practically paid me to take them away.'

'And that new Forum of his is only down the Argiletum. It has a good Temple of Minerva.'

'Yes, though very little wastage came off that site. The contractors were old mates, so I picked up any spoiled pieces but hardly worth taking the cart. It comes and goes. We're still benefiting from that great fire in Titus' reign. Plenty of big public buildings needed restoration, so the old material had to be taken out and it's not all fire-damaged. They are generally glad for us to clear the site or at least pick through the skips. I don't enjoy profiting from a disaster – but you take your chances in life, don't you? If you know when to turn up, it's lucky-dip time!'

Tiberius glanced at me, smiling slightly, as if I was one of the chances he had taken.

I was still considering being a prize in a lucky dip, but now I nipped in. 'I am very glad we found you. We had believed you were a dead man, Gavius!'

'As you see, that's a malicious rumour.' The marble-supplier had a sense of humour; he laughed it off. Other people really take against false reports of their deaths. 'Was my obituary flattering?'

'Yes, I believe there is a very moving ode to you by a court poet . . . I would have known better – I met your parents, lovely people, but they never mentioned your name. All a mistake, so I apologise. The ancient grandma who cooks for the Brown Toad set me straight.' Gavius grinned. He knew who I meant. 'Don't tell me she's *your* granny, Gavius?'

He winked. 'Mine and half the High Footpath. Father's mother.'

'She never said.'

'She likes stringing people along. That would be my gran, all right. She'll ask me what your face looked like when I told you, then she'll wet herself chuckling . . . Gobble up her hotpot if you can get it, but don't believe a word she tells you.'

It would be rather inconvenient to me if her stories about Rufia had been invented. But I did not think so.

'So, Gavius, I expect you have heard we found bodies. At least it's not you and your crew planted out in the garden. One is reckoned to be the barmaid, but five others look male. Faustus and I intend to find out who they are and what happened. We need witnesses. You have been regularly mentioned as one of the customers that night. I hope you can remember?'

'Oh yes.' Gavius had a darker expression now. 'Thales suddenly had a go at us, so we stopped drinking there.'

'It was also the night Rufia disappeared.'

'That was another reason not to go any more.'

'People have described her as rather stern, but you liked her?'

'Kind of. She was a bloody good waitress. They had others there though.'

'If my sources are correct, Rufia also had, let's say, a wide influence in the community?' Gavius looked blank. 'Took a motherly interest in all the bar girls, and the professional prostitutes?'

He shrugged. Women's stuff. Don't ask him.

I knew he had had sex that night. Nipius and Natalis had said all the marble-suppliers went upstairs. Presumably it was regular. Rufia 'looked after them', though that could mean she found a free girl, not necessarily that she went with them herself.

I wondered if their nights out had ever resulted in pregnancies that Gavius knew nothing about. Women who slept with salesmen were not the kind who could name the fathers of their children. Afterwards, if it went wrong, Rufia would have dealt with it; the salesmen would never even be told. Well, not unless a girl badly needed money to cover her expenses and came cooing round after cash. I bet with regular clients the girls kept quiet rather than deter these men from future business.

No doubt paying for abortions was another aspect of bar life that Julius Liberalis would call an overhead.

I could not help thinking about Chia. The threat of a baby was a much bigger issue for her. This was street life: men casual, women desperate.

I asked Gavius the crucial question: did he and his crew see another group of drinkers, five of them, at the Hesperides, the night Old Thales quarrelled? But he said no, not while his crew were there; they must have arrived later.

39

The dogs began to let us know we were reaching their destination. The high road ended beneath a bunch of aqueducts. As we all passed through the Servian Walls at the Viminal Gate, the Three Graces became more excited than ever. They were distracted briefly by wanting to jump up and lick soldiers who were lazily monitoring the crowds under the arches. One of the troops gave them a bread roll, so they may have met these dogs before. Aglaia and Thalia sat pleading for more, while Euphrosyne devoured the free gift. From the way he handled them, roughing up their neck fur, the young soldier knew dogs. Perhaps back at home he had left animals he missed.

The Graces quickly lost interest, keen to move on. Outside the gate, Gavius turned onto the great parade ground of the Praetorians, which lies between the old city wall and the Guards' intimidating camp. In the afternoon, they rarely exercised. Their numbers were low in any case, since many were away in Pannonia with the Emperor.

Gavius, Tiberius and I stood at a corner, taking a welcome breather, as the dogs hared around ecstatically. We watched, while they amused themselves in madcap games. From time to time one or more galloped back to us, panting wildly, seeking approval or a stick to be thrown.

★   ★   ★

An informer must never give up so, I kept on badgering about the five dead men. 'Gavius, I know the Hesperides, and presumably other bars, is a target for extortion by so-called "protection" gangs. Were you ever aware of that?' He shook his head. Any wise person would do the same, unfortunately. Who likes gangsters to think you have ratted on them? Who wants to die now, in some very unpleasant fashion? 'I am wondering if Old Thales decided he had had enough and struck back at them?'

Tiberius put in more questions: 'Could it be that some other outfit tried to muscle in on the rackets? Rival crooks? But Thales stayed loyal, knowing old Rabirius, as someone has claimed?'

'I never heard of any rivals,' claimed Gavius. 'But I have seen Thales and Rabirius having a chinwag like best pals. They played a game of soldiers once when I was there. It's true they went way back. I think they were boys together.'

'You know Rabirius?' I asked.

'To recognise. The ridiculous poser used to come around all the time, leaning on a cane for effect, inspecting his territory. Especially on the Esquiline, which was his real domain.'

'He is a brute?'

'Once in a while he would whack some slave or menial across the face with his cane, so people knew how hard he was. I saw him kick a woman once, knocked her right off her feet, though he wouldn't try that in Thales' bar. If Rufia was looking, she would have cut off his testicles. Haven't seen him anywhere in a while. Like you say, he's probably grown old and someone is taking over.'

I snorted. 'I like the sound of Rufia. I cheer her methods . . . I suppose you saw Rabirius in action, Gavius, because you work with so many bars? Do landlords confide in you? Or do you overhear things?' Warily, he nodded. 'Though at the Hesperides you never saw any threats, or money handed over?'

'Those kinds of men are always discreet,' Gavius replied. 'You glimpse them behind the counter, talking to the landlord as if they are asking how his brother is these days or something – then they shake hands and leave without you even noticing.' He was hedging, like Liberalis earlier. This description belied his earlier claim to know nothing about enforcement. I decided not to challenge him. It was more important to keep him talking.

'Formal handshakes are a nice touch from men of violence!' Tiberius commented in a dry tone. 'Maybe we could ask your colleagues if they know any more, the ones who drink with you?'

'I'm sure all the boys will say the same as me, Legate.'

'Please don't confer,' I urged him. 'Don't suggest what to say. Better they spontaneously tell the truth.' Gavius looked affronted but did not argue.

'I am sure Gavius and his boys are straight, Albia.' Tiberius was playing his 'fair man' role; I knew it was an act, for strategy.

I fell quiet, assessing the situation. Ten years ago, Rabirius was the vicious old clan chief – a different man from the failing spectre he was reckoned to be now. Then he was strong, feared, fully in control, tentacles all over the place. Not only would he come around inspecting his domain, smilingly making himself visible, blatantly striking sudden blows to reinforce his message; he would also listen for any subversive mutters. Such men can be fanatically suspicious. They keep their power by constant vigilance. If Rabirius had been high-born, he could have become a paranoid emperor.

Thank you, Jupiter, he wasn't. The gangster we had in power was bad enough.

Nowadays a clan coup seemed inevitable. No one had seen Rabirius for a while. He must be frail. A nephew called Roscius was starting to flex muscles in the business; Rabirius' hard man, his dark sidekick Gallo, was keen to supplant young Roscius. Had machinations by henchmen and relatives already started at the time of the Hesperides trouble? Or was that too long ago?

Another possibility was that outsiders had tried manoeuvring against Rabirius. Interlopers had tried to shuffle him out of the way, only to discover that, ten years ago, he was still capable of dispatching rivals. Why the Hesperides? Did Rabirius persuade his boyhood acquaintance Thales to cooperate? To provide a discreet location for a criminal death squad to ambush people? Was the graveyard in the garden the body dump after a bout of gang warfare?

40

Tiberius and I left Gavius in the exuberant company of his dogs. First Tiberius said he wanted to call in at the Third Cohort's station house, which was close to the Viminal Gate. We did so, but our contact, Macer, was off duty. We left a message asking him to provide a status report on protection rackets in the Ten Traders bars. He might respond, but I bet Tiberius that Macer would conveniently 'not receive the message'.

We walked back a different way, climbing up onto the Embankment to feel the cooler air. As we strolled along towards the Esquiline Gate, we said little, enjoying each other's quiet company. It seemed a while since we had been able to do this.

The lofty bank of the ancient Servian Wall had once been the city boundary. Now Rome had expanded well beyond the old fortifications, which had never been pulled down but had become a pleasure ground for people walking, lovers escaping, popular entertainers, street theatre and puppeteers. Even in the middle of a working day there were idlers and connivers up here, along with the odd prancing lunatic. Occasionally one of the lunatics was brandishing a knife.

Elsewhere in the city, expansion had taken the form of teeming residential districts, but here we were overlooking a one-time paupers' graveyard to our left; it had such a bad reputation, no one would want to live there. So the area had been transformed into several large gardens. Rumours said it had had to be covered twenty-five feet deep in new soil to cover up the smell of death.

Named for whichever millionaires commissioned them, these luxurious walks were free to the public; well, that was why the wealthy created extravagant city spaces – making sure they were advertised for ever as persons of taste, money and flash beneficence. You might die, but your stone pines ensured your name lived. Topiary was a better memorial than a tomb. I am serious: gardens lay within the city for all to notice, whereas tombs had to be placed along the roads outside.

The Esquiline gardens were beautiful, laid out most elegantly, full of fine trees and plantings and adorned with statues (generally stolen from defeated nations). Some had museums with prehistoric giants' bones or pavilions for the performing arts. The fabulous Stertinius had undoubtedly twangled his cithara to good Hypodorian effect for an invited audience at the Auditorium of Maecenas. The gardens all provided fresh air and peace; they restored the tired soul.

Of course they also concealed pickpockets and hustlers; they were venues for sordid assignations. Generally, as a member of the public, you tried to concentrate on the fine vistas and invigorating atmosphere. Today, as I gazed down from the Embankment, yet again I made the contrast between Rome's civilised heights and its ever-present seamy depths. The lewd and crude jostled the sublime wherever you trod. Side by side; nose to nose. This was a city of stupendous contradiction, which the Romans either viewed as normal or even embraced with crazy pride.

I took a cooler view, of course. I had a reserved northern temperament. Well, not so much in August. At the moment I was too hot and crotchety.

We descended to street level at the Porta Esquilina. While walking, Tiberius had been forming an idea. 'Just along here is the Second Cohort's bolt-hole. Can you bear to come and see if Titianus is home? I know you want to rest.'

'I'm tough.'

'You're tired.'

'I am an informer, I can last out. Mind you, I loathe the thought of dealing with that dreary clown. Of all the lackadaisical, maddening public servants I have ever met, Titianus takes the oatcake.'

'Yes, I knew he was a favourite of yours.'

I understood why the visit had been suggested. Titianus was a vigiles enquiry agent we knew; his beat included the heartland of the Rabirius crime empire.

He was out. Thanks again, to the whole pantheon of delightful gods!

Rather than waste a visit to the station house, I went looking for a certain Juventus. He was a better bet anyway. I knew him and introduced him to Faustus. His name was supposedly secret, in order to preserve his anonymity during a special project monitoring the local gangsters.

According to Juventus, no one was supposed to know even he existed, let alone his project. I for one had been aware of it for years. Operation Bandit King was set up originally by my uncle, Lucius Petronius. I had a better idea of its aims and objectives than Juventus; I had heard Petro maundering on about it for most of my adult life.

246

My uncle would not approve of this idiot being a liaison officer on his legendary scheme.

Juventus was sitting in a room by himself (because of his special mission), doing nothing. Nobody supervised him. No one had ever properly explained to him what his project should entail.

He began by saying he could not talk about his work. That would at least protect him from revealing his incompetence. But the project's secrecy had made him lonely. He was desperate for somebody to talk to.

'Spill, Juventus!' I ordered sternly, watching him weaken.

Tiberius never liked putting anyone in trouble. 'You can safely confer with me, I am Manlius Faustus, plebeian aedile. I heard about you during the Aviola case so I am officially aware of your mission – I'd say, it's a tenet of Operation Bandit King that you should communicate with the aedilate. One day we shall have to take decisions, based on your specialised input.'

'Specialised' was not a concept Juventus grasped. He was leery of 'tenet', too, though he knew for sure 'communication' and 'decision' were words to give him the squits. It was an entrenched rule throughout all fourteen station houses that the vigiles devoted endless time and ingenuity to dodging both. From the day of his induction, Juventus had been taught by his hideous comrades to douse fires, beat up thieves, bully the public, hate his tribune, make rude gestures behind the back of any pompous ass in a toga, respect Vestal Virgins, chat up women (the Vestals do not count as women for these purposes) (though pretty well anybody else does) – and always to avoid telling officials anything at all. Official decisions only led to extra work. The lads in the vigiles had better things to do, for instance loafing about, looking slovenly and going to bars.

Insofar as Juventus was specialised, he went to more bars than the rest, and he went on his own. He could call it work. The purpose was to learn what any criminal gangs were up to. They tended to operate out of eating houses and brothels so Juventus diligently went there to look around and have snacks on expenses. They saw him coming – easy, since he had a mournful expression not suited to such places and he always wore boots tied up with string. While he convinced himself he was properly on observation, he would be lucky if he avoided catching a nasty disease or becoming addicted to drink.

At least if anyone had seen the Rabirius enforcers in action, it was him. Naturally he told us otherwise. He had studied the training manual's section concerning unhelpfulness.

We played on his need for human contact. When he feared we might leave him alone in his room again, he claimed that any events ten years ago were long before his time. Faustus pretended he felt such high regard for Juventus' inside knowledge that any information from him about those far-off days was of high value. I was marrying a sycophant: 'I know you are very thorough.' In reality, after just a few moments, he thought Juventus was shabby, a dangerously unskilled lightweight. The Rabirii would run rings around this dunderhead. The criminal-gangs initiative needed to be taken much more seriously. 'I wondered if you had made it part of your special mission to research past history?'

For Juventus it seemed a startling change to be held in someone's high regard. He made an effort to speculate. Much of it was bluff. Anyone could tell he had not looked into the history at all, but that did not deter him. He reckoned the Viminal bars were enduring more pressure nowadays than previously. Gallo, the right-hand man of Rabirius, had moved over from the Esquiline, extending his influence to the next hill along. He was as ambitious as he was cruel. Strictly speaking, our area of concern lay in the remit of the Third Cohort; they should be able to give more particulars.

We did not admit that Macer of the Third had been our first choice to ask – though we mentioned that he was our contact on the killings at the Hesperides.

Juventus claimed he had liaised with Macer, though I wanted to hear Macer's opinion on that.

Juventus had no more to tell us. We left him, still on his own doing nothing. Tiberius tried to convince me Juventus might now carry out useful research.

'Tiberius Manlius you are such a forgiving man!'

'I am marrying you, Flavia Albia. I have to be an optimist.'

Before we returned to the Viminal, we crossed the main road and went into the Gardens of Pallas. Our walk along the Embankment had made us yearn for more quiet time together. These large gardens, laid out by a millionaire freedman of the Emperor Claudius, would serve as a timeless memorial to a man Nero eventually executed. By the end, Nero had executed everyone he could, as much for owning fine estates as for perceived disloyalty. The richer they were, the more he could snaffle. Besides, Pallas had been the confidant, and according to gossip the lover, of Agrippina, Nero's domineering mother. Yes, he killed her too. Such a nice family.

Pallas had been chief secretary to the Treasury. He was

stonkingly rich. Although it was never suggested that he was guilty of impropriety, even without obvious embezzlement he amassed a fortune large enough to create a notable open-air space. That got him killed. But the fine Gardens of Pallas still memorialised a bureaucrat who would otherwise have been long forgotten.

I sauntered with Tiberius through the western end. This sneaky escape in the late afternoon helped free us of stress. We sat on a stone seat in the warm shade, smiling slightly, thinking that this was what life was for. Free time, time to do whatever you liked, or to do absolutely nothing, alone or in company you valued: of all the luxuries in the Empire, perhaps this was the greatest. To be fair to the Romans, they valued leisure accordingly.

I soaked up the afternoon light, emptying my mind.

It was the time of day when, in the busy built-up areas, the atmosphere was subtly changing. People ended their siestas. Baths prepared to open, so the scent of woodsmoke increased as furnaces were stoked. Military shifts changed; the vigiles would soon gather to go on patrol. Men who needed patrons made their way to the Forum, looking for someone from whom they could wheedle a dinner invitation; men of means either made themselves visible so parasites could ingratiate themselves, or hid from them. Women who could indulge in evening entertainment began to prepare, placing themselves in the hands of their hairdressers, manicurists, adorners with their vials and pots of face colour. The sick were at a low ebb. Workers were weary. Animals barked, bellowed, brayed for food. Above us in the still cerulean sky, swifts squealed as they swooped at high speed after insects. Others careered above water features in the garden.

Tiberius had his head thrown back, eyes closed. He was

not asleep, because his thumb was slowly caressing the back of my hand as he held it. Heat from the bench warmed us through our clothes as we sat.

There, in the peace of the Gardens of Pallas, my brain found its own space to work. Two strands of information came together for me.

'Tiberius . . .' He turned his head, listening. 'Morellus believed one set of bones was from a woman who had given birth: *"female pelvis, child-bearing age, looks as if she has carried some to term, poor unhappy cow . . . "* But other people have told me the missing barmaid was far from young and never had any children: *"I always thought she was one of those women who just couldn't conceive . . . "* If both are right—' Tiberius opened his eyes. He saw my point. '—the skeleton we found at the Garden of the Hesperides cannot be Rufia.'

41

Tiberius reacted typically. He made no comment. His mouth tightened slightly. I observed that he nodded faintly. Twice.

Some people would have rattled on inanely.

'Now I shall have to go right back to the beginning to find out who the headless dead girl is.'

'You will,' replied the understated one.

At least I would never be subjected to interminable chat at breakfast about whether we should try buying better quality carrots from a new greengrocer who might prove to be disappointing, or stick with String-bean Lupius, the vegetable-seller we had always used . . . Tiberius would listen, think, nod, leave it up to me.

I could live that way. Of course, if the new carrots I had chosen turned out to be second-rate, he would say so. When he did give an opinion, he knew how to make his point.

'I'm so annoyed at myself that I missed this.'

'Not your fault, love. So did I.' The fair man spoke.

He left me to dwell on how to reassess the case.

Back in the Ten Traders, before he went in to see his workmen, I watched him conduct a thorough survey of the marble on bar counters. He gave most attention to the Hesperides, naturally. Its two countertops were tiled in the white and grey pieces that we now knew Gavius had supplied. He was coming to inspect them tomorrow, to see where corners had been smashed during the gangsters' raid.

Indoors, the counters' wall faces were plastered, then plainly painted with a dark red wash. Only the staff would see those. On the outside faces, to entice the public, Liberalis had spent more money, with some of the finish in polychrome stones that Tiberius identified for me as Cipollino, which had greenish veins, and Numidian, which was composed of striking yellow patches in purple bonding.

'Rare?'

'No, but you do have to look around. Once you find a source, the material is available – that's assuming you can wait out the long shipping time.'

'And find the cash?'

'That too.'

'I am just wondering whether Liberalis has more money than we think.' I had never expected this enquiry to be about a legacy, but now anything seemed possible.

'A man with a recent inheritance and no family demanding luxuries from him should be able to fund Cipollino misshapes.'

'Right. Mind you . . .' I would not let Liberalis off the hook. '. . . I wonder how much he did inherit?'

'Can you find out?'

'Traceable by the legacy tax.'

'If he paid it,' said Tiberius darkly, in full magistrate mode.

I chuckled. 'And who doesn't under-declare, Aedile? Isn't the chance to cheat on inheritance tax one of the things that alleviates people's grief after somebody dies?'

Tiberius pretended to look stern. He must have a good

253

idea that my father was financing our wedding out of just such smart accounting.

Looking around the other bars, Tiberius found scraps of moulded cornices and even old pilasters incorporated, though mostly the counters were put together from polished slab material. Among the routine white and grey of Luna and Pentelic marble, he picked out with obvious surprise Brescia, alabaster and even a small section of black Aswan granite. The Soldier's Rest, a dingy hole that had mainly escaped our attention until now, even boasted three reclaimed panels of porphyry, set in a triple diamond pattern on its front face. Tiberius reckoned a specialist must have installed those unusual pieces. Since the Soldier's Rest was so unwelcoming otherwise, the fancy front had not improved its customer base. Even the Brown Toad (which only had painted imitation marble) claimed a better footfall, though much of that consisted of clients with peculiar tastes coming to the transvestites; its attraction was untypical.

We stood at the Medusa, having a discussion about marble. Tiberius had a fund of knowledge so it went on for some time. We did not order food or drink; our lunch still satisfied. This kind of conversation must be a great rarity in the bars of the Ten Traders: a man talking to a woman about his long-standing passion, with not a hint of it leading to sex. She listening, not as a prelude to turning out his purse later, but because she liked to hear him talk.

Waiters became twitchy. 'There's no rules for you to check here, Aedile!'

Tiberius broke off what he was saying to me. The interruption irritated him. 'How big a fine are you looking for? Do I see illegal tables, cluttering up the pavement? Not to mention your health hazard: clean up this sauce spill! It must have been festering for weeks, with people putting their elbows in it. Don't serve anyone else until I see this worktop spotless . . . And what are you hiding from me in that hot dish you whipped behind the counter?'

'Chickpeas, honest.'

Tiberius gave him one of his long looks. 'I hope that's right.'

The dish smelled like pork to me, the main meat eaten in Rome, but the stern Manlius Faustus was not really looking for a battle about pulses-only. Well, not today.

I knew him. He would wander past tomorrow. If his order to clean up had been ignored, he would thump the Medusa with every edict in his five-scroll rule book. Selling meat instead of beans and chickpeas would be his first charge. With Manlius Faustus, if people made an effort, he was lenient. If they showed disrespect, he hammered them.

I took careful note of how he worked. It is vital to know how a man reacts to being thwarted before you marry him.

'No need to have a go at me,' the waiter grumbled, feebly applying a wet cloth to the dirty marble. 'If you wanted a dish of hospitality olives, all you had to do was ask.' He paused an insultingly long time. 'Sir.'

I leaned my back against the counter, pretending to take a great interest in a donkey delivering panniers of dry goods to the Soldier's Rest. Out of the corner of my eye I watched my man have his official stand-off.

Faustus folded his arms while he stared at the sorry cleaning efforts. Under this scrutiny, the waiter wilted, went in to fetch a knife, then finally scraped off the dried-on mess. He brushed it carefully onto his palm, then threw the bits in the street. 'That's better, don't you see? Now

255

swab down the rest with a dab of vinegar, then you can officially go back to being in business.'

I smiled quietly to myself, making more mental notes. I would need to ensure we had a very clean kitchen slave. Iberians or Pannonians were supposed to be the most house-proud.

'Now I had better inspect your daily menu,' Faustus told the waiter.

So a board was produced for him, listing the Medusa's offerings. In compliance with Domitian's edict, these alleged-ly comprised Gallic Flageolet Bean Soup and Legionary Barley Broth, while even the salad claimed to feature a sprinkle of pumpkin and flax seeds. The counter pots that might have stored these seeds were in fact empty. I looked.

'This is the board you show us during an aediles' inspec-tion,' Manlius Faustus commented, letting it be known he was not easily fooled. 'I wonder what you really dish up?'

The waiter looked innocent; he sensibly kept quiet.

'I shall be sending someone incognito to test you.'

'No problem, your honour. We are famous throughout the High Footpaths for our delectable pulse casseroles.'

'No need to overdo it!' Faustus chided.

From what I had heard whispered as I moved around the neighbourhood, the Medusa was in fact famous for offering sex with animals.

A tiresome thought came into my mind: was that common? Was the dog bone found at the Hesperides from some poor mutt who had been forced into perverted acts? . . . Settle down, Albia. Garden burials happen. When dogs die, they are often interred at the homes where they have lived as affectionate pets. And what nicer place for a hound to spend eternity than the fabled Garden of the Hesperides? A snake to bark at and bored daughters of Zeus to pat you all day long. Perfect.

Stop being distracted, Flavia Albia. You do not want to feel obliged to investigate the suspicious deaths of dogs.

I stuck with normal questions: 'Tell me, young man.' He was not that young. The period I wanted to investigate should be within his working lifetime. 'Have there ever been rumours of any other women disappearing hereabouts, like Rufia at the Hesperides?'

He thought about it. 'Not really.'

'No?'

'I mean not with everyone saying Old Thales bashed their head in.'

'Some other rumour then? I am particularly interested in the period around when the new Flavian Amphitheatre was inaugurated. You must remember. There were games for days on end. It would have been a very productive time for bars.'

The waiter grinned with gappy teeth as he dredged up a memory for me. 'A pot-washer at the Four Limpets ran away with a one-legged sailor once. She was never seen again. Most people thought losing her improved the neighbourhood substantially.'

I sighed to myself. 'That's very helpful.' This is what informers say to disappointing witnesses. Just in case it makes them think of something more useful. It rarely happens.

I forced myself not to start speculating about the dead man, number four of the five, whose skeleton we found with a leg detached. He wasn't this sailor. Our number four had two legs, even if one went its own way in the fracas and the limb was chucked in his grave with him. That was the clincher. Most one-legged sailors do not carry their amputated pins around with them.

Don't tell me you knew one who did. He must have been a crackpot.

'I don't suppose you are old enough to remember a group that included a man with a serious limp?'

'Ten a denarius. People are always being run over by drays or walking under millstones.'

I thanked him again quietly. Yes, identifying our corpses was going to be difficult.

Let alone the dog.

I nearly didn't bother asking. 'One more question, if you will. Did Old Thales ever own a dog?'

'Pudgy,' the waiter replied, this time not even stopping to think. 'It was always coming over here and squatting on our pavement with galloping diarrhoea. Hades, I haven't thought of Pudgy in years. I've upset myself now . . .' He shuddered dramatically. 'Old Thales bloody loved that hairy thing, but trust me, it was awful.'

I tried to ignore Tiberius grinning at me. 'Pudgy died?'

'It would have been old now if it hadn't! It swallowed the heel off a boot someone chucked it to play with. Choked to death. Thales sobbed for four days.'

I hardly dared continue. 'I don't suppose you know what he did with Pudgy's remains?'

'Oh everybody knew. He made a big thing of it. Buried in a big hole out the back. Old Thales held a very drunken funeral in the garden, followed by a week of massive drinking. He was going to put a plaque up but he never got around to it. Well, it would have cost him. He didn't love the dog – or anyone – enough to open his money chest. Then, just before he did us all a favour and killed himself with drink, he sobered up and immediately forgot all about poor old Pudgy. Talk about a dog's life.'

'And was this around the time, would you say, that Rufia vanished? In the Amphitheatre year?'

'Probably. Perhaps before. Not long.'

'You can't be certain?'

'No. I don't note the death of somebody else's horrible dog in my annual calendar.'

'Apology!'

'Accepted.'

'Why did Old Thales forget his adored pet?' Tiberius suddenly broke in.

'Picked up a new little girlfriend. Adored her even more. Didn't we all? Nobody knew what she saw in him. She was so cute . . . Hercules, I remember her all right! I wonder whatever became of her?'

'What was her name?' I asked, eager to identify this cute creature.

A typical man, he did not remember the beauty as well as he claimed. 'Hades, don't ask me. It's been bloody years. They come and go. How can you expect me to remember one little tart's name among so many on the street? Even if she really was one of the gorgeous ones!'

End of story, so far as he was concerned.

Sighing, I turned to Tiberius. He could see I was despondent; he spoke encouragingly. 'Brilliant, Flavia Albia. Pudgy. You have put a name to one of our bodies.'

'Sadly, my love, it is the one nobody now cares about.' I cursed my luck mildly, in the manner of my father: 'This could only happen to me. I have six bodies from a crime scene, but all I can identify is the dog!'

Not a flicker showed on his face as Tiberius told me deadpan, 'Don't forget we dug up a chicken bone as well.'

'Naturally. Darling heart, I am now working on who the chicken may have been.'

'Good to have priorities,' he answered, smiling. Then suddenly he burst out with, 'Just three days now!'

The wedding.

42

Where next? The day was drawing on. Then as we returned to the Garden of the Hesperides, we saw the waiters, Nipius and Natalis, leaving for their evening shift, which I remembered would be at the Four Limpets.

Tiberius, who found them a louche pair he did not want to talk to now, strode in ahead of me, heading for his site. I managed to greet Nipius and Natalis with a laughing air, as if something hilarious had just happened. 'Hello, you two. I'm thrilled to tell you that with gritty detective work, I have identified one of the corpses!' Perhaps they looked wary; perhaps they only wondered why I found it so funny. 'Here's a test of your memories: do either of you remember Pudgy?'

How fine it would be if this dead dog, who seemed quite incidental, provided my way into the case. *Good boy! Have a bone on me in Hades . . .*

The waiters had been to the baths or a barber; they were swanning about in a reek of hair oil. Both men wore their usual green tunics, probably not laundered since I saw them last. I had forgotten how they exuded unreliability. Still, I didn't want a chickpea flatbread with no fish pickle and a small red wine, only their memoirs.

'Pudgy!' They looked at one another, then jointly assumed postures of exaggerated shock. 'Old Pudgy?' cried Natalis, adjusting his pebble pendant. 'Thundering Jupiter, what's that pooch got to do with anything?'

'I am confident some of the bones are his.'

'Hers,' Nipius corrected me, with a rattle of his bracelets. 'She was a girlie. Ought to have been long forgotten. Hades, Albia, you do like to be thorough. Do you always make a habit of turning up every pet anyone ever shovelled away under a rose bush?'

'I like dogs . . . Anyway I find it satisfying to put on name labels.' I hinted I could be adding more in the near future.

'Pudgy was an awful creature. She caused such trouble – bites, fights, always in heat. Ever tried running a bar where a bitch has a long list of desperate callers but her master wants to keep her pure so he can sell the hulking offspring as pure-bred novelties? We couldn't move for mongrels we were trying to chase away, then Pudgy would have her great lumps of puppies. It was disgusting. Everyone loathed her, except Thales.'

'You got rid of her, though, in the end. Didn't she choke to death on a boot?'

'That's right.'

'Someone gave it her to play with?'

'Rhodina. Gods, she was a dozy tramp.' Nipius had revealed the name before apparently having second thoughts.

'Thales' girlfriend,' I agreed in a light tone, not even making it sound like a question. Since they did not correct me, this must be correct. 'I've heard all about her. Beauty doesn't go with brains. She was a real looker, wasn't she? All the men were after her? So Thales couldn't believe his luck and I suppose he would forgive her anything?'

'Oh he didn't forgive her losing Pudgy!' scoffed Natalis.

'The row about his precious dog went on and on. Even when he pretended to let it go, he kept brooding.'

I had casually positioned myself in the gap between the counters, so the waiters could not leave. Holding them there, I stopped pretending to laugh about it. 'What you say isn't what I have been told. The word elsewhere is Pudgy died accidentally, Thales was heartbroken, he nearly killed himself with drink – and only stopped moaning when he took up with his new girlfriend.'

Typically, the waiters decided it was more important to brag about their own information than to hide the facts. 'You were told wrong then!' Natalis insisted, with some scorn. 'You've been talking to those no-hoper delinquents at the Romulus or the Soldier's Rest. We worked here, we ought to know what happened.'

'Indeed you should, boys – I am happy to believe all you say.' That was a rare promise to witnesses. They were mad if they believed me. 'So the gorgeous bundle called Rhodina worked as a waitress here?'

'Oh she did.'

'A hot favourite with Old Thales?'

'In his bed most nights, from well before Pudgy copped it. He was besotted. She strung him along.'

'Usual story!' I nodded. 'Was she young?'

'Young and pert. He wasn't her first conquest. Nor was she his, come to that.'

'Then she accidentally killed off his dog?'

'She really did not like that dog,' Natalis muttered, with passion. 'None of us did. Pass too close and it would nip you for nothing. Rhodina would not go near it. Customers who sat or stood by Pudgy never got a drink from her. We had to serve them. The dog was a big, powerful thing; she was terrified of it.'

'Well, that was why she tried to distract it with the boot,' explained Nipius. 'She never intended to destroy the creature – or so she said afterwards – though when it started gagging horribly, she made no attempt to help. She was certainly not sorry it died.'

'Not until Thales went up in flames.'

'So he realised it was her fault?' I asked.

'Not to start with. She very carefully said nothing.'

'So he didn't blame her?'

'Not until he found out!' crowed Natalis. Nipius giggled at the memory.

'She told him?'

'She was dim, but not that stupid. Someone in the bar must have snitched. Not us,' Nipius assured me quickly.

'I don't suppose it matters who . . . Then what? Was he furious?'

'Is Etna a volcano?'

I felt my eyebrows lift. 'Was Thales so angry he might actually murder her?'

'Not him. Thales was always all talk and no go. He spent a long time raging at her, but he did seem to cool off.'

'You don't think that was genuine? What made him settle, or seem to?'

'She must have got round him.'

'Know how she did that?'

The two waiters looked at me pityingly. I was pointedly informed that anyone could guess.

29 August

Four days before the Kalends of September
(a.d. IV Kal. Sept.)

Two days before the wedding of
Tiberius Manlius Faustus and Flavia Albia

43

They had no more to tell me about the dead dog or the long-lost waitress, so I let them go.

I gave up my enquiry that day. I call myself tough, but am not as strong as I would like; it is a relic of my early life. Mother had me diagnosed with rickets by the same kindly old doctor who helped her clear me of scabies. Glaucus, at the gym Father goes to, gave me exercises that I have done from adolescence, but I am stuck with soft bones.

Tiberius felt that after the long walk up the Viminal with the Three Graces even he had had enough. We spent an easy-going evening together. We were subdued, and deliberately did not talk about the case.

The Ten Traders area seemed quiet that night too. There were fewer people out and about, as happens for no obvious reason. Just when you think you have taken the measure of a place, people change their habits. Maybe for an evening, sometimes for ever. It reminds you to resist assumptions.

On that basis, I would cautiously avoid deciding yet that Thales, who had for so long been the alleged killer of his barmaid Rufia, had actually murdered his other barmaid, Rhodina. It was tempting. But why would everyone at the time of the murder fix on the wrong woman, not the victim in question?

Did two barmaids disappear simultaneously? Was that possible? People knew Rufia had vanished, but no one said anything about Rhodina. Why the difference? Either could simply have moved on to work somewhere else. A waitress with looks can always find employment; a waitress with only experience may find it harder, but she ought to succeed. If Thales was as awful as he sounded, and angry with her anyway, Rhodina might have slipped away without telling anyone. They might all have guessed why, so that aroused no comment. But why would the other one, Rufia, the queen of the bar, also go?

Stop, Albia! Let it rest. Cleanse your brain.

We retired to our room at an earlier hour than sometimes. Even the lumpy bed seemed attractive.

The ideal Roman wife is welcoming to her husband, not shy of intercourse. I might not be the safest choice for Tiberius now he wanted to remarry, but I would be a good wife to him. Well, once his wedding was over I would be. Meanwhile, when grey eyes turned to me with amorous intentions, he was the lover I wanted; it was easy to be welcoming.

We slept in each other's arms, even though it was a sultry night. The weather must be slowly building towards a summer storm, though so far it refused to break. We awoke to a hot, sticky morning. We were up early, finding the temperature already uncomfortable. I dressed in the lightest gown I had with me, plus my loosest sandals; I wore no jewellery. I hoped I would not be required to chase about. Today would be hard. It was going to be hot.

We bought bread, which we took to eat at the Hesperides, since Tiberius was supposed to meet Gavius there. The nightwatchman told us Gavius came last night on his own for an advance inspection of the counters. 'I'd better tell you – he sped off rather fast. I hope I didn't upset him.'

'Oh? What happened, Trypho?'

'He had two huge dogs with him. We got talking, so I told him you had found the landlord's old pet, and how it died by choking.'

Yesterday Tiberius must have told the workmen about Pudgy while I was talking to the two waiters. They then gossiped with Trypho. All our men were fascinated by the mystery of the skeletons; they were watching how Tiberius and I set about solving it. The foreman was probably holding bets on our success. Gambling for money was illegal but that never stopped anyone.

'So what was the problem, Trypho?'

'The dead dog, it seemed. Apparently, that one they unearthed was the grandmother of the man's own pets. He didn't like the story of the boot, so maybe that was it. He definitely took something I said a bit badly. He's coming back with a price for the smashed counters today. Maybe you can soothe him,' suggested Trypho hopefully, looking at me.

So that was to be my job. I married the firm's owner, then every time his workmen upset someone – Juno, they were builders; how often was that going to happen? – I would be the emissary they sent in. I made another mental note: our very clean Iberian kitchen maid had to be taught to bake must cake with a honey glaze, so I always had treats for peacemaking.

'How do you mean, "he took something a bit badly"? What exactly am I in for, Trypho?'

'I don't know. He seemed to grow very agitated; he said he wanted to talk to you. It's not my fault!'

'No, I suppose it's not. Gavius is very fond of dogs; perhaps he wants to know whose boot killed Pudgy . . . He could have come and found me last evening if he wanted to talk.'

'He said darkly that he wanted to think things through. When he left here, he went over the road to the Brown Toad for a drink, though I saw him leave soon afterwards.'

Trypho scuttled off to sleep. He left looking guilty. Tiberius thanked me in advance for my help with Gavius, twinkling more than usual. 'The woman's touch!' he murmured, subtly satirical.

While we were waiting for the marble-seller, we had another surprise visit from our wedding planners. They had no idea of helping busy people by making an appointment.

Julia and Favonia arrived in Mother's carrying chair, with Katutis obligingly trudging behind. Shrieking that they had something highly urgent to discuss in massive secrecy, they jumped out, grabbed me and rushed me away from Tiberius. I was told I could buy them refreshments while we talked. 'We don't have any money.' I could have guessed that. I managed to steer them past the Brown Toad, and sat them down outside the Medusa. Katutis very sensibly went on his own to the Romulus.

They stared at the Brown Toad. Antistius had described our visit. Presumably he left out the part where he tried to buy a bunk-up from the waitress and was offered Macedonian delight instead.

'How come you've been talking to the brother-in-law?'

'They came last night. Mother thought she ought to give them dinner.' I noted that she had kindly not invited us. 'No, she said you and Tiberius needed time on your own.'

'Mother is always right.'

'That's what she says.'

I summoned olive bowls and whatever could be provided that approximated to mint tea.

'May we have just a teensy snail shell of honey with it, if it's not too much trouble, please?'

'And possibly might I have mine in a glass, not a cup?'

Dear gods, these two were the daughters of an informer who ran an auction house, yet they had no idea.

While we waited the long time this outrageous novelty took to prepare (the chef actually popped out to have a look at us, with a sour expression), my sisters discussed the artistic merits of the painted gorgon's-head bar sign. Despite the stated urgency of their mission, they endlessly discussed the Medusa's wild snake hairstyle, which reminded them we were all to have a specially hired beautician to primp us fashionably on the wedding day. Although they conceded I must take precedence, they begged to be with her first. 'I know you're the bride, of course you are, but it's hardly worth bothering. Anything she does for you will be hidden beneath the saffron veil—'

'Hidden and flattened. Something absolutely needs to be done with Mother; she's so hopeless with hair and she's the matron of honour. The woman can then just fit you in. Albia darling, you do see?'

I saw. My day was really theirs.

'Tiberius will think you are gorgeous; he'll be so surprised you turned up, he'll be up there in heaven, slurping ambrosia on Mount Olympus.'

'Tiberius does not slurp. I wouldn't marry a man who cannot eat nicely. Mother must have told you its importance. Otherwise, it's the fast route to divorce because your husband is so irritating . . . I agreed to have this wedding. Tiberius knows I will be there.'

They wavered. My certainty was alien to these butterflies. They wanted everything to go right – yet they loved frightening themselves with pointless panic over what might go wrong.

Their refreshments came. As usual, they received exactly what they had asked for, delivered without comment. No wonder they never had any idea they were too demanding.

'So, Toodles and Floodles, what's urgent?'

For a moment they looked blank. 'Oh dear gods, Albia, it's *absolutely* terrible. We have forgotten the *most* important thing – we have to go shopping instantly!'

'I can't.'

'You must!'

'Why?'

'This could have been *such* a disaster. Listen – we still have to organise bride-and-groom presents!'

What?

'You know you and Tiberius have to give gifts to each other. Everyone will be s*hocked* if you don't. What are you getting Tiberius?'

'His best present ever: me.'

'Don't joke. We thought of an amazing thing you absolutely must give him: how about a gold torque?'

I sighed, but only to myself. In the fifteen years I had lived as one of the Didii I had become used to gifts with some perceived tribal connection. Anything British, Gallic, Belgic or German, or from anywhere the people looked goggle-eyed in their ethnic art, was deemed especially appropriate for me. Sometimes I pointed out that I wanted to forget mystic Britannia, scene of my tragic childhood. That made no difference.

My sisters were staring at me with new uncertainty. Julia

had the most sensitivity. 'Oh no! You don't think Tiberius is a torque man?'

'I am sure. He is very traditional.'

'Father has a torque.'

I huffed. 'It was a gift from a crazy king. Does Falco wear it? No, he has placed it around the neck of his bust of the Emperor Vespasian in his study. Don't you remember the fuss, because the necklace got bent in the process?'

'Well what instead? We spent ages and ages thinking up that idea. It seemed so perfect.'

'Time spent in thought is never wasted, darlings . . . Do you know what Tiberius intends to give me?'

'He claims it is a surprise. We bet he hasn't organised anything.'

'He will.' I would not waste energy hoping for earrings; his last gift to me was a stone bench. Exactly what I wanted at the time, and we were not even lovers then. Mind you, it was glaringly obvious we would be.

'So, what for him? Albia. Albia, Albia, choose something!'

It came to me of its own accord. When I was ill recently, while he nursed me, he had sometimes read, either to himself when I was sleeping or out loud to entertain me. Horace, he liked. I remembered parts of Juvenal. Cicero's brother on how to win votes in elections. We were close to the Argiletum, supposed home to many scroll-sellers, which would be convenient for the purchase. 'I shall give him a book.'

The girls were entranced. '*Oh – love poems!* You are brilliant. That is such a good wheeze.'

'No. Favonia, settle down and listen to me. Love poetry is either about love miserably denied, or a dead spouse, or it's too pornographic so Tiberius couldn't show people what he received. And on the whole it's terrible to read.'

They groaned. 'So what then?'

'He likes to know everything. I shall give him Pliny's *Natural History*. That purports to contain all the world's knowledge.'

There was a pause. 'It's an encyclopedia.'

'Shitty shit, Albia. Isn't it absolutely gigantic?'

'Don't swear. Thirty-seven scrolls, I believe. He will think this is very romantic, I promise you. Don't tell him.'

'Oh, Albia!'

'Do not tell him, Julia!'

My sisters were horrified by my grand idea. They wanted to argue. However, I sent them packing. A man had arrived over the road at the Garden of the Hesperides. From the way he was measuring up the bar counters, he must work with Gavius. I said I had to go.

I shepherded my sisters back into the chair, allowed them to lean out and kiss me goodbye, then I exchanged greetings gravely with Katutis, asking him to secretly fix up the encyclopedia purchase. By that time Tiberius and our foreman, Larcius, were outside the bar, in conversation with the newcomer.

His name was Appius. He was another hefty man in dusty clothes, one of the colleagues who had been present the night Old Thales quarrelled with Gavius. I went on the alert. That meant Appius knew, and had been entertained by, Rufia. He had been here shortly before the six dead people met their fates. I held back during the professional building talk, but I was waiting. Appius could tell me his version of what happened that night.

He was supposed to meet Gavius here this morning. They would confirm what repairs could be done, then work out costs. Strictly speaking this was a separate job, directly done for Liberalis, but Tiberius would oversee it as part of the main works.

I knew why. Project managers do not like two separately hired sets of builders on their site, in case of conflicts. Fair enough. Informers feel exactly the same way about other people getting under our feet and pinching our materials. My clue is not your clue, sonny. Shove off and eavesdrop on somebody else.

Gavius had said he would meet Appius for a bite beforehand. He never showed up. Appius kept muttering it was extremely unusual.

After a while, we could no longer ignore this. When Gavius still failed to put in an appearance, surprise became puzzlement, then concern. 'This is just not like him. Gavius never lets people down. He may have been delayed, but I'm beginning to think something must have happened . . .'

In the end, I suggested we should walk along to Mucky Mule Mews to look for him.

44

Gavius was a likeable man, with decent parents. I really did not want to see him harmed. But as soon as we reached the end of the alley, we knew.

Women were standing out on their doorsteps. A small knot of short, wide, horrible men with whips must be mule-drovers. A couple of raggedly dressed little children sat in the gulley by the non-existent pavement, watching the adults. Everyone seemed to be waiting. They stood and stared. They knew something was wrong. Nobody took the initiative. I'd like to say it would never have happened on the Aventine, but around Fountain Court it would have been worse; people would have shrugged and quickly gone on their way.

Neither of his parents was visible, thank goodness.

We went up to his door, where we learned what had attracted local attention. Inside, the two dogs who lived with him were howling incessantly. The double sound was so insistent, so mournful, hairs stood on end in response.

We knocked. This produced even more frantic noises from the dogs indoors. Occasional heavy thumps suggested they had thrown themselves against the door. In between the barks, they were now whining desperately.

My two male companions decided who must go to the parents to ask for a spare latch-lifter: me, of course. Appius must have known the old couple, yet he did not volunteer. I wanted us simply to break down the door, but was persuaded against that. Off I went dutifully, to somehow obtain the gadget without mentioning why we all thought it might be necessary. 'Aglaia and Thalia have been barking all night, disturbing people. Appius is afraid Gavius is ill, too many bar snacks maybe. We're just going in to see what is worrying the dogs . . .'

We could guess.

Gavius lay inside. His two distressed dogs were coursing around him. When we went in, they broke off and skittered up to us, making frantic noises and knocking into one another, but to our relief neither was aggressive. We tried calming them, talking to them by name. They at once resumed their howling and agitated running around their master.

He was lying on the floor. He must have been there all night. I saw blood. Not in great quantities, but on his tunic and all around his head.

I managed to grab the dogs' collars and hauled back hard to hold them. I had wondered if they would defend him against us, but we already knew these hulks were friendly; they made no attempt to stop us, though paws scrabbled hard on the floorboards when Tiberius went over. I was having trouble keeping them in check; they were so strong. Appius stood beside me, horrified, not helping.

Tiberius knelt beside Gavius for what seemed a long time. He felt the man's neck for vital signs, tested his wrists for a pulse, murmured something inaudible, then closed the eyes respectfully. He straightened.

'What happened?'

'Stabbed in the neck.' It must have been quick or there would have been more blood. Something slender. Pocket fruit knife? Reed-pen cutter? A blade you could hide about your person to avoid the law. I saw no sign of this weapon. Taken away afterwards.

'Oh, Gavius, Gavius old mate!' Appius crooned. His loss had him shaking his head over and over; we heard hopeless moans of protest. Gavius should not be dead.

Tiberius steadied him. 'Appius, I want you to run for a doctor. Just to make sure, but ask him to come quickly. Say an aedile requests it – and of course will pay for his visit.'

I released the dogs, unable to control them longer. They rushed back to Gavius, but now simply sat beside him whining or occasionally snuffling his body. I could not see his face, which was turned away from me.

Appius left us. He seemed glad to have something practical to do. Tiberius and I stood and breathed slowly, absorbing this.

Gavius had lived in a small rented room, as so many people did. Furnishing was basic. I had seen bleaker places, plenty of them. He kept his accommodation fairly neat. Perhaps his mother came and cleaned; perhaps he had been one of those men who do look after their nests. Various large feeding bowls for pets were in evidence; his own utensils were sparse by comparison. A doggy smell was everywhere; to me it was not objectionable. It looked as though officially they each had a blanket in a corner of the floor, but one or another may have climbed up on the bed every night to sleep with Gavius. Even if he grumbled, he would have allowed it, in reality welcoming them. Most nights he would have had drink in him anyway.

His animals gave him company. They were his children.

He would have been heartbroken to leave his darlings like this. They would be heartbroken too, once they understood their master and best friend was lost to them.

The bed was made, not slept in last night. Evidence on a table implied only one person had sat there with a cup of wine. There was no sign of a meal, though space was cramped; an unmarried man would eat out. We knew Gavius liked to spend his evenings in bars with his friends.

The door and window showed no damage, so whoever had come here, Gavius let them in. Of course a strong man in his own home, with huge dogs, would have felt safe. Or perhaps he knew whoever called. That might make them easier to find when I started looking. Them? I was assuming more than one person could have been involved.

They must have knocked. Gavius allowed them to come in, or they pushed in past him, though there was no sign of a disturbance. Did Gavius realise why they had come?

They cannot have stayed long. With little delay or disturbance, they knifed him to death. They must have brought the knife or dagger; they took it away afterwards. The dogs were no deterrent. They did not have to harm the dogs. So did they know the dogs? Did the friendly Graces recognise them?

Looking around the room, if anyone had stolen anything, I reckoned it was not much. Perhaps they took cash. Even if they did, that was not the primary reason for their visit.

They went, leaving the dogs inside with the body, closing the door. I doubted that anyone else in Mucky Mule Mews had had a break-in last night. If we asked the neighbours, they would all say they heard nothing. Not until this morning, when the desolate howling of Aglaia and Thalia told the world something definitely was not right.

45

Appius brought a doctor; Tiberius spoke to him in a low voice as they knelt to examine the lifeless man. Meanwhile, Appius and I put the dogs on their leads in case they ran away, then took them along to the parents' house. There, I explained as gently as I could how Gavius had been found murdered. Before grief kicked in properly, his mother and father seemed more bemused than anything. Of course they claimed he was the best of men; no one could hold a grudge against him, let alone wish him harm . . .

I had heard this before, on enough occasions to receive it warily. Parents never know as much about their children as they think. The best of men, supposedly, can turn out to be amoral swine. And someone not only wished real harm on Gavius, they made sure it happened.

That he was a dutiful son remained true. He had been to see his aged parents last evening as usual. They spoke of him being a little distracted. His mother had thought he was not taking care of himself, though his father said she always thought that. His father had supposed Gavius had business on his mind.

'Work worries?'

'No, his business ran fine. Just musing on his latest project. He loved his work. He always became very involved in each new contract; he would think about it night and day. We kept telling him to let go a little and enjoy himself, but work was his life. He knew everyone and they all liked him. He had built up the firm until he was the only marble-seller for far and wide. All for nothing! Whatever will become of things now?'

This was tactless, since we had Appius with us. Presumably he, or one of the others we had not yet met, would take over.

Was rivalry the problem? I would have to judge whether what happened to Gavius arose from tensions within the crew. While we were waiting for Gavius at the bar, Appius had already told us that he was the right-hand man, but it was a role he seemed to relish. Things ran smoothly, he implied. They were on good terms. I had no impression that Appius had felt dissatisfied, hankering for more influence. He seemed a natural follower and supporter. His reaction to finding the body looked genuine too. Either he was in real shock or, if he had known about this in advance, he was a good actor.

The parents suddenly demanded to see their son's body; we dissuaded them. For one thing, I realised Tiberius and the doctor were still there, no doubt discussing the cause of death.

Appius went out and found a sympathetic woman neighbour to sit with the old folk, who had both started to look much more frail and confused. The mother was frozen in misery; she said hardly a word. The father had to talk. 'It's always hard. When they are children, you know you must expect them to be at risk . . . once they are grown, you suppose the dangers are over for them. No parent expects to have to bury a fully grown son.'

The neighbour sat them down and covered both with rugs that she found somewhere.

Tiberius came; we left the mews. Appius took us to the marble yard, where we met the other men for the first time. There were two more gnarled, muscled specimens, used to carefully carrying heavy slabs of marble. Quiet men, dry sense of humour. Big men who became soft lumps when faced with trouble. Men whose wives generally dealt with anything difficult.

Tiberius said what had happened. I watched the men's reaction. They were stunned, then overwhelmed by it. With them, Appius now let go and showed his grief. One fellow said they needed a drink, so we could well have ended up in yet another bar. Inertia struck instead. They stayed at the yard.

We all sat around on piles of stone. It felt like respect to Gavius, who had loved his craft and personally selected the pieces we were sitting on. The crew said his knowledge of marble was unmatched, his enjoyment of materials wondrous. The trio talked about him quietly, their memories centred on how truly decent he had always been.

No one had expected to lose him. No one could imagine how their daily lives would be now, coping with the great hole of his sudden absence. Their anxiety was not for their livelihood. The work could carry on as before. Their troubled discussions concerned the loss of this crucial circle member. Their long-time leader. Their lifelong friend. As well as Appius, the other two said they would visit Gavius' parents. They were like a family.

They fretted about the orphaned dogs. The old couple could not be expected to manage all three. No decision was reached, but I could see that eventually these work colleagues would organise a solution. Something would be done. One of these men, or someone they knew, would give the Three Graces good homes.

They wondered about the funeral. They wanted to put up a memorial. A collection was made immediately, while we were there with them. Even the one the others teased for never having any money promised he would borrow some from his brother that evening. These were tight-bonded men. They had worked as a team for many years, socialising together too. Two of them were married to sisters. If there was a festival, they all went to the arena as a group.

What we saw at the marble yard was different from the looser, more fluid, more transient community of bar staff. Those workers often knew each other, but they came and went frequently; they were not linked by family or past history in the same way as the marble crew. I wondered if it was relevant.

We left the yard with Appius; he was going to the stone-recyclers' guild. Gavius had been an official, and the guild ran a funeral club. He walked to the main street with us, stopping at a fountain to scoop up a drink. He gazed at us. Something was coming. 'What's worrying you, Appius?' I asked quietly.

During our discussion at the Hesperides this morning, while we waited for Gavius, Appius had told us he and Gavius had met the previous evening at a caupona. Appius had thought it was a routine supper, to make a plan for a site inspection. Only now did he wonder, he said, whether Gavius had been preoccupied.

I glanced at Tiberius. He seemed quiet, upset by finding the body. Still brooding on it. For no obvious reason at that moment, it struck me that he had not sent for the vigiles. As an official, he would normally make that his first move.

I sat on the edge of the fountain, dabbling my fingers over the big rounded edge of the bowl into the water. My tunic soon felt wet from splashes on the warm stone, but the day was so hot it would dry fast once I moved off. I stared down into the fountain, not meeting his eye, as I pointed out to Appius that everyone would want me to find out who killed his colleague. My immediate line of enquiry had to be whether Gavius had had any quarrels.

I led this conversation unaided. Tiberius stood nearby, apparently lost in his own thoughts.

According to Appius, yes, there was occasional bad feeling, though by virtue of inhabiting the sales territory the locals would generally prevail. Gavius had seen off anyone else who tried to sell marble pieces, whether to bars or anybody else. Appius provided the details fairly willingly. Years before, there had been one tussle with some Numidians who had tried to move in on the trade. Foreigners had to understand they could bring their materials to Rome, but were expected to hold off from direct sales. They had to pass on their imports to local wholesalers, at a suitable price that would allow resident contractors their own traditional profits.

Since I was still trying to identify the five dead men at the Hesperides, I was interested in this competition. Appius agreed it could have been about ten years before. But there had only been two Numidians. Anyway, Appius had seen them a couple of times since, at the Emporium.

Not them then.

Another more minor issue, as Gavius told it, concerned attempts by a certain Arcadinus to undercut the trade in real stone in favour of cheaper painted mock marble, which he created. Arcadinus had made determined efforts to convince bar owners that painting was more fashionable, like putting fake garden designs on interior walls, or even outside in gardens. We had seen imitation marble at the Brown Toad, so at least one proprietor had fallen for it.

'Gavius saw him off. Arcadinus packed up his little fancy paint pots and has never been back.'

'But he was a one-man band?' I asked.

'He sometimes had a little lad to mix his colours.'

The bodies we found at the Garden of the Hesperides were certainly not a man and a boy. This was a red herring.

'How exactly did Gavius deal with such rivals?'

'Warned them off or froze them out.'

'No violence?'

'We are peaceable men. Besides, Gavius could sell a good deal to the clients, and he knew how to get in first. Newcomers could never push past us.'

So was there any more recent trouble not yet mentioned? No, Appius said; there had been no competition for years. Gavius had it all sewn tight.

'That won't be what got him attacked then,' said Tiberius in a sombre voice. His suddenly speaking made me jump.

'He wanted to see me today,' I remembered. 'Trypho told me.' I noticed Appius listening closely. I explained that our watchman had had an odd encounter. 'Something upset Gavius. Trypho had talked to him about Old Thales' dog being accidentally despatched by a barmaid called Rhodina. Does any of that resonate with you, Appius? When you saw him last night, did Gavius mention the guard dog dying?'

Appius now spoke slowly, as if he was thinking. 'He said Pudgy had been dug up again.'

'Just a few bones. And possibly the barmaid too, in her

case most of her.' I decided not to mention her severed head.

Even so, Appius blenched. He was pretty squeamish.

I apologised. 'I am sorry, that was too gruesome.'

For a moment I thought we were getting nowhere, then Appius suddenly admitted that he did know why Gavius had been upset. 'He told me in confidence.'

'He's dead, Appius,' I urged him gently. 'And it may help find his killer.'

Appius capitulated. Last night, Gavius had admitted something, though unknown to him his crew had known it all along: Gavius had had a soft spot for the beautiful Rhodina. They had palled up, even though she was officially the landlord's girlfriend. Gavius thought Rhodina regarded him as a special friend in whom she could confide behind Old Thales' back.

When I was talking to him about Rufia, I remembered Gavius saying, 'They had others there'; in retrospect, now I knew he had a fancy for one of the other staff, he had had a look in his eye. 'Did he sleep with her?'

'Everyone slept with her.'

That was business. For obvious reasons, while she was bedding Thales, any real friendship with another man had to be kept a secret.

'Did the rest of you reckon she saw Gavius as special?'

'We thought it was one-sided.'

'It would end in tears?'

'The poor fellow was fooling himself.'

Even so, Rhodina had confided in him. Gavius had known she was increasingly unhappy with Old Thales, Appius said. She talked about getting away. When Rhodina stopped serving at the Hesperides, Gavius assumed she had finally broken with the landlord. Then for ten years, Gavius meekly supposed she had upped and fled, without letting him know. He was hurt that she said nothing to him. Since nobody was supposed to know they were friends, there was nobody else he could talk to at the time about how upset he was. He simply accepted that she had not really liked him. He had been another part of her problems at the Ten Traders, someone else she must shake off. So he was conveniently dumped at the same time as Thales.

Men and women do delude themselves in relationships. When one party cannot take any more pretence, the one clinging on has a shock.

'Do you think Old Thales was aware Rhodina was close to someone?' I asked. Could her friendship with Gavius have caused what happened to her? 'Was Thales jealous? He owned the bar, I expect he felt he owned the staff too. Could that be the real reason he quarrelled with Gavius and threw your crew out of the Hesperides?'

'We all believed it was,' said Appius. 'We never said anything to Gavius. He was private. He would have hated to talk about it, especially since he thought Rhodina dumped him too. We looked after him, pretending not to notice, until he felt better. Until last night nobody ever mentioned her again. I was flummoxed when her name came up yesterday.'

'And why did Gavius say he wanted to talk now? Because Rhodina was blamed by Thales for killing the dog?'

'Oh no, he always knew that. It wasn't the dog, it was your man telling him Rhodina was buried in the garden. You see, until then we all thought Thales was so keen, he had no reason to do anything to her. Even despite his dog dying. Of course,' said Appius, 'Gavius being Gavius, he

287

was upset that Pudgy choked. He didn't blame Rhodina though. It made no difference to how he felt about her, though he could understand why Thales made a fuss. But last night your man told him Rhodina was dead and that got Gavius thinking.'

'Ah!'

'She was very good-looking.' Appius made this statement, then whistled and outlined with his hands a voluptuous figure. 'Not a young girl, mind. She'd lived with other men. She even had family. And that was why Gavius became curious yesterday.'

'Tell me.'

One reason Gavius had believed Rhodina left the Ten Traders of her own accord was that she had two infant children. She was bringing them up by herself; they probably had different fathers. It had never been a secret; Thales knew, Gavius knew, everyone did. For convenience, she kept them in a more suitable room elsewhere, not at the bar. A minder looked after them while she was working. When Gavius went there looking for her, this woman at the lodging said the children were gone. They had been suddenly collected and taken away; the minder was as surprised as anyone. Nor did she know where they went.

Until now, Gavius had always assumed the little ones were picked up by Rhodina herself, as she secretly escaped. But when Trypho had said her body was buried at the bar, he realised that could not be.

So who took those children? And where were they now?

46

We let Appius go off to the marble-suppliers' guild.

As Tiberius and I walked, I was thinking about who killed Rhodina, and why. And who attacked Gavius? Was it the same person? If so, it couldn't be Old Thales. If Thales killed Rhodina, why would anybody else need to stop Gavius talking to me about it?

I had no doubts the attack was meant to silence him. That meant whoever visited him knew about his plan to talk to me. How did the killer or killers find out? Appius had said nobody else joined them for supper. I would ask at the Brown Toad, where Trypho had seen Gavius go for a drink. Otherwise, he had a discussion with whoever came to his room, and that led to them killing him.

That would mean they habitually carried a knife. In Rome arms were illegal – although, as elsewhere, many in the High Footpath region ignored that. I had a 'fruit knife' myself. In case I needed to slice up an apple, of course, your honour.

I started to discuss this with Tiberius, pacing so silently beside me. 'The big problem is who now benefits from having Gavius dead—'

'No, stop!' he exclaimed. I was half prepared for it. I had noticed he was oddly introspective. His pace quickened, as if he had decided on a new destination. His expression became more open with me.

'What's up, Aedile?'

'I have to go back to the mews. I promised I would return to talk to the doctor after he finished. Then I need to explain something to the parents . . .'

'The doctor will be still there? What are you keeping from me? You examined the body – and you took your time, don't think I never noticed. Did you see something? A clue?'

'You could say that.' Tiberius took my hand as we walked, then he explained. 'Gavius was punched in the neck with a blade. Blood would have flowed straight away. He may have stumbled, he probably fell down. At that point I imagine the dogs became very excited. The attacker might have felt it imperative to get away from the dogs before they went for him. Because of the blood, it would have looked as if Gavius was already dead.'

'But . . . ?' I was already guessing where this would lead.

'The wound was not arterial; that would have been quickly fatal. The weapon must have missed the crucial spot . . . This is why I sent so urgently for the doctor. I didn't want false hopes for the parents – that would be cruel. But the doctor is going to work on him—'

'You mean—'

'Perhaps he can be revived, brought back, saved. He was still warm. I thought I felt a pulse. When I first looked at him, Gavius was still alive.'

47

I gathered my skirts so I could walk as fast as Tiberius; we hurried back to Mucky Mule Mews. Passing through the gawpers, we applied solemn expressions as if we had a further formality to carry out and re-entered Gavius' home. There, the doctor told us the 'dead man' was still breathing even now. The wound had been dressed. With attention, the medico thought Gavius might be saved, though it was not certain. We swore him to secrecy, then paid him off.

The plan Tiberius had was to quickly tell the parents, but nobody else. For one thing, he did not want a killer returning to finish the job. He also felt it might be useful to let any assailant believe the attack had succeeded.

Tiberius discovered there was a narrow walkway behind the buildings here. He went by himself while I sat with the patient. I dreaded to think what an alley behind Mucky Mule Mews was like but it allowed Tiberius to pick his way along, unseen, in order to fetch Gavius' mother and father. With instructions from the doctor, they would secretly tend their boy. They were a devoted family and he was physically strong. If he recovered enough to talk, they would send us a message.

We installed the parents as nurses, then we left; this time we did go back to the Vicus Longus.

★   ★   ★

It was still morning, though after such emotional upheaval it felt as if hours had passed. By mutual agreement, we went straight to the Brown Toad. One of the boy-girls was outside with a hand mirror, applying more Egyptian-mummy eyeliner. He-she called out lewd overtures to me, then when that failed tried Tiberius – even more of a mistake.

'Shut up and show me your registration, please.'

'What?'

'When you first took up your degrading profession, you should have put yourself on the prostitutes' roll. I am a plebeian aedile, you just propositioned me. I never screw illegals. I want to inspect your certificate.'

The pretty thing jumped up and fled with a string of curses.

I gazed at my bridegroom. 'If he had been legal, would screwing be considered?'

'Just talk.'

I left the officious Manlius Faustus on the bench outside, ready to harass members of the public; now he had started being doctrinaire, he needed to work it out of his system. He was in a starchy mood because of what happened to Gavius.

The lethargic waitress drooped out from the bar, to offer him a free drink. She must have overheard who he was. Tiberius asked for a jug of water. She was too limp even to look scandalised.

I passed indoors where, as I expected, Gran was rustling up today's big cauldron of 'staff' hotpot. 'You're too early! Give me a chance, girl.' Since I knew she was grandma to Gavius, Tiberius' plan of secrecy was putting me in a tricky position. I put off telling her.

I squashed myself neatly on a stool, keeping out of her way. I had been in a grandmother's kitchen while she knocked up dishes; I had been trained by many backhanded flips not to be a nuisance as a busy woman worked.

'Himself is outside,' I warned her.

'The girl will look after him.'

'Not his type.'

'Oh I remember. You think you are! Remember, if you can get through the wedding, you can get through life . . . When's the big day now?'

'Two days' time.' I managed to say it without shuddering.

'Better get a move on then,' she commented frankly. She was a true grandmother. 'If you really intend solving whose those old bones are.'

'Don't nag, Gran. I'm not messing about. I will solve it. And I'll discover who put them there. Listen, I only meant let's pretend that gorgeous tripe you're braising is some variety of pulse, shall we?'

The gran gave me a shirty look. She knew the rules; she knew how to get around them, too, but today she wasn't going to give in quietly. 'Now let me see. Pulses – what could that be? Beans? Kidney or broad, what's your fancy? Black, white, green, red, speckled or stripey as a duck's arse? I could do you peas, chickpeas, lentils, millet, barley, oats, vetch or lupins? No, I'm not inflicting lupins on anyone. That's donkey food. Seeds? Nuts? Walnuts, pine kernels, almonds . . . ?'

'Cobnuts. Enough!' I cried. 'Bloody hell, Gran. That's a market wholesaler's catalogue.'

She sniffed. There must be special lessons in being offended yet triumphant, lessons you can have when you are seventy-five and stroppy with it.

'What is it really?'

'What is what?'

I knew that game. 'You know. The tripe?'

'Liver.'

'Yum.'

'Everyone likes a bit of comfort food. I never use a recipe, I just put onions and a bit of pearl barley into everything. Sometimes I do liver, sometimes kidney. I like to put a pastry lid on kidneys. I don't enjoy cooking all the kinds of offal. Udders, stomachs – you can keep those. I feel funny if I have to handle brains.' After this speech, she continued rapidly chopping shallots. Her knife was an old, heavy, wide, wooden-handled one. Luckily I knew Gavius was hurt with a slim blade or I would have wondered whether the attack on him was a family affair.

'I'm drooling. I can wait a bit. Liver will just need a fast flash in the pan . . . I can't keep calling you Gran. What's your real name?'

'Everyone calls me Gran. What makes you so special, young woman?' I wanted to keep talking like this, to be nostalgic. What with the wedding, I must be missing my own grandmothers. She may have sensed my sadness, for she softened, as they do. 'It's Prisca.'

'Thank you. I appreciate the honour.'

I gazed at her. She paused in her vigorous chopping. We understood one another. She realised I had something to tell her.

'Prisca, I am very sorry, I have something bad to say.'

She laid down the knife gently, wiping her hands on her skirts. These were small, formal preparations so she was decently ready. 'Who died?' At her age, there was only one sorry message that solemn people brought to you.

Awkwardly deferring the moment, I asked slowly, 'Did you see Gavius here last night?'

'Who's gone for our Gavius? Is it him then?' She was upset, though perhaps not entirely surprised, I thought. 'What happened?'

'Did you see him when he came over?' She had seen him when he first realised Rhodina had been killed. I had to treat her as a significant witness, press her for her story before she knew what had happened to him.

'I might have been in here, just taking a tot for my arthritis. No harm in that.'

'Little warming drink. Helps you sleep despite the pain. At your time of life, you deserve it, Prisca.' I had been properly instructed in senior people's rights. 'So, tell me. When he came across from the Hesperides, all upset, did he say anything to you? His old grandma?'

'Of course. He's a big enough lump now, but I used to wipe his little pink arse. He can't keep much from me.'

'The story about Rhodina, the one-time barmaid? The one the men all hankered after?'

'Yes. I got that out of him.'

'Tell me exactly what he said, Gran. This is important. He talked to his mate, his backup in the business, Appius—'

'I know Appius. Get a move on. What's happened to my Gavius?' She had not forgotten my threat of bad news.

'You guessed, Gran. I am sorry to be the one who has to tell you.'

'Albia, stop messing with me.'

Obediently I told her. 'He was attacked. Someone went to his house last evening. He let them in. They stabbed him in the neck. We found him lying on the floor a little while ago.'

'He's dead?'

It was no good. I had to ease Prisca's misery. If it was

bad enough for parents to lose children in their lifetime, how was it for a grandparent? Prisca spoke of Gavius as a favourite. So I told her he was in great danger but we needed to pretend he was actually dead.

'I'll have to go and see him.'

'No, Gran. His parents will look after him. This is for his safety while they try to save him. Just make sure everyone knows you're heartbroken.'

She was silent, resisting me, then she burst out instead: 'Were those dogs with him?'

'Going crazy.'

'Who's got his dogs? All he would care about would be the dogs.'

'His parents have all three, at least temporarily. I suspect Appius will help sort something out. The men are all devastated . . . I'm doing what I can to discover who attacked him. So now can you tell me, please, what Gavius said to you.'

She set about it, an efficient storyteller. It was identical to what Appius had said, though flavoured with sneers about her grandson's foolish fancy for Rhodina. 'I forgot all about her years ago, but when he said it, I remembered. I didn't think much of her. Flirty, bosomy little piece. I can tell he really wanted her – and he never bothered with anyone afterwards. I thought our boy had a lucky escape there. You want to know about the barmaid? If you ask me, that one was only interested in finding some man soft enough to be conned into bringing up her children. That Rhodina. She was one of those types, you know – a man only had to wink at her and she fell pregnant. Of course that wasn't her fault. Some women just can't help conceiving.'

'She could have kept to herself.'

'Oh she worked in a bar, Albia! No hope of keeping her legs crossed. She would have lost her job.'

'She bore two little tots, apparently.'

'And some.'

'There were more?'

'I'm sure.'

'So she wasn't young?'

'She *started* young.'

'They all do. Be fair – they have to, Gran. Whether it's their own sad choice or they are slaves and shovelled into it. Did the other babies die naturally, or did she get rid of them? Did Rufia help her sort herself out?'

'I wouldn't know. I never did anything like that, and none of my daughters neither. Well,' said Prisca, being realistic. 'As far as they ever told me.'

I was still thinking about the barmaid's little ones. 'If it wasn't Rhodina who picked up the two children that night, can you suggest anyone else?'

Prisca shrugged. 'Someone who wanted a ready-made family? Must have been someone who knew that Thales or someone had polished off that Rhodina and buried her. Then, since we live in a cruel world, most likely they thought they could make some money selling the brats to a slaver. I expect they were horrible, snivelly little things.' She implied 'not like my grandchildren'. It was probably true, since her descendants would be chubby and contented on kidneys in a pastry lid, oozing with gravy . . .

'I don't suppose their lives were very happy,' I said. 'Weren't they very small? Yet old enough to be left with a minder. If they are still alive, they must be coming up to adulthood; they will remember nothing of their mother or her history.'

'So you can't expect to find them?' Until that moment I had not intended even to look. Damn. As an informer I was always picking up this kind of responsibility.

'Only if I can learn who took them. It's a very small chance.' Almost not worth bothering, Albia. Leave it alone!

'It's not their fault, the life they were born into. If anyone had known, people would have tried to do something for them, I expect. Our Gavius would have looked after them, he was silly enough. Put them down to sleep on a dog blanket. Added two bowls to the row . . .' She was sniffing now, buffing at her eyes irritably with the back of her wrist.

'I know. Your grandson is a good one.'

'The best.' She started crying properly. On principle she blamed the onions, but I was allowed to acknowledge what had really caused her tears.

I had to sit with her while she grieved over the danger her grandson was in. She refused fuss, so I stayed there very quietly.

It struck me nothing is as simple as it looks. I could easily dismiss the Ten Traders and White Chickens as filthy enclaves of vice: all drink, prostitution, extortion and slave-trading, alien to respectable people like me and Tiberius. Yet he and I had both done things we would never talk about at dinner parties.

And here, despite the rawness, it was still possible to expose pockets of normal family life. Some people had skills, held down regular jobs in the community at large. Walk in here, past the peculiar-sexed doll with the livid eyeliner, and you found an ordinary grandmother cooking up a stew using age-old peasant ingredients, utensils and methods. Comfort food, tasty and gelatinous, always with pearl barley because that was her way of doing it. She saw the vice, yet somehow kept apart from it; in her world there was family love and even compassion for orphans of flirty flibbertigibbets.

I myself had once been fostered into that kind of environment. It could be harsh. There was no luxury. But it nurtured life, and where there was life there could eventually be chances.

Maybe, I thought, what happened at the Garden of the Hesperides had nothing to do with drink, prostitution, extortion or slave-trading. Those things only provided a background. It was about domestic emotions, not trade.

Mind you, if so, it had been carried out and concealed rather professionally.

I was on the verge of leaving. I could no longer bear the strain of this fond grandmother's unhappiness for her Gavius. I wanted to trust her, but I probably should not have told her the truth; the point was for the villain or villains to see everyone reacting as if Gavius was genuinely gone. Still, Prisca's tears were perfect. Besides, Gavius might yet die on us.

Just as I took my leave, his grandmother burst out with something: 'You mentioned Rufia.'

'Yes?'

'I don't think she would have helped that other one. She hated her.'

I paused. 'What happened? Jealous of Thales bunking up with Rhodina? Younger, prettier, bustier and more successful with the men?'

'I don't know about jealous. But Rufia had always reckoned Rhodina meant trouble. She tried hard to persuade

Old Thales to get rid of her. Stupid, really. You know men; that only helped make him notice her.'

'I know. If you want a man to do something, Gran, just tell him not to.'

'I never went to the Hesperides,' said Prisca. 'We didn't have much money so I used to put meals together for them all at home. When we had an outing we used to go to the big thermopolium on the Clivus Salutis where they do a lot of fish and they welcome family parties. So I can't tell you all of it. But you hear things. There was a struggle going on there over something, that's a certainty. And Rufia was always going to come out on top.'

So you had to wonder. Could the barmaid everyone always thought had been murdered, in fact be behind the other killings?

48

When I went outside, Tiberius' water jug was empty. He gave me a questioning look, as if I had been a long while, though he had waited patiently.

Coinciding with my emergence, people turned up at the Brown Toad and made for the interior I had just left. Foremost was Menendra, followed as always by her two men. Macer must have let them go. I suppose they had not actually done anything (anything he knew about). Trypho had not identified them and Macer did not want the burden of documenting an arrest.

Today the heavies had satchels slung over them; Menendra was carrying a note tablet and stylus. They looked curiously like a bunch of auditors descending for an inspection.

'Hold it, Menendra! The old cook indoors just heard that her grandson has been killed. She's extremely upset. Give her some recovery time.' Watching closely, I detected some flicker in the woman's harsh features. 'Gavius,' I said softly, letting Menendra know I was checking her reaction. 'He lives in the same alley as the people you tried burgling. Maybe you know something about it?'

'Why should I?' As usual she went into angry mode. 'Shift out of my way, Albia.'

Staying put, I gestured to the writing equipment. 'Doing a fruit-bowl survey?'

She stared. She must have forgotten I had been told by the Dardanian girls that she supplied orchard produce. We all knew that was an invention. Convinced that whatever Menendra did now had once been Rufia's scheme for self-enrichment, I held out my hand imperiously, asking to see her tablet.

Tiberius stood up from his bench and seconded me. 'Show us your notes, please.'

Everything turned nasty. I tried to take the tablet. Menendra refused to let me. I grabbed hold. We tussled for possession, tugging at the wooden boards. I was biting my lip; she was cursing me.

At the same time, her two men fell on Tiberius. They seized his arms, toppled him over backwards onto the outdoor table and started slamming his head against the boards. They looked about to crack his skull open.

'Leave him!' I yelled. I let go. Menendra staggered. Tiberius, who was sturdy enough, was fighting back, though he was at a two-to-one disadvantage and already down. Dammit, I was not prepared to lose my bridegroom before we even sacrificed the sheep. 'This man is an aedile and sacred to Ceres. Touching him offends the great goddess. Stop, or you will be hanged for it.'

This was true. Aediles had no bodyguards because they were sacrosanct. Also true was that Faustus stood little chance. His attackers had no more to lose. 'What can you do?' jeered Menendra.

'Have you all arrested.' My mood had changed. My voice was dangerously quiet. She heard it and signalled to her men, who grudgingly released their victim. Then I shouted to Macer, whom I had just seen approaching down the street with a group of vigiles, probably coming to see us.

*   *   *

'Good timing!' gasped Tiberius, hauling himself upright while the troops grabbed his assailants.

I rounded on Menendra. 'You think you control this area – but see, the rule of law still holds!'

Tiberius held up a hand to indicate I should be calm. Without being told, Macer and his men were searching the three in custody. They emptied out the heavies' bags, adding Menendra's note tablet to a pile of others that scattered on the table. They found purses containing a small amount of money, then stripped each man of lethal-looking knives.

Macer was cheerful. 'Oh joy. I can have them for going tooled up.' Arms were illegal. Even the Praetorian Guards wore togas and pretended to be harmless civilians. The ruthless bastards took a sinister relish in this joke.

Tiberius looked closely at the knives. 'I can't see any blood, but this one—' He balanced a stiletto on one hand. 'This could be what was used to stab Gavius the marble-supplier. It was a narrow blade.' He explained to Macer how Gavius had been attacked, letting it sound fatal.

Macer knew that his cohort had been asked to keep an eye on Mucky Mule Mews after the parents had their attempted burglary. He could have felt he had let that family down – but as a vigiles officer he had no truck with guilt. There were so many worse failures to burden his busy conscience.

He announced, rather pompously, that since the men had been involved in a killing he would haul them to the station house again, Menendra too. They protested – a formality. He laughed and told them on his watch you were guilty until proved innocent. In fact, traditionally, you were guilty until 'proved' guilty. 'Especially if I don't like the look of you.'

Since I was there, Menendra was searched too, by me. I discovered nothing but Macer said, 'I'll find a cell for you too. You look like a whore who is bound to have done something.' Roman justice. It dated back to Romulus. Those Sabine women were delighted to be abducted. What were they complaining about; they got husbands, didn't they?

In her good clothes and in middle age, Menendra did not look much like a prostitute, though she was hard enough to have been one once. While she argued, I examined the various note tablets turned out on the table. I thought if she really had taken over Rufia's full range of activities, they would contain sordid details of women who slept with customers in bars, maybe even client names and brothel accounts. Arrangements with slave-importers and foreign traffickers. Notes of which pathetic mites worked where, what income came in from fornication, hours, percentages, price lists.

Not exactly. Big surprise. There were prices all right. I found rates for the following: barley, oats, buckwheat, millet, peas, chickpeas, split peas, beans in endless varieties, linseed, sesame, even gourds. *Nuts, seasonal, apply for prices ...* One set of notes contained a list of eating houses. It had monetary figures, sometimes with pay-day ticks.

Astonished, I stared at Menendra. She glared back defiantly. I said, 'Either "Mustard Seed" and "Broad Bean" are your secret codes for sex workers, or these figures reveal your trade is far more mundane – you deal in *pulses*?'

She enjoyed my shock. 'That got you! I am the dry-goods queen. Think about it.' Now she looked like a miser counting his gold, salivating over every coin, calling the big aurei his darlings. She positively revelled in her commercial power. Part of her joy was that nobody, including me (especially me), had realised a financial empire could be created in this specialised field. 'How many food shops and bars exist in Rome?'

'Oh I get it. You have identified a real niche market. High commerce is all about three things: wine, olive oil and wheat. But up goes an imperial edict saying "Serve no meat" – then suddenly the food of the common people becomes a vital commodity too.'

'There wasn't enough; Rufia saw that. She started a little lupin round. There still isn't enough of the right stuff – or not conveniently available, not in good quantities, not in enough variety. We make arrangements so the bar owners don't have to. They love us for it.' Her glare was as unpleasant as she could make it. 'This is not illegal. I am helping keep people's bellies full, with foods that the Emperor wants them to guzzle. You cannot touch me.'

'That's right,' I agreed, not disputing her claim. 'Every time some hungry worker orders a pottage of green lentils on his way to his employment, you are acting as Rome's saviour. I shall suggest you be awarded a medal – though that may have to wait, Menendra, until we know whether you had a hand in stabbing Gavius.'

Menendra and the men were dragged away by the vigiles. Macer stayed behind with us. He and Tiberius gazed at me with a mix of amazement and satire.

'So that's it.' Tiberius was gentle in his mockery. 'First you have a garden full of bones, but the only corpse you can identify is the landlord's dog.' Listening, Macer snorted. Tiberius lovingly murmured: 'And now, my sweet, you are investigating lentils!'

49

I was probably not looking at a grocery war; the idea seemed
ridiculous. However, I smiled quietly and said sometimes
the smallest thing can rouse a storm of passion. Macer, a
literalist, flapped the neck of his tunic and answered that
he wished the weather would break and give us a real storm
to clear the air. Though wiry, he was feeling the heat. We
were all sweating lightly.

The fragile creature with the face paint was edging closer
to the Brown Toad, trying to reoccupy his-her propositioning
seat. For a private chat we moved along to the Four Limpets,
which looked quiet. That too had tables illegally blocking
the pavement, where we sat. It didn't matter about us not
wanting to order anything, because all the time we sat there
no staff came out to ask. A board claimed the legitimate
dish of the day was porridge; I had started to make a point
of checking what grains were offered. With the presence of
an aedile in the area, prominent signs offering utterly blameless menus had popped up all over the place. It should do
wonders for Menendra's business plan.

The Limpets' L-shaped counter was in three shades of
grey. I was now noticing that too. The sign depicted only
three conical seashells, not four, though their noduled rays
were finely drawn. I saw a basket for a cat or dog, though
it must have gone out for a walk. Their price list showed

not only wines but how much it cost per session for Orchivia or Artemisia. Virginity was extra. Some joker had added that in different chalk.

Macer was here in reply to our message about needing an overview of extortion in the Ten Traders. It had only taken him a day to respond. He seemed to think we should thank him for making it so urgent. He pointed out that he did have other work; for instance it was the tribune's birthday yesterday, which required a whole day's celebrating. Their governor was a sad case who had no family. Anyone could see why. Nevertheless the lads did their best to compensate him for being so unlikeable. At least, they did when he was buying. 'Was it you who sent me a bright-burning lamp called Juventus? Burbling on about "liaising" on a "special project"? Completely bonkers. What a sad-arsed clown.'

'Must have come of his own accord,' Tiberius assured him gravely. 'We would never do that to you.' So Macer knew it was our fault. He seemed to bear no grudge.

Thinking about Juventus made Macer thirsty. He went into the bar, where he whistled for a waiter, gaining no response. This place was dead. Undeterred, he chose a beaker, selected a wine jar from a shelf, sniffed it, poured a large drink for himself, wiped a drip off the jar with his finger and licked it, then clinked a copper or two in a saucer. When he came back to us he sat for a moment taking his drink. We waited politely.

His gangster overview was short. The Ten Traders territory was currently claimed by old Rabirius, overseen through his hard man Gallo. The young nephew Roscius had his eye on the neighbourhood too, but so far had made no move. Macer agreed that Gallo would try to lean on Liberalis even though his bar was closed for renovation; however, he thought it unlikely the gang would have destroyed our site. It was in their interests to keep places decent in order to earn more money. The Rabirii *liked* improvements to be made. And whatever Liberalis had told us about not paying, he probably had done so, or soon would.

Regarding the attack on Gavius, Macer doubted it had been carried out by the Rabirius gang. It had all the wrong signatures. The key points were: *one*, that the hideous Gallo would have killed the dogs as well, no question, plus *two*, when intent on silencing someone, he would never leave his victim alive. If we needed even more convincing, Gallo's method was to batter people. He wanted the results to look spectacularly painful, to instil terror into others. Anyway, he enjoyed doing it.

We were gloomily silent for a while.

I asked whether Macer knew anything about the pulse-suppliers. He said no, though it sounded very interesting. He might look into it.

I could tell what that meant.

Ha!

50

'Never mind,' teased Tiberius. 'You have plenty to do trying to identify the deceased chicken.'

He had kindly waited until Macer had left before he started ragging. Even so, I felt my hackles rise. If there had been any way to trace the late and unlamented fowl and its one-time owner, or if there was any point in doing so, I would have set about it, just to show him.

Despite knowing better, I started thinking about that chicken bone.

Next thing, I had asked Tiberius the name of the under-takers who had taken away our skeletons – and off I went by myself to have another look. Some informers would not have bothered. I like to be thorough (when I can think of nothing else to do). But do not mock. I was about to prove that diligence pays off.

51

Tiberius and his workmen were going over to Lesser Laurel Street. He looked amused at me going to see the undertaker. 'You're the expert! I reckon the key to this is whether the chicken clucked in the Dorian or Lydian mode . . .' Leaving him, I raised my arm in that universal gesture meaning, *Go wrap yourself around a standard-bearer's pole, Smarty!*

I found the undertaker's. In view of the heat, he had no trade. Even the bereaved were staying at home while they let their dead go blue and bloated on the bier in the atrium. I wondered if the deaths at the Hesperides took place during hot weather; it could have been an extra factor for burying the victims fast.

At the funeral company, I was a welcome surprise. Well, any lone female – especially a live one – was welcome, though the fellow did not push it. Mentally I thanked him. I was too hot to start fending off a grabber. Still, I wished my tunic was less flimsy and not sticking to me in the heat.

His name was Silvinus. He attended the upper level of High Footpath society. This was not a large client base, since people there were either low-born or so lofty they spent all their time in palaces and villas. The Flavian emperors and members of their family owned private homes on the Viminal, but they tended to die either at or on their way to their many country estates. Diarrhoea polished some of them off, though not Domitian, unfortunately.

Despite his empty order book, Silvinus had a hopeful expression and, given the nature of his business, an incongruously bright outlook. I explained who I was and what I wanted to inspect. He gurgled how lucky it was that he had followed the aedile's orders and kept the bones in a box, when he could have spread them around other people's cremation pyres. I answered coolly, yes it was.

He fetched them all out. Realising that the female pelvis almost certainly belonged to someone I could now name gave me an odd jitter. I had seen bodies, but this must have been the first time I looked at bare bones and knew something about their owner. I commented as much; the undertaker nodded. He said most of the bodies he received were strangers to him, and frankly that was how he preferred it. When friends of his died, he asked a colleague to embalm them.

He was more refined than the funeral director I had recently taken to using for unidentified corpses. Unlike the disreputable Fundanus, little about Silvinus suggested he played with the dead for secret sexual pleasure. This did not make him entirely civilised. 'Keeping the skeletons for a while', as requested by Manlius Faustus, meant they were disrespectfully jumbled in a large chest, so broken-up and higgledy-piggledy they could never be reassigned to sets. 'So what will you do if a relative is found? If they want to reclaim one of the bodies?'

'Ask pertinent questions to weed out a description, then use my skill to put together a few bones that look nearest.'

'In fact, we thought the males all looked similar in build. Maybe they worked in the same profession, or came from the same village.'

'Want my expert opinion?' he offered, carrying on whether I wanted it or not. 'One of these men's nasal bones survived, which doesn't always happen. See . . .' He rummaged merrily among the skulls, tossing aside the noseless ones. 'He must have had a hooked snout; could have been eastern. Possibly even North African, but if so, from the Greek end of the Mediterranean.'

'You are talking Egypt?' I suggested.

'This nose would look very appropriate in the Nile basin. But it's only a guess. Half the republican Senate had a beak like this, if you believe the Forum statues.'

'It would cause a stir if I said five senators were buried under the Garden of the Hesperides. A cynic might mutter in that case it was no surprise nobody noticed them missing for the past ten years. But disappearing senators are unlikely . . . I can tell you take an unusually keen interest in features,' I complimented Silvinus.

'The only way the dead can communicate. "*When I was alive I looked like this. Drink up and enjoy your time, for you will soon be ashes*" . . .'

Silvinus himself had a bald head and significant ears. Perhaps they helped him catch the faint sigh if ever a corpse had been brought in mistakenly. It would prevent that nightmare nervous people have, where they are helplessly buried or burned alive.

'Now, Flavia Albia, to work! What are you looking for?'

'A little fragile scrap of rib. One of the vigiles told us it was a chicken bone.'

'Ah, that!'

'You know what I mean?'

'I saw it.'

'I hope you didn't throw it out?'

'Oh no.' Did a strange expression appear then? 'Your man miscalled it.' Well that was Morellus. 'Definitely not poultry in my humble opinion – which is never wrong. Are you here because you suspect as much, Albia?'

'I don't know what I suspect,' I answered honestly. 'I feel uneasy – the more I think about it, the more I have to take a second look.'

'Well, that's understandable!' he commented obliquely.

Silvinus began excavating in his assembly of bones, which took a long time since the rib in question was so small. At first he followed the well-known masculine route of tossing stuff around unsystematically, soon losing track of what he had searched already. Bones were broken in the process. Eventually I managed to prod him into being more methodical. When he had searched through and set aside about a quarter of the remains, he reached in and picked out what we wanted.

I managed not to say wasn't he glad he did it my way? I just smiled and thanked him. Better keep him sweet. I still needed his expertise.

The fragment looked as much like a chicken bone as when I first saw it. I reminded Silvinus that the skeletons had been found in the backyard of a bar, where all manner of food leftovers could have been chucked out for decades. 'It seems reasonable that this should be a relic of somebody's Chicken Vardana.'

'Doubt it. A customer might toss a small bone over his shoulder onto the ground if he was badly brought up. Invariably, a dog or cat or vermin would remove it,' Silvinus demurred. 'How many rats do you think live in the average eating house?'

'Too many! And indeed the bones were buried deep. I accept what you say. So what is it?'

'Did you dig up any other food remains?' I had agreed with him, but he kept pressing his point, clearly proud of his skill. 'Bars cannot afford to hurl their cooking products out into an area where people will sit. Customers will be put off by awful smells, and scavengers running over their feet. No, no, cookshops and bars will take their rubbish to the nearest dump outside. Let the rats run wild at the end of the street or, better, in someone else's street.'

'Right. So was this some hasty sacrifice, buried with the dead?' While he lectured me, I was holding the tiny piece of bone in the palm of my hand. 'I suppose I am now half prepared for your verdict, Silvinus,' I hinted.

He accepted the prod. 'It was a kind of tragic sacrifice. A soul was given to the gods . . . That is from a child, Flavia Albia.' He broke the news gently, so I was braced. 'In my view, that is a rib from a baby.'

I let out an unintended sigh.

Having broken the news, the undertaker went into unrestrained macabre detail: 'It was probably unborn. Could have been lying in the pelvis and became separated when the workmen were digging.'

'It's true they were not careful with the first body they found. The woman had perhaps been disturbed; a lot of her is missing.'

Silvinus would not be deterred. 'Alternatively, sometimes in burials the body's gases expel a foetus into the grave. Don't ask me how I know about that.' Pointedly, I did not ask, so he told me anyway. 'If you are digging a hole for a funerary urn and you come across an old grave, you can occasionally find the baby has been pushed out between a woman's thighs. I mean, after she was put in the ground.'

'Alive?' I revised my opinion: *all* undertakers are grue-some. 'I mean the baby.'

'Not for long!' If he saw my face, he ignored my qualms. 'Almost certainly the foetus would be dead when its mother was interred. However, there is a school of thought that expulsion can happen even while a female corpse is being laid out. It's a horror story directors use to scare their apprentices.'

Since I was not his apprentice, I did not need scaring. I checked that he was certain about the bone. 'It's from a foetus then. Once we knew what we were excavating, care was taken. Why did we only find one rib?'

'How old is your burial?'

'Ten years.'

'No coffins?'

'Bare earth.'

'That's your answer. Lost over time. All the other baby bones must have decayed completely in the soil.'

'Even the little skull?' I really did not want the child to have been beheaded like its mother.

'The head would be soft and unformed, remember. So yes, it could vanish into the earth. I don't know why this single rib should have survived on its own. No reason. Just coincidence.'

I felt the structure of my case shift. If the skeleton was Rhodina, she had been pregnant. From the size of the child's rib, Silvinus believed she must have been showing, and more likely into her final trimester, so everyone who saw her would be aware of it. This could be so relevant. All kinds of dynamics might have been altered by her expecting a baby. It could be simple: this was a reason why she wanted to free herself from Old Thales. It could be why *he* wanted to get rid of *her*. Or it could have affected other people.

Several suspects in my disreputable cast list might have felt annoyed or threatened by the potential child. Sometimes repercussions will depend on who the baby's father is, though with a bar waitress there was no way she could have known. Did that matter? When a father is named by a woman, it can stick, however ridiculous her claim. She couldn't prove who was responsible – but nor could anyone prove it was not the man she named. What might matter in my investigation was who she *said* he was, and whether he accepted it.

If Rhodina was bright, she might have used her pregnancy for manipulation. For her, this baby could have seemed an opportunity to give her family and herself a better life. From what I had heard about her, that was a real possibility.

52

I now felt there were two aspects to this enquiry. Perhaps they were unrelated. One was the tempestuous Thales/ Rufia/Rhodina triangle. I considered Gavius, too, but reckoned he had been merely on the sidelines of the main tragedy.

The other mystery was the five men who died. Their identity remained as unknown as the day we uncovered their skeletons. They could have been from the east, but that might be wide of the mark. I had discovered no clues to their identities, nor could I say why someone had methodically deleted all five from earthly existence.

The second question would have to wait until I turned up something I could bite on. On the first, little by little, as I massaged potential witnesses, I had come to know the characters involved. That helped suggest motives. Motives helped me see what to tackle next.

I knew what I wanted to explore: the inheritance. When I discussed it with Tiberius before, it had not seemed necessarily significant. How much money did Liberalis have, and what proportion of it derived from Thales? I remembered saying I could find out via the amount of tax he had paid on his legacy, at which Tiberius had cynically guffawed. But there was a way to check more accurately. Never mind the tax; I needed Thales' will.

I was ready to leave Silvinus, but on the off chance I

asked, 'You conduct most funerals around the High Footpath, you said? So did you happen to send off Old Thales to his gods? The landlord of the Hesperides?'

'I did.'

'Oh! Can you remember when it was? The new landlord told my partner it happened about six months ago – I'd like to have a more exact date, if possible.' I decided to explain why; Silvinus was a fellow professional. 'I am hoping to track down his will – if they deposited a copy in the archives as they should have. I think he must have had one, because of giving the bar to Julius Liberalis.'

'He did. I heard them read it.'

'Oh wonderful!'

Silvinus was such a very useful witness, informed and willing to volunteer information; he made a pleasant change. 'They didn't bother waiting the nine days of formal mourning,' he said.

'Liberalis was bursting for confirmation the bar was his. He told me that he was the only obvious legatee. That might explain the rush.'

'If he was sure he would get it, why did he seem so anxious?' mused Silvinus. 'It felt as if he was afraid there might be rival contenders.'

'Were they at the funeral?'

'No. By the time Liberalis was appointed executor and sole heir, he was the last man standing.'

'He often seems nervous. He had waited a long time for the bar, so perhaps he just needed formal reassurance . . . You were invited to the will reading?'

Silvinus grinned. 'Not exactly "invited". After we burned Thales, they had a get-together back at the bar. I am a little bit nosy, I'm afraid. I made sure I tagged along.'

'Well practised!' I smiled back.

'Of course. Supervising a pyre is thirsty work. I do feel people want to be appreciative if you take care of their loved ones. Even if they forget to ask me, I assume they meant to.'

'You could save me a very time-consuming trip to the Atrium of Liberty.' Copies of executed wills are supposed to be archived, in case the original is ever lost. But people can deposit them anywhere suitable, in temples for instance. I had been caught out before through not knowing the right place to look. Sometimes I don't want to ask the parties involved.

'I can tell you everything!' Boasting, Silvinus looked as if he was wondering what it was worth to me. We were getting on so well, why spoil it? I had no wish to find out that his idea of payment was something other than coinage.

'Spill then!' I urged, pretending to be taken up with excitement, brushing aside any ideas he had. 'Oh this is so good, Silvinus!' I sounded like Julia and Favonia with a new wheeze. 'Liberalis was given the bar. What interests me is whether there was more to pass on to him? I don't know whether he had any money to start with – or even whether Thales was financially sound, come to that?'

Silvinus let himself be overcome with the fine joy of sharing knowledge. 'Julius Liberalis was left enough to pay for a big funeral, with endless trays of stuffed vine leaves afterwards for a large section of the neighbourhood.'

'Thales was very popular? There were a lot of mourners?'

'He was and there were.'

'Well, I dare say when a bar owner dies, even people who never patronised his place suddenly feel a great fondness for him and want to raise a free wine cup . . . Was it your first visit? Did you drink there normally?'

'No. A lot of my work takes place at night.' Funerals have to happen after dark. 'By the time we get back from the necropolis afterwards, put away the equipment and lock up, all I want is my bed. But I went to that wake and I was surprised. Thales owned a big place. No wonder Liberalis was so keen to have it.'

'What did Thales die of?' I shot in, suddenly wondering. So far nobody in my investigation had mentioned it, but his undertaker would know.

Silvinus enjoyed telling me. 'Age, drink, overeating, shoddy living. Wine, women and song, or as we define it in the trade, natural causes.'

'His time had come?' I was glad to hear at least one person in the Ten Traders managed to pass away in non-suspicious circumstances. 'And tell me, Silvinus, apart from the bar itself and the price of a good funeral, did he leave a pile? Was he very wealthy?'

Once again my informant took huge pleasure in his revelation: 'You mean, Flavia Albia, in addition to the premises and profits – plus his gains from gambling?'

'*Gambling?*' That was a new side to his character. 'Old Thales was a gambler? Successful with his bets?'

Silvinus shook his head; I had misunderstood. 'I expect he did place the occasional wager. I am not talking about that. Of course they keep it very quiet, but the Garden of the Hesperides has always had a secret reputation – at least so people tell me – for serious illegal betting. People came long distances on special nights. A hard core of regulars. I suppose Thales allowed it, always on the basis that he took a cut.'

I blinked. 'Let me guess. Legitimate food and drink sales are out front at the counters; fornication goes on in the rooms upstairs – meanwhile the boards are set up and the gambling occurs privately in the courtyard at the back?' Silvinus pretended that a man like him, who liked an early night at home, could not possibly know. 'Pull a curtain across the corridor and it's out of sight from the street,' I continued. 'Being in the garden gives them time to drop any evidence into a bucket if someone whistles that the law is coming. The vigiles walk in, only to find them all daintily picking at olive bowls.'

'That is assuming the law do not engage in bets like everyone else, Flavia Albia.'

'Of course they love it.' That is why you never see any court cases on the subject. There are even board games scratched onto the steps of the Basilica Julia. Quite often it's barristers playing, with decrepit old judges leaning in to watch.

I remembered the year the Flavian Amphitheatre opened, that long city party with its hundred days of games; it was also a hundred-day-long excuse to make the whole of Rome a gigantic betting ring. Thales must have pulled in lucre by the sack-load. If there was ever a year when he would have done so well it created envy, that was it. The only surprise was that Old Thales survived and was not himself buried deep against the boundary wall.

This explained why Liberalis always sounded so anxious; he must have feared he could lose a fortune. Possibly even Rufia had wanted a share, in return for running the bar. Then along came the fecund Rhodina. Money explained why a barmaid that everyone else hankered after had cosied up to Thales of all people. Liberalis may have realised he himself looked so hopeless that Thales, under pressure, might easily change his mind about who was left the bar.

Liberalis won out but I reckoned ten years ago he nearly lost it. It was time to take a much harder look at him.

The new information offered me reasons why the long-term waitress Rufia might also harbour bad feelings: Thales used her efficiency, only to prefer a much prettier, younger squeeze. No wonder Rufia loathed the incomer. If she thought bosomy Rhodina was after the money, she would stop her and she may even have courted Liberalis as her ally. Meanwhile, if Rhodina was pregnant with a child she claimed Thales fathered, her assertion, though ludicrous, could still strengthen her position. Perhaps he was one of those idiots, past his prime, who would put up with any unlikely story in return for an heir of his own.

On the other hand, Thales might have resented Rhodina's attempted manipulation. He had held out as a single man for years. Why suddenly cave in? Rather than welcome the coming child, he, too, may have decided to be rid of the inconvenience. Did he and Rufia gang up?

Either way, there was Rhodina, pregnant. She had told Gavius she wanted to leave, but he was her only confidant; the rest believed they were stuck with her. Rufia and Julius Liberalis both had strong reasons to remove Rhodina permanently. Even Thales might have been tiring of her. He certainly was not a man to want three toddlers running around in his bar. Rhodina needed to be dealt with, and before she gave birth.

So could the five men who died have been a gambling syndicate? Or did Rhodina possess five hefty brothers who came to the bar to defend her interests? Five would-be protectors with old-fashioned prominent noses, possibly from one of the eastern provinces? Five rather dumb ones, who let themselves be overpowered.

Or were these five men killed for some quite unconnected reason – and murdering them just happened to let Thales and Rufia deal with Rhodina at the same time?

More and more, I felt that both Rufia and Liberalis must have known about, and were closely involved in, the scheme to attack the five men. Rufia vanished the same night, but Julius Liberalis was alive and well, and living around the corner from what was now his bar.

53

I decided to tackle this at once. There was no time to discuss it with Tiberius; I was fired up and ready. Before he and I met, I would have gone in alone immediately. Why wait?

One reason was the attack on Gavius. Whoever was so keen to silence him might attack me too. I presumed they took part in killing the six victims ten years ago. Although they might not all have survived the intervening decade, any who did were dangerous. If Liberalis might be one of them, I should approach him cautiously.

Once it would have been my father's voice mentally nagging me to take more care; now my husband took over the imaginary advice. In true Roman style, control of me had passed from one male head of the household to another.

Still, I ought to take somebody with me. I did consider asking Larcius to release one of the workmen. Then I remembered that all the men had gone with Tiberius to Lesser Laurel Street today, where some great push was being made to complete the house in time for the wedding. Ready for my domestic life? Juno Matronalis! The house might be ready but I was not. When I had time to think about it, I was starting to have very cold feet.

I despised Liberalis too much to feel afraid of him. Apparently he had never worked, just sat on his backside waiting for Thales to die. Now I knew his full motivation, I did assess risks. What would he have done if Thales had found someone else to leave his wealth to? Could it be that under his plaintive anxiety, Liberalis was hiding a vicious streak?

Cobnuts. Nothing so positive was in evidence now. He loved ownership and presumably hoped for a large income, but I could not see him ever amounting to much. Yes, he seemed eager to run the bar, but he was entirely wrong for it. Like Thales, he would lord it over his customers, just hoping they would stand him a beaker of something tolerable and call him a rollicking character. But I doubted that his reputation would ever match that of Old Thales.

Would someone stronger take over the daily running of the Hesperides, as Rufia had done? Surely not Nipius and Natalis, or their Dardanian lady friends. If illegal gambling continued to happen, I could see that being annexed by the Rabirii, through Gallo. The whole bar, with its neat water feature installed by my beloved, might become a gangsters' asset, one more in their black portfolio. Liberalis would be such a patsy I bet the Rabirii would dispense with him altogether. He owned it. So what? That would not stop an organised-crime mob.

These thoughts had made me slow my pace. When I arrived back in the enclave with the bars, on my way to where Liberalis lived around the corner, I was dawdling. I noticed people who had not yet seen me.

There were four, all women. Being female, their gathering point for a gossip was not a bar, but beside the high counter of the bakery. Three I recognised: Gran (Prisca), Lepida from the snack stall and Menendra. Macer must have released Menendra from his horrible holding cell. Here she was the youngest in a mature coven. The fourth woman looked the oldest, a stranger, white-haired, heavily lopsided, struggling on two sticks. Although I had never seen her before she looked at home in this district.

As so often around here, my approach was hindered by beasts of burden. The presence of Menendra implied they were part of her business. As I tried to get around the laden donkeys, the group dispersed as if naturally. The unknown woman managed quite a sprightly step into a carrying chair; she was rushed off before I saw her properly. Lepida galloped away as if she had a busy snack stall to run. Menendra vanished too.

I only managed to block Gran. She tried to sidestep, failed to dodge me, then avoided my questions by introducing the young bread-servers as two of her granddaughters. Lepida was one of her daughters, so Lepidina, the daughter at the snack stall, was another grandchild . . .

Her attitude had changed. She gave me an accusing look as if she did not want to talk to me. Not surprisingly, this was because of Gavius. Tiberius' ploy had failed to work; people had found out he was still alive. The very fact that Gavius belonged to such a large family had led to the truth coming out.

His grandmother had, of course, gone visiting; so, she said, had other relatives. She made a loud announcement, as if informing the whole neighbourhood. 'I thought you was a decent type, Flavia Albia! None of us know how you could do such a terrible thing. The family are going to see him laid out on his bier. When I went, there he was in bed, being fed a spoon of broth.'

I suppose other members of the family thought it was cruel to pretend Gavius was dead. They must have worked on Prisca so she had brooded, then had a rethink – a typical family about-face that ignored all logic. Now Tiberius and I were enemies. She held up a hand and pushed away past me. 'Don't squirm up to me, my girl! You are a nasty, spiteful piece of work and that fellow of yours is as bad.'

I let her go.

The two pigtailed bakery girls were staring at me with open curiosity. I asked for my usual loaf. They served me in silence. Once again it was the last on sale that day, the wonky one with a burned segment.

I tried mollification. 'We were only trying to protect Gavius, and maybe lure his attacker into the open.'

They must have been told not to talk to me. Even so, I noticed they sold me bread. Around here, commerce was everything.

I would not be welcome at the Brown Toad, where old Prisca was the kitchen queen. At the moment, I stood no chance of changing her attitude to me, so I made my way to the snack stall, hoping to see Lepida. She was not there. Possibly she was with Prisca, her mother. At least Lepidina, from the third generation, was there tidying the stall.

She and I had not yet had any conversation. When her mother was at the stall, she only eavesdropped. Lepida for her part had only really opened up to me that time Lepidina was absent. The daughter was another thin, hard-working woman, aged around twenty. Her face was pleasant, her manner subdued, almost to the point of timorous.

I asked for a cold drink. I could see Lepidina wondering whether to serve me, but as at the bakery, commerce or at least good manners won. As soon as she brought the beaker, I weighed in. Though she was an adult, I judged her unmarried and still under her mother's thumb. I bet they lived together. I bet the mother regarded it as her house.

Lepidina was squirming, but had no idea how to get away from me. I repeated what I told the bakery girls. 'I hope your mother and grandmother will believe we meant only good. It hasn't worked—' And what was more, it struck me that Gavius was now once more in danger. 'Lepidina, help me if you will. I am desperately worried what could happen to Gavius if news that he is still alive flies all around the Ten Traders so his attackers hear it.'

'We won't let on.'

'Oh come! I just saw four women having a good chinwag, with two bubbly girls at the bread counter taking in everything as well. I don't blame anyone, but this is no longer a secret. We both know the gossip will be spread through the High Footpath by dinner time.'

'No, it's just in the family.' That was a pretty large family, I knew.

'Well, I really hope it can be kept quiet, though I'd say too many people already know.' I let an indignant note creep into my tone. 'Menendra's not a relative, is she? Why, I don't even know the fourth old biddy who was just now talking to your mother and grandmother! Can you tell me who she is?'

Lepidina shook her head, a fast, nervous movement, while she remained tight-lipped.

'Is it someone you never talk about?' I suggested softly. 'Someone people think is dead?'

At that she was so frightened, she bustled behind the stall, from whose safety she declared with a new boldness that I ought to go. She pulled a heavy leather curtain and hid there.

Their bench was outside. I took it and stayed there. I coughed to let her know.

It is possible that a signal was sent somehow. Whether or not Lepidina passed a message out, after half an hour, her mother bustled up the street. She rattled the curtain, which was pulled up, though her daughter kept out of sight.

'Flavia Albia, I'd like my seat back, if you don't mind!'

I put down my beaker. 'Lepida, listen. Can Gavius talk yet?' Lepida shook her head. He was still too much of an invalid. With a heavily bandaged throat wound, I guessed speech might be difficult anyway. 'It is very important that he be taken to a safe place. Somewhere nobody will know. I am persona non grata so I have to rely on you to persuade the family to fix this. If you want, I can try getting help from the vigiles.'

Lepida unbent slightly.

'If not, Appius and his crew might help,' I persisted. 'You must all understand that he is still at risk. Killers are after him. The big mystery is why did Gavius ever let his assailant in?' Lepida looked vague at the question. 'He knew them,' I told her. 'Whoever attacked him, both he and his dogs knew them. They will think he can identify them.'

Now she looked not just vague but terrified.

I made one last attempt. 'Just now, when you were all by the bakery, there was somebody with you. She was taken off in a chair – not a hired one, it looked private.' We owned one like it in my family, ostensibly for Mother's use, though nowadays it was more often borrowed by my sisters. Ours had the same air: once-smart paintwork that had become slightly battered, two bearers who responded to instructions. Today's couple were the same. Unlike commercial chairmen, they did not annoy the elderly one with a long-winded act of pretending not to recognise any requested destination. 'She has her own conveyance. She said go, they ran.'

Lepida pretended to have no idea who I meant.

I ignored the act. 'I can guess who she is. You once claimed you never knew her.'

'Oh really? Anyway, I have remembered her now.' Lepida was shameless about her previous lie.

'So it seems. I suppose someone contacted her about recent events at the bar? Told her the old bones were being dug up?'

'Somebody must have done.' Lepida had to acknowledge it, but was quick to add, 'She lives far away. I don't know where she stays in Rome.'

'One of your cronies will know. Menendra, no doubt. Send a message. I want a meeting, and I want it soon. The day draws on, so let's say tomorrow.' Tomorrow would be my last chance on this enquiry. After tomorrow I would be a bride in my new home, handing out wedding breakfasts to relatives I couldn't stand. 'She can name the time and place. Tell her she has to meet me,' I said. 'Say that from me to Rufia.'

54

Before I gave up, I made one last call. It was too late to tackle Liberalis; I saw sense. He would deny everything as usual. I was past my best for today. Perhaps the way to deal with such a nervous man was to have him arrested. If stuck in a cell, pure fear might make him talk. Macer could organise that.

Instead, I went to Mucky Mule Mews to see Gavius. His parents let me in but he was sleeping. Guarded by three silent dogs, he lay still, with very laboured breathing. Infection had set in, so I was told; he was delirious. They had managed to feed him once or twice, as his grandmother said, but mostly he would not even take water. To me, he looked so feverish I feared for his life.

Though I was desperate to ask him questions, we did not disturb him. Leaving his father watching, I stepped out into the alley with his mother, Annina. She knew I had suggested moving Gavius somewhere safer, but he was too weak. Having seen him, I accepted that. Instead, Appius and the crew were coming after work and would then maintain a rota to protect him. I was afraid he would die despite them.

'I know you did your best, Flavia Albia.'

'We just want to discover who it was, so they can be punished and stopped.'

'I know you do.' It was the time of the evening when there were more people than usual in the alley. One or two of the women waved and smiled sympathetically at Annina.

'Look, Annina, I am sorry to nag about this, but has your boy said anything at all?'

She shook her head. 'He can't remember what happened. We asked him gently. He just became very agitated. Everyone has been so good, you know. All his cousins have been round to see how he is.' How many was that? No wonder we could not keep his survival a secret. The mother understood what I was thinking, because she said, 'I'm sorry. It's the old fellow. When people come, he does so like to chat with them. This is terrible, but it's really brought him out of himself in a strange way. He lets them in because they are family and, well, you know how it is . . .'

I assured her I did.

I needed to distract her from maundering on about the breach of confidence. I asked abruptly, 'I don't suppose you have seen anything of Rufia today?' Although she had never admitted knowing Rufia was alive, I remembered the way she had spoken when I visited the barmaid's old room. Now, Annina denied having any recent contact. I double-checked. 'In view of all the interest in where she used to live, I wondered if she might have been to see the room again herself?'

'No. No, she hasn't come.'

'But you knew she is in Rome?'

'Well, I heard a little whisper when I was out buying a few provisions . . .' Annina looked relieved that I knew.

'You liked her,' I suggested. 'You kept her room for her, in case she came back. You knew all the time that she was still alive?'

332

She pursed her lips, then admitted, 'Yes.'

'Did everyone know?'

'Oh no! No, they all thought she was under the court-yard.'

'That was what Rufia wanted them to think?'

'I suppose so.'

'And presumably she came and fetched her stuff that night? All her things? And I suppose her money?' I had guessed right, because Annina silently nodded.

I looked at her, perhaps reproachfully. Then she came out with the story: 'She rushed in, saying she was going away, but pleading with me not to tell anyone. One of the mule-drovers was waiting outside with a couple of beasts—'

'Which drover?'

'I was indoors, I never saw him. She carried down her luggage and a lot of leather bags, money bags, I was certain. Then she let out a cry of relief – "All done, we'll be off now! Thanks for everything. Remember, you never saw me!" – and she rushed away.'

'Where was she going? Do you know where she has spent these ten years?'

'No.'

If Rufia wanted people to think her dead, of course she would not leave a forwarding address. 'Somebody must have been told how to contact her,' I insisted. 'Here she is, back after all this time, and it cannot be coincidence. She came because of what we have uncovered at the bar. Somebody sent a message.'

'Menendra perhaps? Rufia left her in charge of her little business.'

'She can't have wanted to come. She looks old. Very infirm.'

'Well, she would be by now. Age wouldn't stop her though. That one will be busy till she drops.'

Would she be busy killing people? I wondered if there were any more bars with skeletons under their sit-out patios. 'So why do you think she did a moonlight flit?'

'Had enough of Thales? Wanted a fresh start? I don't know, we didn't talk about it. She was in a hurry. She just told me she was leaving, and please never to tell anybody.'

'Which you didn't.'

'No. I can keep a secret. Anyway, no one ever asked.'

I smiled reassuringly, turning to go. At that point, Annina had a thought. Her mind must be so much on her son's condition, she was forgetting things, even things that mattered. 'He thought they were Egyptians!'

'What?'

'Gavius. He must have been delirious. I asked, "Have you anything to tell Flavia Albia, son?" He murmured back, "I saw them going in. They were all Egyptians." Straight away he dozed off again, though he looked more peaceful, as if he thought he had said something important. Only that doesn't make sense, does it?' Annina quavered.

Maybe not. Not if you thought Gavius was talking about when he was attacked in his home. But it made every sense if he really meant the night those murders happened at the bar.

55

When I left and walked back down the alley, as I passed the parents' house I did look up at Rufia's old room. It was not yet dark so there would be no lamp lit; I saw no sign of life at all. Mind you, the old woman I had glimpsed struggling on two sticks would find those narrow stairs too hard. Her time of serving customers in rooms above bars must be long over. All she would manage nowadays was organising others to do it.

Tiberius had said he would not come back that evening. He had too much to finish at the house, and he would visit the aediles' office, his last duty call before the wedding. I bought some cold sausage, Lucanian, and a few pickles for a private supper in our room. I went for ablutions, considering whether to walk down to the great new Baths of Titus. An imperial edifice might be run more hygienically than the local pit here. But it was almost as far as the Forum. The day had become ominously sultry. I would only grow hot and sticky again walking back; besides, I was in no mood for the evening crowds.

Enduring a fast scrape and splash at the local baths nearby, I changed into my last clean tunic. Well, it was passable once I turned it inside out. I ate my solitary meal, then sat combing my hair dry. Here by myself, it struck me how much I felt the silence. At Fountain Court I was once so used to it, I never noticed. Now Tiberius lived with me there, a friendly presence even if he was in another room.

I missed that man. Yes, it was time for a new domestic routine; we both needed company.

I was tidying our cramped room, not a long process, when someone hammered on the door below. It was evening now, late evening; clouds had come over even though it was summer. Perhaps my awareness of loneliness had unnerved me. Perhaps I was affected by what happened to Gavius. Anyway, I did not want to go down and answer. For a few moments I sat paralysed, but the thunderous knocks continued. It was not a door-to-door prophecy-seller calling on spec. They were all shysters, but if nobody answered their knocks, most were able to prognosticate that no one was in.

This could be about the enquiry. I forced myself to descend the stairs and call out to ask who it was.

'Morellus! Stop shagging that aedile, dust him down nicely and send the man out to me!'

Feeling shakier than I expected, I opened up. 'Sorry. You're unexpected. I got nervous.'

'Calm down, it's not a rapist, only your cuddly uncle Titus. I've come all the way from the Aventine,' Morellus complained. 'In my state. You know I'm still on "light duties" and even that's only so I can be grudgingly paid a few coppers.' When he was attacked in April, he had come close to death. It was still far too soon for him to return to work, but I supposed his tribune wanted to help. The government has harsh rules on sick leave. Soldiers are either in their fort's hospital or on parade. The vigiles had no hospital, they recovered on their own or they died; but they counted as soldiers for payroll purposes.

'Stop moaning. Here you are, let out to enjoy a pleasant

evening stroll, instead of getting your hair singed off, rushing into burning buildings. You don't have to combat criminals with bad breath who tell you to stuff yourself in a gourd and feed it to a donkey, you get to converse with refined people like me.'

'Where's the man?'

'Not here.'

'Hades with all its phantoms! Why didn't you tell me he would be out?'

'We didn't know you were coming, perhaps?'

'I need to see him. Got something to tell.'

I was cool. 'Have to tell me instead, Morellus.'

'I'm not telling a bloody woman.'

'I'm not a bloody woman, I'm an informer – a bloody good one. Tell me. Then if I think Tiberius Manlius wants to know, I can pass it on with improvements to your grammar and a more elegant speaking voice.'

'Elocution! I bet he likes that.' Being Morellus, he made it sound like an advanced sexual position. 'Give me a drink, Albia, I've come all this way, I deserve something.'

'I am about to become a married woman. I cannot go into bars to buy drinks for strange men . . .' I ended the snooty banter and admitted honestly, 'Morellus, I'm absolutely fed up with nasty drinks places. Let's go for a walk and find somewhere else for a sit-down. And that will stop us being overheard too.'

As we strolled through the streets full of early revellers, off-duty workers and their families, I brought him up to date with my discoveries. The pan pipes player who annoyed the bars passed us on his way to cause torment. A donkey came by with a bean sack.

'Manlius Faustus unearthed all this?' Morellus asked admiringly.

'No, you swine, I did.'

'You're a gem! And eminently—'

'Don't say it.'

'Talking to you was much more fun before you were a bride.'

'Not for me,' I replied bluntly. 'Cut it out, Titus sunshine. I bet your Pullia is looking forward to my wedding. You don't want me spoiling it for her by mentioning that smart woman from the Street of the Plane Trees you tangled with.'

Morellus failed to look ashamed. 'Not me.'

'You were seen! The full carnality.'

'Who told you that?'

'I have my spies.' He was seen by Tiberius and me. 'The word is, you didn't bother to shag her; you just lay back and let the grand lady do the work.'

'People tell such lies,' Morellus disagreed demurely. 'Do you want to hear what I found out or not?'

We decided to perch on a stone bench outside someone's house. I felt revived after my bath and supper, but Morellus badly needed to sit down. I did repent; I went to a bar and fetched him a beaker of mulsum. While I was doing that, he lit a couple of lamps someone had blown out, ordering all the evening loafers to move on. Two pickpockets were cruising that part of the Vicus Longus. 'Trot off and rob somewhere else!' shouted Morellus. They could tell he was from the vigiles. Without complaint they did as they were told.

A porter put his head out aggressively from the house whose bench we were using. Morellus gave him a smiling nod, as we had every right to be there. The porter shrugged and went back inside.

338

'Watch out for pots being emptied from upstairs,' I said. 'Now what have you to impart, sordid Fourth Cohort snoop?'

He had to spin it out, of course. 'I know what you think, Flavia Albia! I could tell it with Macer the other day. You don't believe we ever look into anything, or open a case file, or keep records.'

I nodded. That was what I thought. Why pretend?

'Well, you are wrong.' He dug a finger into me. 'And this is why. I'll tell you, then I'll enjoy hearing you apologise.'

'Better be good then. Speak, Morellus!'

He sipped his mulsum annoyingly. He smacked his lips, wiped his chin, had a drop more, gazed up and down the street. I folded my hands, waiting patiently. I wouldn't ask again. If his information had any worth, he had not marched all this way from the Aventine only to go home without thrilling someone with it.

'Those five men. You said they were salesmen.'

'That's what I was told. Now it's old news. The supposed salesmen were marble-suppliers, who seem in the clear for the bodies. By virtue of them still being alive.'

The joke was lost. Morellus was having none of it. 'You said salesmen, so I proceeded on that basis, woman.'

'They might have been,' I agreed. 'The marble lads have been ruled out, so those corpses could have been anyone.'

'You said salesmen. Foreign salesmen.'

'All right.' I was being quiet with him now. 'Foreign isn't definite, though it seems a possibility. What's your point?'

'You said—'

'I know what I said. So what?'

'So I thought, where do salesmen congregate? Especially foreign buggers? Whatever they are selling?' I let him take his time. Anyone with a good story should be allowed to gauge their moment. 'They all come upriver to the Emporium.'

I nodded.

'Think about it, woman.'

I nodded again, still unable to see why this was so significant.

The Emporium, otherwise called the Porticus Aemilius, lies on the bank of the Tiber, below the Aventine, beside the Marble Embankment. It is a stupendous collection of warehouses for unloading and storing imports. It is noisy, chaotic, full of dealers and swindlers, wharfingers and wholesalers, plus absolutely endless piles of merchandise from all over the world, much of it high range, every kind of desperately valuable commodity and material. Yes, salesmen would go there. No question.

'So this is what I decided,' said Morellus. 'Those five men, nobody around here knew who they were, nobody in the High Footpath missed them ever. Macer's never going to be able to tell you anything about them. If they were lodging near here, the landlord just thought they had bunked off without paying. He stole their luggage as compensation and never said anything. Usual practice. But here's the winning dice for you, Albia. If anyone connected to those dead men wanted to find out what happened to them, they would not come here to enquire. They would start in the one place they knew any salesmen were bound to have gone to. If they wrote from abroad, they would contact the cohort which oversees that place. So,' he said, with his emphasis portentous, 'the missing-persons report wouldn't be sent anywhere near bloody Macer and the cruddy Third. The Emporium is *our* beat. It would come to us, come to the Fourth.'

I reminded him it was a decade past. He said, so what? I laughed.

Morellus thought about his information. 'Now this is where your injustice about our working practices are going to let you down, young woman.' He drained his beaker in a long, slow draught.

Our conversation was proceeding on the usual lines for us: a mix of horrible and useful. Each of us thought the other was a social menace, yet we gave one another credit for reliable work.

I said I apologised.

'Accepted.'

'The Fourth Cohort is always professional and wonderful. So now tell me.'

'This is what I think. Suppose,' said Morellus, leaning towards me confidingly, 'salesmen at the Emporium who deal in anything high quality are going to have people who will raise merry Hades if they don't come home. They could be so well off they are persons of standing in their own society. Their people might even, if they had enough push, persuade high-ups in their province to get involved officially. Even a provincial governor, if they bribed him, might write to Rome asking questions about their mysterious disappearance. Governors love stirring with their big sticks.'

'Agreed. At least if his bribe was big enough . . . So then the vigiles or even the Urban Cohorts, gods deliver us, would certainly be instructed to investigate. But, Morellus, it was still ten years ago.'

'So what? You are speaking not about the ingrates in the Urbans or those loons in the Third, but us, the glorious Fourth. Our patch. Our interest. Our investigation. And

341

with a governorial query, it struck me there would be a scroll concerning this. I had a look for it,' he uttered proudly.

'You big fat darling!' I was genuinely impressed. 'So did you find it?'

'I looked,' stated Morellus, 'in the special place we keep for old scrolls that may be required for embuggerance avoidance in years to come.'

'Where is that?'

'On a shelf in the clerk's office, right at the back with all the horrible spiders, behind the giant beaker we keep for when the tribune visits.'

'Does he?'

'Not if he can help it. But when he does, we can give him his own special cup, can't we? He loves us for that. He's not to know the doctor mixes laxatives in it with a big spurtle, when the lads are all bunged up with constipation.'

'They need to eat more beans.'

'Too farty. You ever been in a station house surrounded by mass flatulence?'

I duly shuddered but let him see my impatience. 'So come on, you swine. Did you, or did you not, find a scroll with old missing-persons records?'

Morellus gazed at me, almost sadly, to think I had doubted. He reached into his tunic and pulled out a scroll, which he handed to me. It was not as sweaty as it might have been.

'Of course I did, Flavia Albia. Ten years ago, we were horribly badgered over five missing men. They were foreigners. Procedures were put in place. That is to say, our duty enquirer went along to the warehouses and asked questions – smart, expertly phrased ones. There was no trace, we never found them. Our verdict was anything could have happened to them; most likely they fell off the boat home and were all drowned. But for twelve months our man kept being asked for further developments, of which naturally there were none. You can see where he has initialled his scroll every time he was asked, very patiently. And he put it away on our special shelf behind the tribune's beaker, so here it is, for you to read.'

I held it as if it were fragile, which indeed in so much time it had become. 'So who were these men the Fourth had to look for?'

Morellus was enjoying his dramatic reveal so much, he looked liable to drop his mulsum beaker. 'I give you their names, poppet: Julius Ptolemaïs was their leader; he had a very bad limp, we were told. The others were Pylades, Hermogenes, Isidorianus and Sesarion. All Egyptian. From Alexandria.'

'And what were these men?'

'They were specialist exporters of very high-quality Egyptian lentils.'

56

I wrote down the missing men's names in my note tablet. I opened the scroll and read it. Questions had indeed been asked of Rome by a provincial governor on behalf of supplicants. Diligent checks were conducted; polite answers were sent to Alexandria. *No trace.* Regret was stated. The initials recording any action were always: *LPL*. That was Morellus' predecessor: Lucius Petronius Longus, my uncle, now retired. He must have hated the waste of time, but he would have been efficient.

I bought Morellus another cup of mulsum, having one myself. It tasted sweet. Progress on what had seemed an impossible case lightened my heart. We shared a laugh that after all I had found myself investigating lentil-supply wars. 'Only you, Flavia Albia!'

'Only me!' I found a grateful grin for him. 'Thank you, Titus Morellus. You are a worthy friend. You shall have double barley cakes at my wedding.'

'Barley!' We both giggled helplessly at the mention of a grain.

Morellus, childlike, made more flatulence jokes. Having four young children, he was very good at sound effects. I lifted my face to the evening sky where the fast clouds scudded, as I enjoyed the unexpected breakthrough.

Promising to keep him informed, I said goodbye to the

raddled enquiry chief before I returned to the hired room. Tomorrow would be a big day. At its end, I must abandon work, whether finished or not, then transport myself to my parents' house where I was supposed to sleep overnight – assuming a nervous bride could sleep at all – before my wedding.

I tried to sleep tonight at least. After a brief session of thinking through the lentil aspect, I went out like a blown lamp. Not long later, when the street noises were still loud, I awoke with a start. Someone was coming upstairs to the room.

Of course I could be under attack like Gavius, but instinct took me to the door. Still bleary, I seized no weapon. I was less alarmed this time, partly because the previous visitor was only Morellus, but mainly because even through sleep the footsteps sounded familiar. The thoughtful arrival carried a small pottery lamp to aid immediate recognition. I wondered which bar counter he had stolen it from.

'Tiberius! I thought you weren't coming back tonight?'

'Missed you!'

He ran upstairs, enfolding me in a hug. After clinging for a few moments to assure himself I still existed, he blew out the lamp. We went to bed, for sleeping purposes. Lying in the dark, I summarised my finds. Then it was his turn. He told me the house was now habitable. 'I hope you like it.'

'Do *you* like it?'

'I do.'

'Then so will I. We have the same taste. We share the same habits, which is what makes a home work. I only remember Lesser Laurel Street as a neglected wreck, but if you think it suits us, I am happy, love.'

Tiberius murmured, satisfied. Just before we fell asleep he felt obliged to give a wedding progress report; I duly listened. 'They are all set to start baking tomorrow. A fashionable cook, highly exclusive, has been ordered. Name of Genius.'

I let out a huge groan. '*Genius!* What is anybody thinking of? I know him. He is terrible. Genius was one of my father's big slave-buying disasters. Every time we hear of him doing some smart banquet, we all fall about in hysterics. His fame is a complete con. Genius absolutely cannot cook.'

Once I stopped ranting, Tiberius soothed me. 'Don't worry, he has become too famous to rustle up anything himself these days, so comes with a battery of elegant, competent under-chefs who do all the work. My wedding planners assure me Genius idolises Falco as the man who gave him his start, and adores him so much he will gratefully produce superb wedding food – all at cost too.'

'My wedding is on the cheap!'

'I don't think so. They tell me Genius is now a legend for his unheard-of exotic ingredients.'

'Oh, not ostrich tongues! That is so out of date . . .' I sighed and gave up. 'I just hope he knows that the best, most desirable lentils in the Empire are produced in Egypt.'

Chuckling, Tiberius cuddled up to me. We slept.

30 August

Three days before the Kalends of September
(a.d. III Kal. Sept.)

One day before the wedding of
Tiberius Manlius Faustus and Flavia Albia

57

Next morning, Tiberius and I rose early. We went out to grab a fast breakfast at the snackery. Lepida was not there but her daughter was clearly waiting to give me a message. She spoke almost angrily. 'My mother says to tell you this. That woman you were asking about has left town.'

I did not believe it.

Tiberius was going to the Hesperides. It was the last day of work. They were planning to connect to the aqueduct, fill up the canal and inspect it for leaks, then he would be handing over the finished bar to its owner in the afternoon, before he stopped work and left for the wedding. His last instruction was that I was not to question Julius Liberalis by myself.

Before he left me, he teased, 'We have never mentioned the appropriate fact that the Golden Apples of the Hesperides were a wedding gift to the goddess Hera.'

'The Apple of Discord caused the Trojan War,' I retaliated mildly. 'Was that golden bauble not brought to the wedding of Peleus and Thetis by an uninvited guest? Who have your planners missed off their invitation list, darling – and are they likely to send us any fruit?'

Tiberius stopped. He looked back at me. Simultaneously we chorused: '*Laia Gratiana!*' His ex-wife.

I said in a sweet voice that I would leave it to his discretion whether the baleful Laia should be hurriedly asked. Tiberius winced, muttering as he went over to the bar that he needed a drink.

I sat on by myself for a while, making notes quietly. It was project-end for me too. I had one last day to solve this case. New leads had appeared but there were still far too many unanswered questions. To organise myself, I made a list:

- Where has Rufia been? Why go? Why pretend to be dead?
- Is it Rhodina among the bodies? Why no head? Where is it?
- Are the corpses the Egyptians? Who wanted to kill them? Why?
- Who did carry out the killings? Who ordered them?
- Who dug the graves?
- Why sever a leg?
- Where are Rhodina's children?
- Who damaged the building site? Why?
- Why did Menendra search Rufia's room? What was she looking for?
- Who tried to burgle Annina and her husband? Why?
- Who attacked Gavius? Was it to silence him?
- What else did Gavius witness after the Egyptians went into the bar?
- Is it about sex? Extortion? Gambling? Or is it lentils?
- What part did Thales play in the killing? Was Liberalis present? Was Rufia?

Well done, Flavia Albia, ace investigator! Even for you, that is some list to have left over on your deadline day.

* * *

As I was putting my notes in the pouch at my waist, along came Macer of the Third Cohort. I called him over, saying I had news. 'By the way, I saw that you released Menendra.'

'I let her men go too. Nothing against them. They produced alibis for the mews burglary and the stabbing. Your watchman maintains they were not who he found breaking up the bar, so that clinched it.'

'Were the alibis fake or believable?'

'Flavia Albia, I don't have time for testing alibis. People give me one, I go with it . . . Believable, I thought. Those musclemen are just two nice boys who sell barley.'

'Not *very* nice boys – but around here, who is?' I told Macer how Morellus had tracked down identities for the five dead men. I made it sound matter-of-fact to avoid jealousy, but Macer accepted being upstaged. It must happen frequently. He had never heard of any Egyptians getting into trouble around the High Footpath; there were none in particular on his watch list now.

He was just going over to the bar to see Tiberius, who had asked him to report on illegal gambling. I went too.

'So this is your next fantasy motive for the murders!' he joked, although he did see that betting rackets could explain a lot. He gave Tiberius quite a reasonable overview.

Gambling for cash was illegal. Most law officers tolerated it on a small scale, so long as it led to no trouble. Most bar landlords were capable of handling any quarrels that sprang up over dice or the draughtboard. The vigiles had other things to do. The big worry was organised, gangster-led syndicates. From time to time, the higher-ups ordered a crackdown. Occasionally that even worked – temporarily.

Tiberius told him I had learned that Old Thales made a huge profit from gambling. Macer was not surprised. Once

Liberalis opened the bar again, he would keep an eye.

Mention of Liberalis prompted me to say he was one of my murder suspects. Since he had an appointment with Tiberius that morning, to sign up for his aqueduct access, Macer and I hung around until he came. Once the formalities were done, Tiberius took the water-board official off for a polite thank-you drink, while Macer and I kept Liberalis back for an interview. We steered him out to the street, where we all leaned on the counters that Appius and the marble crew had now repaired.

'This is how it is, sir.' Macer opened the preliminaries, making it an official vigiles matter, full of fake respect. 'I am going back to my station house now, and if you take the hard option, you'll be coming with me. You will be placed in my cell until you are driven mad by the bare walls and the horrible sounds of fellow suspects under torture. Then you will find you are ready to talk about the night six deaths occurred. Trust me, you really will. The soft option is you can stand here in the pleasant sunlight and tell me what you know. You are known to have been present,' Macer announced calmly. 'We have a witness.'

He had made that up. Anyone familiar with interrogation would have asked him, 'Who is it?' When the question failed to come, Macer discreetly winked at me. Liberalis was an amateur and Macer was on to a winner.

'Someone was waiting at the Romulus to see one of the waiting staff safely home,' I embroidered. I was thinking of Gavius and Rhodina, though of course she didn't need an escort home; she was sleeping with Old Thales. 'Liberalis, you were seen.'

'This is your last chance,' Macer solemnly promised. 'So own up.'

'If not,' I pressed the unhappy witness, 'your smart new bar will have to reopen without you.'

It was his dream. Rather than miss a single day in his beloved bar, Liberalis chose to weaken. 'Other people did it. I had no part in what happened.'

'Come on.' I jumped on him at once. 'We want the people who carried out the killings. Help yourself by helping us.' I had one final lure: 'We know Rufia survived. She is here in Rome. She will be arrested, on suspicion of involvement in murder. Nobody else who knows the truth is left alive. From all I hear, she's clever. So when we question her, she is bound to protect herself by claiming you did everything. Do you want that to happen?'

It worked.

'Yes, I was there,' Liberalis finally confessed. 'But only afterwards.' From a hardened criminal that would be a lie; from him, probably not.

Leaning on his bar counter, he stared at a pothole, transfixed by memories. Macer and I eased off the pressure. In his own time he spilled it all.

'I came back. I came back after normal closing, because I had an idea there was gambling that night. Thales used to hold events, by special invitation, after shutdown. It was the year the Amphitheatre opened. We were profiting from the endless games. He would look through the next day's programme, then take bets. You couldn't do it at the arena, not openly.'

'So you came for betting. What did you find?' I nudged when he fell silent.

'I shall never get over it. I was so frightened I wet myself. It was the most horrible, disgusting sight.'

'Tell us everything you saw.' I spoke quietly, but I was firm. Macer listened. A typical laid-back enquiry officer, at last he chose to show genuine skills – at this point, patience.

Liberalis forced himself to continue. 'It was late. I was alone. My mother thought I had gone to bed; I crept out of the house without her knowing. Nobody was in the Vicus Longus, no one was in our street here. I walked straight indoors, all innocent. I thought there was a meet, as I told you. I could see lights beyond in the courtyard, which seemed usual. But the place was much too quiet. Nobody was serving drinks. I should have gone home again. But I didn't, I stupidly kept going. I went through the passage and into the garden.'

'Who was there?'

'Only Thales. He was all on his own.' Liberalis paused. He looked traumatised. 'Apart from the bodies. I had never seen anything like it. Dead people, lying in a row, all close together, under our pergola.'

'How had they been killed?' demanded Macer.

'Throats cut.'

'Lot of blood?'

'Enough to make me sick.'

'Five men and one woman,' I prompted. 'She was Rhodina?'

Liberalis nodded. He licked his lips in that nervous way he had. Twined his silver points of hair between anxious fingers. 'She had no . . .' He could not say it.

'No head.' I was clinical. 'Was her head lying there?'

He forced himself to remember the scene. 'No. No, there was no head there. Just the rest of her body. Revolting.' He looked as if he might vomit right now.

Somebody had taken her head away already? Strange. 'You knew for sure who she was?'

'Rhodina. She was pregnant. Anyway, Thales said, "This is that poor cow Rhodina. She won't bother me again." I knew she had been nagging him; she wanted a future. He didn't like anyone to tie him down; he wanted to be rid of her.'

Macer leaned sideways, staring at Liberalis' hairy calves below his tunic. The vigilis said, matter-of-fact about it: 'Well look at that! I do believe the poor scared sod is so upset, he's weed all over himself again!' Liberalis writhed. Macer encouraged him to keep talking: 'Publius Julius Liberalis, you sorry man, did one of the dead fellows have his leg cut off?'

'No. Oh don't make me remember it!' He was going off into hysterics. Any moment we would lose him.

'Sure?'

'They were lying with their legs towards me. I would have seen!' So the decapitation and leg amputation were separate incidents.

I breathed in and let it out, a demonstration of staying steady. 'Calm down. Unburden yourself and you may feel better. You have decided to cooperate, remember. So what happened next?'

'Thales had just finished stripping all the clothes off them. He stood up, looked around, and saw me. I couldn't believe his attitude. He treated the scene as if it was nothing extraordinary. He seemed to think I should have been expecting it. He told me he was waiting for navvies who were coming to dig the graves. I could help if I wanted to. I refused. So he said "Bugger off home to bed then." And I did.'

'So simple! Could happen any night in any bar . . . Who were those navvies?' demanded Macer.

'I don't know. A man was sending them.'

'What man?'

'Never said. I don't think Old Thales knew the diggers, but that man was sending them. Thales called it his contribution.'

'What for?'

'Thales never told me.'

'Didn't you ask?'

'Too risky to know. I didn't want to end up lying dead under the pergola myself.'

'Thales cannot have killed six people all alone. So, somebody else, someone you never saw, must have helped him?' I pondered. 'Someone who arranged the bodies in a close line afterwards, out of the way of the gravediggers – but the actual killers left the scene before you came? Then another person was sending diggers?'

'That sounds right.'

'You are quite sure you hadn't seen anybody in the street as you approached?'

'No. Most of the bars were dark then. I might have heard people indoors at the Brown Toad, but that never closes.'

'What happened to the pile of clothes?' Macer snorted. The vigiles have their preoccupations. In a way they are right; at the time those clothes would have been clues to the victims' identity. Still would be, if they existed.

Liberalis went white at this memory.

'Six very bloody tunics and a pregnant girl's bust-band!' Macer chuckled. 'They must have been sopping with blood?'

'We washed them. In the public fountain. Hung them on the trellis to dry overnight.'

'You are joking me? Why not chuck them or destroy them?'

Liberalis confessed meekly: 'The next morning, I was made to get rid of the evidence. Thales told me to go over to Agrippina's Granary. I took the clothes to various second-hand stalls there and sold them.'

'Jupiter! What did you do with the money?'

'I had to give it to Thales.'

'You sound a right little slave baby then! Did you always jump, whatever that bastard said to do?' No answer. 'Is this all you know about the crime?'

'Yes.'

'Really? Didn't Thales explain to you what had gone down here?'

'No. I never asked. I did not want to know. I had night-mares for years, seeing those bodies. I still do.'

'And next time you came here,' I said, sounding hard, 'all the bodies were gone? Was absolutely nothing ever said about them?'

Liberalis shook his head.

'Never?' asked Macer.

'Never. Thales never talked about it.' He paused. 'I didn't even know they were put here. I assumed they would have been taken away and buried so they would never be connected with us. I would never have had work done . . . I was horrified when the workmen started finding bones.'

We all breathed.

'And what about the other barmaid? Rufia?' I asked.

'I never saw her again after that night.'

'She wasn't here when you walked in?'

'No.'

'She is still alive. Did you know that?'

357

'Not always.' He shook his head. 'I found out from Thales' papers, after he died.' Seeing how traumatised he was, I guessed it was Liberalis who panicked when our workmen turned up skeletons, so he was the person who sent a message to warn Rufia. Detecting his hysteria, perhaps she thought she had best come back to supervise.

'What did Thales tell you about her disappearance?'

'Only what he said to everyone. "The bitch has gone." He never explained it.' That did match what Nipius and Natalis had told me about Thales, right at the beginning of my searches.

'And you never questioned any of this?' Macer nagged at him, showing amazement. 'You never told anybody what you had seen? I am puzzled, man. Why not? Why ever not?'

The answer was so tame it seemed quite truthful: 'I never wanted to annoy Old Thales,' admitted Liberalis. 'He was going to leave me the bar one day, but he could change his mind. I kept quiet so he would let me have the bar.'

'It came with a large sum of money?' I suggested.

'It came with some.'

'Profits from gambling?'

'Could have been. I was not privileged to know about the finances.' That had always been his story: he was a young man, forced to stay out of the business arrangements. He sat in a corner dreaming of the day it would all come to him – but had no real idea of anything.

It could not be true. No one hankering after a legacy is ever so vague about what it comprises. People make sure they find out.

'But you always knew there was cash? I am wondering, Julius Liberalis, whether your hopes of a fortune might in fact have lured you into murder?'

358

For the first time, the only time, he stood up for himself. 'In that case,' Liberalis put to me, 'if I murdered anyone, wouldn't it have been Thales?'

He had a point. I nodded in acknowledgement.

'I was surprised when the will was opened,' he maintained, looking innocent. 'The amount of the money was all new to me. I only knew about the bar. It was the bar I had always yearned for; I dreamed of being a bar owner. That is all I ever wanted: the Garden of the Hesperides.'

58

After Macer had asked if that was everything, he said Liberalis would be taken to make a statement. As he was an accessory after murder, he would be held in custody. Furious protests ensued, to which the officer calmly responded, 'I don't believe I promised you a let-off. What witness heard me say that?'

'What about the "soft option"?'

'There's no soft option with the vigiles. A serious note about you will be sent up to the prefect. Only he can decide whether you go to court. If you're lucky, he'll let you out on remand – seeing as you are such a respectable property-owner and businessman!' sneered Macer.

I kept my eyes cast down, taking no part. I wanted Liberalis to be secured somewhere. There were plenty of stupid things he might do in the aftermath of breaking his ten-year-old silence. Now he had cracked, he was going to pieces rapidly.

I reckoned my one last hope of solving this was to let it be known around the neighbourhood that he had been arrested. I would suggest he had told us more than he actually did. Imply further arrests were imminent. Unnerve any others involved in the crime.

Of course it never works. Every previous contact made sure they were invisible. Menendra never put in an appearance all day, nor her escorts, who were presumably lurking

360

wherever she was. Perhaps they were trawling another area with their voluminous list of chickpeas, bulgar, meal flour, sesame and lentils.

The snack stall was now locked up. I could not further challenge Lepida over her story that Rufia had left town. But I received no word on my hoped-for meeting with the aged barmaid. That was never going to happen.

At the Brown Toad, two of the boy-girls were lounging outside, plucking their eyebrows and other, much more intimate places. As I winced and tried not to watch, they told me no one had seen Gran there that day. The staff had been stuck with leftovers for lunch – 'Salad leaves!' – though they had been promised mutton broth tomorrow, as one of Prisca's many grandsons was doing the sacrifice at a wedding.

'Could that be *my* wedding? Is her grandson Costus? Costus who runs the victimarium?'

'No, it's his man, Erastus. He's got himself beaten up in a bar, as usual. We're lending him a face poultice so he'll look pretty.'

This was horrible. My cultrarius was blue with bruises, which had to be disrespectful to the gods, and these importuning transvestites would be eating my sheep, Snowy!

I went along to complain to Costus, but his place was shuttered and he was nowhere to be seen. A boy kicking a ball around outside said Costus had gone to have a tooth pulled; the hunks were in attendance in order to hold him down. I made sure not to look too closely; the lad's misshapen football appeared to be a blown-up sheep's bladder. No doubt part of another sacrifice.

In a desultory mood, I wandered back to the Hesperides. Tiberius and the men were frantically trying to make the water feature work. I sat and watched. First, no water appeared. A red-faced Sparsus conducted the traditional plumbing moves: he banged pipes loudly with a hammer. When the others cried 'Steady on!' he threw down his tools and refused to do anything else.

Larcius and Tiberius went down on their knees, heads together, taking over like men with more experience, men about to do something much more technical. Tiberius hit the pipe.

'That's never going to shift it.'

'Shut it, Sparsus.'

'Ow!' My loved one had mis-aimed the hammer; he whacked his thumb. 'Ow, ow!' As he recoiled, in bringing the hammer up he hit his forehead too.

Larcius took the tool; he struck an expert blow, at which water rushed out. 'Jupiter, turn the stopcock, Serenus!' Water rapidly filled the feature channel. It was soon overflowing. 'Adjust it, adjust it! *Other way, you idiot!*'

They turned off the torrent. All sat down, panting. There were grins, with the endearing mix of sheepishness and triumph that workmen acquire after narrowly changing failure into success. Sparsus applied a filthy rag to Tiberius' brow, where a large cut was now splashing blood. He was also sucking a blood blister on his battered thumb. I said well done all, while going to his assistance. Now I would have a bridegroom who looked like a dying gladiator.

'We should have put in an isolation valve, chief.'

'The client's in jail. Let him sort that one out for himself, another day.'

'He'll call us back.'

'We'll be too busy to come.'

'Promise?'

'Absolute promise!' Tiberius lolled against me as I pressed on his cut forehead. 'We'll clear up, hand him back his bloody bar – or lock up if he isn't here – and get out for ever tonight.'

The others had finished their breather, so they jumped up and began floating little dishes down the canal. Most of them sank. I claimed I had always said it would happen. Serenus knocked Sparsus over, so he fell in the water, splashing everyone. We were all glad to be cooled down, because the afternoon had become stifling.

When they settled again, they began tidying up and removing rubbish. All their tools and usable materials were put on hand-barrows to wheel off to the yard at the Aventine. Everything superfluous was taken from the site and dumped in the back lane. Transport was supposed to come along that evening to take it; it had been ordered and would possibly even turn up. They conducted endless builders' sweeping. Larcius arranged the beaten-up wooden furniture like a meticulous housewife. An oil lamp was placed at the exact centre of each table. The struggling fig tree was carefully watered. The Oceanus mosaic had all its dust washed off so it ended up sparkling.

That was it. Tiberius and I saw the men off. We would see them tomorrow, all in our celebration clothes. 'With big thirsts on!' We two walked slowly to the hired room to pack. Dromo, who yearned for familiar routines, was so eager to go home, he piled everything on his handcart and straight away went off; we heard him moaning about the weight. Tiberius had reminded the boy that tomorrow he could stuff himself with cake made by the fabulous élite chef, Genius.

'Can he cook?'

'No.'

When he left, husband-to-be and I lay down on the appalling bed, intending to wait until the outdoor temperature cooled. Both of us were preoccupied, thinking too much about the lifelong enterprise on which we would embark tomorrow. With a marriage apiece behind us, and after a decade of waiting to risk a repeat, neither could afford this to go wrong. There was no need to talk about it. We were too subdued in any case.

We fell asleep. When we woke, it was already evening. People were expecting us for dinner; by the time we could reach the Aventine, it would probably be over. None who knew us would be much surprised. Any investigation made us unreliable timekeepers; they had yet to hear how this one had run itself into the ground, maddeningly incomplete.

We left the room tidy, locked up, took back the key to the owner. We passed Menendra and a couple of her donkeys laden with grain sacks. They were delivering to the Four Limpets, outside which lolled a group of Macedonian prostitutes, bantering with a tambourine player in the absence of clients.

As we left the Ten Traders for the final time, we passed by the bar. In the course of that afternoon, it had somehow been made ready for business, so it was already open and operating.

Just as it had been when I started this account, the Garden of the Hesperides was a large but otherwise typical eating house on a busy street corner, with two marble counters, five pot-holes for food jars, three shelves of cracked beakers, an unreadable price list on a flaking wall and a faded picture of nude women unsuccessfully guarding an apple tree. This

364

bar had waiters who were very slow to serve anyone and pretty girls who did all the work. A room upstairs was used for assignations; you could bring your own or hire the staff.

Little had changed. Only bodies had been dug up from the back garden and identified. Regulars would no doubt continue to harp on the old tragedy to strangers who might buy a round. I bet they still claimed one body put out there was a barmaid called Rufia.

We could not see whether the new landlord had been released by Macer and was inside, setting about his chosen role of becoming a local character. We did spot the gangster enforcer, Gallo. Both the waiters, Nipius and Natalis, reverently shook his hand as if he were a man of consequence. He accepted their greetings like a lord, passing through the gap in the counters as he made his way indoors. Perhaps he was intending to enjoy a drink in the courtyard, under the pergola beside the water feature, gazing at the lopsided sea-god mosaic. He would probably not give a thought to the murdered waitress who had once been buried where he sat, or her five long-dead companions.

In a strangely muted mood, Tiberius and I set off together for our long walk home. We would saunter down the Vicus Longus, past the White Chickens, ignoring the brothels; we would walk into the Argiletum, gazing at the famous Subura scroll-sellers, cobblers, false-teeth- and wig-makers, though not stopping to browse. We would avoid the Forum Transitorium, which was still partly a building site, but would sidle past the Fora of Augustus and Caesar, emerging into the main Forum close to the rostra. Around the Capitol at the north end, we would pass into the meat market, holding our noses. Thence a quick pass to the Trigeminal Gate, along its elegant porticus on the Marble Embankment, before we stopped short of the Emporium, below the cliff-side of the Aventine, at my parents' town house.

Tiberius would leave me, going on to stay at his uncle's.

That evening, I was supposed to dedicate my locket to my father's household gods (I had never had a locket; Falco never owned Lares). I should put away my childish things. Since I was already fourteen when they took me in, childish things never happened either.

In the small, high-up bedroom I had had as a young girl, where I had once written lovelorn poetry and raged against the world's injustice, I would spend this last night before marriage. Traditionally, I should dream of the day that was to follow.

I, being thoroughly professional, merely cursed and brooded that I had not solved my case.

31 August

The day before the Kalends of September
(pridie Kal. Sept.)

The wedding day of
Tiberius Manlius Faustus and Flavia Albia

59

R ain!
  Whoever thinks of weddings and imagines rain? I
heard it first in the middle of the night, when a great storm
cracked the skies apart. Rain poured down so heavily the
whole house hummed with the pressure of water racing
through its exterior gutterwork. It felt like some pointless
engine in the workshop of Heron of Alexandria, the great
inventor of mechanical curiosities. Rain must be filling the
streets, cooling the air in a mighty gush, waking even me, a
bride who had – let us be frank – drunk too many tiny tots
of something strong with her mother that evening. Unless it
stopped, I would be getting married in a thunderstorm.

This could be a disaster. Having enough to cope with, I
went back to sleep.

Before dawn I was woken again. Urgent footsteps and whispers announced my bridesmaids, wanting to drag me out
for my first task. A bride must rise in the dark to pick
flowers from her parents' garden. These she (not me, oh
please!) had to weave into a garland to perch on her special
hairstyle and hold down her veil. Garlands must be provided,
too, for the bridegroom and any little flower girls who
wanted to take part (many, I had been warned, mainly aged
three, all famous for being sick with excitement). Also there

had to be a bouquet of symbolic herbs: love, honour, joy, fidelity, devotion, long life, fertility and purity. Some powerful bouquets garnis! Quite a prescription for marriage.

Since the parents' house had no garden, I was shoved out alone onto the roof terrace, where the usual pots of roses had been supplemented specially by new containers of herbs.

'We haven't done her six ringlets!'

'She'll get soaked out there. We'll fix the hair when we let her back in.'

It was still raining steadily, so I had to go out with the snips and trug unaided. A gale howled across the terrace, water sheeting sandal-deep. The others just crowded in the doorway to the roof, urging me to hurry up because rain was blowing in on them. I hastily gathered slimy handfuls of what could be rosemary, marjoram, sage, lavender and myrtle – or any old twigs, since I, a city girl, was on my own with this job in the dark.

Fortunately custom says a bride should be pampered with a bath to ward off the evil eye and make her smell nice. I could live with the evil eye, which I viewed as a soul sister, but soaking in fragranced warm water now seemed urgently needed. My mother, sisters, husband's old aunt, plus curious slave women, watched me, gossiping.

The hired beautician turned up in time. For the size of fee she was charging, that woman could not be deterred by driving rain. She dealt with me fast, since my needs were standard: six braided locks, formed with a comb like a spearhead, coiled up as if I was a Vestal Virgin, expertly tied with ribbons and pinned on top of my head. That part was painful. They had to stay in place all day. The pins were long and pushed in very firmly. Women who should

370

know better told me tradition had to be suffered for. My reply was caustic.

The *ornatrix* was keen on little tendrils curled around the face. I quarrelled with her about that, so she huffed off to tend my impatiently waiting sisters and Aunt Valeria, who were all having elaborate court curls – a stupid front head-dress of many tiny pin curls on a frame.

Meanwhile I was dressed by my mother, who had quietly done her own hair. First, a long white tunic, supposedly woven seamlessly on an old-fashioned upright loom and unhemmed. Itchy, of course. Then Aunt Maia's legendary flame-coloured veil, with the droopy garland plonked on it. Moth holes dropped fabric dust like dandruff. The tunic reached the ground, so as Helena crouched to push on my saffron-dyed shoes, I was endlessly instructed to hold it up and not trip over. 'Stop hunching; stand up straight. You're not fourteen now.' Finally, a woollen sash, tied by my mother in a Hercules knot. Only my husband could untie it. Helena got the knot right; she didn't need it, but Father had drawn a diagram.

The saffron veil is intended to be a symbol of submission to your husband. We all guffawed.

I was ordered to wear no jewellery. The only exception was supposed to be my engagement ring. Since my new husband had never supplied one, I wore the old wedding ring I had used as an informer to make me look like a respectable widow (Lentullus and I had never marked our marriage). I refused to go through a whole stressful day now uncheered by glitter.

They poked my wet bouquet into my hands. I was taken downstairs, where my sisters had spent hours decorating

371

the entrance with oriental carpets from the antiques warehouse, tree boughs, ivy and strands of wool. A slave boy
was catching insects that crawled out of the ivy. Julia and
Favonia both had an artistic touch. You could tell either
this was the home of a madman or it was hosting a wedding.

Tiberius arrived. Togate and barbered, he did look like
a man worth marrying. Rather strained, but after a night
trying to survive his family, he probably had a hangover.
He turned up alone; everyone else thought they could skip
the augury and would follow later. I gave him his garland,
which he nervously put on. We shared a private glance. His
aunt Valeria appeared from our kitchen with her gruel bowl.

We had to seek approval from the gods and the omens
confirming divine favour must be taken before sunrise. What
idiot invented that? It isn't always done, but I had traditional
planners.

Now came an unfortunate clash. Nobody had told my
uncle, the elderly master of pompousness Gaius Baebius,
that he could not conduct the sacrifice. 'So thoughtless!'
muttered Aunt Valeria, finding fault with relish. 'The poor
man has even brought his own pig.' The runty thing had
a weird look in its eye.

Gaius Baebius decided to conduct a sacrifice anyway. His
wife, Father's starchy sister Junia, and their son Junillus had
tagged along to supervise, so they had to watch as he placed
a veil over his bald head and advanced on his animal, knife
aloft, while trying to stop the veil falling off. His pig took
one look and made a break for freedom just as other guests
arrived; they pushed in through the front door in streaming
wet cloaks, allowing the frantic porker to dash out.

Next moment, Gaius Baebius was running after the
escapee, scampering along the Marble Embankment,

wielding his unused sacrificial cleaver and weeping with frustration. Even if he caught his pig, it was now defiled by its unwillingness. He would have to start all over again with another animal. The meat market was not open yet.

Junia pretended Gaius Baebius was not her husband. Sweet Junillus hesitated, then obligingly ran out into the storm and chased down the road after his father.

Everybody else stood in the hall and tried not to mention out loud how the escaping pig was a bad omen. Fortunately my professional victimarii turned up, tenderly leading Snowy, the sheep I had ordered. In a wreath and gold ribbons, she let herself be led in, very obediently, then gave us a cute bleat. They had brought their own portable altar upon which to send her to the gods.

Tiberius and I slipped into a side room, prior to our official entry. Favonia put her head into the room. 'Oh shitty shit, Albia! You brilliant sister – they are *so-o-o* gorgeous!'

The three gorgeous experts, barefoot, in long kilts wrapped with wide cummerbunds, and flashing their heavenly pectorals, carried out their duties without fault. I peeked to make sure I got value for money, while Tiberius loftily surveyed a shelf of Greek vases.

They all looked perfect. Passus, my handsome victimarius, gently led the sheep, murmuring to keep it happy. Victor, my muscle-bound popa, whipped out his mallet and stunned it. Erastus, my cultrarius, had been in a brawl, as I remembered the Brown Toad transvestites telling me, but the damage must be cleverly covered up and didn't show. He slit Snowy's throat with one strong slash, enjoying his work; he deftly caught the blood in a special bronze bowl so none splashed on the hall's mosaic, then opened the stomach for inspection.

An old man who looked like a tramp had come with the

hunks. I could see people thinking, *That clown Falco is being kind-hearted again, taking in down-and-outs for a square meal at his daughter's wedding.* However, it was the augur. Staberius was a bunioned old has-been who smelled. He peered at the sheep's bits intently, then quavered: 'The gods approve this union. I see happiness in the home and the marriage bed!'

Tiberius strode up behind me, moved me aside, stuck his head out: 'And no cheek!' The old man nervously added the requested prophecy. We made our formal appearance to polite clapping.

Julia Junilla was mistress of ceremonies, reading out from a list. 'We call upon the gods to be present: Janus, for thresholds, openings and closings, Juno Pronuba for matrimony, Jupiter the father god, Tellus, the earth mother, and Hymen Hymenaeus, god of marriage.' My mother quipped oh dear, we hadn't bought in enough food for so many. 'Our bride will now be handed over by a matron who has only been married once and her husband is still living.'

'There will be appropriate words of advice,' added Favonia, deceptively satirical.

Helena approached me. Suddenly her brother, my uncle Camillus Justinus, cried loudly, 'You're ignoring the rules, Sis!' Well, that was Mother. 'Stop the wedding! Helena Justina has been married twice! Doesn't anyone remember – before Falco, she had that ass who plotted.'

Mother glared at Justinus but stepped back. Someone hissed, 'Don't mention the plots!' Too late. Everyone who didn't know was now asking.

In our family we do not lack independent women. Claudia Rufina beat off all comers, volunteering herself as substitute. She was wife to Justinus, though their marriage was rocky; Claudia loved weddings, where she tended to lock herself in a room, weeping copiously, while Uncle Quintus pleaded in whispers at the door. 'I am a one-man woman,' she declared. 'We foreign brides must stick together, Albia!'

Claudia Rufina then gave me away with such practised panache I wondered whether she and my uncle had conspired. She seized us and joined our right hands, which the augur tied together with wool. This is how I know Staberius smelled. At least Claudia was shedding a fine mist of something aromatic, no doubt a gift after some furious quarrel with Justinus.

Julia announced: 'Tiberius Manlius and Flavia Albia have elected to give their promises in the ancient way of silence.' It was news to us, but had worked for my parents, so I gazed into his grey eyes, making certain secret promises, while he gazed back, seeming more serious, though I knew how to take that.

Tiberius then said steadily: 'By Jupiter, Juno and all the gods, I, Tiberius Manlius Faustus, declare that I do willingly consent to take this woman to be my wife.'

I pretended to have second thoughts, before I quietly agreed: 'By Jupiter, Juno and all the gods and goddesses, I, Flavia Albia, swear that I willingly give my consent to take this man to be my husband.'

We exchanged rings. We kissed. My mother, Claudia and the bridesmaids kissed me. And him. I dragged them off him.

We could not escape gobbledegook. Staberius produced a set of scales with a small weight in one pan; Tiberius placed coins in the other pan until he tipped the scales. I said I hoped that was to show he would be a just husband.

My father presented him with one copper coin as a token dowry. Like many fathers at this point, Falco took huge delight in the low-value singleton coin, as if we had better not hope for any more. Instructed by Julia, Pa nevertheless handed me one further coin to hold in my hand, a second in a purse, and placed a third into my right shoe, making sure he tickled me. I remarked that this was like what he used to give us, his daughters, if we were going out to an evening party – a rather mean fare home.

Joking that this time I'd better *not* come home, Falco then made an offering on the altar in front of some household gods, placing a sample toy alongside. I had never seen that toy before; I noticed a small nephew starting to cry. Mother dramatically produced a spindle and distaff, which she handed to me (emblems of domestic life – though not in Mother's house, or mine). Again, borrowed. Ditto the slightly disreputable household gods. This Lar and his mismatched Penates, dancing with their cornucopiae, looked as if they had been bent in a violent robbery.

Claudia's words of advice were: 'Your dowry belongs to you, don't let him start "administering" it; when children come, always insist he is home every day for their bathtime; be a centre of calm in the whirlwind of the home.'

Someone asked what wise words would be offered to the bridegroom, so my pa ordered Tiberius to treat me well or he would have his head knocked off. This was Falco's first formal wedding of a daughter; he was very emotional.

Next came the dinner.

Tiberius and I were bullied into our seats of honour, two chairs covered by a single sheepskin; skins being smelly, Julia and Favonia had provided a woolly rug. More guests arrived, lured through the storm by the promise of a banquet. Bearing gifts, some not even second-hand, they came up and greeted us. There were more aunts and uncles than I could place on our family tree, some with offspring I had never seen before. If a baby cried, crowds of women vied at jiggling it to sleep.

Tiberius' sister and family had arrived, with Uncle Tullius behaving well; he had decided to treat this like a business meeting where he needed to be pragmatic and clever to secure some tricky deal. Soon the three nephews had found branches from the decorations to use as spears and were running around, hunting down the three-year-old flower girls. After rather too much screaming, the little girls were sick down themselves, so the boys were scolded, which ended in bitter tears. For unconnected reasons, Fania and Antistius took no part in that though they could be heard having a violent row; then they disappeared separately, until Fania reappeared sobbing to Tiberius that she was desperately unhappy and wanted to leave her husband. Women swooped to drag her off for consolation. Only Aunt Maia ordered, 'If you want to leave him, just get on with it, woman – don't spoil your brother's day!'

Men sensibly discussed with each other how to pace themselves with food and drink – before they began sampling amphorae much too fast. The little flower girls were now scampering about naked while their clothes were washed and dried. Aunt Valeria announced three times that she was going for a lie-down, failing to interest anyone.

I had an unexpected encounter with Camillus Aelianus, Mother's other brother. Years before, I had had a severe crush on Aulus, which had ended in heartbreak; we had rarely spoken since. He and Hosidia Meline had divorced, each since marrying other people, yet it was Meline he brought along today.

I could see now that Aulus Camillus was a difficult, truculent, broody man; life with him would have been a disaster, not to mention that since he was my uncle, it was illegal. He had behaved like a bastard to a very young girl who needed security, but since this was my wedding, I unbent. Every bride wants other women to suffer her fate. 'Aulus Camillus, you and Meline are better and closer than ever before. Her interfering father's dead—' The booze-fuelled Minas of Karystos had failed to drown himself in drink, but fell off a ladder one Saturnalia. We all reckoned he lost his balance being sober for the first time ever. 'Why don't you and Meline remarry?'

Aulus was one of the cleverest lawyers to grace the basilica, yet had not thought of that. I left him pondering. Mother would be proud of me.

The food, which was delectable, kept coming. We had to make this feast last all day, so the wedding procession would be after dark. Since the fashionable cook, Genius, did not exert himself in the kitchen, he wandered out looking important, surveying how much all the guests were enjoying his under-chefs' wondrous achievements. I went up to thank him for his expertise. Supervising is hard work.

'Can I ask you a food question, Genius?'

'You are the bride, ask anything.'

'Egyptian lentils – best in the world?'

'Highly regarded. Much sought after.'

'And highly priced? But might few people in Rome want to cough up? Could lentil-suppliers make a killing, or would they need to supplement their income?'

'You are right, Flavia Albia. Upmarket lentils have a limited take-up. Suppliers would need to diversify. Either into other pulses, or some quite different business.'

'Thank you. Genius, you are a genius.'

'So people frequently tell me,' he answered modestly.

Before I placed myself back beside my husband, I inspected the buffet tables. Some of the feast dishes did not come from the sophisticated skills of fashionable food-istas, but were brought by guests. Aunt Junia had given us her famous meatballs, inedible spheres that belonged in a military arsenal. However, one better cauldron was being scraped by eager people fighting to get at what I thought I recognised as one of Prisca's peasant hotpots. There was such a queue, Genius came and requested the recipe.

Katutis, Father's secretary, who was still sober enough to look at his list, said this cauldron had been delivered to me as a wedding present. He retrieved a note from a bundle he was diligently saving, ready for my thank-yous.

The note wished us long life and happiness. When I turned it over, there was intriguing news. *Gavius is dead. He opened the door because it was his cousin. I can't have that but mustn't say who. From a heartbroken Gran. PS Rufia will meet you at Temple of the Flavians an hour after midday. Told her about wedding, but she's going home today.*

What?

That was no use to me. Obviously I could not attend this meeting. Rufia was on the Viminal and I was on the Aventine. It is all very well to be professional, as I always was – but this was the one day in my informing life when work had to stop. I must remain on my woolly-rugged chair, beside my adoring new husband, smiling . . .

* * *

No. I did it. The appointed time was long past but I took a chance. I, Flavia Albia, the bride, left a message that no one would discover for a while, then I abandoned my own wedding.

60

Whatever had made me do this? I realised now I had been enjoying myself. At one with Tiberius. Seeing people who were close to me, all gathered for us. Being the centre of attention, even though I had felt oddly isolated from our guests.

It was steadily raining. I would soon be soaked through. Before leaving, I had dumped my saffron veil, changed my wedding shoes for a sturdier pair, even shed my long white tunic for a more robust one. I stole someone's waterproofed cloak. It was hooded like that of a Celtic god, so probably belonged to Uncle Petro, who, like Falco, reckoned himself an expert on all things northern. I had glimpsed him earlier with my brother Postumus, tending the altar flames: men's work.

Leaving our family home low on the Embankment, I scurried, head down, through the monumental buildings below the Capitol, then was soon skirting the fora to head up the Argiletum. Because of the weather few people were about. Streets were navigable, though in the main Forum even its fine Etruscan drains had too much water to take away, so I had to leap over large puddles. The Argiletum and Vicus Longus were upward slopes, where I struggled against flowing torrents even on the raised pavements.

As I walked, I mentally reran my list of questions. Preparation is the key to a good meeting.

The Temple of the Flavians had been built by Domitian as a mausoleum and a shrine to his family. Previously undistinguished, the Flavian clan needed validation. However, they did now own two deified emperors, along with various nonentity relatives awarded godheads on Domitian's say-so, plus his niece Julia, whom he was rumoured to have bullied into sexual acts with him. Poor Julia's ashes were here, along with the urns of his father and brother and an infant son who had been lucky enough to predecease his paranoid sire. If this imp had lived, Domitian would probably have turned against him.

The weather was too atrocious to admire the place as intended. Relieved to spot a waiting chair, which could mean Rufia was still here, I hurried across a large square enclosure and through an arch to another, containing a beautiful grandiose temple in white Pentelic marble amidst dotted cypress trees. It was extremely tall. An enormous statue of the late Emperor Titus tried to belie Domitian's paranoid jealousy of him. Ditto Vespasian, whose house had once occupied this spot, close to that of his brother Sabinus, in whose home Domitian had been born in a back bedroom when Vespasian was just a poor relation. Ultimately, the purpose of the Temple of the Flavian Gens was to glorify Domitian's own birthplace.

All I cared about was that you could go inside to shelter.

Now I was here, the rain suddenly stopped. Thank you, Jupiter Pluvius and the benign Tempestates!

There were no attendants; any temple slaves must be hiding from the storm. I shook myself on the threshold just as Rufia was about to make her way out.

'You're late!'

'I am here now! Be grateful. I left my wedding for you.' As I pushed back the hood of my borrowed cloak, the six coiled ringlets, still tied in their ridiculous topknot with their now bedraggled ribbons, proved that.

'That's why I waited. Get on with it then.'

Her manner was as gruff as I expected, though she quickly settled. From all I had heard, I was not surprised that Rufia felt a grudging respect when people stood up to her. There would have been so few. She was elderly, badly crippled, her heavy body difficult to support with her two sticks. Her face had never been beautiful and now showed all her years. Thin grey hair was fastened with bone pins like the one I remembered from her old room; she wore the silver bangle Annina had said she put on every day; she had small feet.

I did not take notes. She would never have stood for it. Wasting no time on pleasantries, I began by crisply summing up what I wanted: what had happened on that deadly night at the Hesperides, who did it, and why? And why had Rufia herself disappeared, leaving the world to believe she was murdered?

'I'll tell you what went on, so you can back off and stop prying.'

So that was why she agreed to talk to me. But I would decide for myself whether to stop. I wanted to find the killers.

We both stood in the gracious vault of the Flavian Mausoleum, watched by huge busts of that ambitious family. Rufia had settled her back against a wall for support. I stayed on the opposite side, aware that she could use her walking sticks as weapons. If she lashed out, I was too wet and cold, and too abstracted by my guilt about the wedding, to put up much of a fight.

'Rufia, I know the six corpses found are Rhodina and some Egyptian traders. I also know, and have a witness to support it, that Old Thales organised the murders.'

'He couldn't organise a pissing contest.'

'But he could run bets on it!' I snapped back. 'So did he do this?'

'All the blame for the killings is on him.'

'I thought you would say that. What happened? Tell me about the Egyptians.'

'You don't know it's them,' she attempted.

'Yes I do. They came from Alexandria, they sold lentils: Julius Ptolemaïs, their leader who had a damaged leg, then Pylades, Isidorianus, Hermogenes and Sesarion.'

Rufia scoffed. 'You're good! That's more than I ever knew.'

'What got them killed? Surely not pulses?'

The old woman shrugged. 'Partly. I ran a little lupin round, sold beans and grains to all the bars. I trained up Menendra; she's doing it now. There's money in it. Old Thales never realised, he was too lost in his own grimy concerns.'

'Was Ptolemaïs trying to move in on your patch? Those men sold a very expensive product, for which the market is limited. Did they want to branch out into ordinary bar supplies?'

Again my companion gave me an admiring look. 'Yes, they were thinking about it – and I was determined to stop them. I was doing well. I was a rich woman, training up Menendra to do all the work for me. Not bad, for a one-time Illyrian slave! Those menaces could have taken themselves anywhere; I was not having them lose me valuable income.'

'So you decided to wipe them out – to prevent encroachment?'

'No, Thales took them out. I'm innocent.' That generally

means guilty. 'He was more under threat than me. They hadn't really come to the bar to sell grains. They came for the betting. It was the Amphitheatre year. Those Egyptians had been down at the arena, trying to lay wagers on races, finding it difficult. They met some people from up here who told them we had good nights at the Hesperides, with no official hassle. Higher stakes, more action, all in a pleasant venue with a lively atmosphere.' I could tell Rufia was proud of the offered amenities. 'It was invitation-only, you had to be introduced to Thales. He needed to be sure men who came were a safe prospect – not only that they wouldn't snitch to the authorities, but they possessed big spending money.'

I nodded. This was the usual story.

'People couldn't just knock and walk in.' Rufia was one of those narrators who keep emphasising their point even when you have got it.

'Invitation-only. I see.'

'You're a bright girl!' she sneered. 'But you haven't worked out why Thales took against those Egyptians, have you? It was because of the gambling. He didn't really run it himself, I told you, he was too hopeless; that was all done by a man he knew, Rabirius.'

'The crime lord.'

'Oh you have been working hard!'

'I know of Rabirius and Gallo and their protection rackets. So they involve themselves in gambling too? No surprise! They killed the Egyptians?'

'Not that stupid. Rabirius was keen on the Egyptians. All Gallo did was send trusted diggers afterwards for the graves.'

'And why did Thales want the Egyptians dead?'

'Because they had spotted what a good little earner we

had. They palled up with old Rabirius, that cheating devil, to take over the syndicate. Thales would have been cut out altogether. But that Gallo was just establishing himself at the time, so he put a different idea to Thales. They would remove the Egyptians, outmanoeuvring Rabirius, so Gallo could start building his power base. He was making the rackets all his own. The only thing was, Thales had to fix up the deaths, to stop Rabirius knowing Gallo was behind it. He didn't have the oomph to kick out Rabirius altogether, not then, so he still wanted to pretend to be loyal.'

'I get it,' I said. 'Rabirius was cheerily double-crossing his old friend. Gallo came along behind his chief's back, spelled out how Thales was being cheated, offering to help out. But Thales had to find someone to carry out the killing; he had to host the incident, and take all the risks.'

'Gallo's a smart operator!' Rufia scoffed. 'And Thales was a fool. In the end, Gallo did practically nowt.'

'So who did Thales commission for the deed?'

'That I don't know.' She must be lying, but I guessed she would never change her story. This woman was as tough as everyone said. She had spent ten years avoiding any comeback for that night at the Hesperides; she would not lose everything now by confessing.

'All right, change the subject. How did Thales persuade his killers?'

'Money, of course.'

'Oh what else! I understand why the Egyptians, but why Rhodina?'

Rufia spat. 'That silly little cow. Juno, how I hated her. Girls who build their lives on cosying up to men . . . As it happened, she was dreaming. Thales was never prepared to share his cash. If he had been, let's face it, I would have tied him up myself. Sure, I despised him, but the money would have sweetened it.'

'You had earned your share.' I showed that I realised her situation. 'You spent years running that bar on his behalf because he wasn't capable. He never gave you credit. You were only ever known as a barmaid.'

She grudgingly agreed. 'And Rhodina would never be anything different, but the silly woman never saw that. Let's get on. So, those men came to the Hesperides, thinking it was a gambling night. Thales said the others weren't there yet, so while they waited for things to kick off, he got them drunk and we used Rhodina to distract them. The boys came in—'

'These boys whose names you never knew?'

'The same.'

'You didn't recognise them?'

'Oh no.' Barefaced lie.

'How did they kill the Egyptians?'

'Cut their throats. Slick and quick. They did for two before Rhodina, the idiot, started squealing at the blood. The rest were slurring and tipsy, but took in what was happening; one of them grabbed her. She couldn't move fast, she was a lump when she was pregnant. He broke her neck, so one of the boys broke his for him, then they finished off the rest in no time. Very professional. We laid the bodies in a line, ready for their graves. That's it.'

'Not quite. What about you, Rufia? Your disappearance?'

'Thales didn't know, but I already planned on leaving. What happened that night, well I could bear it, I have a strong stomach, but that was enough aggravation for me. I told him I had put together such a nice little nest egg I was pissing off out of it. I was starting a new life and if he wanted to avoid trouble, he would agree to my plans. He was very surprised. Well, he didn't know that as well as my tips money and what I got from the lupin round, I'd taken extra from his bank box – he'd find that out later. I said I would never come back to bother him, so long as he co-operated. He was so weak and pathetic he did. Be fair, he always honoured the bargain afterwards.'

'I bet it was your suggestion to behead Rhodina?'

'Of course. Chip, chop! That way, if the bodies were ever found, no one would realise it wasn't me who died.'

'Why pretend you were dead?'

'Oh . . . I just didn't want any fuss afterwards.'

She would never admit the truth, but I thought she probably took more of a part in the deaths than she was claiming. She needed to flee. People could have fingered her for murder. If, despite her denial, she really knew who 'the boys' were, they must have known her. I wondered, was it actually Rufia, not Thales, who had organised the killers?

'I suggested they take off that man's twisted leg, too, for the same reason,' she went on. 'Just in case anyone came looking for the Egyptians. And I told Thales to remove their clothes and get rid of them.'

I told her they had cut off the wrong leg, to which she replied, that was men for you. Thales himself, probably. He was always an idiot. 'Right, Flavia Albia, is that all you want?'

I had a few more questions, so started to shoot them at her. Wet through as I was, I felt frozen, while clearly her diseased joints would not support her weight much longer. We needed to conclude. Juno, I had to get back to that wedding.

I tackled recent events: who damaged the building site

and who attacked Gavius – killed him, as his grandmother's message had now told me? Rufia claimed to know nothing about that.

What had happened to Rhodina's head? Rufia took it away with her. Nobody was told what she did with it; that was why Menendra, who remained her ally, went looking at her old room, in case it had been hidden there. 'So what did you do with it?'

'Sent it to a farm. The pigs ate it. We couldn't take all the bodies, there were too many to move. People would notice. The cart might be stopped for inspection.'

'Someone tried to break in. Was that Menendra too?'

'No, her two men were leery. She asked someone else to do it, but they messed up. After that I arrived back and said she needn't bother.'

'Who first told you we had found the bones and made you come back? Was it Liberalis?'

She spat again. 'Another idiot!'

'That bar attracts them . . . What happened to the children?'

Rufia admitted she took them. 'They've grown up lovely. My boy's an accountant for the filthy rich; the girl is a musician. Respectable – she doesn't take her clothes off or go with the customers. She could have won a prize at the Neapolis Games, if they still held them.' They ended after Vesuvius erupted. 'Of course she's that age now – boy-mad. I gave them good lives, Flavia Albia. I made up for everything.'

'Neapolis is where you went?' I deduced.

She agreed she had settled there in a discreet property; she ran a list of very high-class prostitutes that rich men in the expensive Bay of Naples villas could order for their beach parties. Exclusive call girls. 'Clean. Well groomed. Lovely manners. Sophisticated services.'

'I suppose you are good at it?'

'The best. They love me. I take good care of them.'

Yes, that was the Rufia I had heard about.

I considered trying to arrest her – difficult on my own. She watched me weigh up options, sneering at my helplessness. 'I did nothing. I killed no one. All you can ever say against me is I knew the truth but never spoke of what I saw. I shall deny that.'

I would nevertheless have passed the story to the vigiles, but she caught me with her final thrust: she was now a good mother to two young people whose lives I would destroy if they lost her. Still too young to fend for themselves in respectable ways, they would be orphans, at the mercy of a sordid world. Did Rufia know my own history? That was possible, if she had been talking to the Macedonians. I had spoken to them of my own horrible childhood. I could not wish that fate on anyone else, anyone who might instead be given a normal life, as I had been.

I do think Rufia knew. Certainly at the end she must have seen it in my face. On my wedding day, with my heart full of gratitude to Falco and Helena who gave me a second chance in life, Rhodina's innocent, living orphans had a claim that surpassed even obtaining justice for the dead. If the vigiles or anyone else worked out how Rufia was involved, she would have to take her chances. I myself would make no further move against her.

We had finished. I accepted this was as much as I would ever know.

We went out together through the decastyled gabled porch,

across one enclosure to the second, where her carrying chair now stood alongside another. Poor Tiberius must have read my message. My bridegroom had sent transport to fetch me back to him.

We parted. As the splashing bearers cursed and hurried home through the wet, deserted streets, in the privacy of the carrying chair I gave way to long-ago sorrows and I wept.

61

People were already gathering outside the house. Everyone loves a torchlit procession with obscene jokes and songs. I was glad to see a small crowd, despite the weather. For us, making a racket on the Aventine was the whole point of today. It was just about fine still but heavily overcast and thunder growled, further along the Tiber.

I rushed in. I fled upstairs. While I was drying off as best I could and re-dressing in my bridal clothes, Tiberius came. He was cradling a wine cup. 'Tiberius Manlius, dear heart, you look like a desperate man whose wife has left him.'

'During the wedding – the ignominy!'

'I am sorry.' I truly was.

'Well you came back.' The grey eyes were quiet. 'Is this how our life will be?'

'Not if I can help it . . . Next time you can come along.'

'I appreciate that . . . Well, I knew who I was marrying. When I read Prisca's message, I saw you had no alternative. I would have followed, but I felt at least one of us ought to be here for our guests!' The reproach was muted. 'Come here.' He straightened my half-dead garland, then took hold of me and kissed me, letting me know how glad he was to see me. 'So did Rufia tell all?'

'Yes, except I could not persuade her to admit who carried out the killings. Forget it,' I said, holding that dear man's face between my hands, smiling tenderly for him. 'Let us go down for our procession.'

'Ready?'

'All yours, husband.'

'Hmm. I hope nothing else happens,' he replied, rather warmly.

Some of the guests had never noticed me missing. They had had all the food and drink they could take. To amuse them further during the afternoon, my father had hired the fabulous Stertinius.

'I don't think we needed to hear him twice!' blared Antistius. He was jealous that my parents had, apparently without effort, managed to secure a private concert from this sought-after virtuoso.

Fania Faustina and Antistius must once have had a wedding like ours. Perhaps they were equally full of hope at the time – yet this week he had thought nothing of asking a Rome waitress for paid sex. For a wild moment I thought, *There is no way you can know*. However sure of each other Tiberius and I felt at this moment, anything could happen . . .

You have to have faith.

'Albiola!' murmured Tiberius, as if he knew what I was thinking.

Then he and I were swept up and put in a private room, where the fabulous Stertinius improvised on his cithara especially for us. My mother had devised this.

Close to, this time we could watch his hands, feel his emotion, hear every fine note. He played almost as if it was for his own pleasure, yet allowing us an intimate share in his skill. The music seemed to reverberate right through us, carrying us into rhapsody. For the first time that day we had private time together, sitting in silence, holding hands. Our souls emptied, then filled up with love. Stertinius was enjoying his own talent and mastery. Sometimes he tossed off shimmers of notes almost arrogantly, then he pulled back into meticulous, skilful patterns. After that he would turn to us with a half-smile, deliberately serenading us as the bridal couple with his exquisite music.

When he finished we emerged, stunned, for our procession. It started to rain again. Well, of course. However, the resourceful men of my family had spent hours that afternoon making a large canopy. Supported on four poles, it would be carried over me, to protect me on my journey to my new home. They explained proudly that they had even put taller poles at the front, so when water collected on the roof it would run backwards and cascade off safely behind me.

The front doors were opened just as the determined drizzle started. Gathered outside were many friends and colleagues. Some, like the victimarii, had left earlier but returned for the procession. There were Tiberius' workmen, people I knew in Fountain Court, Rodan, our horrible porter at the Eagle Building, members of the vigiles.

Those taking part in the procession itself were bossily marshalled by my father and Uncle Petro. My cousin Marius, Maia's son, was playing his flute. A marriage hymn was sung, rather raggedly. The bridegroom took me with a show of force from Mother's arms (those Sabine women have so much to answer for).

'Try harder, Albia, you're not struggling enough!'

'Oh, just take her!' cried Mother, shoving me into his grasp. I felt like a wool sack in a shepherds' dispute.

I was led under my canopy, a dry haven. Behind me Julia Junilla Laeitana bore the damned distaff and spindle. My brother Postumus was trying to control the naughty nephews; at least they would not set anywhere on fire, not in this rain. Two of the little boys, who had been eating something sticky, took my hands, while one in front brandished the torch.

'Hawthorn, I hope?'

'No, oleander. Closest we could find.'

Tiberius set off first. I felt a momentary pang, not wanting to be parted from him. He was distributing to the crowd nuts, sweetmeats and sesame cakes, which Dromo had in a sack on his handcart. Dromo, I heard afterwards, kept back as many cakes as possible, which he then hoarded.

I, too, began walking, amidst cheers and wild laughter. Walking fast at first, because everyone wanted to get out of the rain. Soon slowing as I had to climb the steep stairs to the Aventine summit.

Along the route, rude songs called the Fescennine verses were sung; they would have been much ruder if anybody had known the words. Improvising feebly, the crowd also shouted the ancient marriage cry, or since it is 'obscure', they simply shouted. Once up the hill, I dutifully dropped a coin as an offering to the crossroad gods, if they could ever find it in that enormous puddle.

The Aventine is extremely steep, especially on the cliff side. You just try it, wearing a very long, soaking wet skirt and new saffron shoes you are trying to keep out of puddles. After we climbed the Stairs of Cassius, we turned past the Temple of Juno the Queen (hail, goddess of matrimony). That took us in a detour down the Street of the Armilustrium, until we passed around the back of the Temple of Liberty and into the Vicus Altus, by definition a high point on the hill. We came out in Lesser Laurel Street, turning left briefly so we could make a show at the Temple of Ceres.

395

There, others of the aedilate had assembled to cheer on their colleague. I was breathless, though my mood remained buoyant as I saw Laia Gratiana, my austere predecessor, standing on the steps of the temple, where she ran a religious cult. 'Wave to the lady!' My small attendants stuck their tongues out. I blew her a kiss; we were all girls together now – officially the two wives of Manlius Faustus.

As we turned about in front of the temple, thunder was approaching Rome, rolling downriver, while the rain began beating down harder. I kept walking valiantly until older members of the party demanded a breather. Everyone had hair plastered to their heads, including my sisters and Aunt Valeria, whose pin curls had all unwound.

Even my canopy started leaking. Waiting impatiently, with water running off my garland's herbs and down my neck, I chatted to the workmen who had volunteered to bear the canopy poles. I grinned at the nightwatchman. 'You look a bit sick, Trypho. Too many titbits?'

'I'm just thinking what a narrow escape I had when the site got busted. He could have cut my throat.'

Shaking water off my saffron veil, I wrenched back my concentration. 'Who could?'

'That one in the crowd over there. One of the fellows who sacrificed your sheep. That Erastus.'

Well, thank you, gods.

There I was, with my two midget attendants guarding me like jailors, all eyes upon me. White tunic, flame-coloured veil, saffron shoes, drooping headdress. At last the truth came to me, but I was stuck

Horrified, I looked at them. They looked at me. They were no longer perfect: Erastus must have used the transvestites' skin potion that morning to cover up his birthmark, plus serious bruises and a black eye; now the rain had washed off his disguise, letting Trypho recognise him.

Erastus regularly used knives. *All* of them used knives. They were allowed to take them everywhere. They were experts in the quiet kill. *Quick and slick* . . . So that was it. These were 'the boys' Old Thales, or more likely Rufia, commissioned to kill the Egyptians. Locals, younger then but up for anything, open to cash offers for their specialist skills. Costus owned a farm – *'Sent it to a farm. The pigs ate it . . .'* He had not come to the wedding; did he realise the game was up? Had he gone on the run? Or was he innocent but now realised how his men had gone moonlighting ten years ago? The three victimarii had slit the throats of Julius Ptolomaïs and his four colleagues, presumably Rhodina's as well.

And Erastus must have killed Gavius. Erastus was one of Prisca's grandchildren, a cousin of Gavius. If Erastus knocked, Gavius would let him in, as one of the family.

They saw that I had realised. They started to move away from us. Surreptitiously, then faster.

There was nothing I could do. Someone else would have to hunt them down, later. I would not abandon my bridegroom a second time. He was tolerant, but a wise wife knows not to push too hard. Ahead of me, Tiberius reappeared, coming back to see what had delayed the procession. I had seen him set off, the happiest participant, waving, smiling, tossing his nuts and cakes to people, showing the world he was my proud, joyful new husband. He was looking towards me in enquiry. Somehow I shook off a clinging child and waved, frantically pointing at the victimarii. He understood. He began running towards them.

Lightning flashed around the Aventine tops, almost simultaneously with the thunder,. Then, the sky burst with the loudest roar I have ever heard. Rain poured down on us. As a full storm broke right above our heads, a huge flash lit the streets on the heights.

At the corner of the Vicus Altus, the three victimarii were caught in the open, helpless. Tiberius was very close to them. The lightning struck earth right where they were. I covered my face, but looked again at once, to see four bodies lying on the ground.

62

When my first husband died in an accident, I was alone at home. At least at your wedding your whole family is there to swoop in and hold you. 'Don't worry, pet. Father and Petro are going. No, Albia, stay here.' No use. I was running, running to him.

My father raised an arm. One of the prone bodies moved. Tiberius was still alive. He was being stood up, bolstered, sent back to lead the procession. Despite their differences, his uncle Tullius was there, one arm around him, virtually dragging him along. Marius ran to help. Tiberius looked completely confused, unaware of his surroundings, unsure what was happening.

Uncle Petro stopped me. 'Later. People are with the lad. Don't look at these, don't upset yourself.' The culprits were already dead. Petro was conducting checks, but his head kept shaking. Their knives drew the heat, Father told me afterwards; they died of burns.

I congratulated my uncle quickly: 'You can be proud. Those men killed the missing Egyptians you were asked to trace in the year of the Amphitheatre. Your scroll provided names.'

He was thrilled. 'Go on now. Enjoy your procession. You're a good girl, Falco's eldest, and your fellow is not bad at all. He's just a bit singed. You and he deserve a decent bash. Only you could arrange one with three people going up in smoke . . .' Agreed. Only me. Three dead. Bridegroom struck by lightning. We would never live it down.

'You go on, girl.'

So, under my canopy, I set off once more for my new home.

When we reached Lesser Laurel Street, I saw that our porch, once propped up on scaffold poles, had been reinstated and handsomely painted in shades of cream and dark red, with wonderful panelling and trellised woodwork, beautiful mock-marble pillars. I had been warned that indoors still had bare plaster, but the elegant front doors were an indication of the lifestyle Tiberius was intending for us. I was now desperate to see him.

The doors were flung open to greet me. Bemused and in shock, held upright between his uncle and my cousin, Tiberius anxiously tried to welcome me. I shushed him as I wound the smart doorposts with bands of wool, a supposed symbol of my future household occupation. I quickly anointed the door with oil and fat, emblems of plenty, wincing at the mess on the new paint. Petro and Father turned up in time to carry me in carefully, using a vigiles' lift, while Julia and Favonia grabbed my feet to make sure I did not accidentally kick a doorpost; we had to avoid any bad omen such as a slip of the foot.

In the atrium, Tiberius was helped to offer me fire and water, tokens of the life we were to have together. 'Blazing rows and tears!' muttered a female guest satirically.

I handed another coin to Tiberius as an emblem of my

supposed dowry. I was almost afraid to touch him in case he crackled.

I laid the third coin as an offering to his Lares, which appeared to be the crooked ones from my parents' house; someone must have whizzed them up here. I tried to kindle the hearth with the sodden marriage torch; male cousins got a flint to spark, then lit the hearth for me. I tossed the dead torch among the guests, who fought for it as a lucky charm – more fool them.

We exchanged gifts. Uncle Tullius spoke for Tiberius, saying that his gift to me was our new house, though he also gave me pearl earrings, from which I shall never be parted. I had bought him Pliny's *Natural History* – but only one scroll.

'I have to explain, love. This first scroll is an enormous table of contents – from which you will discover, I am sad to say, that the book you want most, on precious stones and marbles, is the last but one. My plan is: I give you the first book now at our wedding, then every year on our anniversary, you shall have one more scroll. When we have been happy together for thirty-seven years, your collection will be complete. You can either choose another book, or you can leave me.'

Tiberius was smiling as he managed to croak, 'If we divorce, can I keep the library?'

'Argue when we get that far.'

He would own the entire encyclopedia one day. I was sure of it.

Our ordeal was almost over. I recited a prayer – 'Heaven help me!' – and was led by my matron of honour to the wedding chamber. Our bed, our comfortable bed from Fountain Court, would be waiting for us.

I let Claudia Rufina come only as far as the bedroom door, which I closed very firmly. Only then could I take charge of my stricken lad. I put him to bed, trying not to weep over him too much. So many brides have to cope with new husbands who are too drunk to move. Half paralysed, mine could barely groan, but he was blameless. 'Tiberius Manlius, you are favoured of the gods. Jupiter Best and Greatest struck you with his thunderbolt, yet allowed you to live.'

I undid the damned Hercules knot myself, but afterwards he always said that was only what he would have expected of me in any case.

We lay still and quiet together, listening as our guests, drenched and exhausted, prepared to depart. Tomorrow they would all be back and we must give a dinner (Julia and Favonia had booked Genius again); on following nights, other festivities. Being married is no holiday. But the point was to make a big public statement and our wedding had surpassed all hopes. *Aedile bridegroom struck by lightning* would even make it to the *Daily Gazette*.

I heard the last guests milling about. There were tired women's voices as they collected up young children. Men sounded less in evidence. I had glimpsed Father and Uncle Petro, heads together, dumping their women while the women deplored them. If I knew them, it was prearranged, though I had lip-read the classic mutter of, 'Let's get to a bar; I need a drink!'

The bar crawl would be decorous, because they were taking my young brother Postumus and Marius, who was very refined, a philosopher. They excluded the loathsome Antistius, though as a gesture to new unity, Uncle Tullius was discreetly invited.

Some landlord would do well tonight. It would probably be at the Stargazer. But wherever they went, I knew it would be a better bar than the Garden of the Hesperides.